OH, YOU'RE SO COLD

BAD BOYS OF BARDSTOWN
BOOK TWO

SAFFRON A. KENT

This is a work of fiction. Names, characters, places, and incidents are either the product of the author's imagination or are used fictitiously, and any resemblance to actual persons living or dead, business establishments, events, or locales, is entirely coincidental.

Oh, You're So Cold © 2024 by Saffron A. Kent
All rights reserved. No part of this book may be used or reproduced in any manner whatsoever without written permission of the author except in the case of brief quotations embodied in critical articles or reviews.

Cover Art by Najla Qamber Designs
Editing by Olivia Kalb and Emily A. Lawrence
Proofreading by Virginia Tesi Carey

June 2024 Edition

Published in the United States of America

DEDICATION

This one's for A.
My best friend. My soulmate. My husband.
You make me who I am: a writer, a wife, a mommy, and a girl who had the courage to seize her destiny. It is my greatest hope that all the girls out there meet an A of their own someday, if they haven't yet.
This is also for the other A in my life. My baby girl, Adora. I'm so blessed and privileged that you're a part of the destiny that your daddy helped me seize.

BLURB

I swear I didn't do it on purpose.
All I wanted was a harmless kiss from the handsome stranger at my eighteenth birthday party. But when he said—with a cruel twist of his cigarette-smoking lips—that he doesn't kiss 'annoying little girls,' I stupidly decided to flirt with a random guy to make him jealous.
I never wanted that random guy to fall in love with me. Or worse, accidentally start a relationship with him. But now I have a new boyfriend while I can't stop thinking about the guy who doesn't care that I exist.
So it's time to move on and focus on my new relationship.
Only the moment I make that decision, he decides to notice me.
He decides to stare at me a little too hard and in a way that makes me blush. Oh, and one day when my boyfriend isn't looking, he decides to corner me in a lonely hallway and put his rough and heated hands on me that feels equal parts forbidden and familiar.
But I'm not stupid.
I'm not going to ruin my new relationship for someone people call Stellan 'The Cold' Thorne. Especially not when the random guy I'm dating isn't random at all.
No, my new boyfriend happens to be the brother of the guy I'm inappropriately obsessed with.
And I'm not the kind of girl who comes between two brothers.
Twin brothers...
Or am I?

AUTHOR'S NOTE

Dear Reader,
    I have so many things to say about this book so I'm going to list them all in bullet points because I don't want to leave anything out:

- Isadora is my very first Indian (Desi) American heroine. Her dad is American, and her mom comes from India (Punjab specifically, where I come from as well.) Even though, she was born here, in the US, and hasn't been to India ever in her life, she's still enamored by the culture, the language, the traditions, the movies. As you read along, you'll find many such references but don't worry, she's learning right alongside you.
- She has a grandmother whom she calls *Biji* (as they do in India; I call my own grandmother that) and who comes from bits and pieces of my own grandmother.
- Her love for Bollywood movies comes from my love for Bollywood movies. Again, you'll find many references to such movies as you read on. They're all her favorite movies and mine too. For a full list of movies mentioned, see below.
- She also loves Bollywood music. To listen to what she's currently listening, go here.
- She also has a Spotify playlist, which you can find here.
- This book has the D word in it and not the D word that I usually have. This word starts with a D and ends with a Y. You've been warned.
- I would never have been able to write this book without the support of my husband. Being able to balance being a new mom and a crazy

writer who doesn't sleep or eat until the book is done was hard. And he not only supported me, he saved my sanity during this time. This here is my personal declaration that he is the GOAT and is above all book boyfriend and Bollywood heroes combined.

Movies mentioned:

- Act 1, Chapter 5: Dilwaale Dulhaniya Le Jaayenge.
- Act 1, Chapter 13: Kuch Kuch Hota Hai
- Act 2, Chapter 5: Dil Se
- Act 2, Chapter 15: Maine Pyaar Kiya

PROLOGUE

The Beginning

CHAPTER 1

ONE YEAR AGO

I'm a slut.
    Or so my mom calls me.
She also says that one day it'll get me in trouble. The kind I won't be able to get myself out of. I don't think that's true, though. In fact, I think being a slut is what usually gets me *out* of trouble.
    It at least gets me out of locked rooms.
    Like it did tonight.
    As always, I made my mother angry. I chose to wear a dress I liked instead of the one she'd picked out for me. In my defense, it's my birthday—my *eighteenth* birthday—and I wanted to wear something of my own choosing for a change.
    Yes, it's short and yes, it shows off my cleavage.
    So what?
    I like it and it's my birthday tonight.
    Don't I deserve *some* leeway?
    Apparently not.
    Because as soon as I came down the stairs in my pretty white dress, my mom lost it. She dragged me upstairs, locked me in my room, and told me I wouldn't be coming out until I put some decent clothes on. My dad—who loves my mother to death and will do anything for her—posted a bodyguard at my door for good measure too.
    Well, they always have bodyguards posted around me.
    Because apparently, I'm too out of control and need to be kept an eye on.
    Anyway.

My parents thought he was tough, the bodyguard, but he folded and let me go the second I screamed out for fake help and batted my dark curled eyelashes.

And look, here I am.

Sneaking out of the back garden exactly like I'd planned.

I knew this area would be empty and therefore a safe passage for me because people would be busy with the party around the pool. And with any luck, I'll be back before my parents figure out I'm not where I'm supposed to be.

Although I *will* say that I'm late.

But it's okay.

The moon is bright. The early winter air is crisp and fresh. Not to mention, I'm finally seizing my destiny or rather making an attempt to seize it.

So I'm not going to despair.

But the moment I decide that, I stop mid-run.

I have to.

Because suddenly, the blissfully empty back garden is not empty anymore.

There's someone here.

Someone I can't see because even though the moon is shining at its brightest, whoever it is, is standing under the pink magnolia tree, shadowed by the branches and the flowers.

All I can tell is that it's a he.

It's a darkly dressed he.

With dark pants and a dark shirt.

It's also a tall he.

In fact, he's such a tall he that he won't have to stand on his tiptoes to pluck the flowers from the branches. Actually, he won't even have to raise his arm fully to get to them. Both of which I have to do and even then, it's a hardship.

Who is he?

And what is he doing with my flowers?

"Who are you?" My loud voice cracks through the silence.

If he's another one of my new bodyguards, I'm going to be very pissed. And he could be because my dad did say he'd hired a bunch of new ones from a very famous Bardstown-based security company, The Fortress, after he caught me almost making out with the last one. Spoiler alert: I wasn't really going to make out with him. That was also a ploy to get myself out of another tricky situation.

Again, anyway.

I simply *do not* have the time to flirt with another clown.

He doesn't get my urgency, though.

Because he doesn't reply. It's like I never even spoke.

Which pisses me off even more.

Putting a hand on my hip, I ask, "Are you another one of my bodyguards? Because if you are, then I'm going to be very angry. And trust me when I say you do not want that."

That gets me an answer.

Not right away, though. First, it gets me a movement.

His arm.

Lifting in the darkness, reaching up.

Going up to his face.

Actually, going up to his lips.

A cigarette is pinched between his fingers, bright and glow-y, and he puts it in his mouth, sucks in a breath—I squint my eyes and notice his chest moving that I have to say seems really broad—and then, a whorl of smoke is being released into the air.

Then, "Why not?"

I get momentarily distracted by not only his smoking—all casual and careless—but also his voice.

Which is deep.

Deeper than any other voices I've ever heard.

Like he's got a bottomless well inside of him.

And that bottomless well is filled with gravel. Because his voice has that quality too.

Gravelly and deep.

Keeping my hand on my hip, I declare, "Because I'm dangerous when I'm angry."

"Define dangerous."

"I bite."

"Do you?"

"Yes, I also scratch."

"That does sound dangerous."

"It is." I nod. "The last man I bit had to go to the hospital."

It's not all a lie.

I did bite one of my bodyguards last year.

Because he took my flirting a little too seriously. He actually thought that if he let me go to the party my parents didn't want me to, I'd really show him my breasts. I wasn't going to and I told him that. So when he started to get mad and a little handsy, I bit him.

Plus scratched his face.

He bled a little, but other than that, he was fine. No hospitalizations.

I, on the other hand, was grounded.

For a *whole* month for injuring a member of the staff. Who tried to force himself on me, hello? But my mom said it was me who'd provoked him, so I was the one who needed punishment.

"So?" I prompt him. "Are you? One of my bodyguards."

"Sounds like the world needs protection from you," he says in that deep voice of his. "Not the other way around."

"So what, is that a no?"

"Although I will say you probably shouldn't do that."

"Do what?"

I detect another movement.

This time he uses the hand, the one with the cigarette, to first point at me before taking in another drag and releasing a puffy cloud of smoke. "Take that off."

"Take what off?"

"In front of me."

"I don't..."

Oh.

Oh!

Okay.

I get it now.

He's talking about my bra. Which I was in the process of taking off as I ran through the garden. Mostly because I hate wearing bras. To be fair, what girl doesn't? In any case, I believe in being free and unencumbered. That's why instead of wearing winter boots, I only have slippers on—the kind you wear on a beach—and I left my sweater behind in my room.

What can I say, I also love the cold.

But anyway, one strap dangling down my arm, I ask, "Why not?"

"Because I don't think it's very safe to take off an article of clothing in front of a strange man."

"Why, are you a perv?" I ask instead.

"I could be," he replies.

I tilt my head to the side, thinking about him.

Of course he could be a perv.

He could be anyone.

But for some reason, as annoying as the interruption is, I don't think so.

"Nah, you're not a perv," I tell him.

"Why is that?"

"First, because you gave me that advice and I'm assuming it's well intentioned and you don't even know me," I inform him. "And second, I don't think a perv would admit they're one."

He studies me for a beat.

I don't know how I know that because as I said, it's dark and I can't see anything at all. But I do feel like he's running his eyes over me. Which I have to say, I like very much.

And that's intriguing.

Because even though I flirt and use my charms as much as I can to get what I want, I don't enjoy it. I don't enjoy men's eyes on me. I don't enjoy the thoughts running through their heads when they look at me.

I don't *enjoy* being a slut.

But back to him.

The mysterious man takes another drag of his cigarette as he replies, "Well, then allow me to tell you all about the white van I drive with a big mattress in the back. And how I use candy to lure unsuspecting girls in so I can take them away."

Nah, definitely not a perv.

After dealing with them most of my life, I don't get that feeling from him.

"I don't think girls like candies anymore," I share, chuckling.

"No?"

"No."

"So what do girls like these days?"

I shrug. "Tequila maybe." I tip my chin at him. "Definitely a smoke."

Again, he studies me for a beat and I get the feeling that he's trying to figure me out. Then, holding the cigarette up, "First, I never share my cigarettes. And second, I don't think you're old enough to drink."

"Why don't you share your cigarettes?"

"Because I only smoke one cigarette a day. They're a precious commodity."

"You only smoke one cigarette a day?"

In response, he takes in a long drag.

"Why?"

"It's a rule."

"Whose rule?"

"Mine."

"Do you have a lot of rules?"

"Some."

"Wow," I go because who the hell is he? "I can barely *remember* the rules, much less follow them."

"I had a feeling."

"How old are you?" I ask next.

"Older than you."

"When was the first time you tried alcohol?" I fire off.

"When I was old enough to."

Even though I suspected such an answer, my eyes still pop wide. "Shut up."

In response, he takes a drag of his cigarette.

"You're kidding! You actually waited until twenty-one to try alcohol? That's *crazy*. I had my first drink when I was eleven. I got my period and it hurt like a fucking bitch, so I tried my mom's wine to dull the pain."

A puff of smoke before he says, "That's more information than I needed to know, but good for you."

"What, periods make you uncomfortable?"

"Seeing that I've got a sister your age, I would say no, but I'm okay if you think that."

"You have a sister my age?" I ask excitedly. "What's her name?"

His response is to let out another string of smoke.

"What's *your* name?"

No response.

Well, except for more smoking.

And the more he does that, the more he doesn't answer me, the more I want to know. And I know that I have to be somewhere, but damn it, I'm intrigued now.

I sigh dramatically. "Well, if you don't tell me, I have no choice but to call you Mr. Adorbs."

He hums. "That's a new one."

"So why don't just share what people call you?"

"Cold," he replies. "People call me cold."

"Cold, huh." Tilting my head to the side even though I know there's no way I'm going to catch even a little bit of what he looks like, I reply, "Then we're perfect for each other."

"How's that?"

"Because I love winter."

"I'm colder than winter."

"And because my middle name is Agni."

"What's Agni?"

"Fire," I inform him. "In Sanskrit."

He releases another puff of smoke as if to emphasize my name. "Fire."

"Yup. My mom's from India, born and brought up, and when I was young, they said I was unpredictable. I'd cry one second and laugh the next. I'd throw tantrums in the middle of the laughter. So she named me Agni, unpredictable like the fire. I'm Isadora Agni Holmes and even if you're colder than winter, I can melt you"—I snap my fingers—"just like that."

"Isadora Agni Holmes," he repeats as if he wants to get a taste of my name.

Of me.

Or maybe I want him to want that.

Because apart from finding him more and more intriguing as the seconds pass, I realize with a certain level of shock that I want that too. I want to get a taste of him.

And that's definitely never happened to me before.

Definitely.

Who *is* this guy?

"That's me," I murmur, still taken aback by my realization.

"A mouthful," he murmurs back.

"So?" I prod. "What's your name?"

"Nowhere near of a mouthful as yours."

I study him then. Or rather his silhouette.

All shrouded in mystery and intrigue.

"So is that how we're playing it?" I shift on my feet.

"Games are for children"—he shifts on his feet too and I notice him lean against the trunk as if settling himself in for the long haul—"but why not."

"Okay then." I nod, accepting the challenge. "We already know you're not my bodyguard. Which means you must be a guest. And since I just told you my name, you probably also know that this is my party and—"

He jerks his chin at me. "Happy birthday, by the way."

I lift my chin at him in response. "So how about you tell me your name as a birthday gift?"

"Can't."

"But—"

"I already bought you gifts."

Forgetting my disappointment for a second, I ask excitedly, "Yeah? What'd you bring me?"

I detect a shrug.

"A gift basket from one of those spa places. My sister assures me girls like that."

I don't know why, but I find that really adorable.

Him going to his sister to ask about what girls like.

"But now I'm rethinking it," he finishes.

"What, why?"

"Because from what I hear, girls like tequila and cigarettes these days," he drawls.

"But then again, you don't share your cigarettes and I'm not old enough to drink. So a gift basket works. Thanks." I chuckle, deciding here and now that as soon as I get a chance, I'm going to hunt down his gift first.

"You're welcome."

Then it occurs to me what he said. "But wait, you said gifts. Gift*sss*. You brought me more than one? What's my other gift?"

"Keeping your secret."

"What secret?"

Releasing a puff of smoke, he goes, "That you're sneaking out of your own party."

"I'm not—"

"Because that's what you're doing, aren't you?" he cuts me off. "Sneaking out."

Normally, I'd debate how much to tell him. Because if he's a guest, then that means he's a friend of my parents. And who knows how trustworthy he is.

But this is not normal.

What's happening right now, what I'm feeling right now, is not normal.

"Maybe," I say.

He straightens up from the tree and nods. "Well then, don't let me keep you from whatever it is you're sneaking off to do."

"What do you think I'm sneaking off to do?"

He pushes a hand down his pocket and with the other puts the cigarette back in his mouth. "Meet a boy."

"A *boy*?"

In the wake of smoke from his lips, he replies, "And just a little piece of advice: Keep your bra on."

I smile. "Yeah, why?"

"Because boys can be assholes."

"And you know that because you've got a sister my age?"

"She's a little older than you but yeah."

Actually, forget being intrigued.

I'm totally and completely obsessed.

"I'm going for an audition," I tell him truthfully.

That gives him pause. "An audition."

"Yeah, for a play." And then to test it out, I add, "I'm an actress."

"An actress," he murmurs.

"Yes. Or at least I wanna be, and if I get the role, I could be."

"What's the role?"

And my heart blooms.

There's no other way to put it.

It blooms that he's asking me about the play. That he's taking an *interest*.

No one in my life has ever done that before.

Not one person.

Well, except my *biji*.

Except my grandmother, they all think it's a frivolous hobby of a spoiled little rich girl rather than a passionate dream since childhood. A passionate dream I've always been persecuted for because it's not conventional or something my mother—and therefore my father as well—approve of.

It's not something good girls do.

Good girls go to school, get good grades, and follow all the rules. Good girls wear modest clothes, don't go to parties, only date boys their parents approve of. Good girls grow up to become high society wives who don't make waves, look pretty on their husbands' arms, and don't generate negative attention from the media.

Good girls aren't like me.

"It's, uh, from a book called *Lolita*," I tell him, my breaths all fast and hazy. "I'm auditioning for the lead role."

For which, I've prepared for weeks in secret.

In my defense, I wasn't going to.

I wasn't going to disobey my parents. For all my rebellious ways, I don't enjoy pissing them off. I don't enjoy being punished or grounded or made to feel like an outsider in my own family. I don't think any kid likes that, the very people who're supposed to love and support you making you feel like an alien. So I was going to let this role go like I've let all the others go before.

So far, all I've done is perform in front of my bedroom mirror. Or in empty classrooms or auditoriums. I have never, not ever, performed in front of people or taken part in any stage performances. Every time I even broach the subject with my mother, she loses it and grounds me, and my dad lets my mom do whatever she wants and disappears into his study.

But then my *biji* told me I needed to stop being a chicken and do it. If I want to prove people wrong and show them I'm serious about acting, then I have to take a chance. I have to put myself out there despite the fear, despite all obstacles.

So I flirted with one of the men on the casting team and they're letting me audition this late into the night. Because I told him my parents don't approve. He's also the one who's picking me up tonight, a couple of blocks away from my house, and giving me a ride to Bardstown—which is where the play is and not in New York where I live with my parents. It's being put on by Bardstown community center and if I get the role, I'm sure he can be my ride to and from Bardstown. And I'm also sure he'll expect some favors in return, but I know how to both dodge the attention and keep it on me at the same time.

In any case, I'm doing this.

I'm seizing my destiny tonight.

On my eighteenth birthday.

And no one can stop me.

"A teenage girl who ruins an old man's life and drives him to break all rules of morality," he says, breaking into my thoughts.

"You've read the book?" I ask in excitement.

"I was right," he declares. "The world needs protection from you rather than the other way around."

"You—"

"So if you're Lolita, what are those for?"

He points toward what he's talking about and suddenly a chilly breeze flits through, making them flutter and graze the backs of my bare thighs and my arms.

My wings.

That I'm wearing.

Along with the white slip dress I have on, I'm also wearing a pair of gossamer wings. Another thing my mother found objectionable but I love to pieces.

"They're my good luck wings," I reply.

"Good luck wings."

"Yeah. They belonged to my *biji*." I smile and explain, "My grandmother. She wanted to be an actress too."

"So what happened?"

"Life," I reply. "From what she tells me, Indian society back in the fifties wasn't very conducive to women working, let alone women working in the film industry. So her dreams never became a reality. She's the one who gave me the acting bug, much to my parents' dismay."

"Is that why you're sneaking out," he asks, "because your parents are dismayed?"

"Yes."

"Good."

My heart blooms harder. "No advice against sneaking out then?"

"Just, as they say in theater," he murmurs, "break a leg."

"Why do they say that?" I wrinkle my nose. "That can't be good."

I think his lips twitch, but I can't be sure.

"Back in the olden days, if you didn't get to perform, you stayed behind the 'leg line' and wouldn't get paid. So it grew as a term to say, hope you get an opportunity to perform and get paid. In modern times, however, it simply means good luck."

I study his shadowed form for a few seconds, completely flabbergasted.

Awed.

"You're a scholar, aren't you?" I breathe out, impressed.

"Absolutely fucking not."

"I bet no one here knows that. Not one single person at this party knows where 'break a leg' comes from." I shake my head. "Except you."

"It's a simple Google search. And people here have more of a reason to know what a penalty means than anything else."

"Ah, soccer," I conclude.

My dad owns one of the pro-soccer teams, New York City FC, more or less as a status symbol than anything else. His actual business is a group of hotel resorts all over the country. So everyone here is a soccer enthusiast.

"Soccer," he confirms.

I wrinkle my nose again. "I don't think I like soccer very much."

"I don't blame you."

"You don't like it either?"

"I like it enough."

"But—"

"In any case, don't let me keep you," he says, cutting me off.

And it feels like a hint.

A hint that he wants me to leave.

"Fine," I tell him. "I'll go. But I have a condition."

I think he shakes his head a little. "I think you should give up."

I know he assumes that I'm still playing the game. That I still want to know his name, and I do.

But I want something else more.

So standing there, watching his smoking silhouette, I finish what I'd started to do before I ran into him. I take my bra off, despite his advice. I slide the other strap down my arm, then reach back and under my dress to unhook it. When I'm done sliding the thing off my body and the garment is hanging off my index finger, I drop it on the ground. And then sidestepping it, I take off.

On a run.

My fake wings flap behind me; the hem of my dress flutters against my bare thighs.

And my long, wavy hair whips back in the chilly breeze.

It's like I'm flying and I love it.

But at this speed, I'm going to crash.

Against a mountain.

Or a body that grows bigger and bigger the closer I get to it.

It's okay, though.

That's my intention.

Crashing against him.

Because when I do, he'll catch me.

I get that feeling from him. The feeling of safety.

And I'm right.

Because he does.

The moment I make impact, my front colliding against his, his arms go around my waist. His feet shift and he widens his stance to absorb the force with which I tackle him.

And I'm saved.

In fact, I'm more than saved.

I'm all warm and cozy.

And the first thing I say is, "Whoever calls you cold is crazy."

"What the—"

"Because I think you're as hot as a wildfire."

"Are you fucking insane?" he grumbles, his arm tightening around my frame.

My arms tighten around him as well. "A little."

He stares down at me for a few beats, a frown between his brows, and I'm happy—I'm super fucking thrilled, actually—that I can see it.

That I can see *him*.

Finally.

And immediately, I realize his face isn't meant to be looked at in one go. You can't just look at him and move on, no. You have to take your time. You have to study every angle because like his voice, his features have a depth to them.

His features have nuances.

They're meant to be taken apart and analyzed and *mooned* over.

That arch of his dark brows; the crest of his cheekbones; the deep wells beneath them. The slanting angle of his jaw; the bridge of his nose and those lips.

God, those lips.

They're luscious.

They're curved at the ends, bowed in the middle, so very soft and plush-looking. Like petals of a dusky rose maybe. And when I imagine his mouth with a cigarette in it, it makes me tingle. When I imagine the orange embers making that mouth glow, it makes me feel heated.

It makes me picture a rose set on fire.

The petals of which I want to lick and eat.

And swallow and burn with.

"Dora."

My eyes snap up at his voice. "No one calls me Dora."

His jaw clenches. "Let go of me."

"I like it."

"Let me go."

"You're very handsome."

"Let. Me," he growls. "Go."

"Kiss me."

He stiffens. "What?"

I glance down at his lips. "That's my condition. For you to kiss me." Looking up, I add, "You do that and I'll let you go. I'll leave."

The frown in his brows thickens. "Do you always throw yourself at men like this?"

I fist the collar of his jacket. "I do throw myself at men but not like this."

His eyes—that I'm very pleased to announce are dark—flare. "You—"

"Usually, I throw myself at them when I want something. I tempt them. I make them false promises. I dangle myself as a prize." I fist his collar tighter. "But that's not what I'm doing here."

"What *are* you doing here?"

"I'm seizing my destiny."

"What?" he snaps.

"Yeah." I nod, looking into his eyes, thrilled beyond belief. "I wasn't going to do it, the audition. I didn't want to make my parents mad. But then my *biji* convinced me. She told me to seize my destiny and so that's what I was doing tonight, on my eighteenth birthday. But then I run into you."

His body's still and rigid, his eyes narrowed.

I don't think he's liking my explanation all that much.

But it's okay.

I'll still keep going, despite my fear.

Despite all obstacles.

"And you're unlike anyone I've ever met," I continue. "Someone else, a different man, would've tried something with me by now. There's a man waiting for me, two blocks away. He's here to take me to Bardstown for my audition and I bet he's thinking what he can get in return. I bet he has all kinds of bad intentions toward me. Because men always do. Sometimes I encourage it, sometimes I don't. Sometimes I use it to get myself something, like a ride to a different town. But they always, *always* want to try something with me in return. Not you, though. You haven't tried one thing. You've tried to give me advice and protect me. So—"

"First," he growls, his body so tight that it's like I'm plastered against a rock, "you're *not* getting into a car with a strange man."

"I won't," I agree readily.

"You—"

"If you kiss me."

His jaw clenches. "This is not a fucking game, do you understand? You could seriously get hurt. You could—"

"Kissing you is not a game for me."

His chest expands on a breath. His nostrils flare.

Then, with his arms that are still keeping me safe, flexing around my waist, he growls, "I'm not fucking kissing you."

"Why not?" I ask, exasperated.

"Just let go of me."

"I've never been kissed before. You could be my first kiss."

"Fuck no."

He looks so horrified that I'm compelled to add, "How about I sweeten the pot?"

"No."

"How about I let you go further?"

"What?"

My arms are still hooked around his neck and so I almost dangle against him now, my feet leaving the ground, my back arching, my neck craning up. And yet again, he saves me. His arms around my waist tighten to the point where I feel the shift of his muscles through layers and layers of our clothes.

And an involuntary shiver runs down my spine at his strength.

Making me even bolder and shameless and determined.

Looking into his dark eyes, I ask, "How about I let you touch my tits?"

"*What?*"

"Yes, no one has ever touched them before. I'm a total virgin. I promise."

"That's—"

"Plus I have nice tits." I rub myself against him. "See? They're all soft and perky."

He moves his arms and grips my hips, stopping me.

But other than that, he doesn't say anything else.

"I also have cherry-colored nipples."

His jaw clenches in response.

"You could suck on them."

His jaw clenches harder.

"You could even bite me, leave your mark on me."

His jaw clenches even harder than before.

As if he's testing the sharpness, the strength of his teeth.

"Men like that, don't they? They like to leave their marks on girls. You could leave yours," I offer, "on me."

He mashes his teeth.

"And I also know men like to be all dominating and rough. Like a daddy. You could be that. You could be my daddy tonight and I won't tell anyone. Ever. Not my dad or my mom. Or anyone, really. I—"

"No." His fingers dig into my flesh harshly, *painfully* before pushing me away from his body.

Forcefully thrust away from him, winter attacks me.

Sharp claws of chill dig into my skin.

And rubbing my hands over my bare arms, I say as a last-ditch effort, "If I figure out who you are, will you kiss me then?"

He watches me rub warmth back into my arms and his chest moves again. "You should go back. Get inside. Get away from the cold. Get away from that fucking man."

See? He's still trying to protect me.

"You're new," I say instead. "You have to be. Because I've never seen you before. I would've remembered if I had. And since this party is full of soccer people, you have something to do with..."

It finally occurs to me then.

I know who he is.

The man I've become obsessed with in such a short amount of time is someone everyone's talking about.

"You're Wrecking Thorn," I say, awe clear in my voice. "You're the *legendary* Wrecking Thorn. Shepard Thorne. Aren't you? Why didn't you tell me? You're a god or something. People can't stop talking about you. My dad, my mom, everyone. They all think you're going to change the fate of the team. You're going to bring back the glory days. You're the hottest soccer player of the season." I shake my head, chuckling. "You have to kiss me now so I can brag about it to all my friends."

When all he does is stare at me, I clarify, "That was a joke, by the way. I don't have very many friends." When he still doesn't laugh, I go, "You can laugh now."

"No."

"What?"

"I'm not him."

I frown. "You—"

"So unfortunately, kissing me won't give you bragging rights."

Something in his voice alerts me to take stock of his stance.

To study his face, his demeanor.

And I realize that it's all tight. His voice, the muscles in his body.

Rigid and aloof.

Somehow, I've offended him, I think, made him angry.

"I'm sorry," I say, taking a step toward him. "I was just—"

"I'm the lesser-known version of him."

This time before saying something, I think. I weigh his words.

Try to put them together.

And then it hits me.

Who he is.

Shepard isn't the only man my parents talk about. They also talk about someone else. Someone who's just as new as Shepard. Someone people call cold.

Oh my God, it was so obvious.

He did tell me who he was, didn't he?

Earlier.

He's not a player, though.

He's the new assistant coach.

"You're the Cold Thorn. You're his twin."

"I am."

"I didn't know. I—"

"Well, now you do," he says, his voice low. "And let me also tell you that if you want to be kissed, then you picked the wrong twin. I don't go around kissing spoiled little rich girls who can't take no for an answer. Him, though, he'll indulge you. He doesn't have a lot of standards and from what I hear, desperation turns him on. Not me, though. I find desperation annoying. I find little girls like you even more annoying. So you should run along and find him. Maybe he's your destiny, because I'm absolutely fucking not."

I do as he says then.

I run along.

And I find him.

His twin brother.

Not because he's my destiny but because I'm Isadora Agni Holmes and I'm going to melt Stellan 'The Cold' Thorne and make him eat his words.

CHAPTER 2

THE WILDFIRE THORN

I'm cold.
 Or so people call me.
They say I'm a block of ice. They say I'm frozen.
That I'm feelingless, emotionless.
That beneath my chest there's a heart that doesn't beat.
 It's because I want them to think that. It's because there are things inside of me I don't want anyone to see. Things I don't want myself to see. So I keep them hidden, buried under six feet of ice. Like people bury their dead.
 But that's not the point.
 The point is that I'd much rather be home, smoking my one cigarette of the day in peace while losing myself in the pages of a book. Only for an hour, though. No more.
 That's why my plan was to get in and get out. Show my face enough that they know I was here but mostly stay in the shadows, undisturbed and undiscovered. Much like those things inside of me. Besides, I'm the assistant coach. My team is in attendance; my players are here. So being here is more or less my job and I take my job seriously. Even though I'm not a fan of it.
 I'm not a fan of soccer, not like these people here.
 Never was. Never will be.
 Which suits me just fine.
 But anyway.
 What I hadn't planned on was her.
 I hadn't planned on being discovered by her.

Being *seen* by her.

You're as hot as wildfire...

No one ever sees me, which again suits me just fine. I want it that way. So I'm not sure how an eighteen-year-old could. How was it that she saw me, *found* me in the dark?

How was it that I found her interesting?

Her reckless advances. Her endless chatter. How was it that the more unpredictable and whimsical and wilder she became, the more I couldn't make myself leave?

Maybe because I'm none of those things and she's the polar opposite of me.

And maybe that's why I was so harsh with her.

Because I don't want to find people interesting. I don't want to be intrigued.

I've heard about her, of course. She's the boss's daughter; this party's in her honor. People know who she is. Not to mention, there are rumors. I've heard how Mr. Holmes is disapproving of her. And how he needs to be because she's out of control. She ruins men, lays waste to their careers with her seductive beauty.

A real-life Lolita.

Mr. Holmes has had to fire two junior coaches ever since he bought the team two years ago. He's had to fire three security guys, trade in a player, all because they were found in various compromising positions with her. Personally, I've never put much stock into rumors and considered her none of my business.

Not tonight, though.

Tonight, for some reason, she seems like my business.

Tonight, I'm watching.

Her.

With him.

Dancing.

I'm watching her with him, laughing. With abandon, without a care in the world. Without a *care* that I'm only a few feet away.

A ticking time bomb is only a few feet away.

A bomb that's going to explode at any moment.

Any moment, I'm going to march across the dance floor, grab my brother's collar, and beat that smile off his face. I'm going to break his legs into pieces, one by one, so dancing is a distant memory for him. I'm going to rip her from his arms and steal her away. I'm going to start a fight with my brother because I saw her first.

Which isn't good.

Me feeling like this—angry, agitated, *jealous*—is not good. Her making me feel this way is not good at all.

It's very fucking bad.

It's downright dangerous.

She's dangerous.

So much so that I need to step away. I need to contain myself. I need to contain this fire inside of me. These things I don't want anyone to see. I need to go back to the shadows where I belong, remain undiscovered and hidden.

Which is what I do.

I leave the party, determined not to give a single thought to Isadora Agni Holmes.

The girl in a white dress and fake wings.

With enough fire to melt the fucking Arctic.

With enough fire to melt even me.

ACT 1

The Asshole, The Slut, & The Boyfriend

CHAPTER 1

PRESENT

He stands away from everyone and at the edge of everything.
Like always.
This ballroom is filled with people, every nook and cranny overflowing with glossy gowns and dashing tuxes. But he's managed to find one corner, *one tiny corner*, by the exit to the grounds. He stands there, leaning against the wall, sporting a tumbler of whiskey. That he hasn't drunk from, I bet, or taken more than a few sips of. He's not a big drinker.
As he watches people.
As if he's here to observe and not participate.
He's separate from all this nonsense and frivolity. He doesn't care for it. It doesn't move him or inspire him.
He rejects it.
This charity event New York City FC threw together.
I don't blame him.
Even though such events have been the norm for me growing up, I have also never liked them. They're too stuffy for me. Too fake, too artificial, with practiced smiles and rehearsed dialogues. As an *unofficial* theater minor in college, my love for fake is big but not this big. So I understand his disdain.
Besides, I don't think he has very many things common with the rest of the men here.
Well, except for the clothes.
He's wearing the same shiny tux and a crisp white shirt underneath like the

rest of them. His dark brown hair's combed and styled exactly like the rest of the guys. And his wing-tipped shoes are polished to perfection.

He still stands out, though.

Because I know him.

While everyone here would break all the rules the first chance they get, he will follow them no matter what. While people here will talk about the weather or soccer stats, he can probably hold a conversation about history and politics; I've heard him do both on more than one occasion. When he does deign to speak, that is. While a weaker man would succumb to temptation, I know he'll stick to his one cigarette per day come what may.

Oh, and I also know he's cold.

So, so cold.

Not that I care about any of those things I mentioned above.

I don't.

In fact, I'm not even really watching him right now.

Nope.

It's just that he's in my line of vision.

And every time I look up from my drink—a white wine—my eyes inevitably pass by him. So it's a *passing glance*, is what it is. Any second now, I'm going to pass him by and look at something else.

I am.

It's going to happen.

"Isadora?"

I jerk, sloshing my wine dangerously close to the rim, and turn to the voice beside me. "What, I'm sorry."

It's my mother.

Which I knew, of course.

I knew I was standing with my mother. I knew I was getting a drink with my mother, which is why the drink is a tame white wine instead of something tequila based.

I knew all that.

It's just that as soon as I spotted... a certain someone by those exit doors across the ballroom, I kinda forgot.

Which was stupid.

Because now my mother is looking in the same direction as I was just now as she asks, "Who are you looking at?"

"No one," I reply quickly.

A little too quickly maybe because my mom's eyes come back to settle on me.

I look like my mother. There's no question about it.

We have the same honey-toned skin and jet-black hair. The same nose, the same bow-shaped lips. The same almond-shaped eyes. Mine are gray, though—I get them from my father—and hers are dark brown. They border on black when she looks at me, however.

Because her gaze fills with displeasure.

Always.

No matter what.

When I was young, it was hard for me to understand why my mother was like that. Strict and stern and always unamused by me. No display of emotions. No overt expressions of love. Just a bunch of rules and annoyance about me being too loud or too rambunctious. As I grew older and started to know more about where my mother came from, I realized that maybe it was because she grew up in a different culture. A culture that values traditions and obedience and structure.

I mean, if we think about it, Aarti Arora Holmes—Arora is her maiden name—has never done anything unconventional. Well, except marry my dad—an American—and move from Punjab, a state in the northern part of India, to a different country. But even that was because my dad's family had been friends with my mom's, and my grandfather—he's deceased now—thought it was a good match.

So since I was none of the things that her culture valued, my mother just didn't know how to deal with me except be angry and reprimand me at every turn.

But then I grew up more.

And realized that's not the case either.

It's not the culture that has made my mother the way she is. It's just her.

Because my *biji*, my mom's mom, is exactly like me. Or well, I'm like her. She's free-spirited and fun. She doesn't care about the rules or being good. So maybe that's the problem. That I'm like her mom. Whom she doesn't like very much either.

"Are you sure?" my mother asks after a few seconds of silently and suspiciously studying me.

I fidget. "Yes."

Another few seconds of tense silence. "Let's go over it again, shall we?"

And my gut clenches.

Because even though my mom will never love me, *I* love her. I want her to approve of me.

I want her to accept me for who I am.

Just like the dream of becoming an actress despite my mother's wishes, it's a dream I've had since I was a little girl. That one day my mom will realize how much she loves me, despite me being the way I am, and we will live happily ever after.

I wave all these thoughts away and reply, "Yes." Then, "Uh, only one drink."

She eyes the glass in my hand. "Just one."

I swallow, clutching the glass tighter. "No dancing on the floor if no one else is dancing."

"Good."

"No laughing too loud or talking too loud."

"What else?"

"No"—I clear my throat—"making a scene like I usually do. No attracting attention to myself."

"You're not an animal in the zoo," she reminds me. "You don't want a bunch of people staring at you."

Even though this isn't the first time my mother has said something like this, my cheeks still burn with embarrassment. In her defense, though, I have done every single thing on her list of rules.

I have gotten drunk at parties.

I have danced when no one else was dancing. One time, I actually got up on the table and started slow dancing. But only because everything was just so boring and lifeless, and I wanted to have a little fun. I have also laughed too loud and talked too loud. And yes, people have stared at me and the next day, I have ended up in gossip magazines and websites.

Embarrassing the shit out of my mother and my father.

"Keep going," she says. "There's more."

I know there's more.

This last one is somehow harder to say.

Because it's also the one I'm the most famous for.

Or infamous for.

But I know my mom won't stop looking at me like I'm a criminal if I don't say it. "No other m-men."

Her jaw moves back and forth.

Of course in displeasure.

While my mom can still tolerate me being all brazen and inappropriate, too unpredictable for her liking, what she absolutely cannot tolerate is the reputation I have with men.

The reputation I've more or less cultivated myself.

This time, though, I have a defense for myself.

And it's that I didn't know.

I had *no clue* that I was cultivating a reputation for myself if I flirted with my bodyguard to go to a party. I was just thinking about the party at the time. I had no idea that if I batted my eyelashes a little at the bartender so he'll let me taste whiskey for the first time, I was painting a target on my back for being too easy; I was just thinking about the whiskey and how I wanted to try it even though I was thirteen. Or the time when I was failing my science class, so I thought why not be nice to Mr. Sanders. Why not smile at him and laugh at his unfunny jokes so he'll give me a passing grade. Which he did. He also tried to get me alone in a classroom one day and when I refused, he went to the principal about my inappropriate behavior.

I've explained all this to my mother multiple times. I've explained each and every situation to her, but she always says that it's my fault. That I shouldn't have smiled or flirted or batted my eyelashes. She thinks it's a girl's responsibility to keep guys in check. And girls who are irresponsible like me are sluts.

"Not when the whole world is watching, Isadora," she adds, coming closer and grabbing my elbow. "Is that clear?"

I jump. "Yes."

She digs her nails into my skin and insists, "Not when every eye is already upon you."

I gasp at the pain. "I won't…"

But my mom isn't happy with that.

She pinches my flesh, her eyes harsh. "Not when you're so *tied* to the team."

Tears sting my eyes then.

From the pain. The burn.

From the way my heart's pounding in my chest. "I'm not… I won't do anything."

"You'd better not," Mom says. "I mean it, Isadora. I won't have you embarrassing this family. Especially when the season's starting and everyone's watching the team. Everyone's talking about us. And if we end up in the media for *anything* other than the team winning the championship for the second year in a row, I'll make you regret it. Is that very"—she twists my flesh—"*very* clear?"

I can't stop my grimace then.

I can't stop myself from squirming and trying to get away from her.

"Mom, you—"

She doesn't let up, though. "Answer me, Isadora."

A lone tear slides down my cheek. "Y-yes. I won't do anything. I won't screw up. I won't embarrass you or D-dad."

She grits her teeth, studying me, probably trying to figure out if I'm telling the truth. "Good. Now go clean yourself up and find your table."

So I do that.

I escape.

I go clean myself up, wipe my tear off, freshen up my lipstick. Then I go find my table.

I'm seated with other players and their wives and girlfriends. And even though my conversation with my mother has put a damper on my spirits and my skin burns where she pinched me, I'm still happy to see them.

There's Tempest Thorne, wife of one of the players Ledger Thorne; Bronwyn Littleton, girlfriend to Conrad Thorne, the team's head coach; and Meadow Brooks, Riot Rivera's—another one of the players—fiancée. And they're all friendly and warm, and immediately draw me into a conversation after their initial greetings. Apparently, they're all talking about the last time they had sex.

"You're kidding," Bronwyn, or Wyn, says to Tempest, her eyes wide.

"Nope," she answers, an impish grin gracing her lips.

Meadow addresses Tempest as well. "Here? You"—she lowers her voice—"did it *here*?"

Tempest takes a sip of her drink and nods.

"At the event?" Meadow keeps going.

"That's what I'm saying." Then, "Hey, listen, okay. I have not one but *two* six-month-olds. Twins. And they both have a killer radar. They somehow always know when Mommy and Daddy are getting busy. So we need to get creative." She takes another sip of her drink. "Mommy wants a large family and Daddy has promised to give her everything she wants. Besides, Mommy always has a hard time keeping her hands off Daddy."

She looks over at the daddy then.

With wild dark hair that curls at the ends and cascades over his brows in a fringe, and a face that seems carved from stone with the most beautiful angles, Ledger has to be one of the most handsome men I've ever seen in my life. And his handsomeness only increases by the fact that every few seconds or so, his eyes find ways to stray over to his wife even though he's engaged in a passionate discussion. It makes me feel like he wants to make sure that Tempest is still there.

Or that she is safe.

Or maybe both.

It's very sweet.

"Where?" Wyn asks, fascinated.

"Why, you want suggestions?" Tempest smirks.

Wyn blushes. "I mean, kind of."

At this, I chime in, "No way."

Wyn turns to me. "Why not?"

Now I lower my voice and all the girls lean in. "I don't think your man would go for something like that."

At this, Tempest bursts out laughing, causing Wyn to swat her arm.

While Meadow and I simply look at each other in confusion. Then Meadow goes, "I think Isadora's right."

I nod. "I mean, look at him. He looks so controlled and professional."

We all do.

Conrad Thorne.

Along with being the head coach of New York City FC and Wyn's boyfriend, he also happens to be Ledger's oldest brother. When I first heard that, though, it was a big surprise. Because they look nothing alike.

On the outside, I mean.

If Ledger has dark hair and dark eyes, Conrad has dirty-blond hair and navy blue eyes. While Ledger, also known as the Angry Thorn—his soccer nickname—perpetually looks thrumming with a violent energy that he can unleash at any second, Coach Thorne is more reserved. I'm not fool enough to think he's a cool guy with zero temper issues, but where others may resort to violence, Conrad Thorne appears as if he will wither you away with just one look.

And so again, I can't imagine him getting busy in a public place.

"I bet he only does missionary," Meadow murmurs and then claps a hand on her mouth. "I can't believe I said that about Coach Thorne." Then, turning to Wyn, "Oh my God, I meant no offense. I swear."

It just makes Tempest laugh harder.

And rolling her eyes, Wyn swats her arm again. "Stop laughing."

Tempest wipes the tears of mirth from her eyes. "Sorry, sorry. It's just..." She wheezes some more. "It's just really funny that they think he won't jump at the chance to do dirty things to you in a public place."

Wyn shrugs, a small, secretive smile on her lips. "I like it. They all think he's grumpy and colorless. That he's so serious"—her eyes shift to him—"but he's not. He has colors. He has nuances. He's my muse."

As if Coach Thorne heard it, he swings his gaze over to his artistic Wyn. And his navy blue eyes smolder in a way that for the first time I can actually see why Tempest was laughing at us. Because I do think Coach Thorne would jump at the chance to do dirty things to Wyn in a public place. In fact, he may clear out this ballroom with one of his legendary stares just so he could be alone with her.

"What are we all laughing about?" a new arrival, Jupiter, asks.

She's a redhead and is so stunning that I can't. She's not a wife or a girlfriend, but she's been hanging around the tables, dropping in for a chat here and there. Because she's good friends with the other girls—Meadow and Jupiter grew up together, in fact—and she's working the event as one of the waitstaff.

I'm extremely new to their girl group, but from what I understand, their gang is much larger, with a few more girls who aren't here tonight, but most of them went to high school together, called St. Mary's School for Troubled Teenagers, a girls only reform school in the neighboring town of St. Mary's.

Their friendship is the kind I would've loved to have when I was in high school. They've all been through a lot and have supported each other through thick and thin. And if I'm being honest, I'm a little envious of that kind of love.

Tempest pulls Jupiter down and whispers in her ear, probably telling her what we all have been talking about. When Jupiter's all up to speed, she gives Meadow a look first, then me before rolling her eyes. "Children." Then, "Trust me when I say, they both set our school on fire with their longing, pining gazes."

"Shut up," Wyn mutters, swatting Jupiter instead.

Oh yeah, Coach Thorne—before he was the head coach for New York City FC—used to be a coach at St. Mary's. Which is where they fell in love. They should probably make a movie about it. Actually, they should make a movie about all these girls' love stories.

"What about you, Meadow?" Tempest moves on to her, breaking my thoughts. "Do you think Riot and you would do it in a public place?"

This time, Jupiter cackles knowingly and Meadow swats *her* arm. "Oh yeah, they so totally would."

"Shut up," Meadow mutters, her cheeks flushing. "Well, I don't think... I... He..."

Surreptitiously, we all look at her beau, Riot, and sigh.

He's busy in a discussion with Ledger and Coach Thorne, his dark hair mussed up and long, almost kissing his eyebrows. I think of all the men at this table, his hair's the longest right now—even longer than Coach Thorne's, who's famous for his long-ish hair. Not to mention, his skin is the most tanned too, owing to his Latin heritage. And hence glows the most, inevitably drawing your eyes toward him.

God, he's handsome.

Like all the other men, his eyes check in on Meadow as well. Actually, he checks in on Meadow the most. Because they just started going out. They got engaged right away, though, because they've known each other a while; Meadow used to be Riot's daughter Sophia's nanny. In fact, she just got a wedding dress; she invited me along to go shopping. See? Friendly.

And I corroborate Jupiter's statement. "Oh yeah, totally."

Wyn chuckles. "Yup."

Tempest laughs too. "Yeah, that was a silly question."

Meadow blushes and ducks her eyes.

"What about you?" Tempest settles on me. "Would you guys do it in public?"

I mean, I should've expected it.

I should've been ready for it, the question.

As I've mentioned before, that's the good thing about these girls. Even though we've only met a handful of times, they've all been very good to me. They've all been welcoming and inclusive. So them posing this question to me while going around the table, so to speak, is normal.

But for a second or two, my brain shuts down.

For a second or two, I don't know what to say.

What words to use.

What gestures to make.

What should I *do* exactly?

Which is so unusual for me.

Because I'm good at lying. I'm *good* at acting.

It's just that... They're all so friendly and the more I get to know them, the more I find that I hate lying to them. And that's what I'm doing, aren't I? I'm lying about certain things.

I'm saved, though, when the room explodes with applause and their attention diverts.

Thank God.

Instead, we all focus on what's happening on the raised platform, which serves as the makeshift stage where my dad has begun his speech. He talks about how much money he's raised for the team via charity events and his campaigning during off-season. Followed by how he built the team that's all set to be on its winning streak, all by himself.

I'm not going to lie, it makes me feel bad for the team.

For the people who actually do the work.

Like the players and the coaches.

I've never been interested in soccer, but I can imagine how hard they work. How disciplined they have to be in order to achieve this level of excellence.

But my dad's always been like that. He cares about himself, his money, his status, his reputation. And my mom, who's sitting up front, is a perfect match for him. Despite being from two very vastly different cultures, my parents are actually happy together. Or as happy as they can be with their suppressed emotions and negativity.

When my dad's done talking about his achievements, he dedicates the last ten seconds or so to the coach of the team. Meaning he introduces him by the name and welcomes him on the stage, and that's about it.

Applause breaks out once again as Coach Thorne takes the stage. While my dad described his cleverness in much detail, Coach Thorne is succinct and to the point. He rests all the success on his players' and his staff's shoulders. He praises them for their dedication and hard work during the off-season, and talks about how they need to keep doing what they've been doing because the new season's upon them. When he's done, he welcomes the next person: the captain of the team.

The captain of the team is just as succinct as his coach was. Who also happens to be his brother, by the way; yeah, there are a lot of Thornes and they're all affiliated with the New York City FC. Only his speech is laden with the F-word and a couple of jokes of the dirty variety. Which earns him copious amounts of laughter and a side-eye from his big brother, who's back at the table we're all sitting at. But when his speech is over, the laughter and applause and whistles that break out can probably be heard throughout New York City. If I didn't know any better, I'd think that people were relieved that he was leaving.

But I do know better.

They're not making this ruckus because their captain has left the stage.

They're applauding because of *where* he's going.

They're jubilant because of who he's striding toward. All purposefully and determinedly.

Toward his girlfriend.

And when he reaches her, he leans down and offers her his hand, and the applause that I didn't think could get any louder does. So much so that I don't think I can hear my own heartbeats anymore. I don't think I can hear my own thoughts.

Maybe that's why it takes me a second or two to realize that he's offering his hand to me.

That people are clapping and cheering for *us*.

Because I'm her.

I'm the girlfriend.

Me.

Isadora Agni Holmes.

Shepard 'The Wrecking' Thorne's girl.

CHAPTER 2

*H*e's staring at me.

From his spot across the ballroom, where he's watching everyone else at this party, I imagine his eyes on me. That he's watching me dance with him.

His twin brother.

That he's watching and he's *seething*.

His fingers are tightening and tightening around his still almost full whiskey tumbler. His dark eyes, chocolate brown like his hair, are narrowing and flashing. His jaw, always clean-shaven and so angular and hard, is clenching in anger.

I imagine he wants to push off that wall and stride across the room.

And he wants to do it in a hurry.

So much so that he shoves people away. He puts his large hands on their body and physically removes them from his path. And he can do it too. He's so tall and broad and built. Not in a brutish way, though. In a way that all soccer players are built: sleek and sculpted, with dense bones and streamlined muscles. Even though he doesn't play anymore, he still looks the part. And he's going to use his quiet strength to destroy all obstacles in his path to get what he wants.

Me.

And when, at last, he gets to me, I imagine him ripping me from his twin's arms. I imagine him spinning me around and crashing me against his muscular body. And when I gasp at the force, at his violence, he captures it with his cigarette-smoking mouth.

He finally, *finally* gives me what I asked him for.

A year ago.

On my eighteenth birthday.

A kiss.

A soul-wrecking, gut-clenching kiss.

But it's not going to happen.

He's not going to kiss me.

He's probably not even looking at me right now.

First because this isn't a movie. He's not a tortured hero and I'm not a tragic heroine. Our love isn't star-crossed or written in the wind. And second because it's been a year now and he hasn't done any of those things. In fact, he hasn't even spared me more than a passing glance. So instead of making up scenarios in my head, all cinematic complete with a background score, I should focus on the present. I should focus on what I'm actually doing right now.

And what's happening around me.

I'm on the dance floor and I'm kinda being watched.

Not by whom I want but by Jupiter.

Okay, don't quote me on this, but I think, I *think*, she has a little crush on the man I'm dancing with. I've caught her staring at him a few times but haven't broached the subject with her.

Because well, he's with me.

I mean, he just claimed me in front of everyone.

That's what he did, didn't he?

He claimed me.

This isn't the first time he has done that, though. He's offered me his hand, his arm to hold on to; he's pulled out chairs for me; he's opened doors for me. One time, he even carried me in his arms because my heel broke while we were walking down the street, and instead of letting me limp along, he bent down and carried me to the restaurant we had been headed to, to meet his teammates.

And I'm not going to lie, I've encouraged it.

I've encouraged his hand holding, hugging, carrying me around.

His claiming.

Because it served a purpose.

A very selfish purpose he's unaware of.

"Are you ready for the season?" I ask.

I know it sounded abrupt.

Given that we haven't said a single word to each other ever since he dragged me out here on the dance floor with several other couples who are swaying in each other's arms to slow music.

Which is very unlike us.

If we're both good at one thing, it's the talking.

Sharing jokes.

Making each other laugh.

Something that was apparent the very first time I met him at my eighteenth birthday party. The moment I found him by the pool chatting with some of his teammates and asked him to dance with me, I knew. I *knew* from his arrogant smirk and the impish look in his eyes that we were going to be best friends.

Oh, and then there were his words: *Let me guess, you're trying to piss someone off. Your dad, most likely.*

And when I asked if he'd help me, he went, *Fuck yeah. Not a huge fan of your daddy.*

Instant best friends.

It was like I found a kindred soul.

Ever since then, we've been inseparable. And it would be amazing if our forced proximity was only because I very unexpectedly found a best friend in him when I was, in fact, trying to piss someone off—just not my daddy.

But it's not, is it?

And it's becoming increasingly difficult to bear that burden.

"Are we making useless chitchat now?" he asks instead.

My eyes snap up from his Adam's apple—the spot I've been looking at all this time—and go to his face. His dark eyes shine with mischief. Thick, curly lashes, that mussed up hair he runs his fingers through. That arrogant nose and those lips, always on the verge of smirking. Like he knows a secret joke no one else does.

Shepard Thorne is a quintessential bad boy.

A rule breaker. Fun, irreverent.

Popular and arrogant.

Life of a party.

And a complete and utter opposite of a certain someone I can't get out of my head.

I wave all that away, though.

"What?" I try to pinch his arm but fail. "It's a legit question. The season's starting next week. Are you ready or not?"

He gives me a look. "All right then. To answer your question, Miss Holmes, yes. I am ready. The entire team is ready. We brought home the trophy last time and we're doing it this time too. Because we don't fuck around when it's something that belongs to us."

I raise my eyebrows. "That was a little arrogant, don't you think, Mr. Thorne?"

"Arrogance is just confidence with a few extra inches," he shoots back. "And if you know anything about me, you know I've got a lot of those."

"Are you saying *you've* got a few extra inches?"

"I'm saying I've got a lot of few extra inches."

I shake my head, trying to curb my smile. "Maybe you're not aware, Mr. Thorne, but you've just made a double entendre on national TV."

"Oh, I'm aware, Miss Holmes."

"I don't know if it's appropriate for our delicate audience, however."

"Well, you're just going to have to bleep me out, then."

"I guess so."

"What about you, though?"

"What about me?"

He dips his face toward me. "Are you too delicate for my double entendres and extra inches?"

I pretend to think. "Well, I'm going to have to think about that. On one hand, I *am* a lady, but on the other, I'm also very well aware of your pre-season rituals, so I don't know, Mr. Thorne. It's a tough choice."

I laugh then.

Because until I said it, I had completely forgotten about that.

About his pre-season ritual.

Or more like start of the season ritual.

Something he'd told me about the same night we'd met. While dancing together, we started exchanging crazy things we'd done in our lives. Mine was streaking through a party on a dare—I was drunk and in a playful mood. And his was the twins story. So for the lack of a better way to explain it: every start of the season—ever since his high school soccer career—he somehow finds two girls who are identical twins and has a threesome with them.

Yup.

A threesome.

With identical twins.

First of all, it's so hard to find identical twins, or at least I imagine it would be. And second of all, if he did find them and if they're age-appropriate, so many things have to align: they have to be willing to have a threesome with him. They have to be willing to get naked in front of their sibling. Not to mention, they have to be willing to *be* a one-night stand. And when I raised all those questions to him, and I did at the time, he told me it just happened for him. That he never had to put in a lot of effort in finding these girls; they just showed up and everybody banged and then everybody left.

The girls for his last season came all the way from Chicago.

But anyway.

The important thing is that I'm laughing. That all the heaviness from earlier, all the awkwardness I'd built up in my head, my encounter with my mother is gone and it's all because of him.

Is it any wonder that I love him?

As a friend, I mean.

Which puts an instant damper on my mirth.

And I realize that the heaviness is still there, after all. Because he isn't laughing.

He doesn't think anything is funny.

"Yeah, you know about that, don't you?" he murmurs.

"I don't…" I shake my head. "I didn't mean anything by it. I—"

"Just for the record, I didn't this year." He shrugs, kinda sheepishly. "Not that it makes me a prince or anything. I—"

"It does," I interrupt him, trying to put his mind at ease. "I-I mean, you already were. A prince. With or without it. And, Shep, I don't care if you sleep with other girls. You're my friend and I know you, and it doesn't matter to me that—"

"I'm your friend, huh?"

I realize that heaviness that was lingering in the air has now reached his frame. His expression.

His eyes.

And my heart squeezes.

It squeezes and squeezes, and I just... I want to turn back time.

I want to go back to the moment when we first met, and when he'd said that thing about pissing off my dad, I want to tell him the truth this time. I want to tell him exactly who I was trying to piss off.

I want a do-over.

Please.

Or actually just let me go back to any of the other moments that came after, when I started to get the feeling that he thought of me as *more* than a friend.

"Shepard," I begin. "I—"

"It was a big surprise for all of us when my brother got hooked up," he begins.

And I stumble a little.

At the mention of his brother.

At the mention of... *him*.

That's who Shepard is talking about, isn't it?

He is... Oh God, is it?

Is it him?

Did he hook up with someone? Who did he hook up with?

Who is she?

I've been watching him for the past year.

Obsessively. Sickly. Madly.

How did I not notice that he's with someone? That—

"Conrad," he clarifies and my frantic thoughts break.

I'm able to take a breath that was caught up somewhere in my chest, tangled up with the veins in my lungs, the chambers of my heart.

Okay, so Conrad.

Right.

I mean, it's not as if Shepard has one brother only. He has three.

Conrad Thorne, the oldest Thorne sibling and the head coach. Ledger Thorne, the youngest Thorne brother—not the youngest sibling, though; they also have a sister and she's the youngest of all.

And well, *him*, his twin.

"Especially when we all heard that it was with a student of his," he continues, his eyes now settled on something over my shoulder. "A student who's fourteen years younger and also happens to be Callie's best friend."

Callie, their baby sister.

That I am a year younger than.

Calliope Thorne, or, well, Jackson now. Because she's married to Tempest Thorne's—formerly Jackson—brother, Reed. They were supposed to be here too, but Callie's pregnant with their second baby; they have an adorable little girl, Halo. I've only met Callie once, so I don't know her that well, but I've heard good things about her. She also belongs to the girl gang with Tempest and Wyn that I was talking about earlier.

"I actually took a bet," Shepard confesses, his focus still somewhere else. "Thought it wouldn't happen. Lost two hundred dollars to Ledge. That fucker."

"You took a bet against your own brother?" I ask, incredulous.

He comes back to me and shrugs. "I knew he'd fallen for her. We all did. I just didn't think Con would ever admit to it. That he'd fallen for someone inappropriate like Wyn." Then, "I'm happy that he did, though. He deserves it."

I think so too.

I've only known the Thorne brothers personally for a year now, but I know their story. I knew it before I knew them. It's almost a legend in town. And like every legend, it has tragedy and perseverance embedded in the very core of it.

Everyone knows their father abandoned them when Callie was only a few months old. Leaving their mother to take care of all the Thorne children, and since Conrad was the oldest—and in his teens by the time Callie was born—he took the brunt of all the responsibility. Meaning that Conrad stood by their mother, supported her in every way possible while she worked three jobs just to keep the roof over their heads.

As sad and tough as that sounds, it still would have been fine. They were surviving. They were happy even, from what I hear. But then a few years later, tragedy struck again when their mom got sick with cancer. She died when Conrad turned eighteen after her long battle with the disease. At which point, Conrad dropped out of college, left his still-in-the-making but stellar soccer career so he could take care of his siblings.

Honestly, it makes my heart ache just thinking about it.

Just thinking about everything they went through and they did it all alone. I don't even know *how* they did it. Just that I can't help but admire their courage and strength and want to shower them in hugs. I want to even hug Coach Thorne, who looks all kinds of scary to me, and Ledger, who appears so unapproachable with his anger and handsomeness; I regularly hug Shepard and if I met Callie again, I'd give her a hug as well.

And him...

Well, I don't want to think about him right now.

Not when my best friend is trying to tell me something.

"I was even more surprised when Ledge hooked up," he informs me as we sway lightly to the music. "Not because he doesn't deserve it, but because I never thought he'd settle down. He was just too wrapped up in himself and in the game to get involved with someone."

"But that's a good thing, right?" I prod when he doesn't speak for a bit. "Your siblings settling down, finding love."

"Yeah, it is," he replies, his eyes boring into me. "Now."

"What does that mean?"

His answer is to sigh, his broad chest undulating. "I felt betrayed."

"What?"

"At first." Another deep breath before he explains, "I felt like I was left behind. Like we were a team, all five of us, or at least all four of us brothers, who took care of our baby sister. But then suddenly, they had someone else they needed to take care of. That they brought into the family when it had always been just us. *We* were a family. Us and no one else. We knew how cruel the world could be, how cruel fate could be. Everyone who'd loved us or was supposed to love us either died or disappeared. And for the longest time, all we had was each other. We shouldered responsibilities. We wiped each other's tears. We cheered each other up. We made each other laugh, and... I resented their love in the beginning. I resented my siblings moving on, expanding their world. But then I..."

"Then you what?"

As soon as I ask the question, I know what he's going to say.

I *know*.

And my heart breaks.

My heart bleeds for him.

Not only will he hate me if I tell him the truth now and I will lose his friendship—something I've never had much of in my life—I will also hurt him.

God, I will hurt him so badly.

And I don't know how to deal with that.

I don't know how to prevent that from happening.

From the pain I may cause him one day.

"Then I met you." He looks back at me. "You were different."

And I want to stop him.

I want to open my mouth and tell him to stop talking.

To not say the things he's going to say.

They're lovely things, wonderful things.

But I don't deserve to hear them.

He should hear the truth first.

But my voice is gone.

All I can do is stare up at him and his serious expression. Something that's a rare sight.

His resting face is irreverent and full of playfulness.

"You made me laugh. Not many people can do that. You weren't impressed by me and my soccer skills. Again, not many people can resist that. Girls definitely can't. You called me out on my bullshit. And I never thought I'd like that. Every time I put my moves on you, tried to use my charms on you, you remained unaffected. And I thought to myself," he scoffs, "she's going to be a challenge. I thought to myself that I liked that. I liked that you were going to be tough to crack. I liked that you weren't starstruck, that you weren't intimidated by me.

You held your own. You *can* hold your own. And so I thought maybe she just needs time. Maybe I need to be patient with her, chase her a little. So this is me chasing you."

I grip the sleeves of his jacket. "Shep, listen, there's something you need to know. There's—"

"I want you," he says, his eyes on me, penetrating, dark. "I want us to be together. I want what other people already think we have and they do, don't they?"

They do.

They *do*.

And that's the whole point.

Oh my God, that *has been* the whole point all along.

I wanted that.

I wanted them to think we were together, Shepard and I.

I *wanted* the world to think we were a couple.

It didn't start out that way, though.

When I asked him to dance with me on my birthday a year ago, that was all it was going to be.

One dance.

A few minutes of flirting and that's it.

A few minutes of talking and laughing together and pretending that I was into him. As it turns out, I was—just as a friend, though—because I genuinely found Shepard wonderful and amazing.

But when that one dance wasn't enough, I deliberately started showing up wherever Shepard went. I deliberately started taking an interest in soccer games and practices. I purposely made dates with Shepard and showed up at team events and parties.

All because of one thing and one thing only: *him*.

The Cold Thorn.

Who feels as hot as wildfire.

To make him jealous. To move him. To melt him.

To get him to eat his words from that night.

To get him to kiss me.

Like a selfish, immature girl with a heart swollen with too many feelings, I pursued him with a one-minded devotion. I pursued him with everything in me, uncaring of consequences, unbothered by the means I was using.

Means being his twin brother.

I thought it was the perfect plan. I thought even though the world thought we were together, Shepard wouldn't. I thought a player like him—with pre-season rituals and one-night stands galore—would never be interested in me.

But I should've known, shouldn't I?

My mom calls me a slut for a reason.

She calls me a temptation to men. She says I'm the one who provokes them into doing things, and that's what I did here. That's what I *always* do.

I use men.

And while I never felt bad about that before, I do now.

I feel bad for using Shepard. For throwing myself at him to make *him* jealous.

For making him want to be with me while every time I dance with him, I imagine it's *his* arms around me. I imagine *him* finally being overcome with jealousy and claiming me with a kiss.

God, I'm awful.

I'm an awful human being.

"They do," I whisper at last.

Shepard watches me for a few beats and I know I could use this silence to finally tell him the truth about me. But like a coward, I stay silent too.

I wait for him to say whatever it is he's going to say.

And when he does, I blink in confusion.

"Our first home game is in eight weeks," he informs me.

"First... Okay."

"You've got until then to decide."

"D-decide what?"

"Whether you want to be with me."

"Whether..."

"Because as it turns out, patience isn't my strong suit."

I run his words in my head over and over.

I try to make sense of them.

I know it's there, right there, the implication of things, but it's taking me some time to figure it out.

Then, "Are you... Is this an ultimatum?"

His jaw clenches, stubbled, unlike *him*. "Yes. Because I don't think I can take it anymore."

"Take w-what?"

"Being your friend." Then, studying my face, "Just your friend."

My fingers tighten in his suit jacket.

As if I can stop him from doing this. As if I can stop him from making commands he already has. "Shepard, I—"

He steals my words when he says, "I love you, Isadora. And I want you to be with me."

Then he bends down and places a soft kiss.

On my forehead. "Good night."

And then he turns around and leaves.

I should go after him.

I know that.

I should stop him from leaving.

I should tell him the truth. I should put him out of his misery.

If he knows the truth, he'll hate me and that's better than wanting to be with me, isn't it?

Isn't hate better than love?

Oh God, he loves me.

Loves.

It's the worst. Because I know what it feels like. I know what it feels like to be in love with someone who doesn't love you back.

I *know*.

I also know I can't go to him yet. I can't.

I have to...

I have to go to *him*.

For some reason, I need *him* in this moment.

When I glance at those doors, though, he's not there anymore. He's gone and I have to find him.

I have to find my wildfire.

CHAPTER 3

I shouldn't be doing it.
 I shouldn't be searching for him when my best friend's in pain. When the reason he's in pain, unbeknownst to him, is because of the man I'm going after.
Because of these crazy feelings I have for him.
Not to mention, searching for someone who claims to be colder than this winter night is not advisable.
I don't even know *why* I'm searching for him.
All I know is that if I don't find him, my heart is going to beat out of my chest and I'm going to perish.
So here I am.
I scan the ground as best as I can in the wintry darkness. Snow clings to the air and the ground as I make my way farther and farther away from the ballroom. When I can't find him anywhere in the vicinity, I venture into the part of the grounds that's flanked by bare and scary-looking trees and seems more slippery and chillier. The winter air's more brutal as it slashes through my bare arms and shoulders, making even me think—the girl who loves the sharpness of cold— that I should've put on a coat at least.
"Running away again?"
My gasp is loud.
Louder than probably that voice.
That deep, deep voice.
That reminds me of a bottomless well.
I whirl around and for the first time in a year, come face to face with him.
I know it sounds dramatic—in a year and all that—but it's true. Even though I've seen him around, I've been to the same places as him, deliberately

put myself in his path so he can stumble upon me, we haven't been alone since the night we met a year ago. We haven't talked to each other or come in contact with each other in any way whatsoever since then.

He's always been there but only in my periphery.

I always looked at him from the corner of my eye, with surreptitious side glances. And now that I have him in front of me, I can't stop staring.

He's standing under a tree like he was the night I met him. It's not a pink magnolia, but it doesn't matter. Because everything else is the same. His casual lean against the trunk; his dark clothes; the fact that he's in the shadows and that cigarette of his.

Dangling from his plush lips, all orange and glow-y.

Sending out curls of smoke.

Reminding me of a rose set on fire.

"You scared me," I say after a year of not saying anything to him.

He gets that cancer stick out of his mouth and, sending a puff of smoke into the air, speaks, "You don't look scared."

I think he's right.

I probably don't. I probably look the opposite of scared.

I probably look all flushed and breathless.

Because I'm the same too.

From a year ago.

I'm feeling the same feelings. The same emotions, the same thrill. The same ecstasy running through my veins that I'd felt when I'd stumbled upon him.

"I am, trust me," I insist because maybe if I keep saying it, it'll become true.

All my ecstasy will turn into fear.

All my thrill will turn into revulsion.

"Well, then you shouldn't be out here all alone at night," he shares.

"Or maybe you shouldn't be standing out here hidden in the night like some sort of a thug."

"A thug," he repeats.

"Yes."

His silence feels thoughtful. "And here I thought I was a bodyguard."

A jolt goes through me like I've been electrocuted.

Like I stuck my finger in the power socket and now every corner in my body is filled with electricity, every cell buzzes, every nerve crackles.

All because he said something completely inconsequential from that night.

"And here *I* thought," I shoot back, watching his silhouette, "that the world needed protection from me and not the other way around."

"Old men, specifically," he reminds me as if he needs to.

As if I don't think of that night—also enact it on some occasions—every single day.

"And then," I keep sharing, "we decided that you're safe because you're not that old."

"But now you know that I am," he returns.

He is.

Or at least *he* thinks he is even though he's only seven years older than me. And since I'm only nineteen, that puts him at twenty-six. Not old by any means whatsoever and even if he were, I know I wouldn't care.

When it comes to him, I don't care much about anything at all, to be honest. And that's the problem.

That has *always* been the problem.

"So maybe," I say, "it's *you* who should be scared."

He takes a drag. "I guess so."

"Well, it's not too late. You can still go back inside and save yourself from me."

"Maybe I should."

"You—"

"Because I don't think I'm in the mood to be mauled by a half-naked girl tonight."

"I didn't *maul* you," I say, taken aback.

He lets out another puff of smoke. "Forced yourself upon me then."

"I did not do that either," I say vehemently.

"No?"

"Absolutely not."

"So what would you call it?" he asks.

He sounds so genuinely curious that I can't help but answer, "Seizing my destiny."

"Ah"—he lets out another cloud of toxic smoke—"somehow I'd forgotten about that."

At this, I'm burning in the middle of winter.

With embarrassment.

"You don't have to—"

"So what about tonight?" he asks, cutting me off.

"What *about* tonight?"

He sucks in a drag, his cheeks hollowing out and his chest expanding before he lets it out. "Any particular reason you're half-naked?"

"What?" This time, my voice sounds squeaky. "Are you... I'm not half-naked!"

"It's forty degrees out."

"So?"

"So you should probably wear something more than that flimsy thing you have on."

The flimsy thing he's referring to is my scarlet Vera Wang dress. And yes, it's tight and short and hardly a cover against this brutal weather, but how dare he. It's pretty and has spaghetti straps. It has a slit running down my left thigh and a huge rosette-style flower on the right side of the bodice that makes it both edgy and feminine.

"I'm fine," I announce.

"If you keep standing out here for too long, you won't be."

"Are you saying you're worried about me?"

"I'm saying I'm not in the mood to interrupt my smoke of the day to haul a dead body inside," he says, taking a long drag to emphasize his point.

"Smoking is injurious to health," I inform him primly even though there's nothing prim or proper about me.

"Your point?"

"So you shouldn't be doing it."

"Now, are you saying you're worried about me?"

"No."

"Good."

"Why's that good?" I keep arguing.

"Because I'm not him."

"Who's him?"

"Your boyfriend."

"I don't..."

It's like I slammed into a wall.

And all my words, my breaths, my heartbeats get knocked out of me.

Leaving me empty.

Breathless. Thoughtless. Speechless.

I'm just... less.

Than I was a second ago.

A second ago, while I was going back and forth with him, I felt alive. I felt like I was flying on my fake wings. But now it feels like someone—him—froze them.

Froze *me*.

With his chill.

Leaving me a little less alive.

"And I'm not sure if your boyfriend would like it that you're worried about me," he finishes.

"He—"

"Actually, I'm not sure if he'd like it at all that you're out here, talking to a strange man."

I can't help but rub my arms then. "You're not a strange man. You're his twin brother."

I notice his chest moving then.

Expanding and contracting with the next drag he takes. The longest until now.

Then, "I wouldn't."

My heart races. "You're—"

"So you should probably run along to him."

"That's what you said to me that night too," I say before I've had a chance to think it through.

I also do what I try to avoid doing before I've had a chance to think it through.

Study him.

Or in this case, when I can't see him: map out the differences in my head.

Differences between Shepard and him.

Even though they're identical twins, they never looked similar to me, let alone identical.

Their hair may be the same color, dark chocolate brown, but one keeps it deliberately mussed up and longer, while the other keeps it short and pushed back from his face. They both may have the same heavy-boned and square jaw, but one keeps it stubbled and the other clean-shaven. And the shape and dusky color of their lips may be the same but only one has the perfect pout that I think has come from years of smoking one cigarette per day and slowly killing himself.

Even their voices are different.

As in, they *sound* different.

One sounds friendly and easy and open, while the other blends in calmness and condescension so easily that it hurts and feels good at the same time.

I'll give you one hint who that brother is.

The one with shorter hair, clean-shaven jaw, and pouty lips. That hurt-y voice.

It's not my best friend Shepard.

It's the guy who pushed me toward him.

He did that, didn't he?

Not only did he reject me that night, but he told me—*explicitly*—to go to him.

He *told* me to go to his brother.

So it's not all my fault that I did, is it?

It's not all my fault that I used Shepard to get to him and now Shep's hurting. It's not all my fault that he wants to be with me. With a girl who's obsessed with his twin brother. He deserves better.

He deserves so, so much better than me and *him*.

"You *told* me to run off to him," I accuse, my hands fisted, anger coursing through my veins.

"And you did."

I'd like to think that his tone is accusing as well.

That he's mad about it.

About the fact that I ran off to his brother minutes after trying to get him to kiss me. That I didn't even *wait* to go flirt with someone else after flirting with him, mauling him half-naked as he called it.

I want him to be angry about that.

I want him to be *jealous*.

I want him to think that I'm a slut. The only time I *know* I'd like being called one: by *him*.

But I don't think he does.

Because he sounds calm, his tone soft.

In fact, more than *saying* those words, he *murmured* them. Instead of standing up straight and taut like I am, he's still leaning against that tree, cigarette dangling from his lips.

It pisses me off.

That he can remain unaffected like that.

While the world around me is burning.

"Yes, I did." I narrow my eyes. "Because you were an asshole to me. You humiliated me. You made me *cry* that night."

He did.

After I left him at the tree, I ran back up to my room. I cried in my pillow like the heroine from a melodrama whose destiny was just ripped from her fingers. Then I pulled myself together. I let anger consume me and shed my wings. I changed into the clothes my mother had picked out for me and did my makeup to give myself a smoky, seductive look before going in search of his twin brother. I invited him to dance on the floor that no one was dancing on, not until Shepard accepted my invitation and we started slow dancing to fast music.

And every second I spent in the arms of his brother, I missed his.

I missed their quiet strength, the steely muscles, the way they curled around me, keeping me safe from falling as if he really was my bodyguard and his job was to save me from myself.

From all the insane things I do.

"Well, from where I was standing, you looked pretty fucking happy to me," he declares.

"I wasn't," I tell him, accusation still laced in my tone. "And you weren't looking."

"Is that why you were dancing with him," he asks, "because you wanted me to look?"

"I was—" I pull myself back once again.

I catch myself in time from uttering the truth.

I'm not going to betray Shepard like that.

Not after what happened tonight. Not after how he laid himself bare in front of me while his twin can't even be bothered to conjure up one little emotion for me. If someone deserves to know the whole truth first, it's Shepard.

Not *him*.

So I say, "I was dancing with him because I wanted to."

He waits to respond back because, once again, taking a drag is more important to him than me. "I'm glad you got what you wanted then."

I'm clenching my teeth.

I'm clenching my belly too, holding my muscles tight lest I burst out of my body.

"I did," I agree and then add because I just can't help myself, "Because he's more my type than you ever were."

"Is that so?"

"Yes." I raise my chin, rubbing my arms anew. "He's more fun and adventurous. Impulsive."

"Yeah, he's that."

"I know you're twins, but nothing, *not one thing*, about you and him is the same. You don't even look alike."

"Hmm. Not sure you know the meaning of identical then."

I scoff. "Technically, yes, you're identical twins. But not really. Not to me. I can tell you both apart with just one look."

I totally can.

And I still can't believe that others can't.

Again, he chooses to smoke first. Then, "Sounds like you've done a lot of looking."

Yes. You.

I've spent a lot of time looking at you.

I dig my nails into my arms. "Of course I have. He's my boyfriend."

After this, I take a few seconds to recover.

Because this is the first time I've said it.

The first time I've said *these words*.

Directly.

I've never said them before. To anyone. I've danced around it. I've beaten around the bush when people talk to me about it. I've never corrected people when they've assumed. But actually using the exact words, *that* I haven't done.

Not until now.

Not until him.

I didn't think, though, that it would be so hard. To lie. Not only because lying is a skill I'm good at and very comfortable with but also because this is exactly what I wanted.

This is my dream come true.

To throw these words at him and watch him burn with jealousy.

Only I can't see him all that well and the only thing that's burning is me.

"So I guess I was your destiny after all," he muses after a few seconds.

"You... What?"

"Because you wouldn't be with him"—he releases a puff of smoke—"if you hadn't met me."

God.

God.

I just...

I can't contain myself.

I can't contain all these rioting feelings inside of me.

I *can't*.

"You know, people think you're this great guy," I say, my nails cutting into my flesh. "Stellan Thorne, great coach. Great ex-soccer player. Great brother. Great, great, great. But you're not, are you? You're a fucking asshole in disguise."

The whole Bardstown thinks he's one of the good guys.

A straight A student while growing up; an amazing soccer player just like the rest of his brothers who could've gone pro if he wanted to but chose to be a coach; a saint of a brother who stepped up and took care of his siblings when their dad took off and their mother tragically died.

He's the quietest of the bunch; even quieter than their oldest brother Conrad Thorne. All the Thorne brothers have always had a spotlight on them, either from the way they grew up or from the fact that they're the soccer royalty of this town. Conrad Thorne, the greatest soccer coach there ever was; Shepard Thorne, the captain of the team that he's helped resurrect from the dead; Ledger Thorne, one of the most promising up-and-comers with a bright future in the European league.

But somehow, Stellan Thorne has always been the one who has managed to fly under the radar. Somehow, he's always been the one who has managed to stay in the shadows, avoiding this glaring spotlight that seems to follow these brothers everywhere they go.

The mysterious one.

The cold one.

The one who gets overlooked but maybe shouldn't.

But perhaps it's all a facade, huh?

Perhaps it's all fake. He's nothing like the good guy people think he is.

Which begs the question: why the hell am I so obsessed with him?

"So then what the fuck are you doing here?" he asks, his voice almost a growl.

A growl that reaches my clenched belly.

Because this is the first sign he's shown that my presence affects him.

That anything at all about me is affecting him.

In a whole year.

And I can't help but say or try to, "I'm... I want..."

I want you to kiss me.

I want you to want me.

I want you to be jealous. I want you to feel something for me. Someone else wants me. Your twin brother wants me. Why can't you? Why can't you want me enough to put a stop to all this?

Why can't you want me at all?

That's why I came.

Because I want him to want me. Because the game I started playing in my craziness, in his name has gotten out of hand and he *still* doesn't care about me.

I burned the world down for him, but he's still cold as winter.

But then again, I can't force him, can I?

No matter how angry I am, how frustrated, how utterly devastated that he feels nothing for me when I feel everything for him, he doesn't owe anything to me.

So my posture sags and my hands fall away from my arms. I look down at the ground that seems so icy that nothing will ever grow here. "I-I think I need to go."

And try to find a way out of this mess I've made.

But as it turns out, I can't do that.

I can't go anywhere.

Because as soon as I tell him that I'm leaving, he comes out of the shadows. He shows himself, all towering and broad chested. And it's not as if he comes at me in a flash, though, no. He takes his time. He *prowls* instead of *strides*. He leisurely approaches me, his cigarette clenched between his teeth, his hands in his pockets, his eyes pinned on me.

So saying that I *can't* go anywhere may be an exaggeration.

I can absolutely leave if I want to.

I have time to run away.

But I don't do that.

Like an idiot, I stand there and wait for him to reach me.

When he does, he slides his hands out of his pockets. Looking down at me and keeping the cigarette in his mouth, he pulls the front of his jacket apart. I watch the stick burning at the end, wispy smoke wafting as he rolls his broad shoulders and shrugs it off. Then, reaching forward, he swings it behind me and drapes it over my shoulders.

With my arms limp at my sides, I look up at him. "What are you doing?"

Adjusting the jacket on me with one hand and taking the cigarette out with the free one, he replies, "Saving you from yourself."

This is why, I think.

This is why I'm obsessed with him. This is why I'm in love with him and I am, aren't I?

Love at first sight.

Things that only happen in the movies, happened to me.

And it's because he has a habit of protecting me. Because under all that ice, I have a feeling he's got a heart that beats and beats oh so fiercely.

Oh so hotly.

As hot as his coat.

Hot like wildfire.

"I—"

I stop on a flinch.

Because his fingers brush against my elbow.

My left elbow.

Even though it's through the fabric of the tux and his touch was light—he was simply fiddling with the sleeve—I still feel a sting on the tender spot where my mother pinched me earlier.

"What was that?" he asks, a frown between his brows.

I immediately fold my arms across my chest, cupping my elbow, protecting it. "Nothing."

He glances down at my arms.

And I try to stand straight and tall, holding my posture from before.

When he still doesn't look away, I say, "I think I'm going to—"

He looks up. "What did your mother say to you?"

"What?"

"Earlier. By the bar."

His eyes are penetrating. So grave.

As bottomless as his voice that I can fall into.

"How do you know"—I lick my lips—"I was with my mother at the bar?"

"She said something," he replies, his features sharp and tight. "What was it?"

"I thought you don't look at me," I say instead. "I thought—"

"Was it about your acting?"

I draw back. "My acting?"

"Yeah." He keeps digging, his voice thick and low. "Was she giving you a hard time about that?"

I squeeze the bruised area as I keep looking at him.

I don't know why I can't answer him just yet.

I just can't.

Maybe because my heart's so full. My body's so full.

Of feelings. Of emotions.

He's still the only man I've told about my dream—other than my *biji*—who didn't laugh at me. Who didn't make a joke about it, dismiss it.

He was interested.

He was curious.

And God, he still is.

"Dora," he prods when all I do is stare at him.

And now there's no way I can answer him because... *Dora*.

He called me Dora.

"No one calls me that"—I swallow—"still."

A muscle jumps on his cheek. "She still give you a hard time about it?"

I nod, my heart racing in my chest. "Yeah. She doesn't want me to be an actress."

"And are you?"

"I'm what?"

"An actress"—his gaze flicking back and forth between mine—"yet? Because last time you were on your way to an audition to be one."

I don't know why I blush at this.

But I do.

Maybe it's his direct gaze. Or maybe because I'd sounded so hopeful back then.

So young.

Even though it was only a year ago.

"I never made it," I tell him.

I guess he already knows, though; I spent the night dancing with his twin brother in my quest to make him jealous.

"What happened to that guy who was waiting for you?" he asks next, his voice raspy now.

And I can't believe it.

Even though I know he remembers everything from that night; he's already proven that. I still can't wrap my head around the fact that he remembers the guy I'd mentioned to him in passing.

"He said I wasn't worth it," I share on a whisper.

"What?" he bites out.

When I didn't show up to meet him at his car, he called me nonstop. Something I noticed the next day. He left me numerous texts and voicemails, ranging from being concerned and cajoling to angry and ranting.

"He said that"—I remember the exact words from his last voicemail—"I couldn't be that good of a lay to make him wait for over an hour, and that I didn't have any talent to begin with anyway. So I kinda did him a favor by not showing up."

I'm used to men being angry at me.

It's the name of the game when you tempt them and refuse to put out. I don't mind it. But apparently, this man in front of me does. There's no question about it.

He is angry.

"What's his name?" he asks, his voice raspy sounding once again but in a way that's dark and threatening, and his jaw is tensed.

My heart's spinning in my chest. "Why?"

"He live in New York?"

"Bardstown."

"Then he'll be easy to find."

My eyes go wide. "Are you going to?"

Another clench of his jaw. "Yes."

"Why, so you can beat him up?"

"So I can teach him how to talk to a girl, yes."

"And how do you talk to a girl?"

"Nicely."

"Is that another one of your rules?"

"Yeah."

"You never talk nicely to me, though."

"What can I say," he murmurs, "you're fire and I'm ice. You're the only girl I melt for."

I close my eyes then.

Because it's music to my ears.

It's poetry.

It's a song for the ages.

But it's also a lie.

He doesn't melt for me.

I want him to, but he doesn't. And his mocking words are the proof.

Opening my eyes, I find that his are roving over my face. His are drinking my features in like he drinks that smoke.

Hungrily, compulsively.

Or so I think.

"You don't," I whisper, shaking my head. "So you don't get to ask questions like this. You don't get to ask about my dreams or my mom or that guy. If anyone is going to beat him up, it's *him*. Your twin brother. My boyfriend. And you're not him, are you?"

It's none of his business what my mother was saying to me. What my mother did. What she's always done—pinch me, dig her nails into my skin when no one's looking, smack me away from everyone's eyes. Something that's increased in the past year ever since I started hanging out with Shepard. Because she thinks I'll do something to screw it up. In my usual slutty fashion, I'll do something to cause a scandal and ruin the team. They already had to transfer or fire or trade in players and staff members in the last two years because of me, and now that team's finally on its winning streak and making money for my father, I'll mess things up.

So a few months ago, she banished me to Bardstown.

Where I could be away from New York and the team.

I think she always wanted to do it mostly because she wanted me away so she didn't have to deal with me and my scandalous ways, and also keep me closeted in a small town where I may not be able to pursue my dream. So when I started hanging out with Shep, she saw it as an opportunity and finally sent me away.

So here I am, living in one of their houses that I share with a housekeeper and a couple of bodyguards, going to the Bardstown community college where their theater department has one teacher and probably five students who double and triple and quadruple as writers, prop managers, costume designers, and set designers.

My *biji* was really mad when she'd heard about it. She didn't want my mom to send me away like that, make it even harder for me to pursue my dreams, but I promised her I wouldn't give up. I wouldn't let lack of funding or enthusiasm or resources or the fact that I'm not even officially registered to be in one of their classes deter me from my path. That's why ever since I started my freshman year, I've been trying to rally about funding, organizing bake sales and whatnot to gather funds. And we're so close. We may get to put on a show soon.

But again, he doesn't get to know any of that.

"So how come," he murmurs, "you're going to let me do it?"

I frown. "Do what?"

"Kiss you."

Once again, it feels like I've slammed against a wall. And I've slammed so hard that not only are my breaths knocked out, but this time, there's going to be a bruise on my body.

Purple and pulsating.

Painful.

As painful as this ache in my chest.

This longing.

"What?"

His eyes drop down to my parted mouth. "You will, won't you?"

I lick my lips and his eyes flare slightly. "I... No."

"How about I sweeten the pot?"

"No."

"And go further?" he goes on.

I wince. "I... Look, I don't know what—"

"You know what I'm talking about, don't you?"

"I don't think—"

"How about when I'm kissing you, I slip my hand under that flimsy dress of yours and touch your tits?"

And God, I know I'm the one who said it to him first, but in his voice, on his tongue, these words take on another meaning altogether. They were dirty before, but now they sound obscene. They sound so erotic and filthy that I can't help but feel all shy and innocent.

I shake my head. "I-I... Please stop..."

"And I bet you're not wearing a bra tonight either, are you?"

"I'm not telling you that," I say, finally able to complete a sentence instead of stumbling.

"It's okay," he soothes, "it's not that hard to figure out."

"You—"

"So then," he begins, leaning closer, "it'll be real easy, isn't it? All I'll have to do to get to your cherry tits is hook a finger in the middle of that ridiculous dress you have on and give it a tug. Not a hard tug, mind you, because I don't think your dress can handle that. I don't think your fragile little flowery dress can handle my big, rough fingers without crumpling like tissue paper, can it?"

His eyes go down to my dress, to my heaving tits. And I, before I can think it through, cover them with my arms. I even pull his coat closed for good measure.

His lips twitch.

Keeping his chin dipped, he lifts his eyes. "Do you think that'll save you?"

"I—"

"Hiding them from my view like that."

"I don't think you should—"

He leans in even further. "Because let me tell you, it'll only make things worse."

My heart jumps. "H-how?"

"Because then I'll have to *make* you show them to me. I'll have to force your arms away and pin them behind your back and fucking make you show me your cherry tits. And I'm sure you won't like that. I'm sure you'll struggle. And in all of your struggling and my subduing, your dress will be the one to suffer. Your useless but pretty dress may get ripped down the middle, not only spilling your tits out but also leaving other parts of your honey-dipped body bare. And that's not what we're trying to do here, is it? I'm not trying to strip you fucking naked. I'm just trying to get to your tits." His eyes are glinting right now, wisps of smoke wafting from his mouth. "I'm just trying to suck on them. Lick them, bite them, leave my teeth marks. Be your new daddy. So what do you say, Dora, my mouth, your tits, let's make fire and melt this goddamn snow."

God.

God, my chest is heaving. My tits are feeling heavy and swollen and so achy.

"C-can you stop repeating everything I said to you," I say breathily, "that night? I don't think it's very appropriate. I'm with your—"

"Twin brother," he finishes for me. "I know. So again, what the fuck are you doing here, writhing in ecstasy and going to pieces, just because I said I'll kiss you and suck your tits. Because let me tell you something. I'm an asshole in disguise. I'm a fucking thug. And if you keep looking for trouble, *I* am what you will find. And if you do find me, I'll keep you, you understand? Not forever, no. Because you're still an annoying little girl, but until I teach you what it means when you tempt a man like me to be your daddy. I'll make you forget every fucking thing you *think* you know about it and teach you a new definition of the word that you'll remember for the rest of your fucking life. And then I'll send you back to my brother as my sloppy seconds. So next time," he goes on, his eyes shiny and dark, "you want to look for me after dancing in my twin's arms, next time you get the urge to flit from one brother to another, remember that. *Remember* that I don't play games. Now one more time: run along and find my brother and leave me the fuck alone."

CHAPTER 4

THE WILDFIRE THORN

TWO WEEKS LATER

*I*f you ask my siblings what their earliest memory is, they'd probably say of our mother. Of her running around the house, probably tired but loving. Her waking up early to get to one of her jobs, kissing everyone goodbye.

My earliest memory, however, is of my father.

I know it's strange and I'm the outlier among all the Thorne siblings, but it is what it is.

But when I was five, I remember waking up to his cries in the middle of the night. When I went to him and asked about it, he said he'd done something bad. And that he was sorry. When I asked what, he told me that he got angry. He told me that he got so fucking angry that he'd hit our mother. He couldn't stop himself, he said. That it was as if he was outside his own body. As if someone else was doing those things, not him. And then he told me that it was because he'd had too much to drink and that it was okay because he was never going to do it again.

Of course he broke his promise.

Because he did both things.

Drink and hit.

I watched him drink himself into a stupor. I watched him lose his temper and then I watched him hit our mother. Sometimes he'd hit her even without the liquor. And the more I watched him do that, the more I remembered this earliest memory of mine. The more I remembered how *I'd* felt when he'd confessed his crime to me. I remembered that I felt frozen even though it was the middle of July. I felt afraid for my mother. I felt afraid of him.

I felt afraid of myself.

I'd felt afraid because of what he told me. *After.*

After he confessed that he'd done something bad, he told me that I'd done something bad too. He told me that he'd been watching me do bad things for quite some time. In fact, that very day, I'd done something similar. I'd had a fight with Shepard. He'd stolen one of my books and in my anger, I'd hit him. I'd hit him so badly that I think I broke a couple of his teeth. And he told me that the reason I did that—I fought so viciously and so brutally—was because I was like my father.

I had anger inside of me. I had fire. It made me do things without realizing that I was doing them. He told me that one day I was going to turn into him.

It scared me because he was right.

I did have anger inside of me. I did have this fire, this urge. This *need* that made me violent. That stole my thoughts and turned me into a monster who just wanted to roar and scream and destruct and destroy.

So that was the last time I fought with my brother.

Ever.

Because that night when our father was sobbing into the beer bottle and telling me I was like him, I made a silent promise to myself that I'd never ever hit Shepard again. I'd never ever lose my temper at him, or anyone, for that matter. Sitting next to my drunk father, I'd made a promise that I'd be good. I'd follow all the rules. I'd always be there for my family. I'd make peace rather than waves. I'd be in control rather than lose it.

And as I watched my father break his promises over and over, I became determined to keep mine. I became determined to win against this thing inside of me. This thing that lives deep inside and feels like fire. This thing that ticks like a bomb and can explode if I'm not careful.

It was hard.

But I did it.

I did it because I never wanted to be like my father. Because I could see how *tempting* it was to be like him. How tempting it was to lose control like Ledger and destroy things rather than build them. In fact, for the longest time, that was what he did, Ledger. He destroyed things, relationships, broke a girl's heart because of his issues with his temper. He's fine now, but it was hard to watch him spiral like that.

Which is why I still do it.

I take every precaution, every measure to keep myself in check. I do every fucking thing I can to protect my control, to protect this thick layer of ice around me. To not get angry or agitated. I do everything to keep people around me safe.

From me.

Although I have to say that I'm failing right now.

And my anger only grows the more I watch him.

My twin brother.

We're in the locker room after the game. That we lost badly. This is only the fourth game of the season and we've lost three of them so far. Con's not happy. Team's not happy. The board is definitely not happy and the pressure from them has already been at an all-time high.

Conrad has just chewed them out, including laying down the rules for the next few days, and the mood's somber. So laughing and joking around in the locker room is not really an appropriate thing to do. But of course, my twin brother has never cared about what's appropriate or not.

I'm about to do what I always do, remove myself from the situation, when Ledger calls out, "Hey, Stellan, a bunch of us are going for a couple of drinks to get over the disappointment." He raises his hands up before reassuring me, "Nothing crazy. We know the season's on. We'll just get Kombuchas, I promise. You wanna come?"

No is at the tip of my tongue.

I don't like get-togethers—never allowed myself to like them; too many people and too much stress.

And stress is an obvious trigger.

Lots of things are a trigger for me and I've always tried to keep away from them. Things that threaten my control. Things that make me angry. Things that have the potential to turn me into a threat to my promise. I keep away from any excitement, any thrills. I keep my head down and stay away from everyone.

Growing up, I kept my head down and focused. On my studies. On my books. On soccer, on chores around the house. Besides, me doing my chores was the only way I could be there for my siblings. My entire energy, my entire attention was taken up by leashing this thing inside of me that I never had the time to be there for them any other way. Helping them with materialistic things was the only way I could contribute.

Not to mention, someone like me—a ticking time bomb—didn't deserve any sort of comradery anyway.

All this to say, no I won't be going out with them. I don't like to drink even if it's Kombucha. And at the end of a long, grueling day at a job I don't like very much, I'd like to get back to the hotel and unwind. But before I can say it, someone else answers for me.

"Forget it, Ledge. He's never going to say yes."

As always, my twin's voice has a provocative quality to it. It's because he likes to provoke. And he likes to provoke me the most.

My twin brother is my biggest trigger. Probably because we're as different as they come. He likes to be in the spotlight while I like the shadows. He likes to be loud and abrasive while I like to keep my head down. He likes to fight while I like to keep the peace.

In any case, I've learned to ignore him. I've learned to ignore our differences.

I've learned to keep myself at a distance, withdraw into myself from time to time so I can be around him without posing a danger to him.

Although sometimes I do wonder.

What it'd be like to get to know him.

What it'd be like to have a real relationship with him.

But I don't have the luxury for that.

"Thanks for answering for me, Shepard," I say.

He shrugs. "You're welcome, Stella. Thought I'd save you the trouble."

Stella is a silly nickname from childhood. It's Callie who coined it because when she was little, she couldn't stay Stellan and so Stella it was. While she doesn't call me that anymore—of course—my twin uses it to provoke me.

Ignoring it as always, I give him a short nod. "I appreciate that."

Again, I try to leave, but he has more to say. "I mean, it's not as if the head coach will ever fraternize with the lowly players."

Head coach.

Yeah, that's me.

I've recently been promoted. Actually, it came through at the beginning of the season a couple of weeks back. It's not something I wanted and for the longest time, I kept turning it down. I was happy where I was. I didn't want change. Change is not a good thing for a man like me. I need equilibrium. I need routine, structure. I need boundaries.

Besides, I would have liked someone else to get the job. Someone who was more passionate and driven. Passion and ambition are not the luxury I can afford. That's why I'm in soccer in the first place. It's safe. It's predictable because I've played it all my life. And it comes to me easy.

But that's not the reason I won't hang out with them. And if I'm being honest, it's not also because I don't like to hang out all that much.

The reason is something else entirely.

Before I can answer, though, again Shepard gets there first. "But then again, you still act like you're Con's errand boy, so"—he shrugs—"what do you say, wanna hang out with us?"

Suddenly, the atmosphere gets tense.

It was somber to begin with, but now there are currents of discomfort.

As I said, Shepard likes to provoke and this isn't the first time he has done it in front of the team. In fact, he's been doing this a lot, especially over the last year.

Shepard has been poking me and prodding me and egging me on. And as dangerous as it is, as dangerous as I am, I've tried to do my best to let it go. To ride it out and let him off the hook.

But now I'm the head coach and shit like this can't fly.

And I guess he knows that.

I guess he *knows* I can't let him go this time.

This is *exactly* the kind of situation I try to avoid. Where I'm *this* close to losing it. I've imagined it a million times in my head, of course. A scenario where

Shepard is provoking me and he thinks it's all fun and games. But unbeknownst to him, I'm burning inside. I'm getting ready to explode. Where *he's* the one who's going to come out with third-degree burns.

I'm not sure how I do it, but I know I have to go really, *really* deep inside of me to find the strength to keep my voice even and my features made of ice as I say, "In my office."

He watches me for a few seconds.

Then as if coming to a conclusion, he throws me a cocky smirk and a chin lift.

For his sake, I turn around and simply walk out of the room.

I head toward my office across the hall. It's not my office, per se, because this isn't our locker room. We have a few away games before we get to go back to our home base. So this is a temporary space, but it's as good as any. When I hear him enter the room, I turn around to face him.

I ignore the little smile that's still lingering on his face and say, "Close the door."

He eyes me for a few seconds before doing as I say. Then he goes ahead and leans against it, folding his arms across his chest like everything is fucking fantastic and he isn't summoned by one of his coaches.

"What was that?" I ask, standing by the desk.

"An invitation," he says both casually and meaningfully.

"To get your ass kicked?"

He cocks his head to the side. "Are you going to kick my ass?"

Ignoring his jab, I announce, "I want you on that field an hour before everyone else tomorrow. Is that clear? And don't make me wait or it'll be two hours earlier the day after."

Not that it affects him one bit because his cocky tone's still in place. "That's it?"

I jerk my chin up at the door. "You can leave now."

"That's all you're gonna do?" he goes as if he can't believe me.

He better thank God that that's all I am going to do. But I don't say it like I don't say or do a million things on a daily basis. What I *do* do, though, is round the desk to go sit in my chair. "Close the door behind you."

"Come on, Stella," he keeps talking. "Give me something here. I fucking insulted you in front of the whole team."

Ignoring his childish nickname for me as always, I stare at him impassively. "I'm waiting."

"I'm waiting too," he insists. "Be a man. Grow a pair."

My knuckles tingle like they do a lot when he's around. My teeth clench too and my skin feels heated. Still, I say, "You don't want me to grow a pair. Now leave."

He watches me for a few seconds, all earlier playfulness gone from his face. His eyes, so much like mine, are grave. Then, "Are you serious?"

"Leave," I say, steel in my voice.

Maybe now he'll get the message.

Now he'll understand how much of a danger he's in. How he needs to get away from me so I don't hurt him.

His jaw clenches now. "Jesus fucking Christ, you're something, aren't you?" Then, shaking his head and raking fingers through his hair, "Look, I'm not a very patient guy and last year has tested my fucking patience more than you can imagine. So I'm trying to live in my fuck it era, all right? Maybe you can take all this tension. Maybe you can thrive on sweeping things under the rug, but I'm not you, yeah? I'm not fucking you and I can't take it. So we need to talk."

"There's nothing to talk about," I tell him, my voice vibrating now with the strain of keeping it even.

"Yeah, that's where you and me are different," he says. "Because I think we should've had this conversation months ago."

I grit my teeth. "Don't."

He doesn't take my advice. "Do you remember Sarah Ann?"

My body tightens at that name.

I haven't heard it in years now. Mostly because she was in my high school math class. And once upon a time, she used to be Shepard's girlfriend. But only because I used to like her. I don't even remember her face anymore, but back when I was fifteen, I do remember having a little crush on her.

Just for the record, I don't do crushes. Girls have a knack for bringing out your emotions, your baser instincts, and when your baser instincts are black as the smoke I inhale, it's better to keep them at an arm's length. So that's what I do. I use them when I need them, but I don't keep them.

But Sarah Ann was different.

Not that I was going to do anything about it for obvious reasons.

But when Shepard came home with her one day, it pissed me off. It pissed me off to the point that I almost broke the coffee mug I'd been holding in my hand. And then I saw the smirk on his face, that cocky, irreverent smirk that let me know he was doing it to provoke me. He wanted to see me lose my cool for his amusement and I loosened my hold. I let the mug go, set it down on our old kitchen island, and went back to my room. Where I stayed for the entire night.

For the next six weeks, until Shepard broke up with her, I made sure to either stay late at the library or stay closeted in my room until she left. Because if I hadn't, I would've broken my promise and become like my father.

Before I can protest again, he continues, "I can see that you do."

"Don't," I say again, the same anger burning up inside of me.

At the fact that he used her to provoke me.

He used her to make me angry and for what? So he could watch me blow up, isn't it? So he could play me like he plays his lackeys who worship at his feet.

"We never talked about her either," he says.

"There is *nothing* to talk about." I keep my fingers laced even though it's taking a great effort, but if I let go, I'm going to curl them into fists and put them through his fucking face.

He ignores me. "All you had to do was ask and I would've given her to you. All you had to do was talk to me."

"I have no *interest* in talking to you," I say.

Because if I talk to him, I'm going to hit him. I'm going to fucking destroy him right now. And that's not something I want to do.

He scoffs. "Yeah, that has always been established. But that's not the point."

I know that's not the point.

I know.

That's why I've been avoiding this conversation. That's why I've been avoiding him in general. That's why I don't hang out with the team. That's why I turn down invitations, but since I always turn them down, people don't notice. Which is how I want it to be.

"Shut," I growl lowly, "your mouth and leave."

"The point is that I'm not going to do it here," he states. "I'm not going to do it with her."

And I imagine my control dangling off a cliff then. In my head, I see it. I see that the only thing holding it in place is a thin thread that's built out of years and years of practice.

Years and years of suppressing myself, holding myself back.

Years and *fucking years* of remembering and reliving that one moment. That one night with my father. Where he was sobbing while my mother slept upstairs with a black eye. That the next day she had explained it away as walking into a kitchen cabinet. Only I knew the truth. And probably Conrad. But none of them, none of my other siblings and that includes this reckless asshole in front of me, knew what had happened.

None of them knew that a time bomb lived among us.

Along with a time bomb in the making.

Me.

And that's the only reason, the only fucking reason I stay sitting. Because if I unlace my fingers and spring up from my chair that 'in the making' will turn into 'made' and I won't let that happen.

"I know you want her," he says, his jaw clenched. "I know you watch her when you think no one's looking. I know that's why you've been keeping your distance from me for the past year. That's why you don't hang out. That's why you avoid me. And while we've never been close and I've never been a huge fan of you and vice versa, this is different. She is different. *She* is not Sarah Ann."

I'm mashing my teeth right now.

I'm on the verge of breaking my own fingers.

"I love her," he declares. "Not that you'd know what it means, but I do."

I know that.

I know he loves her.

I also know that I don't know what it means. I don't have the luxury to find out. And while it never bothered me before—love isn't something that I remotely gave any thought to; most of my thoughts are occupied with how not to break someone's teeth and shove them down their throat—it bothers me now.

It *bothers* me.

Not because he's in love but because he's in love with her.

It makes me want to roar. It makes me want to pick up this chair and throw it through the door that he's so casually standing against.

But all I do is say, "And?"

"And," he bites out. "She's mine. No matter how much you want her, how much you want to act pissy about it, she will stay mine."

No, don't do it.

Don't do it.

Do not fucking kill your brother.

"And don't get me wrong," he goes on. "I feel bad for you. I do. I mean, we both know you've got"—he searches for a word—"a handicap, for lack of a better word. You have a... flaw, let's say. A defect. You don't know what to do with emotions. In fact, I don't even think you have any." He chuckles harshly. "People say a twin is your soulmate and well, I got stuck with you. So I know. I *know* that what they say is true. You're cold. You're fucking freezing. You're dead inside. You have no feelings. No emotions. You have no ambition. You could've gone pro but chose to become a lowly assistant coach. And then they try to promote you and you keep turning them down. Well, until recently. When Con had to force it upon you."

His words are like darts to me.

Stinging and burning.

But it's fine.

It's okay because he's right.

He did get stuck with me. He did get stuck with a brother with a handicap, with issues, with baggage instead of a fully functioning twin.

So it's fine if this is what he thinks of me.

It's just that...

It hurts.

That this is what he thinks of me.

"So yeah, I feel bad for you," Shepard continues. "But you have to understand that even if I gave her to you, you wouldn't know what to do with her. She's bright. She's colorful. She deserves someone like me, not you. I'm the right guy for her and you know that. And that's been your only saving grace. That's why I haven't come for you before today. The fact that you're completely wrong for her and so far, you've kept your distance. But I saw the way you were watching her. At the charity event. I saw the way you followed her every move, and I didn't like it. I have never liked it. I've never liked the way you watch my girl. And I've given you plenty of opportunities to come talk to me. But since you won't, let me make it very clear to you that it won't end well. If you come after her. If you keep watching her, if you keep *wanting* what's mine, I'll make you regret it. So I'm asking you to stop. I'm asking you, *very nicely*, to stop obsessing over my girl."

He watches me for a few beats before pushing off the door and saying, "So don't be pathetic, Stella. Not more than you already have been for the past year. Find your own girl and leave mine alone."

Before he can walk out, though, I call out, "Or what?"

He turns around then. "Or I'll fight you."

"You'll fight me."

"I'll go to war with you."

I keep watching him, my fingers numb now. "First rule of a war: pick an opponent who's equal to you. Or it wouldn't be a fair fight."

"Second rule of war," he begins with a cocky smirk. "Don't bait your opponent or you'll lose your teeth."

I have to smile at that.

I have to.

It's a small smile, but it's one of amusement. "Yeah, you've got no clue."

His eyes narrow. "Why don't you clue me in then?"

Mine remain the same, covered in ice and expressionless. "Nah, that'd be too easy. How about you think about it while you sit out the next game."

It takes a second for him to get what I'm saying. "What?"

"You're benched."

His expression ripples with disbelief. "What the..."

"Third rule of war: don't pick a fight with your coach or it'll be for the rest of the season."

~

*I*sadora.
      Dora.

Do. *Ra*.

The misery of my life. The torment of my heart.

My crime. My corruption.

If I were a writer, say Nabokov, I'd describe her in such flowery terms. Since I'm not, I'd say that she's a girl I find everywhere I go. At games, at team events, at parties. And no matter the occasion, she's always laughing her throaty laugh. She's always smiling with her bow-shaped lips that look perpetually stung. In a sea of pasty and dull bodies, she always shines with her honey-colored skin and jet-black hair. Her eyes—metallic gray and her most unique feature—have an impertinence and mischief to them that makes you think she's perpetually up to no good.

And wherever she goes, she does it with my brother.

Because she's my twin brother's girlfriend.

But before she was his, she was the girl I'd met one night. A girl in a white dress and fake wings. A girl who saw me in the shadows. A girl who tested my control when it's always been ironclad and legendary.

She was the girl who made my heart beat a certain way.

When you've lived your life by monitoring your heartbeats, keeping track of your pulse rate, you get familiar with it. You get familiar with how your heart beats, its cadence and its rhythm. Its triggers. Things that mess with your heart.

She's one of them.

She messes with my heart.

She makes my heart race.

And I know what happens when I can't control my heartbeats. The world starts to disappear. My vision gets blurry. The edges of my body start to strain, and it feels like I'll burst out of my bones if I don't find something to ground myself.

So I should stay away from her, shouldn't I?

But it's hard.

I thought my initial fascination with her would go away, but it hasn't yet.

My brother was right.

I *do* want her.

To put it mildly.

To put it accurately: the want of her keeps me up every night and torments me every day. The want of her makes me feel like I have a thousand paper cuts all over my skin.

To put it even more accurately: It constantly makes me want to punch a hole in the wall. It makes me want to break my rule of one cigarette per day and smoke the whole pack away. The *want of her* keeps me on edge every second of every day, and I have to physically stop myself from hunting my twin down and hurting him.

And that's why she's dangerous; I knew that the first night.

Because she makes *me* dangerous.

Because if my twin brother is my biggest trigger, she's my fucking kryptonite. Nothing, not one thing, has tempted me, threatened my control, fucking chipped away at my sanity, like she does.

So even though it's hard, I'm not going to go after her.

She's the very last girl on this planet I'd go after.

Instead, I'll do what I've done for the past year: keep my distance, ignore all this, bury it somewhere deep, and go about my day. So I watch the games and prepare a strategy to discuss at tomorrow's meeting. Once done, I go back to the hotel we're staying at and spend an hour on the treadmill and then another hour with the weights like I do every night.

Structure is the key.

And if I hit the weights harder than usual and run at a higher speed than what I normally do, I don't pay it any mind. Anything to put that conversation with my brother behind me. Anything to curb this want that seems to attack me the hardest at night.

When I go up to my room, I quickly shower and then do what I've been itching to do all day: grab a smoke and look for a book to read. I know I won't be getting much sleep like I haven't gotten any in the past year. I also know that I won't be able to focus enough to make it past page one, but like always, I try.

Just as I'm settling down, though, I hear a chime.

It's not my phone, it's Shep's.

In his usual fashion, he'd left it in the locker room. He has a habit of leaving things behind: his phone, his books, his soccer cleats. And since I always kept myself busy by doing chores, cleaning up after my siblings, I have a habit of picking up things he forgets. And so, in my usual fashion, I picked up his cell phone as I was leaving.

When I go to switch it off, though, I see the reason why it chimed up in the first place.

A text.

From her.

ISADORA

Hey

And the anger that lives deep in me surges up.

The jealousy I'd felt the night she ran across the garden in a sheer white dress and fake wings only to end up in my brother's arms rages in my veins.

It rages and rages.

To the point where the world starts to disappear.

Where it's hard to remember things.

Remember who I am: the ice.

Or who she is: the fire.

It's hard to remember that I have rules. That I need to stay away from her.

It's *hard*.

So much so that before I know what I'm doing, I open the text message—we may not be similar in any way, but we do share a face and his password is facial recognition—and my fingers start typing.

CHAPTER 5

A FEW HOURS BEFORE THE TEXT...

She's running toward him.

Her dark hair's flowing behind her, along with her *dupatta*. Her traditional Indian-style *lehanga* is whipping around her legs. Her arm is outstretched toward him just as his. She's trying to catch up to him. She's trying to take his hand, but I don't think she will.

I think she'll miss it.

Because he's on the train that's leaving the station and she's not fast enough to get there in time.

So when she does, when she does catch up to him and their hands meet and he grips her fingers oh so tightly and pulls her on board, I take a breath that I've been holding throughout this scene. A deluge of happy tears flows down my cheeks and my skin bursts with goose bumps.

Every. *Time*.

Every single time I watch this movie—and I've seen it thirty-seven times including today and all with my *biji*—I think it won't happen. I think they won't get their happy ending, that she'll miss the train and the love of her life will be gone forever. And then she'll have to marry the guy her father wants her to and she'll spend her life heartbroken and pining for the guy she's in love with.

But thank God, it's a movie.

A Bollywood movie at that, where happy endings are almost guaranteed.

Not in real life, though, is it?

In real life, the guy you love turns out to be a big jerk and you end up regretting the day you ever met him. You end up regretting all the things you've done in his name and all the hearts you've broken.

In real life, you have to face the consequences.

Which is why as I watch the credits rolling on the TV, I blurt out to my *biji*, "I'm doing it."

We're sitting side by side on the bed with a large pink-colored margarita glass between us that we're sharing and two straws coming out of it. I'm in my heart-print bikini and so is my *biji*; although hers is a one-piece. We both have pink-colored, heart-shaped glasses on, and we both are sporting blood-red lipstick. We are absolutely twinning in her old age home room and pretending to get tans because in reality, it's fucking snowing out there and we're trapped.

At my announcement, she looks at me.

Even though I can't see her eyes behind her glasses, I know she's studying me shrewdly. She's in her eighties, but my *biji* is a very sharp woman. She just *knows* things without me having to tell her. And her knowledge about human emotions and life's curveballs is unparalleled.

I love her to pieces.

She's been with me almost all my life. She moved to America after *Dada ji*, my grandfather, died when I was about three or so. And since my mother never liked her, she always made sure that *Biji* stayed in a different house than us and always supervised our visits. And then when the time came, my mother sent her to live at an old age home. Just like she sent me away to live in Bardstown.

Although since my *biji's* home is in Bardstown too, I don't mind it all that much. I hate that she has to live here, though. I wish she could stay with me, but my mother would never ever agree to that. She already thinks I'm the way I am because of my *biji*.

The only consolation that my *biji* lives with strangers is that these strangers love her too. Well, I mean she has not one but two boyfriends—one younger than her by five years and from Nebraska, and the other older by two and from London. They both adore her equally and know that my *biji* is a firecracker who doesn't believe in commitments, not after her being married to the love of her life. There's another resident here with his eyes on my *biji*, but she isn't interested in him all that much. He's from India and she says she's already dated, loved, married an Indian and so she needs variety now.

Anyway, back to her and her scrutinizing eyes.

"Doing what?" she asks.

I take an innocent—not—sip of my margarita before mumbling, "Saying yes."

I keep my eyes trained on the rolling credits on purpose and thank God for my shades. Because I don't want to look into her eyes directly. I know what I'll find: disappointment and displeasure. And while I can deal with my mother's disappointment—it hurts like hell but still—I can't deal with the same from *Biji*.

"Tell me you're joking," she says.

"Well, I would"—I take another sip and still keep watching the TV—"if I could."

"Look at me," she commands.

"No, thank you."

I can feel her staring very severely at me. "Isadora."

"*Biji*." I employ the same tone.

"Look at me," she says again.

"I think I'm fine."

She sighs sharply. "Isadora, *meri bacchi, aakhein idhar kar.*"

So that was Hindi.

I don't understand Hindi all that much or Punjabi, predominantly spoken in the northern part of India where my *biji* and my mom are from, that my *biji* also speaks in sometimes.

This I understand, however.

Meri bacchi means my girl, spoken affectionately most of the time. And the other part, even though I don't understand quite literally, I can deduce from the context. She's probably asking me the same thing—to look at her—like before.

"You know, *Biji*, this is really not fair." I squirm in my seat a little, still stalling. "You know I don't understand Hindi all that much and it makes me feel very stupid when you—"

"*Haye Rabba, iss ladki ke natak,*" she mutters. When I go to tell her that I don't understand that either, she doesn't let me. "It means stop being a drama queen because I know you understood what I said before. You're not an idiot. Unfortunately, neither am I. So can we get to the point?"

Sighing, I do as she says and finally look at her.

She points to my shades and I reluctantly push them up.

Then, she asks, "Why?"

"Because I want to. Because I think it's the right decision for me," I say.

"Right decision," she repeats.

I nod. "Yes."

"Saying yes to his ultimatum is the right decision for *you*?" she asks again.

"You know, you can ask it a hundred times, in a hundred different ways. My answer is not going to change."

"Explain it to me then," she pushes.

"Because I want to move on, okay? It's high time, don't you think? I should move on with my life. It's been a year, and it hasn't happened yet. And it's not going to happen ever. So I'm getting smart."

I sit back and slurp my drink from the straw.

Because I think she should be happy after what I've told her.

For the past two weeks, ever since the charity event, I've been thinking about what to do. How to tell Shepard the truth. *If* I should tell Shepard the truth. In between rehearsals, classes, homework that I mostly neglect in favor of rehearsals —because hey, we're finally doing a show and I got the lead role—I came to the decision that if I say yes to his ultimatum, there's no need to tell Shepard anything.

When I decided that, I knew I'd have to tell my *biji* because I tell her everything. And I knew if I went the self-care route, she'd be totally on board.

My *biji* is a big believer in self-happiness.

She thinks the first thing and the most important thing that you could do in life is love yourself and care for yourself. Go after what you really want and what your heart desires.

I guess it comes from living in a society and time where women weren't valued all that much. Where they didn't have a voice. My *biji* was never given a choice on what to do with her life—be an actress; or where to go—she always wanted to travel, but she lived the majority of her life in a very small village in Punjab; who to marry—she says she was in love with this guy in town, but she never had the chance to tell him before she was married off at the ripe old age of sixteen to my *dada ji*. Although she did eventually fall in love with *Dada ji*, it was very hard for her in the beginning and it made her feel suffocated.

"And there's no other reason?" she inquires.

I keep my eyes on the TV. "Absolutely not. As I said, it's the right decision. Shepard is the right guy for me."

"Is he?"

"Yes." I begin counting on my fingers. "One, he's amazing. He's funny and he makes me laugh. I never feel awkward around him. Or shy. I never blush like I'm some innocent who's never heard the F-word. I've heard it. I've said it. I've never done it, but so what? It's disgusting when I blush over it.

"Two, he's easy to talk to. It's not like I'm pulling teeth while I'm talking to him. He answers my questions. He doesn't hide things from me or act like he's so superior and condescending. Three, he's kind. He doesn't insult me or humiliate me or make me cry. And yes, he's not that into plays and books and acting, and he kinda gets bored when I tell him about the scene we're workshopping or the character I'm trying to nail down. But that's okay. Not everyone's going to be interested in art and theater. But despite all that, he supports my dreams. But most of all, *Biji*, he wants me. He wants to *be* with me. He likes me. He likes me so much that he gave me an ultimatum, okay? And for the first time in my life, I'd like to be with someone who wants me back and not chase after them and their love and approval like I've always done. *There*. Are you finally happy now?"

Okay, after *this*, she should definitely be happy.

Everything I've said is true.

Shepard *is* amazing. He *does* make me laugh. Exhibit A: he made me laugh at the charity event when everything felt so awkward and heavy. He *is* easy to talk to. Exhibit B: He confessed about his twin ritual the first time we'd met. Our conversation flew even when we were strangers. Whenever I talk to him, it's not like I'm trying to bang my head against a wall, trying to get information about him. He laughs with me. I don't have to rack my brain to come up with the last time he cracked a smile. He jokes around and his jokes aren't mocking. They aren't condescending.

And it's a good thing that he doesn't make me blush or make my heart race. Who wants to live with perpetually flushed skin and a pounding heart? It's like walking on tightrope all the time.

It's not comfortable.

It makes you act like crazy and do borderline compulsive, stalker-y things.

So this *is* the right decision for me.

Only that's not why I'm making it.

But my *biji* doesn't need to know that.

"Yes," she says at last, turning back and sipping on the drink.

"You are?" I ask, surprised.

She takes another sip. "I am. Because I agree."

"You agree with what?"

"That it is high time."

I smile, relieved. "It is, right?"

"Yes." She keeps her eyes on the TV as well. "Because maybe *ab uss khote de puttar nu akal aayegi*."

"*Biji*," I say, exasperated. "You know I don't know what you just said."

Well, except for *khote de puttar*. Which more or less means asshole.

I also know who she's talking about because she's used this term before in his context.

She huffs. "I meant maybe now that asshole will get his head out of his ass. When you've moved on. *Enni changi kudi hai meri* and if he can't see that, then *aag lage usko*. And to translate, it means if he can't see how amazing my granddaughter is, then he can go to hell. But not before he learns his lesson first and comes to you begging."

Needless to say, she knows everything. She knows the whole story. Mostly because even if I wanted to hide things from her, I wouldn't have been able to. As I mentioned earlier, she knows everything and she definitely knows everything about me. She knows about how I ran into Stellan that night, how instantly obsessed I became with him, how different he'd seemed to me. How then I went to Shepard to make Stellan jealous.

She told me, numerous times over the past year, that I should come clean to Shepard. That I should tell him everything, confess my feelings for Stellan, but I didn't listen. First because I was convinced that Stellan would come around, that he would come back to me begging and crawling. And after that because Shepard had become my friend, truly, and I didn't know how to tell him. Every time I pictured telling him, I'd see him look all betrayed and angry, and I'd just chicken out. And after, *after that*, when I realized that he wanted me as more than a friend, there was no way I was going to break his heart.

In any case, she knows.

And she has grown increasingly unhappy with *him* over the past year. Him being the love of my life who doesn't want anything to do with me. She thinks he needs a bigger push.

"But I wish that was why you were doing it," she finishes.

"What?"

She turns back to me and pushes her shades up. "That's not why you're saying yes, however."

"I don't—"

"You're not saying yes because you want to get smart and you want to move on or even light a fire under his ass. You're saying yes because you think it's your fault."

I squirm in my seat and look away. "That's not true."

"Oh, my baby, I wish it weren't true, but it is."

"*Biji*, I—"

"Because I know you. You're saying yes because you don't want anyone to get hurt; you think it's your fault Shepard fell in love with you and you want to make amends."

I stubbornly remain quiet.

And she stubbornly goes on, "I know how you think, *meri bacchi*. How you like to take the blame on yourself when more often than not, it's not yours to take. And I also know where that comes from, who's responsible for it."

I swallow thickly then.

As the spot around my elbow smarts with a dull pain.

My bruise—something I hadn't noticed until I got back home that night—is gone now. But the slight pain remains. Probably because I had one more encounter with my mother when she'd dropped in unannounced to check on things; she does that. Thank God, I didn't have rehearsal that day, so I was home when I should've been. Even so, while she was leaving, she dug her nails in the same spot, worrying the wound.

My *biji* doesn't know that, though.

No one knows what my mother likes to do out of the public eye.

Which is how I want it to be.

She already doesn't approve of how my mom treats me and growing up, always made sure to shower me with love and care when my mom didn't. But if she knew how angry my mom gets and what she does when she gets like that, my *biji* would lose it. But mostly, it'll break her heart and I don't want that to happen.

Not because of me.

So I keep it a secret.

Besides, it's not as if my mother actively beats me, she just... grips me too hard or smacks me a little here and there, and mostly those bruises and stings go away in a few days. And I become good as new.

But back to the situation at hand.

"I can't hurt him," I tell *Biji*.

"I know."

"He's my best friend."

"I know that too."

"He didn't deserve what I did to him. How selfish I've been all this time. He didn't deserve to be played with. And that's what I did. I played with his heart. I played with his feelings. I deliberately sought him out. I deliberately went after him knowing that it will create rumors. I held his hand; I danced with him. I smiled at him, flirted with him. I did it all because I... Because I wanted his twin brother. I *made* him fall in love with me. So now it's up to me to fix it. It's up to me to grow up and stop being selfish."

I need to face the consequences of what I've done.

I've used a man.

A good and kindhearted man.

I cannot let him suffer for that. I absolutely *cannot* hurt him by telling him the truth, no. Maybe one day, I will tell him. But by then, we will be firmly in a relationship, and I will be the best girlfriend he could've ever imagined.

Because that's step two of my plan.

Step one is saying yes.

"But more than that," I keep going, pain stabbing my chest. "I know."

"What do you know?"

I look at *Biji*. "I know what it feels like when you want someone and they don't want you back. I know how painful that is. How it makes you ache. How you pray and hope. How every night you ask the sky, why me; what's wrong with me; why can't *I* get lucky in love; what can I change about myself to get that; what can I do; why can't he love me, why can't *anyone* love me. Why... And when no one answers, it hurts."

It hurts so badly.

It makes you question everything about yourself, about your life. And in my life, I know that my *biji* loves me, but she's the only person. Maybe my dad loves me a little, but he loves my mother so much that I don't think he can be disloyal to her by loving me. And we all know that what my mother feels for me is so far away from love that it's not even funny. And while I know Shepard is loved by people, his family, going through unrequited love is something else altogether. It is arguably the worst kind of love there is. The loneliest kind of love there is and I'll be damned if I let him go through that.

So there's only one solution, isn't there?

All the love that I have in me, I will give to him.

He's the only one who deserves it anyway.

Biji keeps looking at me for a few beats. "I hate my daughter. I do."

"*Biji*, that's not—"

"I hate what she's done to you. I *hate* that all your life, she's put you down, torn you apart. Made you feel bad for being yourself. I *hate* that. You should be cherished," she says fiercely. "You should be treated like the treasure you are and everyone has failed you. Every single person in your life has failed you and I..." Her beautiful dark eyes that I wish I had well up with tears. "If I could beat some sense into your mother, I would. But nothing works with that girl. She's always been bitter for one reason or another. Nothing we did worked with her. And if I ever meet that *khote da puttar*, rest assured that *juttiyon se maar maar ke seedha kar dena hai maine usko.*"

"*Biji—*"

She grabs my cheeks and squeezes them. "It means: if I ever meet that asshole, I will beat him so hard that he'll fall at your feet and promise to love you forever."

God, I love my *biji*.

She's the best grandmother in the whole wide world.

"That'll make a good movie story," she finishes.

I chuckle with stinging eyes and decide to focus on good things. "Will you tell me your story? With *Dada ji*."

She watches me for a few moments, her thumbs still rubbing my cheeks, her eyes roving over my face. Then she reaches forward and kisses my forehead. "Of course, my love."

With that, she moves away and settles against the pillows. I put our giant margarita glass away and put my head on the pillow in her lap, lying on my side. And she begins as she runs her fingers along the long strands of my hair, smoothening them and slowly braiding them like she used to do with her hair back in her village where she lived with my *dada ji*.

"I was young. I was headstrong. I wanted to travel the world. No one had done that in our village. I wanted to be in movies. I wanted to fall in love. I did fall in love with this neighbor boy. The one thing I didn't want to do was get married. And I specifically didn't want to get married to this stern-faced man who came to our house one day. He looked like he'd never cracked a smile in his life, let alone laughed. And he was so tall and broad. Taller than all the buildings in our village, broader than the mountains I once saw in a book. He had this really big mustache. I swear he looked like a movie villain. A handsome movie villain but a villain nonetheless. I wanted to run away on our wedding day and when I couldn't, I ran away on the wedding night. There was no way I was going to sleep with him in the same room. Plus, I had to go find that guy I'd loved. I was going to find him and convince him to run away with me to Mumbai. It was called Bombay back then but still. Your *dada ji* found me, though. But I was determined. I told him I didn't love him. That I would never love him. I hated him for ruining my life. That if he ever touched me, I'd cut off his fingers. I'd poison his food. You know what he said to me?"

I smile, looking up at her, and ask, even though I know the answer, "What?"

"He said"—she's smiling, her eyes full of love—"no one wants to be married to a witch, so I was free to go. Plus, my one eye was bigger than the other, my nose was crooked, and he didn't really like how loud I laughed. It gave him a headache. So he said I could leave if I wanted to."

"But?"

"But I had to give him six months. Because he had a reputation and if I ran away on the first night, no one in the village would ever agree to marry their daughter to him."

What bullshit.

He wanted more time with her because later, he told my *biji* that he'd fallen in love with her at first sight. And he couldn't bear to let her go. So he wanted six months to see if she could learn to love him too.

Spoiler alert, she did.

I chuckle. "*Dada ji* had moves."

"He sure did."

"He knew where to strike."

"At my pride, yes."

"Because you've got the prettiest eyes and a cute button nose."

She laughs. "He used to kiss me on the nose. Every morning when he woke up and every night when he went to sleep."

My heart bursts with joy. "To make up for what he said?"

"Yes. I wasn't going to let him off the hook." She tweaks my nose. "He insulted my looks."

"And you have the most magical laugh," I say.

"That's what your *dada ji* used to say too."

"I love him," I say.

"He loved you too."

My handsome *dada ji* passed away when I was very little. So I don't remember him at all, but my *biji* has told me enough stories all my life that I feel like I already know him.

"I wish I'd gotten to meet him," I add.

"Me too."

"I love you, *Biji*."

She takes me in for a beat or two. "I love you too, *meri jaan*."

This I know as well.

Meri jaan means my life.

My heart. My soul.

Just like my *biji* was for my *dada ji*.

Hours later, when I get back home full of love stories from my *biji*, I sit in my bed. With my window open and the white curtains billowing from the winter breeze, I put my plan into motion.

I send him a text.

ISADORA

Hey

I know we decided on a timeline for the ultimatum. That I'd give him an answer when he gets back. But now that I've made up my mind, I'm not going to make him wait another second. I know he's busy with his practice and games and the season, and I usually try not to bother him when he's on the road, but desperate times call for desperate measures.

Hence the text.

Only he doesn't get back to me.

Not even after fifteen minutes. I know he's read it, though; I can see the receipt at the bottom of my message. But I'm nothing if not determined. I'm about to send him another text when my phone chimes and I sit up in my bed.

SHEPARD

Hey

CHAPTER 6

$\mathcal{I}$ stare at the phone.
Stare and stare.
Unblinking.
With wide eyes.
With *disbelieving* eyes.

Even though I wanted him to reply and was fully prepared to keep texting him until he did, I still can't believe that I don't have to take any of those measures. That he replied on his own. For some insane reason, I thought the charity event would be the last time we'd get to talk to each other.

Well, not *really* insane because he issued an ultimatum, so not getting to talk to him was a valid concern.

In any case, I'm both surprised and relieved that he replied.

And I'm rendered stupid by it, I guess, because my next words are these:

ISADORA

You're still awake?!

Of course he is awake.

Of course I *knew* he'd be awake; that's why I texted him in the first place. He's a night owl. Which is a surprise because he always needs to be up super early for practice. And if Shepard has one rule—and he doesn't have that many—it's that he's never ever late for a practice.

I watch the dots come and go on the screen. They keep doing that for a long time too and it makes my heart clench. With fear. With desperation, with sadness. That we've gotten to this place where we're so awkward with each other. And my heart clenches harder when I see his response show up on the screen.

SHEPARD
Clearly

Damn it.
I hate one-word answers. I do.
They're so hard to crack. They make it so difficult to keep the conversation going.
That alone makes me want to say it.
That alone makes me want to go all caps lock on him and tell him yes. That yes, yes, *yes*, I will be his girlfriend, cue all the exclamation marks and a clown face and heart emojis.
But I refrain.
I pace myself.
Because I don't want to scare him with my enthusiasm. I don't want him to think of me as crazy and wonder what he's gotten himself into.
I mean, he knows me, of course, but he knows me as his best friend, not as a girlfriend. And I've never been anyone's girlfriend before, but I assume I'm going to be very gung-ho about it. I'm going to be overly dramatic, super lovey-dovey with perpetual heart eyes and throws-pink-glitter-and-confetti-everywhere kind of girlfriend.
So I go with something I would normally go with.

ISADORA
I saw your game tonight.

I'm so sorry you lost.

I see the dots going on the screen once again and I pray they don't last as long as they did before. And they don't, thankfully. It's only a little progress, but I will take it.

SHEPARD
Yeah, it was shitty.

I know my next words won't help all that much, but still, I send them to him. Because another thing about Shep: he's always so hard on himself when it comes to soccer. Which I find both admirable and heartbreaking at the same time. He's one of the best players out there, but he's always competing against himself, trying to be better and better. Sometimes I wish he'd stop and celebrate his hard work too.

ISADORA
It was. But you played like you always do, amazingly.

SHEPARD

Did I?

ISADORA

Yes!

SHEPARD

And how would you know that?

ISADORA

Because I know you!

SHEPARD

But you know nothing about soccer.

ISADORA

I do too! You taught me.

SHEPARD

What did I teach you?

ISADORA

The first thing you taught me is that when the ball hits the net, it's a goal.

SHEPARD

I do sound smart.

ISADORA

And you did that tonight. You hit the net.

SHEPARD

Can't deny that.

ISADORA

In fact you were the only one.

SHEPARD

Can't deny that either.

ISADORA

See? So you should at least be happy about that.

SHEPARD

I would. Except only the captain hitting the net doesn't really cut it because soccer's a team sport.

Did I forget to teach you that?

ISADORA

You're hilarious.

> **SHEPARD**
> That should've been lesson number two.

> **ISADORA**
> I have lesson number three for you.

> **SHEPARD**
> Yeah, what's that?

> **ISADORA**
> Stop moping around about a loss because there's always a next time.

> **SHEPARD**
> Very inspirational.

> **ISADORA**
> I can be inspiring. 😊

> **SHEPARD**
> I probably should get a bumper sticker with that.

> **ISADORA**
> You probably should.
> Along with that thing you always say.

> **SHEPARD**
> What thing?

> **ISADORA**
> That arrogance is just confidence with extra inches.

> **SHEPARD**
> Yeah I do say that, don't I?

> **ISADORA**
> And from what I remember you have a lot of extra inches.
> Oh and yes, that was a double entendre. 😊😊😊

I chuckle as I send the message off, and in a rush of happiness, I realize something. That the awkwardness is gone. As always, our conversation just flowed and what do you know, I forgot about everything else.

In fact, this is the first time in *days* that I haven't thought about anything else. I haven't thought about my rehearsals, the upcoming play. I haven't thought about my mother and my smarting skin. I haven't even thought about... him and—

Oh great.

I just did that, didn't I?

I just thought about him while celebrating the fact that I *hadn't* thought about him for five minutes. And now that he's popped up in my head, I can't help but also think that the only time I forget the world, the *only time* I forget everything else that exists in the world, is when I talk to him.

But maybe it's not unique to him.

This phenomenon.

This amnesia that seems to occur only in his presence.

Maybe Shepard can make me forget things too.

And that's wonderful, isn't it?

Yes, it is, I tell myself. It is a good thing.

When my phone pings with a text again, I forcefully push all the thoughts of *him* away and focus on my goal. On my best friend.

SHEPARD

Looks like you've learned from the best after all.

I go to type something cheeky, but his next text that immediately whooshes in gives me pause.

SHEPARD

But I'm afraid I should really stop talking out of my ass.

ISADORA

What?

SHEPARD

Because if I keep doing that there won't ever be a next time.

ISADORA

What? What does that mean?

SHEPARD

I got benched.

My eyes go wide as I stare at his reply. For a few seconds, I can't make sense of it.

Is he joking?

Because he does that a lot. He jokes around. He makes fun of things; he keeps things light. But I don't remember him ever, *ever* making a joke about soccer. He takes it way too seriously. And I can't type fast enough.

ISADORA

Are you joking?

SHEPARD

No.

His one-word reply, so unlike him, by the way, makes my heart race. It makes my heart pound and *pound* in my chest. With dread. With confusion.

> **ISADORA**
> But what happened? Why would they bench you? 🌼

> **SHEPARD**
> Because as I just said I was doing the thing that I always do, running my mouth.

> **ISADORA**
> Running your mouth about what?! 😩😩😩

> **ISADORA**
> It doesn't make sense. Did you have a fight with Coach Thorne? What happened? Why would he do that? 😩😩😩

> **SHEPARD**
> There was a Coach Thorne, yes. But not the one you're thinking of.

I'm frowning harder now.

My heart is galloping harder as well. The more I talk to him and ask questions, the more confused I become.

What is he talking about?

What does he mean by not the one I'm thinking of? There's only one…

But there isn't, is there?

There's also *him*.

And maybe it's all in my head—in fact, I'm pretty sure it is—but I feel like the temperature drops in the room. The air gets colder. The air gets harsher too, blowing the curtains up in a large wave. And my skin breaks out in goose bumps.

I try to type, but my fingers keep slipping and hitting the wrong keys. But his text comes in first.

> **SHEPARD**
> I see you've figured it out.

This time I'm successful in getting my trembling fingers to cooperate and respond.

> **ISADORA**
> He benched you?

> **SHEPARD**
> Yeah.

> **ISADORA**
> Why?

> **SHEPARD**
> Apparently power got to his head.

> **ISADORA**
> What power?

SHEPARD

He's the new head coach.

At this, I drop my phone.
I do.
I have to.
Because oh my God. *Oh my God*, he accepted?
He finally accepted the job?
I know he wasn't.

I've heard my dad talking about it. I've heard other people talking about it at parties. How they've been wanting to promote him, and he keeps turning them down. They've been wanting to fire their old coach—the coach *before* Coach Thorne came on board—and promote *him* to the head coach. But he always kept saying no, that he was fine where he was. In fact, one of the biggest reasons he convinced Coach Thorne to take the job in the first place was because he himself didn't want it. For some unknown, *bizarre* reason. That I've wanted to find out.

Every time I heard people lamenting about the fact that Stellan Thorne wouldn't take the job, I wanted to go to him. I wanted to shake him and ask him what the hell he was doing. Why the hell would he keep turning such an amazing opportunity down?

I mean, isn't that what he's working toward?
Becoming the head coach.

But I guess he stopped being an idiot and took the job. And I'm so happy about that, so ecstatic and thrilled and excited that I fire off a response without thinking.

ISADORA

He is?!!! He took the job?!!

SHEPARD

Well it was more or less thrust upon him but yeah.

ISADORA

Oh my God!!!!

SHEPARD

You're not kidding, are you?

What if I was?

ISADORA

Shut up. No. Don't be kidding about this.

SHEPARD

Why not?

ISADORA
Because this is serious, okay? This is amazing!!! 😤

SHEPARD
Amazing.

ISADORA
Yes! This is beyond amazing. 😤😤😤

SHEPARD
You're using that word a lot today, aren't you?

ISADORA
Shut up! Do you know how many times I've heard people talk about it at parties?

SHEPARD
How many?

ISADORA
God, I don't know, a hundred?!

A million! 😂😂😂

SHEPARD
It couldn't have been that many.

ISADORA
Stop.

The point is that so many people wanted this! 🙌

SHEPARD
Sounds like you're one of them.

ISADORA
Of course I am! He's responsible for the majority of the changes in the team.

SHEPARD
Ah, I forgot that you know everything about soccer now.

ISADORA
Again, shut up.

And he is. Ask anyone!

SHEPARD
I don't think some people would agree with that.

> ISADORA
>
> Then some people need to get a clue. He was the first one who came on board when the team was almost dying. He was the one who trained so many players, helped in drafting them. He did all the initial work. He lay the groundwork for others to come in and shine. In many ways this is his team.

It is.

People always see the shining trophies and praises *after* the fact. And no, I'm not denying all the work that players and other coaches have put in. But *he* truly was the one who whipped the team into shape in the beginning. He truly was the one who came on first and changed so many things around the locker room and game strategies. He did lay the groundwork for others to build on.

But maybe it's not so glamorous as scoring a goal or shooting a commercial. Pair that with his reluctance to go on camera or do interviews or any sort of press and the fact that he insists on staying as the assistant puts him at a disadvantage.

And despite everything, my heart squeezes for him.

For this man who loves shadows more than light.

Who wouldn't even take credit when it's overdue.

I wish I could...

I wish I could do something about that. I wish I could understand *why*.

But then again, it's none of my business.

Shaking my thoughts away, I fire off another text.

> ISADORA
>
> Besides do you remember the old coach? How obnoxious he was?! He totally gave me the creeps. I was so happy when he was let go.

SHEPARD

He gave you the creeps.

> ISADORA
>
> Yes.

SHEPARD

Why?

> ISADORA
>
> Because he hit on me.

SHEPARD

He hit on you.

> ISADORA
>
> Yes!

SHEPARD

When?

> **ISADORA**
> I don't know, a lot of times.

> **SHEPARD**
> Define a lot of times.
>
> And if your answer begins with I don't know, it's probably the wrong answer.

I frown down at my screen. Is it just me or does he sound bossy?

I mean, Shepard can be bossy sometimes, sure. Like when he's talking about soccer. Or when we're riding in his car—he loves cars; that's his other passion besides soccer—and he's always like, no eating in my car, and all that.

But not like this.

Never ever like this.

It reminds me of... damn it.

There's only one person it reminds me of and I'm trying so hard not to focus on him right now.

> **ISADORA**
> That's not even the point.

> **SHEPARD**
> It is now.

> **ISADORA**
> Can we just drop it?

> **SHEPARD**
> How many?

> **ISADORA**
> Please.

> **SHEPARD**
> How the fuck many.

> **ISADORA**
> Oh my God, I don't know! And that's the right answer because he'd do it at every party, okay? And multiple times during the party. Sometimes he'd come over for dinner and I'd be up in my room and he'd come up and strike up a conversation with me. And the whole time he'd stare at my chest or try to touch me. It creeped me out. He creeped me out. There. Are you happy now? 🤢🤢

I know I'm making light of it, but he did make me super uncomfortable. Actually, he scared me too. I'd avoid him as much as I could. Usually, I can handle myself with men. Be it sheer luck or skill, I've always managed to come out unscathed in tricky situations. But for some reason, I always thought my luck would run out when it came to the old coach.

My mom obviously didn't believe me, meaning my father didn't too. Whenever I complained about him, she would just tell me to stop being provocative or wear different clothes. Or just not be so *myself*.

So I was glad when they let him go. And they did that because they were able to bring on Coach Thorne. And *that* happened because of him. Because he somehow pulled his older brother out of his self-imposed exile and convinced him to take the job.

So in a way, I've always thought he saved me.
Like he has a habit of doing.

SHEPARD

I will be.

ISADORA

What?

SHEPARD

When I make sure he gets fired from his current team and never gets a job again.

ISADORA

What?!! Why?

SHEPARD

Because someone needs to teach him a lesson.

I stare at the screen for a few seconds.
Then, without thinking, I type up and fire off my reply.

ISADORA

Are all Thorne brothers like that?

SHEPARD

Like what?

ISADORA

Ready to teach lessons to assholes who don't treat girls nicely.

Because that's what he said too.
The night of the charity event.

SHEPARD

Pretty much.

ISADORA

Is it because you've got a sister my age?

SHEPARD

She's older than you. But yes.

I clench the phone tighter then.

Because a giant wave of emotions goes through me that makes me shiver and reminds me so much of him, so very much that for several seconds, I don't know what to do. But I try to stay focused.

ISADORA

Well, no need to waste your protective instincts on me. I'm fine now. He's gone and he's never coming back. So can we please get back on track?

SHEPARD

Which is what?

ISADORA

Which is how amazing it is that he's the head coach now. Well, co-head coach along with Coach Thorne.

Right?
Everything else aside, I'm glad for him.
I really am.

SHEPARD

I don't think that was the track we were on.

The track was how as the head coach the very first thing he did was to bench the captain of the team. But can't deny that this has been a revelation.

I had no idea you were such a big fan of him.

My heart drops then.
At his words.
And something occurs to me. That how strange it is that we've been talking about him without really mentioning his name. That how it is understood that the *he* is him. I don't know why I'm thinking about such useless things when there's something else at stake.
The fact that I forgot.
I completely forgot about Shepard being benched because of the news of his promotion.
God what a fucking idiot I am.
Forget being a girlfriend. I acted like such a shitty best friend just now. Instead of supporting him through this, I'm going on and on about the man who caused this in the first place.
Not to mention, this is so against all my promises and plans.

ISADORA
Did you guys have a fight?

SHEPARD
You could say that.

ISADORA
About the game?

SHEPARD
No.

ISADORA
About how you played tonight?

SHEPARD
No.

ISADORA
So then about what?

SHEPARD
About inconsequential things.

ISADORA
What inconsequential things?

I wait for his answer then, growing restless by the second.
I don't know why, but I have a bad feeling about this.
Bad and angsty.
Twisty and achy.

SHEPARD
He wants something.

ISADORA
What does he want?

SHEPARD
Something I have that he thinks belongs to him.

ISADORA
What is it?

I see the dots going and going, and this achy feeling only grows.
And it grows so much that it gets harder to contain it within the limits of my body. The seams of my skin and the borders of my bones seem to be pulling taut.
Just when I think I will come apart, he replies.

SHEPARD

It doesn't matter. He'll let me keep it.

I have zero idea of what he's talking about.

Zero.

All I know is I don't want them to fight.

I *don't.*

Even though I know there's some tension between them. There always has been. You couldn't miss it or at least *I* didn't. Probably because in the beginning, every time I'd strike up a conversation with Shepard about him, he'd wave it away. He'd avoid talking about it. Sometimes he'd get irritated and I'd back off. And so from all that I've seen, it looks like Shepard doesn't like his twin brother all that well.

And it always made me curious.

It also made me think that maybe this stupid plan I have—using one brother to get another—should be stopped. Of course I didn't stop, though, and now look where we are.

In any case, I still try to approach this albeit delicately. Not only because he may not like it but also because for some reason, I can't shake that bad feeling. I can't shake this restlessness in my chest.

ISADORA

He's your brother.

SHEPARD

I'm aware of that.

ISADORA

Twin brother.

SHEPARD

Aware of that too.

ISADORA

So you should talk to him. Whatever it is that you guys are fighting about can be resolved. I mean, he's one of the good guys, right?

SHEPARD

Can I tell you secret?

ISADORA

What secret?

SHEPARD

He may look like a good guy but from what I hear he's a fucking asshole.

My whole body shakes then.

My whole body goes in an uproar. My heart, my breaths.

My soul.

For a few seconds, I think that maybe he knows.

He knows what I said to *him* that night. I called him an asshole in disguise, didn't I, so maybe Shepard overheard it. Not only he overheard what I said, but he can read my mind. He can read my thoughts. He can hear my heartbeats and if he can, then he probably knows that every beat of my heart, every pulse, every thought is of one and one man only.

Him.

ISADORA

Yes.

SHEPARD

Yes what?

ISADORA

Yes, yes, yes. A thousand times yes, I want to be your girlfriend!!!

And then comes the longest pause in the history of all the pauses in the world.

I know that was abrupt, me going all yes on him like that. But I needed to get the situation and my traitorous thoughts under control. And now that he's not responding, I think maybe I should call him instead of this stupid back and forth via texting. But then I realize that this is all I can do right now. This is all the courage I have in me, so I fire off another text, a long one.

ISADORA

I know I've been a shitty friend. I know this whole past year I led you on. The whole world thinks I'm your girlfriend when I'm not. I never was. Instead, I gave you mixed signals. I knew you were starting to feel more for me, but I didn't say anything. I pretended not to notice and that was awful of me. It was so fucking awful of me to do that to you, to my best friend. I watched you feel so shitty and did nothing. I strung you along. I dragged my feet. I forced you to give me an ultimatum that night and I... I'm so sorry about that, Shepard. I'm so so sorry. I never wanted you to feel that way. I never wanted to hurt you. I just... I was so blind. I was so wrapped up in my own head that I couldn't realize that you were the one for me. You are the one for me.

You gave me until the home game to give you an answer but I'm giving it to you now. I want you. I want to be with you. I never ever want to make you feel the way I have this last year. I want to be your girlfriend.

I want to say more.

I want to keep saying it.

I also want to curl up in a ball and disappear as the winter breeze swirls inside my bedroom. Because this is it, isn't it? This is the end of an era. The end of my obsession with *him*. Because now that I've given my answer to Shepard, I'm going to cut all ties with *him*. I'm going to firmly push him out of my mind and focus all my devotion and love on my best friend.

No more watching him. No more obsessing over him.

No more making him jealous or angry.

I knew it was coming, the end. I wanted it to come, but maybe I wasn't fully prepared for it. For the death of my love. For the murder of it.

At my own hands.

But it's okay.

It's always better to kill the love that will only be mourned by one heart. Because that love is unrequited and therefore useless.

Once again, those three dots come and go, and I stare at them and stare at them, waiting with bated breath for his response.

> **SHEPARD**
> The world does think you're my girlfriend.

I swallow as I watch another one come in.

> **SHEPARD**
> But you're not.

Followed by another.

> **SHEPARD**
> Because you gave me mixed signals.

And another.

> **SHEPARD**
> You strung me along. You dragged your feet.

And yet another.

> **SHEPARD**
> Even when you knew I wanted you.
>
> Do I have all of that right?

I don't know how I do it, but I reply to him.

> **ISADORA**
> Yes.

SHEPARD

And you're sorry.

Do I have that right as well?

ISADORA

Yes, you do. Because I am. I'm sorry, Shepard.

SHEPARD

But now you want to be my girlfriend.

ISADORA

Yes, I do. I want to.

My chest heaves, going up and down. My breaths are cold and papery as I once again stare at the screen like my life depends on it. And maybe it does because the moment he answers back, my heart stops.

SHEPARD

No.

ISADORA

What?

SHEPARD

What makes you think I want you to be my girlfriend.

After everything you've done.

This hadn't occurred to me. I have to admit.

Not once did I think he'd... refuse. Not once did I think he'd say no.

He is, though, and... And I think it makes sense, right?

It makes perfect sense because I've hurt him. Not only did I string him along for almost a year, I made him wait for two whole weeks after I forced him to give me an ultimatum. After he told me he loved me.

God, I should've thought of that. It should've been obvious.

I hasten to reply back.

ISADORA

I know you're mad at me. I know that. I understand that. But I just need one chance.

SHEPARD

One chance for what?

ISADORA

One chance to prove that I mean it. That I won't ever do anything to hurt you.

> **SHEPARD**
> Yeah, see that's the thing, isn't it, from the sound of it you already have.

> **ISADORA**
> Please, Shepard.
>
> I'll do anything.

> **SHEPARD**
> To be my girlfriend, you mean.

> **ISADORA**
> Yes! Whatever it is that you want me to do.
>
> I'll do it all.

I'm gripping my phone with both hands now, sitting up in the bed. My breaths are louder than the wind whipping outside. And then they explode when he replies.

> **SHEPARD**
> Okay.

> **ISADORA**
> Okay, I can be your girlfriend?

> **SHEPARD**
> Okay, I'll let you do anything to be my girlfriend.

I chew on my lips as I respond.

> **ISADORA**
> What does that mean?

> **SHEPARD**
> It means that you should rest your knees tonight. Because starting tomorrow you'll be spending a lot of time on them. Begging me to stop stringing you along and playing with your emotions. Starting tomorrow you'll be begging me to show you mercy. When you didn't. For a whole fucking year.

CHAPTER 7

Sitting on the window seat, I stare at the icy panes. I stare at the flurries of snow falling beyond it. They're the kind that stick to the ground, to everything they touch, morphing the world into the land that's either made of wonder or waste.

Kind of like love.

Making a heart bloom or taking away its last beat.

Looking away from the window, I glance down at the phone in my hand.

Unable to sleep, I read and reread the messages with Shepard. My boyfriend or rather my would-be boyfriend when I'm done repenting for my sins against him. It's okay. I don't think it's unfair by any means. After everything I've put him through, I think I'm getting off easy.

It's the other thing that's stealing my sleep in this moment.

I'm telling myself I shouldn't do it.

That there's no reason for me to do something like this. Yes, *he's* benched Shepard for whatever reason, but it's not my fight. It's theirs. They should resolve it. I have no reason to put myself in the middle of it. In fact, I've already tried to come between them and I should be thankful it never panned out.

But for some reason, I can't help myself.

From pulling up his number—he never gave it to me, of course; I lifted it off Shepard's phone one day—and firing him off a text.

ISADORA

Put him back on. 👑 🐺

His reply comes back in seconds as if his phone was in his hands and he was just waiting for it to ring.

WILDFIRE THORN

Who is this?

Even though he has no reason to know who this is, his innocuous response makes me angry. It makes me want to punch him.

ISADORA

This is the girl who's going to kick your ass! 😈😈😈

WILDFIRE THORN

I thought you were going to burn me down and melt me. Or something to that effect.

I gasp.
Asshole.
You know what, I'm changing his name to asshole just as soon as I get off from chewing his ass out.

ISADORA

You knew who I was.

WILDFIRE THORN

I had a feeling.

Although I don't remember giving you my number.

ISADORA

I stole it from Shepard because I'm just so obsessed with you.

That was sarcasm by the way. Something you're so familiar with.

WILDFIRE THORN

I am familiar with it, yes. That's how I know sarcasm is just a fancy way of telling the truth.

Although what I don't know is do I need to change my number now that you have it.

I grit my teeth.
I narrow my eyes at the screen even though he can't see me.

ISADORA

Relax. I have no interest in you. Not anymore.

WILDFIRE THORN

So then to what do I owe this annoyance in the middle of the night?

OH, YOU'RE SO COLD

> **ISADORA**
> You benched him.

> **WILDFIRE THORN**
> Who's him?

I grit my teeth harder and stab the screen with my fingers as I respond.

> **ISADORA**
> Don't be an asshole.

> **WILDFIRE THORN**
> Can't help it.

> **ISADORA**
> Put him back on the team!! 😈 😈 😈
> Now!! 😈 😈 😤

> **WILDFIRE THORN**
> I would. Except you still haven't said it.

"God, I hate him," I grumble to the phone, but instead of typing out a response, I just hit call. This back and forth is ridiculous.

"Looks like I may have to change my number after all," he murmurs, picking up before the first ring ends.

And I have to draw up my knees to my chest and wrap my arms around my bare legs, physically holding myself together with his gravelly voice filling my ear. "Why are you being such an asshole?"

"Probably because I *am* such an asshole," he responds flippantly.

I breathe out sharply. "Okay, fine. Shepard. Shepard Thorne. Your twin brother, remember him? Put him back on the team."

"Ah," he goes. "You mean your boyfriend."

I think he puts emphasis on the 'boyfriend.'

A great emphasis. As if saying it in underlined italics. As if saying it with an underlying *meaning*.

But maybe it's just me.

Maybe I'm making things up in my head.

"Yes, my boyfriend." I swallow, still uncomfortable lying to him. "You benched him. You need to fix it."

"Hmm." He almost purrs in my ear and I dig my nails into my thighs. "That's not how you do it."

"That's not how you do what?" I snap.

"Beg on your boyfriend's behalf."

My spine straightens. "What?"

"That's what you're doing, aren't you?" he drawls. "Begging me."

I press my phone to my ear and say with clenched teeth, "I'm not begging you. I will never beg you."

"Although I will say that I'm a little surprised," he says without paying attention to what I said.

"There is no need for you to be surprised. Because I'm not—"

"Didn't know he'd send a girl to make his case," he finishes. "But it's understandable if he's a little intimidated."

And I'm gritting my teeth so hard that it becomes tough to speak.

But I manage it somehow.

"He is not intimidated," I tell him. "Okay? He is so not intimidated by you. In fact, *my boyfriend* will kick your ass any day of the week."

"And twice on Sunday, I assume," he inquires with a mocking tone.

"Oh, you think it's funny?"

"No, I just think he'll probably be too busy running laps around the field come Sunday, and every day of the week for that matter, to kick anyone's ass, let alone his coach's," he drawls. "So I wouldn't get my hopes up."

My nostrils flare with a large, angry breath. "This is an abuse of power. You know that, don't you?"

"I know," he says simply, casually.

I shake my head. "What's wrong with you? Why are you doing this?"

For the next couple of seconds, all I hear is my own breaths, fast and loud. Like I'm waiting for a bomb to explode. I'm waiting for him to tell me something that's going to blow my mind.

"I think you know," he murmurs, but there's still an edge to his words.

But I'm not concerned about his tone right now. Because that bad feeling I couldn't push away while talking to Shepard comes back in full force. It feels more like an instinct now. A gut feeling.

More solid. More undeniable.

I notice flurries picking up speed from the corner of my eyes as I say, "He said you guys had a fight."

"We did," he confirms.

"What did you guys fight about?"

Again, for a few seconds, I hear my loud breaths. But this time, it's against the backdrop of the wind whipping and howling outside. It's against the backdrop of this dread in the pit of my stomach.

"I think you know that too."

And then it feels like everything stops.

My heart, my breaths.

The snow.

The flakes suspend in the air, floating like feathers.

"You think…" I begin with a trembling voice. "I don't… I don't belong to you."

My words sound bizarre to my ears.

They don't make any sense, except they do.

OH, YOU'RE SO COLD

Because that's what Shepard said, didn't he, when we were talking about the fight. He said that he has something that Stellan thinks is his.

Those were his exact words.

Exact.

So if they fought about what I *think* they fought about—me—then in conclusion, *I'm* the thing that Stellan thinks belongs to him.

Right?

I know I sound like a crazy person right now, putting things together like a puzzle, but I just... I think I need a minute.

To gather my wits.

To pull myself together.

Because... What?

What the *fuck*?

"That's where you're wrong," he says again with an edge to his voice.

This time, more pronounced, though.

"What?"

"You do belong to me."

And then, with his words echoing in my ear, the world begins to move. The breaths slam back into my chest. My heart pitter-patters before pounding. The flakes finally make their way down to the bare branches of the tree I've been staring at all through this.

"I... What?" I ask on a whisper.

"Not him," he whispers too, but again his is edgy, dangerous, full of sharp and icy thorns. "*Me.*"

"I... I don't," I finally manage to say. Finally manage to pull myself together and *think*. "I don't even know why you'd think that. I'm with him. I'm—"

"Only because you're not with me," he cuts me off.

"But you didn't *want* me," I say, clutching my phone tighter.

"Which is why you went to him." He pauses then, "Didn't you?"

And I realize I'm still very much in danger.

Because again I become thoughtless and speechless.

I freeze.

And not from the cold.

"The reason you went to him in the first place is because I didn't want you. Because you *wanted* me to want you. You wanted me to look at you, so you gave me something to look at. Isn't that right? You danced with him that night. You danced in his fucking arms. You laughed with him, flirted with him. You made it look like he's the center of your fucking universe. Because I was the center of yours."

"That's not..." I burst out, but words fail me. "H-how do you..."

"You use men," he says, his voice low. "Isn't that what you told me? That night. You use them to get what you want. You throw yourself at them to get them to do what you want. And you wanted me. So you used my twin brother to get to me. Wasn't so hard to put together if you look closely. I just wasn't looking. That's why you came after me that night at the charity event. Not because you're some spoiled little rich girl who can't make up her mind, who flits from one twin to another, but because you want just the one twin and you've been using the other to get him." Then, "I have to admit it doesn't feel very good. Not being able to recognize what was right in front of me. I'm usually better at paying attention than this."

"You—"

"On the other hand, though, maybe you should take solace in the fact that this bodes very good things for your acting career. If you can fool me with your stellar acting skills, you could fool anyone."

I clutch the phone with both hands, my belly churning. "Please don't... Don't tell him. Don't... I'm... I'm not using him anymore. I'm not... I want him, okay? I want to be with him and—"

He hums. "Very touching."

"Please, I'm begging you."

"I thought you didn't beg."

"God," I burst out again. "Can you just... Look, yes, I wanted you. Back then. I wanted you badly. I wanted you so much that I used Shepard. I made it look like I was into him. Because I wanted you to be jealous. I wanted you to want me back, to eat your words from that night. I wanted you to regret not kissing me, for rejecting me. I just... I don't know what had gotten into me, okay? I'd never felt this way about any guy and... I thought... God, I actually thought you were my destiny." I shake my head. "It sounds so stupid when I say it now, but... I thought you were the one I dreamed about. But I was stupid, okay? I was petty and immature. It was before I knew how big of an asshole you are. I don't want you anymore. I want him. I want to be with Shepard. So I need you to stop messing with him and put him back on the team."

"I will," he says.

"You—"

"But I want something in return."

Dread is hard and cold in my stomach.

Because I know. I know what he's going to say.

I *know* it.

"Don't," I warn him. "Don't do this. Don't—"

"You."

"No."

"Because I think such devotion and persistence should be rewarded, don't you? I'm sure there's a lesson in there somewhere: be careful what you wish for or more like, don't play the game with someone who can play it back harder. But let's focus on the reward rather than the punishment, shall we? You've been dying for me, haven't you? Well, congratu-fucking-lations, I'm putting you out of your misery."

"I don't—"

"So this is how it's going to go: when we come back for the home game, I want one night."

"O-one night?"

"With you," he goes on. "One night to do as I please. To do whatever the fuck I want with you. To give you what you've been begging for. One night where you belong to me. Where you're mine and mine *only*. You agree to that and in exchange, I'll give you what you want. I won't mess with him. Or you. I won't abuse my power. I'll keep your dirty little secret so you can live your happily ever after with my brother."

"Don't do this," I beg again. "Please don't do this."

"I kinda have to. I'm the asshole in disguise, remember? But unfortunately for you, Dora, I *am* also your fucking destiny."

CHAPTER 8

THE WILDFIRE THORN

I'm gripping my phone so hard that I know if I don't let up, I'll break it.

I also know if I let it go, I'll break everything else in the room.

So in a way, this phone is my lifeline, my grounding object.

There have been many occasions in my life when I could've lost all control and given in to my fiery urges. A lot of times where I could've broken my promise and succumbed to my genes. But I've held fast.

So I'm not going to lose it now.

Not over some slip of a girl I couldn't get out of my head for the past year.

A girl who's been *lying* for the past year.

That's what she's been doing, isn't it?

She's been *lying*.

She's been fucking torturing me for the past year. She's been playing with me, with my control. With my fucking emotions that I chose to bury and *bury deep* so I could keep it together.

Except when it comes to her.

When it comes to her, I can't keep it together.

I can't. *Fucking*. Keep it together.

One year.

One whole year of seeing them together, of her walking around on his arm, of her laughing with him, dancing with him, fucking looking at him like he's the only thing she sees.

One whole *goddamn* year of this jealousy.

This burning in my gut, this restlessness.

I don't know what's worse. That a teenage girl, a girl younger than my sister, my boss's daughter, a girl my twin brother is in love with, can make me feel things. Or she could do it to this extent that I couldn't tell what was real or not.

I don't know what's worse: trying to hold on to my control or burning this whole world down like I want to.

Maybe if I give in to my urges, once, just once, it wouldn't be so bad. Maybe if I explode and break everything in this room, if I break my twin's face, I could calm down.

But no.

I'm not hurting my brother. I'm not going to turn into my father.

But I will end this.

I will fucking end this.

I will forget about her. I will push her out of my head, out of my life. And I know how to do that. If I can't give in to this fire within me, then I'll give in to her.

I know she's the love of my twin brother's life, but she'll be mine first before I'll let her go to him. She'll be mine first to play with, to toy with. Mine to torture and to twist in pretty little knots before I'll let her be anyone else's.

With that thought, my fingers slip from around my phone but instead of throwing it against the wall, I set it on the nightstand and pick up my book. I read the same line over and over until exhaustion claims me and I pass out.

CHAPTER 9

THE NEXT NIGHT...

*H*e's bluffing.
  He has to be.
 He's just messing with me. There's no other explanation.
 And I've tried to find one too.
 All day today, during classes and rehearsal, I've tried to find an explanation as to why he'd be doing this. I think it's because he's angry at what I did. He's angry that I lied to him and all of the world. And since he *is* mad, he's trying to scare me.
 Right?
 Because the alternative is that he's blackmailing me. For *real*.
 And oh my God, I cannot believe that.
 I cannot believe that I'm getting *blackmailed*. By someone like him.
 By someone who everyone thinks is such a good guy. And yes, I have had my doubts about his goodness, but even so, I never expected him to stoop to this level.
 Well, maybe you pushed him there...
 Like you pushed Shepard to give you an ultimatum.
 God.
 How is this my life?
 How in only a matter of two weeks, one twin gives me an ultimatum and the other blackmails me? And maybe if *he* was only hurting me, I could bear it—somehow—but I'm not the only one at stake here, Shepard is too and I...
 I don't know what to do.

I absolutely *do not* know what to do about it.

Okay, you know what, I *know* what to do. At least right this moment. I'll figure the rest out later but for now, I need to stop thinking about *him* and focus on my boyfriend.

My would-be boyfriend.

If I earn his forgiveness.

So I pick up my phone and fire off a series of texts to him.

> ISADORA
>
> I'm wearing a nightie.
>
> It has cherries on it.
>
> And lace.

I'm sitting on the bed like last night and the windows are open and the curtains are billowing. It's all the same as yesterday, except I'm a lot more nervous and as the last whoosh fades, I think that was so out of the blue. All my texts sounded so random and context-less.

God, I'm an idiot.

This was supposed to be the perfect plan. But in my nervousness, I botched it up.

I pick up my phone again, ready to explain to him what I just did, when his text comes in.

> SHEPARD
>
> What color?

My heart bangs in my chest then as I reply.

> ISADORA
>
> Pink.

> SHEPARD
>
> Are the cherries pink or the nightie?

I look down at my nightie as if I don't remember what I'm wearing. As if I didn't deliberately wear it in the first place.

> ISADORA
>
> The nightie.

> SHEPARD
>
> What color are the cherries?

Again, my heart races and races in my chest as I type out my response.

> **ISADORA**
> Red.
>
> Well, dark pink.
>
> So I guess they're both pink...?

I'm fucking this up, aren't I?
I totally am.
This is *not* how you sext your boyfriend.
Which is what I'm trying to do. But I don't think it's coming out that way.

> **SHEPARD**
> No, I think there's a difference.

> **ISADORA**
> What difference?

> **SHEPARD**
> Only one of those is the color of your mouth.

Finally, all the racing and pounding that my heart was doing stops and my body goes still.
I freeze.
But thank God my fingers are working, so I can ask,

> **ISADORA**
> The color of my mouth?

> **SHEPARD**
> Yeah.

> **ISADORA**
> Which one's the color of my mouth?

> **SHEPARD**
> The cherries.

My fingers inevitably go up to my mouth.
It's tingling. It feels swollen.

> **ISADORA**
> You think my mouth's the color of cherries?

I know, I know.
It was stupid. Again.
But I can't help it. I can't help being stupid in this moment.
Because did he just describe my lips as cherries?

SHEPARD

I think your mouth's the color of ripe and swollen cherries, but yeah.

ISADORA

Ripe and swollen cherries.

SHEPARD

The kind of cherries that are so ripe and so swollen that the moment you sink your teeth into them, they can't help but overflow with juices. That kind of cherries.

ISADORA

I didn't know.

SHEPARD

You didn't know what?

ISADORA

That you could talk like that.

SHEPARD

Probably because we've never talked like this.

ISADORA

No, we haven't.

SHEPARD

So what else do you want to talk about?

ISADORA

Do you think about my mouth a lot?

SHEPARD

Define a lot.

ISADORA

Um... At least once a day maybe?

SHEPARD

If you think that's a lot, then we both have a very different definition of it.

ISADORA

What's your definition of it?

SHEPARD

Probably once every hour, if not every minute.

I let my lip go then.

Before this, I've been biting my lower lip. The moment he sent me that text about sinking his teeth into them, I sank mine. I don't know why I did it. Maybe because I wanted to see if he was right. If my lips really feel like ripe cherries that overflow with juices.

But that's all beside the point now.

In the face of this revelation.

Because I...

As I just mentioned, I didn't know.

Even though I knew how he felt about me, I didn't really *know*.

I didn't realize the extent of it. I should have, though.

ISADORA

That's... actually a lot.

SHEPARD

Yeah.

ISADORA

And is it always about sinking your teeth into my lips, your thoughts?

SHEPARD

No.

SHEPARD

Sometimes I want to leave a mark.

ISADORA

A mark?

SHEPARD

Maybe on your neck.

Or the triangle of your throat.

And you know what the color of that mark would be?

ISADORA

What?

SHEPARD

The color of ripe and juicy cherries.

To match the color of your lips.

ISADORA

What else?

SHEPARD

If you want me to tell you what else, you better finish what you started.

ISADORA

What did I start?

SHEPARD

This.

Which I can only assume is your way of sexting.

My eyes go wide, and I rush to reply.

ISADORA

You got that?!

SHEPARD

Yeah, I'm surprised too that I did.

ISADORA

I thought I was fucking it up!

SHEPARD

You were.

But when a girl tells you about what she's wearing, it isn't exactly rocket science.

ISADORA

I was just trying to cheer you up.

SHEPARD

I think I'm getting that too.

ISADORA

Because I saw the game.

And you looked upset. On the field I mean.

He did.

Tonight's game was a disaster. Not because the team lost—they won actually—but because their captain wasn't playing. They kept bringing the camera back to Shepard, who was sitting in the box, to get his reaction after every goal or a miss or a pass, a foul, and every time they did, his face would look like a stony mask. The commentators kept making speculations as to what had caused their captain to be benched, and if tonight's win, *without* him, means something more and indicates to a deeper issue. So far, the story's that Shep got injured during practice, but it's minor and he missed the game as a precaution.

But of course the truth is something much worse and far uglier.

The truth is me.

A girl who came between two twin brothers.

And now Shepard is paying the price.

SHEPARD
So you thought like a good girlfriend you'd cheer me up.

ISADORA
Yes.

That's exactly what I thought.

Because I know how important soccer is to him. How important winning is. The team's finally doing good. They won last season and despite the losses in the previous weeks, there's still hope that they'll do it again. And imagine potentially not being a part of that. Of something you worked so hard to achieve.

I know my poor attempt at sexting won't fix things, but I *have* to do something.

Something to make him feel better.

Until I find a permanent solution to the problem, to somehow get him reinstated on the team.

Well, you could just give him *what he wants and then all of this will be over, won't it?*

No.

No, no, no.

Haven't I just decided that he's bluffing? He has to be.

He can't expect me to... give him what he wants.

SHEPARD
But you're hardly good, let alone my girlfriend.

ISADORA
I want to be.

SHEPARD
Good or a girlfriend?

ISADORA
Both.

For you.

I do. I want to be.

So that while I talk to him, I don't think about his twin brother.

Because that's what I've been doing, haven't I? I've been wondering what *he* thinks about my lips. If he ever thinks about them at all. Does he think my mouth resembles an overripe fruit? Does he want to sink his teeth into me? Does he want to give me bruises on my neck that match the color of my lips...

My phone pinging breaks my thoughts—thankfully—and I grab it with both hands, trying to stay in the moment.

SHEPARD
So then you gotta pay your dues.

> **ISADORA**
> Tell me how.

> **SHEPARD**
> That's a very good question, isn't it? How do you pay your dues?
>
> How do you pay for a year worth of torture.
>
> For a year worth of stringing me along. For making me watch you from afar. Forcing me to fucking watch.

I couldn't respond to him even if I wanted to.

And he doesn't seem to need any as another one of his texts arrives on the screen. But I can't decide if it's a good thing or not, him not needing a response from me just yet because every word he says hits me like a sharp dart.

> **SHEPARD**
> As you smiled at other men with that cherry pink mouth of yours. As you forced me to listen to your throaty fucking laughter.

> **SHEPARD**
> Do you know what your laughter does to men?

It's hard, but I pull myself together enough to fire off a reply.

> **ISADORA**
> What?

> **SHEPARD**
> It makes them go insane.
>
> It makes them go feral.
>
> It chips away at their control, slowly, piece by piece until all what remains is that feral instinct. To possess it. To gorge on it, to eat it up. To kill every man who's ever heard it. Your laughter, Cherry Lips, turns men into murderers.

> **ISADORA**
> Did you just give me a nickname?

> **SHEPARD**
> Seemed appropriate for a girl whose mouth is the color of ripe cherries.

And God help me, I can't stop thinking about how *he* calls me by his own name too. How Dora, even though derived from my own name, sounds so new and unique. How I like it more than...

Okay, no.

I'm not going to think about that. I'm not going to compare stupid nicknames.

ISADORA
I'm sorry. I'm so sorry.

I'm not sure what I'm saying sorry about, though. The fact that I immediately thought of his twin brother and the name he gave me or because of all the ways I've tortured my best friend because of him.

SHEPARD
Well sorry isn't enough, is it? When not only have I had to hear your laughter and watch you strut around in your frilly skirts and skimpy dresses, but I've had to watch you dance in them too.

ISADORA
But you know that I like to dance.

SHEPARD
That's the thing though, you don't dance, do you. You put on a show.

ISADORA
What's the difference?

SHEPARD
The difference is that when you dance it looks like you're getting paid to do it. It looks like you're a cam girl and your only job is to make all the men who've been eye-fucking you on their screen, blow in their pants in under two minutes.

When you dance it looks like you want something between those honey-colored thighs of yours. You're aching for something to dance against and I'm not talking about a pole. Or not the kind that you'll be dancing against if I have a say about it.

I jolt in surprise.
My thighs clenching. My belly clenching too.
And I have a very strong urge to lie. A very strong urge to tell him that no, I don't dance like that. When in fact I do. I have. Like I'm putting on a show. Like I'm getting paid to do it. Only I've done it for his twin brother.

SHEPARD
You know that you do, don't you? You know you dance like that.

You dance like you want someone to watch.

ISADORA

Yes.

And as always, in the quest of this, I never paid any mind to my best friend. I never paid any mind to what he must be feeling, watching me put myself out there like that.

In my defense, though—if there could ever be any—I never thought Shepard had any feelings toward it. He's not the jealous type. He's just not. In all the time I've known him, he's never, not once, said or expressed anything to this effect and...

Well, I'm lying about this too, aren't I?

Because he did once.

We were at this bar with his team for a victory party. There were drinks and dancing and revelry. And until that night, Shepard had never cared about what I wore or how I danced. So when he gave me his jacket to put on in the middle of the dance floor, I was taken aback. I didn't even think he was wearing a jacket—he's not a suit jacket wearing kind of guy. But apparently, he was and when he draped it over my shoulders, I looked at him in confusion. He said something about some guys watching me and that it was better if I covered myself up. And since he'd never made a demand like that, I agreed and did what he said.

But even back then, I didn't get the jealous vibe from him.

I thought he was being protective like a good friend. And I don't have siblings, but it felt... brotherly, for the lack of a better word.

Now I know, though.

And it twists my heart.

I never wanted him to feel that way.

God, there are so many things I never wanted but did anyway.

SHEPARD

So how do you make up for something like that?

My fingers type and send the text before I've had time to think about it. And when I watch the screen, waiting for his reply, I realize it's the right thing to do.

ISADORA

I'll do it. I'll dance for you.

Only for you.

SHEPARD

Only for me.

ISADORA

Yes! I've made you watch, haven't I? While I've danced like that for other men. So from now on I'll just dance for you and no one else.

It makes perfect sense.

Besides, why would I want to dance for someone else anyway? Now that I'm with Shepard, I don't need to put on a show for someone else. Or rather the only man I've ever deliberately put on a dancing show for.

So yeah, this is a perfect plan.

A perfect way to pay my dues.

SHEPARD
Do it.

ISADORA
Dance?

SHEPARD
Yeah, for me.

ISADORA
You mean like when you come back?

SHEPARD
No, I mean like right now.

ISADORA
Right now?

SHEPARD
Do you remember the white dress you wore the night we met?

I straighten up in the bed then. I move away from the pillows as my fingers shake and fly on the keyboard.

ISADORA
The white dress from my eighteenth birthday?

SHEPARD
Yeah, the one that was sheer and flimsy. So sheer that your parents locked you up in your room that night.

I told him about that dress when we were dancing. I told him how I got into trouble for wearing it and how I thought I should be able wear something of my own choosing because eighteen was a kinda big birthday; selecting your own wardrobe should be allowed.

I know I keep saying it, but once again, for the millionth time, I didn't know Shepard remembered. We've never talked about that dress after that night.

Not until now.

ISADORA
Yes.

SHEPARD

I want you to find that dress and put it on.

I read his words a few times before I can manage to unglue my fingers from the screen and type out my reply.

ISADORA

You want me to wear that dress?

SHEPARD

And wings.

ISADORA

My good luck wings?

If I told him about my dress, then I definitely told him about my wings. The ones that always make me feel that I can fly. The ones I don't wear anymore.

I don't wear that dress anymore either.

Not in public, no. Not for anyone's eyes.

In secret, yes.

In the dead of night, I wear that dress and those wings.

And then I go into the back garden. I like to stand under a tree and pretend it's the pink magnolia tree. I like to smoke too. Like he was doing that night. I like to pretend that I'm him. That I'm inside his head, taking up all his thoughts. I'm in his chest, curled around his heart. I'm on his tongue so all he tastes is me. I like to pretend that I'm in his body, possessing him like he possesses me.

Sometimes I like to play the character of a witch. A witch in that white dress and fake wings, that brews a love potion that I somehow trick him into drinking. So he falls in love with me.

So yeah, I do remember that dress and I do remember those wings.

But to wear them for Shepard right now feels... wrong.

It feels disloyal.

It feels like I'm giving away a part of myself I'd kept reserved for the man I love.

But he doesn't want that part, does he? He doesn't care about my white dress or my fake wings. He doesn't dream about that pink magnolia tree, and he doesn't care that I color my lungs black for him.

And even if he does, *I* don't care.

I only care about Shepard.

About fixing things for him and facing the consequences.

SHEPARD

And when you're ready for me, I want you to pick up my call.

ISADORA

Your call?

> **SHEPARD**
> Yeah. Because tonight, you'll dance and you'll be on display. But only for me. Only where I can see you.

> **ISADORA**
> Will I be able to see you?

I don't know why I ask that. Maybe because it feels... strange that I'm going to see him after how we just... After all the things he said to me. I mean, he's my best friend and...

> **SHEPARD**
> I'm not the one paying my dues, am I?

> **ISADORA**
> No.

> **SHEPARD**
> So then you'll see me when I decide you have.
>
> You've got two minutes.

I breathe out a sigh of relief even though I shouldn't. As I dress and follow his instructions, I keep telling myself that I'm not breaking any rules. I'm not breaking any promises. I'm not doing anything wrong.

In fact, I'm doing the right thing.

For the first time in months.

When I'm done, I put on the music—something slow but bass heavy—I prop the phone against my pillows like I've done countless times before. Not to dance for him or anyone for that matter. But to record myself doing scenes or reading lines. As soon as two minutes are done, he video calls me. I pick up on the first ring and my nervousness reaches new levels.

Because all I can see is the darkened screen and moving shadows, the silhouette of his body. Which I expected, of course. But oh God, I can't...

I can't cope.

I can't... This is exactly like the night I'd met *him*.

This is exactly how *he* had looked—covered in darkness, his body shadowed by the pink flowers and sturdy branches. And for a second, all I can do is imagine him. That he's the one I'm dancing for.

Like I've always, *always* wanted.

But it's not.

It's Shepard.

So somehow, someway, I make myself move.

I keep my eyes on the screen where I can see the broad strokes of his frame, the hills of his shoulders, the planes of his chest. Where I can see the slopes of his thighs that I think are spread as he lounges in, from what I can gather, his bed. I let that image ground me. I think he's got his phone propped up against something too. As if he doesn't want any responsibilities right now. He doesn't want to divide his attention but rather wants all his focus on me.

I watch him and follow the beat.

I sway and writhe my hips. I throw my arms in the air and put myself on display.

I bow my back and thrust my chest out.

But as I lose myself in the beat, in the music, it gets harder and harder not to float away. Not to become untethered and unmoored until the seams of my body become attached to *his*.

Until suddenly, I'm doing exactly what I didn't want to do.

Dance for him.

Like he's a king and I'm one of his slaves, a dancing girl.

I remember my *biji* telling me stories of Mughal emperors who used to rule India, the king of kings, the *shehanshas*. They used to have dancers in their court, the pretty slave girls, who would entertain the king whenever he desired.

The legend goes that there was once a prince, the heir to a kingdom, who fell in love with a common dancer. It was against the rules, of course, so they would meet in secret. They would meet under the moonlight, in the darkened corners of the castle. But one day, their forbidden love is discovered by the king. To protect his love, the son goes to war against his father. He loses, though, and is sentenced to death. However, the king says that the prince's sentence would be revoked if he handed over the slave girl. The prince refuses; he was ready to die for his love.

And so was the slave girl.

So she gives herself up and the king orders her to be entombed alive.

That's what it feels like in this moment.

That he's my king and I'm his slave girl, and I love him so much that I'm doomed to give my life for him. That I'm doomed to love him forever. I'm doomed to dance for him until my feet turn bloody and the last breath in my body leaves.

And this thought, that I'm at his disposal, that heats me up so much, that arouses me so much that even the chilly breeze through the windows can't cool me down.

I'm so fucking aroused right now that even my shame won't stop me from getting wet and slippery between my legs. So much so that I think I'm soaking my thighs. The droplets of my lust slide down my legs, making a puddle on the floor.

Which is why I slip, I think.

Or maybe it's from how fast I'm spinning as I put on a show for him.

Whatever it is, I stumble and fall to the floor. My knees crash against the hardwood and my breaths are somehow both broken and loud. Even through that, though, I hear when my phone dings with a text message. I snap my eyes up and scramble on my hands and knees to get to it. I don't even know when he disconnected the call.

SHEPARD
Tomorrow.

ISADORA
Tomorrow?

SHEPARD
Same time.

ISADORA
For the call?

SHEPARD
Don't keep me waiting.

I won't.
But first.

ISADORA
Did you like my dance?

SHEPARD
Did I like your dance?

ISADORA
Yes.

SHEPARD
Does the fact that I'm texting you with bloody fingers because I had to punch a hole in the wall, something that I'm going to point out that I've never done before in my entire fucking life, answer your question?

My eyes are wide as I stare down at the screen.

ISADORA
You punched a hole in the wall?

Me: Why?

SHEPARD
Because I got pissed.

ISADORA
Why did you get pissed?

SHEPARD
Because Houston is over fifteen hundred miles away from where I want to be right now.

Panting, I read and reread his words for a few seconds.

ISADORA
And where you want to be is with me?

SHEPARD
You have a very annoying habit of pointing out the obvious.

ISADORA
Yes.

SHEPARD
Yes what?

ISADORA
That answers my question.

Good night, Shepard.

Despite myself, I can't help but feel happy about the outcome. He liked it. Maybe it did help him a little bit and maybe this is a step in the right direction.

But every love story has a villain, doesn't it?

Mine has one too.

It's his twin brother and with a deep breath, I dial his number.

CHAPTER 10

"Put him back on the team," I say as soon he picks up.

For a few seconds, all I can hear is silence.

Actually, no.

There's silence, but there's also something else. Something thick and heavy, panting. Something that matches my breaths. Only his are punctuated with low growls.

Confused and concerned, I go, "Stellan?"

I swear his growls become louder then.

And somehow, I feel them in my own chest, further messing with my breaths.

"Are you okay?" I go on. "What... What's wrong?"

Finally, he breaks his silence and in a voice that sounds even rougher and more gravelly than usual, he replies, "This feels like déjà vu."

"What—"

"And since I don't like repeating myself, all I'll say to end this matter is you know what to do if you want me to put him back on the team."

Now it's my turn to remain silent and growling.

God.

I'm an idiot for being concerned for him.

Even for a second.

Breathing deep, I declare in a firm voice, "I'm not going to do that."

"Then I'm afraid we're at an impasse."

"You know, I've been thinking about it," I begin, still sitting on the cold floor, propped up against the foot of the bed. "And I think you're bluffing."

"Yeah?"

"Yes." I nod. "You're trying to scare me because you're angry."

"I *am* angry," he agrees. "And as I'm coming to find out, I do like you scared of me. So yeah."

"You're doing all this to teach me a lesson," I continue.

"Correct again."

"Which means you're not *actually* going to do anything," I finish.

"Why don't you wait and find out?"

With my heart pounding in my chest, I seethe. "Are you seriously saying that you'll keep him benched for this?"

"Yes."

"Your brother, the captain of your team," I keep insisting, "one of your best players. A *player* you need to be able to bring the trophy home. You need him to win. You'll keep him benched just because you…"

I can't say it.

I absolutely cannot say it because it isn't true.

It can't be, right?

I mean, he doesn't *actually* want me.

Not really.

He had an entire year to do that. An entire fucking year where he hardly looked at me. Where he hardly was aware that I existed. That I was in the same room as him. Where all my efforts—and there have been many as evidenced by the conversation I just had with his twin brother—to get him to notice me have failed.

So no, I refuse to believe it.

"I know it may be surprising to hear," he says, his voice rough, "but I don't care about a trophy or a win. I never did. At least not as much as it matters to him, your boyfriend. So yeah, I will keep him benched for this." Then, after a pause as if he knows the effect it'll have on me, "For *you*."

I clench my eyes shut at the jolt I feel.

It goes through my entire body, stopping and jumpstarting things, making me dizzy.

I want to scream that he should stop this.

He should stop saying it, stop *lying*.

Stop making me go crazy with want and desperation when I'm finally doing the right thing.

But I gather my control and my dignity and open my eyes. "Fine. So how about this? You can't *possibly* keep him benched for the rest of the season, just because you have this insane urge to mess with me. It's impossible. Coach Thorne won't let you. And if somehow you dodge him, which I don't think is ever going to happen, you have my dad to contend with. He will lose his shit, okay? He probably is already losing his shit right now. And in case you don't remember, he's your boss."

As soon as I finish, I want to take it back.

At least that comment about my dad.

I don't like using my father in arguments or as an excuse. It makes me feel exactly what he'd called me back then, a spoiled little rich girl. Not to mention to be a spoiled little rich girl, my father actually has to spoil me and since he prefers to keep his distance from me, it makes me nothing but sad to drop him into conversations like this.

But in this context, it's the truth.

My father *will* lose his shit and he *is* the boss.

Which means Stellan can't possibly keep this up for long.

"Yeah, that's a valid argument," he agrees, and I finally breathe out in relief.

"So then I just have to wait for either Coach Thorne or my dad to—"

"Except *Coach Thorne* has a habit of placing his absolute trust in me. Something about me being his responsible younger brother. And your father"—a puff of air escapes him as if he's both scoffing and chuckling at the same time and doing it with arrogance—"he doesn't know the first thing about soccer. If I tell him that we don't need your boyfriend to win, and we don't, trust me, he'll get with the program. So again, I can and I will do this. And no one can stop me. Least of all my big brother or your daddy."

"You—"

"And besides, from what I remember, you wanted *me* to be your daddy, didn't you? So here I am," he says, his tone laced with mockery. "Your new daddy and as long as I have you, the rest of the world can go fuck itself."

But like a pathetic girl, it makes my belly clench.

Him calling himself that.

It messes with my head, my breaths.

My heart.

I clearly have issues. Big ones.

But I keep my focus on here and now and just burst out the words, "Oh my God, stop, okay? Just stop. Stop saying these things. Stop *acting* like this. You don't act like this. You're one of the good guys. Yes, you're an asshole to me or whatever, but I refuse to believe that you'd do this to your own twin brother. And for what? For *me*. You don't even like me. You think I'm spoiled. You think I'm young. You think I'm annoying and desperate. You said that to me. And I have tried, believe me. I've fucking tried to make you see. I've tried to make you realize that I'm different. That I may be young. That I may be reckless and impulsive and a little crazy, but I *could* make you feel something for me. But you haven't. You *don't*. So I don't know what this is, but whatever it is, you need to stop. Stop fucking messing with him and—"

"You think I like this," he says in a thick voice.

Thick and low and growly.

And I realize I've never heard him sound like this before. I've never heard this tone from him. Is this... anger? If it is, then again, I've never heard him angry before and so my entire body takes notice.

My own voice grows lower when only a second ago I was screaming into the phone in *my* anger. "Like what?"

"This. Whatever *this* is," he says through clenched teeth.

And I feel the snap in my jaw. "I don't—"

"I'm a shitty fucking brother, all right," he says, his words low but his breaths loud. "I know that. I *realize* that. I know that he got stuck with me as his twin. And even though I've done everything I can to step up, I know it doesn't make up for everything that I am. So do you think I like this? Do you think, even for a second, that I like *watching* my twin brother's girl? As if she's mine and feeling absolute zero guilt for it."

I go still then.

He's turned me into a stone with his words.

"Do you think I like following your every move? Tracking them like a fucking stalker. Do you think I *like* this burn I feel in my fucking gut when you smile at him? Or when you laugh." Another puff of air, but I think this is more anger than anything else. "Do you think I like straining my ears to hear it? Do you think I like pushing people away, shoving them out of my way so I can somehow get closer to you, without anyone noticing, mind you, to catch it?

"Or maybe you think I like going to parties. I like going to bars and clubs and team events. Things I try to avoid at all costs and stay home in peace and quiet. So I can smoke one cigarette a day and read my fucking book. But I still make sure to show up at these fucking things because you'll be there. You'll be there laughing and flirting and fucking dancing. And you'll be doing that without a care in the world. So then it's up to me, isn't it? It's up to me to keep you safe. To keep an eye on things. To make sure no one's fucking bothering you and if they do, then it's up to me to gouge their fucking eyes out for looking at you. It's up to me to break their fingers if they dare to touch you. It's *up to me* to break their goddamn brains for even thinking about touching you. Do you know how many parties I've attended ever since I met you?"

"H-How many?"

"Forty-fucking-three."

"I—"

"And there are 52.143 weeks in a year. Fifty-two weeks and one day. So I've been to a party pretty much every single week, more or less."

"You—"

"And do you know how many books I've read since I met you?"

"N-no."

"Zero," he bites out. "Zero fucking books. Because A: I don't usually have time to read them because as I've explained to you, I'm having such a fucking fantastic time being out and about in the world. And B: Because every time I do pick up a book, I can't focus because I'm either thinking about this guy I've had to warn against looking at you or how loud you were laughing at my brother's joke to *make* the said guy look at you."

"But—"

"So do you think I like that? I like being your bodyguard who keeps you safe from yourself. Or maybe you think instead of the game and my players and doing my fucking job, I like watching you at the stadium. I like remembering your laughably flimsy outfits more than remembering who made the pass or who scored the fucking goal.

"No, actually, what I enjoy the most is this incessant urge to beat up my twin brother. This incessant urge to ruin him and get him out of the way. *Creative ways* to ruin him and get him out of the way. Ways that defy all logic and reason. Because that's the only *way* I can keep myself from doing something drastic, from actually turning them into reality. Tell me, Dora, do you think I enjoy any of it, any of *whatever the fuck* this is?"

He doesn't wait for me to answer as he keeps going, "You're a virus, you understand. You're a disease. You're an epidemic. The fucking CDC should issue guidelines for the kind of health hazard that you are. And I'm *sick* of being sick with you. I'm fucking sick of being infected by you. I want you out of my system, my mind, my body. I want you gone. I want to be myself again. I want my peace back. I want my life back. I want my fucking control back and if I have to deign to touch you to make that happen, then I've decided that I will. If the only way to get you out of my system is to fuck you out of it, then I've decided that I will do that too. It doesn't matter that you're not my type, that you'll never be my type or that my twin brother's in love with you. I want you and I will do *anything*, break *any* rule, fuck *anyone* over to have you. Until I don't want you anymore."

I'm not sure whose breaths are louder, his or mine.

Whose heart is racing more.

It has to be mine.

It *has* to be.

Because he's the Cold Thorn, isn't he?

The one who's always emotionless and aloof. The one who doesn't get affected. Who's made of ice.

But maybe not.

Maybe what I thought was right. He's as hot as wildfire.

"Y-you..." I begin, halting and stumbling. "You really think about creative ways to—"

"The other day, I thought about him slipping in the shower and hitting his head."

"That's awful," I gasp out.

"I'm awful," he agrees.

"And what about other guys? Do you really... threaten them t-to keep me safe?"

He waits a few seconds to answer. "Someone has to do it."

"And that person is you?"

"That person is always me," he says. "When it comes to you."

I bring my knees up to my chest and wrap my arm around them. "Do you really watch me more than you w-watch the games?"

"I missed last season's winning goal."

"The one..." I lick my lips. "The one at the championship game?"

"Yeah."

"It was Ledger. He made the goal," I inform him even though there's no way he doesn't know by now.

"Which I found out about thirty seconds later."

"What was I wearing?" I ask then.

"What you always wear."

"Which is what?"

"Some flimsy contraption made of strings and laces. This one was orange in color."

"It wasn't a contraption," I protest.

"It had more strings crisscrossing your back than any dress could possibly ever need," he protests.

"That's not—"

"But then again, for how flimsy it was and how it kept whipping against the wind while basically showing off those two dimples on your back, maybe it did need those strings to hold it all together."

"You noticed the dimples on my back?"

"Along with a small mole, yes."

I bring my hand back then and touch the mole through my white dress. It sits just above one of those dimples and it's really small.

"It's really small," I repeat to him.

"Your dress was really revealing."

"It was just a normal backless dress with a few strings spanning the back."

"It was also a dress where I could not only see those dimples and that mole but also the crack of your tight little ass."

I sit up even straighter. "You couldn't."

"I could."

"My dress wasn't that revealing."

"It was exactly that revealing."

"Well, then you should've looked away."

"Is that why you wore it?" he shoots back. "Because you wanted me to look away?"

No.

I wore it specifically so he'd look.

I've worn other dresses over the last year for that specific reason alone.

For him to look. For him to watch.

For him to *want*.

And he does.

God, he does.

That's the conclusion of it all, isn't it?

He does want me.

After all this time, after all these tears, all this frustration, all the times I thought even if I dropped dead at his feet, he'd simply hop over my dead body and walk away without sparing me a glance, turns out he won't. He probably would bend down and carry me somewhere safe.

Because he protects me.

Because he *wants* me.

"So I did it," I whisper.

"Yeah," he rasps as if he knows what I'm talking about.

And I guess he does.

"Me, Isadora Agni Holmes," I keep whispering.

"Yeah."

"I melted Stellan 'The Cold' Thorne."

"That's what you wanted, didn't you?"

Yes.

I wanted that.

I wanted to be his fire.

His flame.

His Lolita.

The only girl who can move him and melt him.

But it's too late now, isn't it? I've already promised myself to someone else. I've already promised myself to my best friend whom I've used and hurt. I can't hurt him twice. I can't break his heart.

"It's too late now," I tell him.

"Is it?"

"Yes, I'm with him."

There's a pause here.

Thick and heavy.

Clinging to the air like the chill of winter.

Then in his gravelly voice, he says, "And you can stay with him."

"But—"

"After I've made you mine."

"You—"

"I'm not asking you to be with me. You understand that, don't you?" he goes on to explain. "I have no *interest* in being with you. This isn't a marriage proposal. All I want is one night."

I dig my nails into my thighs. "Right." Digging them a little harder still, I say, "I understand."

"Shouldn't take more than that. He can have you once I'm done with you."

I don't know why I brought any of that up when I already knew the answer.

But I just... Maybe I needed a reminder of it all.

Of what *this* is.

Before I completely drown myself in delusion of what I *want* it to be.

"No," I tell him.

He holds his silence, but I do hear a sharp breath.

"You can't have me. Not even for one night. For the millionth time, I'm with your brother." Then I add, "And you can stop now."

"Stop what?"

"Watching me, *watching out* for me. Looking at me, looking at my dresses," I clarify. "What I wear is none of your business. I wanted it to be, yes. But as I've already said, it's too late now. Besides, he..."

"Besides he what?"

"He does that. He keeps me safe."

He does, doesn't he?

He told me that tonight.

He told me so many other things tonight. Things that made me feel awful. Things that made me regret everything that *I* did in pursuit of the man I'm obsessed with. But of course he's not my only victim.

I have played games with both of them.

I've gotten everything so twisted and snarled.

God, what a mess I've made.

But I'm cleaning it up now and if anyone has the right to keep me safe, it's Shepard.

Not *him*.

A few seconds pass in silence before he says, "Does he now?"

"Yes," I reply. "My boyfriend protects me."

"Except your *boyfriend* isn't exactly known for being chivalrous and observant."

"Well, he is. He's more chivalrous and observant than you think," I tell him, defending Shepard. And then because I can't stop myself from bragging about him, I go, "Exhibit A: one time when we were at a bar, he put his jacket on me because there were a bunch of guys there who were watching me. And he didn't like that."

Again, a few seconds go by in silence, followed by, "Is that right?"

"Yes." I nod. "Which means I don't need you because I have him."

"And his jacket."

I grit my teeth.

God, he pisses me off so much.

And so easily too.

How can anyone have such power over someone?

It's disgusting.

It's...

But wait.

I have some power over him too, don't I?

I do.

He just admitted to it.

And maybe, *just maybe*, I can use it. I can use my power over him to make him feel powerless for a change. To make him feel as if he's at my mercy rather than I'm at his.

Just a little. Just for tonight.

"So it doesn't matter how Shepard and I started," I continue, feeling giddy and tingly. "What matters is that we're happy now. We're perfect for each other. We have insane chemistry. We're in love and you need to get that and back off."

"Insane chemistry."

I do realize that I'm doing the same thing.

I'm using Shep to make him jealous.

But whatever.

Even if these things aren't true right now, they will be one day. I will make it so. So all I'm doing really is using the future to make him jealous and that's fine.

"Yes, we do," I agree, my tone snotty. "We have insane chemistry."

"How insane?"

"*In. Sane,*" I say, emphasizing all the sounds and the syllables. "The kind of insane that you probably won't be able to understand."

"Try me."

"Are you sure?" I ask with a smile in my voice. "Because given what you've just told me, about how crazy you are about me, I don't think you'd be able to handle it. And no matter what you've done to me, I'm a good person. I don't want to hurt your feelings."

"By all means, hurt my feelings."

His dry yet arrogant tone just fires me up even more. And I straighten my shoulders and eye the white billowing curtains and the winter night with challenge. "Do you know what I was doing before I called you?"

"What?"

"Talking to him."

"Yeah?"

"I was trying to cheer him up," I go on.

"Is that so?"

"Because as you may have heard, his asshole coach benched him."

"I'm liking his coach already."

"And do you know what a girlfriend does to cheer up her boyfriend?"

"I'm sure I'm about to find out."

"She does whatever he wants."

"Whatever, huh."

"Yes. *What. Ever.*"—again, I emphasize all the syllables—"he wants."

"So what did you do?"

I lift my chin. "He likes the way I dance."

"I bet he does."

"And remember the white dress I wore the night I met you?"

"Vividly."

Despite myself, my breath gets stuck in my throat at his *vividly*. "Well, he likes that dress too."

"I don't blame him."

"And remember those wings?"

"I don't think I can ever forget."

Again, despite myself, my heart stutters. "He absolutely loves them too."

"So then what happened, Dora?" he asks somehow both flatly and mockingly.

And I get so mad and so fucking tingly at him calling me that, that I just let loose. Or rather let loose in a way I know is going to affect him. I'll *make* it affect him.

"Well, then, Stellan," I begin, "as you can guess, I danced for my man. Actually, no, I wore that dress and those wings and then put on a show for him."

"Yeah, what's the difference?"

"The difference, asshole, is that when *I* dance, I don't just dance, I put on a show," I explain. "I move my body like I'm doing it for a purpose. I twist my hips like I'm doing it to drive someone crazy. To drive someone out of their mind with want. I want him to lose control, see. I want him to want me with such intensity that he forgets who he is. He forgets his rules and morals. So he not only crosses all the lines he's drawn in the sand but also completely erases them. So he not only dreams about me in his sleep like a rational human being, but I also want him to see me when he's awake. I want him to hallucinate about me. I want to be his delusion, his madness. So the difference is that when I dance, I dance like I'm Ecstasy and I'm running rampant in his bloodstream. When I dance, Stellan Thorne, I do it like I'm someone's biggest temptation. Like I'm someone's Lolita."

Never mind that when I say someone, I mean him. Because I've done all that for him. Never mind that his twin just told me the same thing and I almost died with embarrassment. And never fucking mind that I have zero shame in me right now even though there's pin drop silence on the other end.

No, wait.

There's something beside the pin drop silence.

It's his breaths.

Kinda like how they were when we had first started the conversation. Which makes me curious once again as to what exactly he was doing before I called. But I'm *not* going to make the same mistake as I did before.

I'm *not* going to ask him about it.

Instead, I'm going to keep going. "So, well, again, as you can guess, things got a little heated. You know, between us. Given our chemistry and all that. Which they always do when I put on a show for him, but tonight was different. Maybe it was the way he was watching me, watching my every move. Tracking it, hanging on to it like his entire existence depended on how I twisted and spun, I don't know. Whatever it was, it turned me on. Big time and..." I sigh and then just go for it, "I got so wet."

I can't believe I said that.

I can't believe I'm moaning right now. As in a little moan and a hitch of my breath as I continue, "So, *so* wet, Stellan. I don't think I've ever been this wet in my life and that's saying something because the way your twin brother gets me going"—I sigh and moan again—"it's no joke. It's no fucking joke. My panties are perpetually soaked around him and oh my God, I'm dripping right now, Stellan. I'm aching and—"

"No."

His fervent growl makes me jump. "What?"

"We're not doing that," he growls.

"Doing what?"

"We're not playing this game."

I pretend to be innocent. "What—"

"*You're* not playing this game," he cuts me off, his voice even thicker now. "You're not fucking with my head. You're not fucking with *me*. Not anymore."

"I'm not—"

"And just for fucking lying like that, you're going to show me."

His words, spoken even more roughly and commandingly, jolt me. "S-show you what?"

"How wet you are."

"*What?*"

"Show it to me."

"Y-you... What?"

"Dancing for my twin fucking brother got you wet, didn't it?" He keeps growling. "It got you wet that he was watching you like his goddamn life depended on it. He was. He was watching like he always watches you. Like if he moved his eyes away from you even for half a second, his heart would stop beating. His *breaths* would stop coming and he'd fucking choke to death. And if that gets you wet, then show it to me. Show me what dancing like a fucking Lolita does to you."

"You are right. I was lying," I tell him quickly. "It d-didn't."

He barks out a laugh. "If you think that's going to get you off the hook, then you really don't know what I'm about. You really don't know how insane you've made me."

"Stellan, you—"

"Show it to me."

"I'm not showing you my—"

"I'm not *asking* you to show me your pussy."

I don't know why I jolt when he uses the same word I was going to use.

But I do.

Maybe it's his thick, growly voice. Or maybe it's the fact that all that bullshit I spewed was not exactly a lie. As in I did get wet. Only it wasn't because of his twin brother but him. And now he's asking to see it.

"What is it with you, huh?" he asks impatiently and angrily. "I ask for one night and you think I'm pledging my undying devotion to you. I ask to see how wet you are and you're ready to flash me that pussy. Why the fuck are you so desperate?"

"Oh my God!" I scream into the phone. "You're the one who... I can't believe we're having this conversation. I don't understand—"

"So let me explain it to you then," he bites out. "If you flash me your pussy right now, I'm going to have to abandon everything. Tomorrow's prep meeting, tomorrow's practice, my job, my fucking team. And I'm going to have to get on the first flight back."

"What?"

"To you."

"M-me?"

"Yes." Then, "If you flash me that wet fucking pussy of yours, then I'm not going to be able to sit here, am I? I'm not going to be able to sit in this fucking hotel room, in my bed, in the middle of all the scattered books that I don't seem to have any interest in anymore. I'm not going to be able to smoke my cigarette that I was very much looking forward to all day. Or focus on the game reruns and play strategies. If you flash me that fucking pussy, Dora, then I'm not going to be able to *function* until I get a taste of it. Until I lap up all that pussy juice and analyze exactly what you taste like, exactly what your flavor is. I think you're tart like the cherries. But you could also be sweet like honey. Or maybe you're a mix of both.

"But until I find out, I won't be able to concentrate. I won't be able to think of anything else and you've already messed with my control enough. You've already fucked with my head, my fucking life enough. So we're not doing this. We're not fucking doing this. You're not lying to me and spewing some bullshit about how you have an insane chemistry with my twin brother or how wet he makes you when I know for a fact, *I know*, that you're still a fucking virgin. And you're definitely not showing me your wet virgin pussy when I'm not there to actually do something about it, is that clear?"

"Y-yes."

"Good," he says. "Now, what you're going to do is slide those messy panties of yours down your thighs and take a picture of them. And then you're going to send me that picture right the fuck now. And before you get any ideas, if there isn't a picture of your wet panties on my phone in the next five minutes, I'll make sure that he pays for it at practice."

My heart somehow both pounds and seizes to beat for a moment. "If... If I send you the picture, will you let him back on the team?"

He exhales sharply.

"Stellan, please. I—"

"Fine."

CHAPTER 11

THE WILDFIRE THORN

TWO WEEKS LATER...

"What the fuck's up with you?"

From across the locker room, I hear Isiah's, team's halfback, voice as he addresses Shepard and snaps a towel against Shepard's ass.

Shepard pokes his head out of his locker. "What the fuck, man?"

Isiah digs into his own locker but keeps talking. "You ignoring me now?"

Shepard grumbles something under his breath. "Why, are you a clingy chick who can't take a hint?"

Pulling a shirt over his head, Isiah goes, "If I were a chick, my smooth and curvy caramel ass would be so out of your league, it wouldn't be funny."

"You already *are* a smooth and curvy caramel pain in the fucking ass, so you're halfway there, man."

Isiah makes an annoyed sound in the back of his throat and pulls his gym bag out of his locker. "What, you're too much of a princess to get back to my texts?"

Before Shepard can reply, Riot joins in the conversation. He has his bag slung over his shoulder and looks to be on his way out. But at Isiah's words, he stops and adds, "Yeah, what's up with that? I sent you a picture of Sophie riding a horse for the first time the other day and no response. You're too good to send even an emoji back?"

Shepard looks annoyed. "Shut the fuck up, both of you. I lost my phone, okay?"

I've been looking at the meeting notes that Con left for me, trying to tune the conversation out. But I switch my complete focus on them now.

"What, where?" Isiah asks, snapping the locker shut.

"If I knew where, it wouldn't be lost now, would it?"

Riot scoffs. "Well, genius, there are things now called Find My Phone and stuff like that. You've got an iPad, don't you? Or a laptop. Use it to find your phone."

Shep's not into technology like that. He doesn't care about laptops or iPads. Despite having numerous discussions with him, his passwords across all of his accounts are the same, where it's not a face ID, that is, and the one that he's had since high school.

Shepard gives him a look and proves me right with his next words. "You think I'd bring an iPad on the road? Or a laptop. What am I, a college nerd or a Wall Street stuck up? No, I don't have any of those on me. Besides, I needed a new number anyway."

"Why?" Riot asks, smirking. "A chick going stalker on you?"

Isiah smirks too before tackling Shep in a bear hug that Shep breaks out of easily. But that doesn't deter Isiah from expressing, "Aww. Look at him, being all loyal to his girl and shit."

Riot chuckled. "Yeah, who would've thought."

"That a girl named Isadora would tame the lion," Isiah completes the sentence, high-fiving Riot.

I flinch at the crackling sound.

At the name.

Not because the sound's loud or this is the first time I've heard her name from the guys or around the locker room. The team's loud and they like to give their former-playboy captain a hard time about his changed and monogamous ways. And while previously I've simply walked out—not only because her name's come up but also because it's easier for me to ignore the urge to join in their banter when I know I can't; I don't deserve to—I find I can't do that now.

I find I'm glued to my spot.

Every part of my body attuned to the conversation that's happening. Maybe because I know the truth now. I know that while the world thinks they are together, they are not.

Not really.

That it all started with a lie.

That along the way he fell for her, and I can only assume he never corrected any assumptions about them because he wanted them to be true. Or maybe it was his ego. Maybe it was a little of both. Whatever the reason, I can see that he wants her. I can *see* that he's in love with her.

And yet, I'm doing what I am doing, what I've been doing for the past two weeks.

Yet I don't plan to stop.

It makes me an even shittier brother; I'm aware of that. It makes me an even shittier fucking person for taking what doesn't belong to me. But that's the thing, isn't it, it feels like it. It *feels* like she belongs to me. That she has belonged to me since the moment I met her.

It feels like he's the intruder, not me.

He's the one in between us, not the other way around.

"Why don't you both shut the fuck up and leave me alone, okay?" Shep breaks into my thoughts with his irritated words. "Jokes about my girl are getting old now and it's none of your goddamn business why I need a new phone."

From there, they go on to argue about phones and how they're good for everything except one thing. And it's to watch porn because porn is meant to be watched on a big screen, or you don't get the same effect. Again, I tune them all out and focus on my notes. Until I feel a prickling.

I look up to find my twin staring at me from where he's leaning against his locker. Apparently, all the guys have left and we're alone now. Which hasn't happened ever since our encounter where I benched him. Over the last two weeks, I've kept my distance from him. Until I know I can handle being around him without posing a danger.

But from the looks of it, the time-out is over.

I fold my arms across my chest, tucking the clipboard to my side, and stand straight. "Who's the stalker?"

His shoulder jerk slightly. "What?"

"The stalker you were talking about."

He watches me a beat before dismissing, "None of your business."

"So there is one," I conclude.

"Told you, it's none of your business."

"Is it serious? Should we call—"

"She's none of your concern, all right," he snaps. "Just drop it."

Well, that's curious.

I've never seen my brother agitated like this.

Not over a stalker. Who happens to be a girl.

"It's a girl," I keep going.

"She's not a fucking stalker, yeah?" he snaps again. "And what part of just drop it didn't you understand?"

Now I'm even more curious.

Because he was angry, yeah, but now his expression is thunderous. And it's not a word I associate a lot with him. Shepard doesn't get angry or thunderous or any of the things that have a serious and grave connotation.

And I've always been grateful for it. That he isn't cursed by the intensity of emotions like I am. Better me than him. I wouldn't wish this life on anyone let alone my twin brother.

So this is novel.

But if he doesn't want to talk about it, he doesn't want to talk about it.

I can respect that.

"Fine." I widen my stance. "I'm guessing there's a reason you didn't head out with the guys."

"Kind of."

"So what is it?"

Finally, his posture eases and he stares at me with his usual arrogance. "Just that you haven't thanked me yet. But you're still welcome."

"For what?"

"For taking great pains not to beat the shit out of you this last week."

Despite everything, my lips twitch.

I bet he did.

This was an unprecedented situation, what I did.

While I have very little guilt about what I'm doing behind his back, I do feel guilty for giving in to that moment of impulsiveness and benching him. He didn't deserve that, no matter how fucked up I had been in my head.

And needless to say, people weren't happy with my decision either. When Con asked me about it, I told him the truth. That I'd lost control, and I did it out of sheer anger and recklessness. I thought he'd be disappointed in me, that I let personal feelings affect my job. But he wasn't. He had my back and defended me to the board even though I didn't deserve his support.

"Well, in that case, you have my gratitude," I reply gravely. "But just to say, I wouldn't have hit you back. Or blamed you."

His jaw clenches. "Yeah, why's that?"

My chest moves with a breath. "Because I was out of line."

His jaw clenches again, but otherwise, he remains silent.

"I shouldn't have lost my temper like that," I continue.

He studies me for a few moments before asking, "Are you saying that as my coach or my brother?"

It's my turn to clench my jaw.

Because once again, I'm guilty of losing my control and benching him; I shouldn't have done that. I shouldn't have messed with his game. But I can't muster up the guilt as to *why* I lost control. I can't muster up the guilt for wanting to punch the shit out of him because he's between me and her.

Because he gets to be with her while all I get to do is be on the sidelines.

It's all irrational. It's all fucking insane.

I don't even want to be with her. I don't even *want* to want her.

I *can't* want her.

I just want my peace back.

But there you have it.

"As your coach," I reply back.

He keeps his gaze steady as he goes on, "And as my brother?"

As his brother, I want to go to war with him. I want to fight him for her. I want to fucking steal her from him.

As his brother, I want him out of the way.

"She's our boss's daughter," I tell him almost accusingly.

"Fuck him," he retorts.

My jaw tics. "She's young, younger than our baby sister."

"Doesn't matter to me," he says before adding, "And apparently, it doesn't matter to you either."

I clench my fists. "She's not my type."

"Again, you don't seem to care."

"She's *yours*," I say finally, my fists clenched so hard—so fucking hard—that my knuckles pulse.

"And somehow"—his jaw moves back and forth—"you still want her."

Keeping my gaze steady, I tell him the truth, "Yeah."

And that's why I'm doing this.

That's why I'm going behind his back.

Because I want to put an end to this madness. I want to put an end to this want, this craving, this uncontrollable desire for her. Because even though I think she belongs to me, she doesn't.

She belongs to him.

He loves her. He's my brother.

He should have her.

I'm the villain in this story, not him.

"I do," I continue, without taking my eyes off him. "I do want her. I've always wanted her. But you're my brother. My twin brother."

His eyes are narrowed, his jaw tight as he bites out, "So?"

"So as I said, she's yours. And she'll stay yours," I promise.

After I've made her mine.

After I've used her and thrust her aside.

It's not the most selfless thing in the world, but it's the only thing that will put an end to this all. The only thing that will get me my peace back, my life back. The only thing that will save my control and stop me from turning dangerous and destroying my brother.

With that promise in mind, I go back to the hotel. I run. I lift weights. I shower. I pretend to find a book to read. I open the first page and then abandon it to look at the time. I watch the clock as I wait for her call on my brother's phone like I do every night. When it doesn't come, I pick it up and stab the keys on the screen, firing off a couple of texts.

SHEPARD

Where are you?

You're late.

It takes a minute or two for her to get back to me.

A minute or two that seem like a day.

Such a long day that I'm ready, so fucking ready, to call her and fucking demand to know where she is, blowing my cover. Thankfully, the text comes at the last second, though. Or rather a flurry of texts.

ISADORA
OMG! I'm so sorry!!! 😮 😮

I totally forgot!! 😔 😔 😔

Well, I didn't forget. Time just ran away from me.

I let out a sharp breath.

SHEPARD
Are you going to stop it from running away then?

Another minute passes that seems like a very long day. Longer than before and I'm not amused.

ISADORA
Okay, don't be mad but I can't call you right now. 😳 🙈

I sit up straight in the bed, my chest heaving with agitated breaths.

SHEPARD
Why not?

ISADORA
Because I'm not at home.

SHEPARD
Where the fuck are you?

ISADORA
You're getting mad.

SHEPARD
Answer me.

It's a point in her favor that she doesn't make me wait like before and answers immediately.

ISADORA
I'm on my way to go see this guy.

But I don't think earning points with me is going to help her right now. Not after her reply.

SHEPARD
Explain.

ISADORA
God, you're scary. I never knew how scary you could be.

I'm *this* close to saying *fuck it* and giving her a call when her next text flies in.

ISADORA
Okay, fine. So I have this huge assignment due day after tomorrow and I'm sort of struggling with it.

SHEPARD
What assignment?

ISADORA
History assignment. It counts toward half of my grade.

SHEPARD
Struggling how?

ISADORA
Struggling as in, I haven't really finished it.

SHEPARD
How far along are you?

ISADORA
On the first paragraph...?

I stare at the screen for a few seconds.
Then, pinching the bridge of my nose, I type:

SHEPARD
Are you saying that you haven't even started the assignment that's going to count toward half of your grade?

ISADORA
I did start it! I wrote a whole paragraph!

Well, half of it.

I breathe out a sharp sigh.

SHEPARD
How many lines?

ISADORA
Three.

And a half.

Another sharp sigh.

SHEPARD
What does this guy have to do with your assignment?

OH, YOU'RE SO COLD

ISADORA

Okay, so he's a genius, see. He sits in the front row, always has his hand up during class. He tutors people. He was supposed to go to Harvard.

SHEPARD

So what's he doing at a fucking community college?

ISADORA

Hey, don't knock community college!

SHEPARD

Fine. What's he doing at an establishment as fine as Bardstown Community College?

ISADORA

☺

He got kicked out of Harvard in his first semester, okay? But that doesn't mean he is any less of a genius. So I want him to help me with the assignment. I looked all day for him but no one knew where he was. Until I got a text from one of my friends that he's at this party. So I'm going there to find him.

SHEPARD

Why did he get kicked out?

ISADORA

That's not important.

SHEPARD

Why.

ISADORA

God!!!

For dealing weed on campus.

Again, I stare down at the screen for a few seconds. Then, with as much patience as I can muster in this situation, I type out my reply.

SHEPARD

So you're going to a party in the middle of the night to look for a drug dealer so he can help you with your history assignment.

ISADORA

He's not a drug dealer! He just sold some weed. It's not a big deal.

I know you're an athlete and all that and you have high standards but I've done weed. Weed's harmless, I promise.

> **Not to mention, legal.**
>
> SHEPARD
> **You still can't deal it without a proper license.**
>
> ISADORA
> **So he made a mistake, so what. All I need him to do is help me with my history paper, for which time's running out.**
>
> SHEPARD
> **And why's that?**
>
> ISADORA
> **Why's what?**
>
> SHEPARD
> **Why's your time running out? What were you doing before? If it's half your grade, I'd assume you'd pay more attention.**
>
> ISADORA
> **You know what, Shepard, these days I don't even recognize you anymore. You sound like an eighty-year-old stuck-up professor.** 😉😉😉

My fingers flex around the phone.

In agitation. In anger.

Every time she says his name, I want to command her to say mine. I want to demand that she keeps saying it. So she only knows the taste of me on her tongue.

Soon, though.

Four weeks.

In four fucking weeks, I'll teach her my name in such a way that she'll never forget.

> SHEPARD
> **Why didn't you do your homework before?**
>
> ISADORA
> **Because I was busy with rehearsals.**

My brows bunch up. That's news to me.

We've been talking for two weeks now and she hasn't mentioned any rehearsals to me. As my twin brother or myself.

> SHEPARD
> **What rehearsal?**

ISADORA

So omg get this!!! 🎭🎭🎭🎭 My department finally has enough funding to put on a show. We're doing this amazing play in a few weeks and I have the lead role! Can you believe that?! My debut!! Finally!!! 🎭🎭🎭🎭✨✨

But it's been crazy busy. We're doing everything on our own. Costumes, set, music. It's been exhausting!!! And I got busy with practice every day that I completely forgot about this stupid assignment and now I'm in this bind and only Jordan can help me. So I REALLY have to go find him, okay?

She is in a bind; I can see that.

And it's not really her fault either.

Acting is her passion. Even though I don't know the first thing about passion and don't have the luxury to find out, I know how it can drive people. I know how it drives *her*. How reckless she was the night we met. How she was running off with that fuckface. Sometimes I wonder what would've happened if I hadn't been there. If I hadn't stopped her.

Sometimes I wonder if I could ever see her on stage. I bet she'll shine like a star.

Actually, no.

She's Isadora Agni Holmes. She'll burn bright and set the stage on fire.

SHEPARD

If you've been so busy with practice for your debut, then why is it that this is the first time I'm hearing of it?

ISADORA

Because you're busy with your season and practice and traveling and all that. So I didn't want to bother you.

Plus I know whenever I start to talk about theater and acting and scenes and stuff, you start to drift away a little bit. Which is fine. Theatre isn't for everyone. So I just... let it go.

Renewed anger pulses through my veins at this.

He thinks her passion is boring? To the extent that he starts to drift away. To the extent that *she notices* he starts to drift away and doesn't feel comfortable sharing her dreams with him.

I know she's trying to make light of it and wave it away, but what the fuck is he *thinking*?

What the fuck is going through his thick head?

This is the girl he's in love with and he can't gather enough enthusiasm—pretend or otherwise—to support her through it.

With my heart pounding in my chest, I fire off my reply.

> **SHEPARD**
> First, I want you to stop and turn around.

> **ISADORA**
> What?

> **SHEPARD**
> Go back home.
> Send me the topic of your assignment.

> **ISADORA**
> What? Why?

> **SHEPARD**
> Because I'll do it for you.

> **ISADORA**
> You'll do my assignment?

> **SHEPARD**
> That's what I said.

> **ISADORA**
> What? That's crazy! 😵 😵 😵

> **SHEPARD**
> Go back.

> **ISADORA**
> But you hate homework. You hate assignments. Every time I tell you I have homework, you thank God that you don't have any. That you're out of the hellhole that people call school.

Yes, he does hate homework, schoolwork, assignments. He hates anything that requires him to get away from soccer. And I've helped him. I've helped him practice. I've done his homework. I know soccer's his passion and so I've done what I can to be there for him. The *only way* I can be there for him.

So I can do the same for her.

> **SHEPARD**
> Not tonight.

> **ISADORA**
> But, Shepard, you have practice in the morning!! You had practice today! 😵 😵 😵 😵
>
> You can't do this. You must be exhausted!!

I clench my teeth at his name again.

> **SHEPARD**
> Go back and text me the details.
>
> Right now.

I see those dots going again.

> **ISADORA**
> Is this you being jealous?
>
> Because I'm going to go see another guy.

I stare at her texts for a few seconds before replying truthfully.

> **SHEPARD**
> Yes.

> **ISADORA**
> You don't have to be.
>
> I only want you. I promise.

My jealousy roars.

My jealousy is set on fire and is now engulfing my veins.

Every time she says something like this, something that's meant for my brother, I want to out myself. I want to tell her that it's me she's been talking to. It's *me* she's been dancing for. It's *me* she's been paying her dues to every fucking night.

Me. Me. *Me.*

> **SHEPARD**
> Go the fuck back.

> **ISADORA**
> Okay. Okay, I'm going.

> **SHEPARD**
> And next time you're in a bind, you text me first.

> **ISADORA**
> I will.

> **SHEPARD**
> Next time you're spending your days in practice; getting exhausted at practice; next time you fucking practice period, you tell me about it.

> **ISADORA**
> Okay, yes.

> **SHEPARD**
> And if you think about taking some motherfucker's name in front of me, don't.

Her reply is slow in coming and I swear to God, I'm going to fucking lose it.

> **ISADORA**
> Why?

> **SHEPARD**
> Because it makes me want to fuck him up.

> **ISADORA**
> I won't. Shepard's the only name I want to say anyway.

I stare at her words for a few moments.

Then I shut off the phone and toss it aside. I get up to make myself a pot of chamomile tea, hoping to calm the fire in my gut from her last message. Not to mention, it's going to be a long night if her assignment really consists of half her grade.

Actually, it's going to be a long fucking four weeks until the home game.

Until I get to go back and put an end to this madness.

CHAPTER 12

FOUR WEEKS LATER...

He's not bluffing.
I wish he were, but he isn't.
This blackmail is very, very real.
So my only recourse is the truth. My only recourse is taking matters into my own hands and telling Shepard the whole truth when he comes back. So *he* doesn't have any leverage over me.
So he doesn't get to tear me apart from my boyfriend.
I know nothing is final yet, but he still feels like my boyfriend.
Especially when he asks me about my day. When he listens to all my costume woes and lighting disasters. He listens to me about my classes and how I wish I could be outside, soaking the snow in, instead of being cooped up inside, learning about things I don't really care about. He listens to me about my *biji*, how much I love her, how I wish I could live with her. Not that he didn't before, but before, for some very strange reason, we didn't have the intimacy we have now.
He didn't feel like... mine.
Maybe all I needed was to let myself open up to him and now that I have, he feels like someone I could share anything and everything with.
Not to mention, it definitely feels like he's my boyfriend when he helps me with my assignments. Although we've had to make some adjustments there. That history assignment he did for me got me an A, which was a huge surprise for me because I had no idea Shepard was so into history, and also for my profes-

sor. Who's never known me to be that hardworking. So when next time he offered to do my homework so I could focus on my upcoming play, I told him not to be so good about it. Which I don't think he took very well.

SHEPARD

Why the fuck not?

ISADORA

Because! You did so well the last time, my professor got suspicious. 😒😒😒

SHEPARD

He got suspicious because you got an A?

ISADORA

Yes! Because I never get As. I'm mostly a straight C student, okay, and you know that!

SHEPARD

Well you're turning your life around now.

You're going to be a straight A student if I have something to say about it.

ISADORA

No, I'm not and I don't want to be. All I want is to just fly under the radar and be able to do my play.

Because if my mom finds out that something is wrong, she could take me away. She already does her surprise drop-ins to check on me. I don't want her getting suspicious when I'm this close to FINALLY performing on stage.

His answer came back a few seconds later and even though it was succinct, I could feel his struggle through the screen.

SHEPARD

Fine.

ISADORA

Fine what?

SHEPARD

I'll hold my genius and get you a C.

ISADORA

You know, you don't have to. You work all day and then you have games at night. I can handle it myself.

SHEPARD

Just send me the details.

So I did.

So I *do*.

Whenever I have assignments and things to do for class, I ask for his help. Because he's not only my boyfriend but he's the best boyfriend in the world. And while I'm very, very happy about that, I'm also very, very guilty.

Because a best boyfriend deserves the best girlfriend.

I do try to be that—that was always the plan to begin with—but I don't think I'm succeeding all that much.

Especially when I think about *him*.

The Cold Thorn who feels like wildfire.

He *forces* me to think about him because every night, he asks me to send him my pictures. And it would be okay if they were all dirty photos—no, seriously, it would be okay if he asked me to expose myself to him on a nightly basis—because then I could put a label on it all and call him a pervy asshole and move on.

But he doesn't.

He asks to see the most innocuous things.

My panties wet from my juices after dancing for his twin brother; yes, I dance for Shepard still. Sometimes he asks to see my wet fingers in addition to my wet panties. He doesn't let me put my fingers inside me, though, no. That was his demand the first night he asked me to show him my fingers. He specifically told me not to put my fingers inside and when I asked him why, he said that it's *his* first right to enter my body. And that made me so mad, his arrogance, his dominance, his fucking entitlement that I couldn't help taunting him.

"But something's already been inside me," I told him.

"What?" he bit out.

"Tampons."

"Tampons," he parroted in a flat tone.

"Yup." I nodded even though he couldn't see me. "So sorry, asshole, someone or *something* got to my pussy first."

I heard his breaths for a few seconds.

"And you should thank your lucky stars that my dick can't do the job of a tampon or you'd walk around with me in your bleeding pussy twenty-four seven for a whole week, on a monthly basis."

I had to clench my thighs at that.

I also had to tell him, "That has to be, *has to be*, the craziest thing anyone has ever said to me. Or to anyone, for that matter. You know that, right?"

"Yeah."

"So you know you're insane," I went on.

"I wasn't, though. Not until you decided to barge into my life like a fucking highway crash."

My mouth fell open. "Are you comparing me to a deadly road accident?"

"Actually, you're more akin to a plane crash."

I gasped. "What?"

"Because instead of barging, you *flew* into my life wearing a white dress and fake wings."

"I hate you."

"You don't need to love me to let me fuck you."

"I'm not fucking you, okay?" I told him firmly. "I'm so not fucking you."

"Well, then it's your boyfriend who's going to pay the price for it, isn't he?" he threatened. "Either way, someone's getting fucked before the home game."

I wanted to call him an asshole again.

I wanted to say that I hated him.

But I've already said all those things a million times. So I decided to seethe in silence. I also decided to think that it's almost... flattering.

In a way.

If you really think about it.

The way he's obsessed with me. With having me. With ruining me.

With using me and possessing me.

The way I drive him crazy.

So much so that along with the photos of my panties and wet fingers, he also asks me for pictures of the nape of my neck; the underside of my elbows. The webbing of my toes; the hem of my dress grazing my upper thighs. My chipped nail polish; the apple of my cheeks. My two dimples and that mole on my back. One night, he asked me to show him my belly button. Another night, he wanted to see my dark hair strewn about on my white pillows. It's like he's trying to make a collage of me. Catalog details about me that no one has ever bothered to. *I* didn't even bother to.

It makes my heart race more than I want to admit.

In any case, this will all be over soon, and if I'm looking at the clock on my nightstand right, it should happen in two days. In two days, Shepard is coming back for the home game and I'm telling him everything. To say that I'm nervous and that I want to hide away from the world is an understatement.

Not to mention, my debut's happening tomorrow, the night before Shepard's due back, and my heart isn't exactly in it. Plus, I'm struggling with a couple of scenes and I just want to back out of everything.

Picking up my phone, I decide to text Shepard.

ISADORA

> Hey, I know this isn't our usual time to talk and you must be busy with practice and stuff. But I wanted to text you anyway because I... I'm nervous. About the play. About a couple of scenes and I wish... I just wish you were here. That you could see my play. You'd be the only one I'd know in the audience. Since you know my biji isn't coming.

> Anyway I'm going to go practice now. Have fun out with the boys and text me when you get back!

Sighing sadly, I pick up the stapled, well-worn copy of the script, ready to run lines, when the phone I hadn't even put down on the bed starts to ring. It's a video call and before I've had a chance to think about it, I hit accept.

And I realize that I made a mistake.

I should have thought about it.

I should have *waited* to think about it.

Because of who is on my screen.

"Stellan," I whisper, the phone in my hand trembling.

Something moves over his face.

His beautiful, *beautiful* face.

The face I haven't seen since the charity event.

Well, I mean, I have seen it. On TV. In passing, during the games.

But not like this.

Not where I could take my time and as always, you have to take your time when staring at him. You have to give him your full attention or you could miss out on details. You could miss out on all the sharp turns and harsh terrains of his features. You could fail to notice the exact way his thick eyelashes curl or the way his dark eyes glint. You could definitely pass by on how his rose of a mouth pouts and curves at the ends.

And holy God, if I wasn't taking my time right now, I totally would've missed out on seeing his usually clean-shaven jaw all stubbly and gruff. Not to mention that hair. That's always neatly combed and pushed back, grazing his broad forehead.

Is that what he looks like at the end of the day?

In the privacy of his room?

Is that what happens to his shirt, a white button-down? Does it get wrinkled with the top *three* buttons open? Showing the sliver of his massive chest.

He looks like a fever dream.

A dream made of snow and thorns and pink magnolias and cigarette smoke.

"Say it again," he commands.

I blink. "What?"

"My name," he rasps, his eyes glinting. "Say it."

I want to ask why. Or at least I should. That would be the prudent thing to do. But the look on that beautiful face of his makes me obey him without question.

"Stellan."

His chest moves with a breath, that tanned skin drawing my eyes toward it once again, as he says in a raspy voice, "Yeah, that's my name."

Looking up, I comment on his strange tone, "Did you, uh, think that I..."

"You what?"

"Did you think that I wouldn't"—I lick my lips, wondering if mentioning this is a good idea—"know you were... *you* and not... him?"

His eyes flick back and forth between mine. "No, I knew that you'd know."

"Even if I didn't," I go on, "there's a thing called caller ID."

"There is."

"I have you saved as *Asshole*."

I don't.

I never got around to it for some reason.

He's still my Wildfire Thorn.

His lips twitch. "Even if you hadn't saved me as *Asshole*, you'd still know."

I wish I could deny it.

But I don't have secrets from him, unfortunately, like I have from the rest of the world. Which is kinda ironic that he knows me more than my own boyfriend does, but it is what it is.

I sigh. "Why are you calling me?"

He studies me for a few seconds. "Because you need my help."

"What?"

"You have your play tomorrow," he informs me like I don't know. "And from what I've gathered, you're nervous."

I stare at the screen for a couple of seconds. "How do you... How do you know?"

"Because I got your text."

"*You* got my text?"

"I have his phone," he explains simply.

"You have his phone."

"Actually, I've had his phone for the past few weeks," he explains again and this time even more simply.

"You have..."

"Which is how I know that you've been practicing for your big debut for the last couple of months," he keeps going, his face blank and his expression cool. "And you've got the lead role. I also know you're helping with the costumes, the stage design. You've had a hand in the script writing too. And all of this is because your department hasn't had a lot of interest or funding. There's one faculty, hardly any students. If it weren't for your and your classmates' efforts, they'd shut down the department."

All throughout his talking, his tone has been calm. His tone didn't have *a tone*.

But my heart was slowly speeding up in my chest. My blood was slowly speeding up in my veins too. To the point where now my heartbeats are deafening, and my blood is roaring. My skin is so hot in the middle of my chilly room that I'm sweating.

Still when I speak, I do it without screaming. "If... If you have had his phone for the past several weeks, then... H-how is it that I've been talking to him?"

His gaze is steady, unhurried and calm. "You haven't been."

"I... I'm sorry?"

"It was me." Then he repeats it in case I didn't get it the first time, "It has been *me*."

And he's right because I don't get it.

Not at first.
Not even after five beats of silence.
On the sixth beat, though, I say, "Y-you."
"Yes."
"So you've been..." I stop to take a breath; it's like I'm having to consciously remind myself to breathe. "You've been pretending to be him."
"Yes."
"Why?"
"Because I... I couldn't not," he says, looking into my eyes. "Because when I found his phone, I had every intention of giving it back, but then I saw your name flashing on the screen and it was like... a switch flipped. Something happened. Something I don't know how to explain. Something rearranged itself inside me. And I..."
"And you what?" I ask, looking back into his eyes.
"And after a year of stopping myself, keeping myself in check, keeping myself *contained*, I couldn't. I couldn't stop myself from bursting out. From reaching back out," he says after a few seconds of pondering. As if he's coming to this conclusion himself right now. "From getting to touch you somehow. From getting to know you. Even from hundreds of miles away. Even through a screen and under the guise of him."
I keep staring at him for a few seconds more.
I keep staring and staring.
I study his fever dream of a face and that messy dark hair. I study the jut of his Adam's apple and the veins on his throat. The peek of his collarbone. I study how unaffected he appears, how calm while confessing his secrets. Recounting his crimes.
I believe him.
I believe him except...
When I'm done, I go back to his eyes and try to sound just as unaffected as him. "You couldn't stop yourself from getting to know me."
His eyes rove over my face before he replies, "No."
"Me," I emphasize because I don't want there to be any confusion.
"You," he confirms.
"So..." I take a deep breath. "Does that mean you care about me?"
That gives him pause. "I... I'm..."
He can't say it, can he?
That liar.
That fucking asshole.
That stupid fucking asshole who thinks *I'm* stupid.
I'm the stupidest, most foolish girl he's ever met.
Who will believe everything he just said.
Because I want this to be true so badly, don't I? I want this twisted thing to be true *so fucking badly* that he's mocking me. He's being condescending to me like he always is.

"About the girl who's tortured you for over a year," I begin.

"That's—"

"The girl you don't even like. You called me a virus," I continue.

His jaw tenses. "You—"

"You also called me a plane crash," I cut him off, my voice rising.

His jaw tenses further. "I—"

"Oh, and on top of all that, you're blackmailing me. All because you could get one night from me. Just one night. Where you could fuck me and leave me as sloppy seconds for your twin brother. That's not getting to know me, Stellan. That's the *opposite* of getting to know me. That's saying that you don't respect me enough to get to know me. You don't care about me enough to get to know me. That's saying that all I'm good for is spreading my legs for you and—"

His nostrils flare. "Maybe you should be happy about all this. About the phone, about the blackmail, about me breaking all the fucking rules for you. You wanted to be my Lolita, didn't you? Well, there you fucking go. And besides, I never said that's all you're good enough for. I—"

"You didn't have to," I snap—no, actually, I scream because see? He *is* mocking me. "What you're doing says everything, isn't it? What you're doing says that all you care about is yourself. What you're *doing* is saying that you're a selfish fucking asshole who will not only get his hands on Shep's phone and read our messages, our *private* correspondence, but you will lie about it. You will make a mockery of it. You will *violate* our privacy and you will sit there and you will fucking lie about it. You will sit there and you will insult this awful situation even further. What it says to me, Stellan, is that you're *dangerous*. You're dangerous to my happiness. You're a danger to my heart. To my happily ever after. You're fucking dangerous," I breathe out sharply. "You must think I'm *sooooo* stupid, don't you? You must think I have no sense in my body. You know what, I'm not talking to you. I'm done talking to you. This is over. This bullshit is—"

"You don't need to talk to me," he finally bites out, putting an end to my tirade.

And I realize that... he looks stricken somehow.

He looks taken aback. Shocked, surprised.

And I don't know what it was that I said that's making him look that way. All harsh and white.

Harsh as ice. White as snow.

"S-Stellan," I whisper.

It's as if he wakes up, his eyes blinking. "But you still need my help."

I want to ask him about it.

I want to ask him about what just happened. Why he looked like that. What did I say? I mean, I said a lot of things, but what exactly was it that made him look like he's seeing a ghost?

But I don't.

I won't.

It's none of my business. Not after what he pulled.

"I do *not*, in any way, shape, or form, need your help," I deny.

"You texted that you're nervous."

"And the fact that you read it makes you an absolute asshole."

"I—"

"No, it makes you a devil," I speak over him. "That's what you are. You're a devil."

Tightness ripples on his face. "And if you refuse my help, then you'd be as stupid as you just called yourself."

I'm gripping the phone so tightly that I should be worried I'll break it.

I'll smash it into pieces with my bare hands.

But that's okay.

Because I want that. I want to smash it and crush it.

I want to climb inside it and smack his pretty fucking face. Because yes, I am stupid. And for a second or two back there, I wanted to believe him. I wanted to believe that he really got his hands on Shepard's phone and it's him I've been talking to for the past weeks. That it's him I've been dancing for.

All because he really wanted to get to know me.

He did it for *me*.

To chase after me.

To woo me.

He did not. He's lying.

Because if he really wanted me, if he really cared about me even a little bit, he wouldn't be blackmailing me. He wouldn't be playing with my emotions. He wouldn't be pretending and shame on me for even entertaining the thought that somehow all of his is flattering instead of what it actually is.

Despicable and disgusting.

"Fine." I clench my teeth. "I'm stupid then. Are you happy now? I'm—"

"Look"—he clenches his teeth too and I hate myself for thinking how sharp that turns his already killer jawline—"this is your debut. This is your fucking dream, isn't it? This is the reason why you were sneaking out that night, the night I met you. This is your destiny. So then fucking seize it. You're nervous; I can help. Let me help. You can go back to hating me when I'm done running lines with you. So stop wasting both our time and send me your script so we can start."

I don't.

I choose to once again stare at him for a few moments.

Then, in a voice that's much lower than before, "You want to run lines with me?"

His chest moves again with a breath. "Isn't that what you're supposed to do in rehearsals?"

I nod. "Yeah."

"So then that's what we're doing."

"Why?"

"Why what?"

"Why do you want to"—I swallow—"help me?"

It's his turn to study me for a few moments. Not that he wasn't already doing that but still. He takes *pause* to do it now. He takes pause to flick his gaze over my face, from the top of my messy bun down to my stubborn chin. He also takes in my sleep T-shirt. A loose boyfriend T-shirt with Minnie Mouse on it that I got at a thrift store and that I wear when I mean business. Business as in when I'm trying to practice in front of the mirror and not sit around and... well, think of this cold and cruel asshole.

When he's done looking for whatever it is he was looking for on my face, he replies, "Because I can."

Then something occurs to me and words are out of my mouth before I've thought it through. "Is it because you think that'll get me to sleep with you?" I sit up straight. "Is that why you're being nice because you think I'll give in and—"

"I don't need to be nice to get you to sleep with me," he says, his features hard. "You'll sleep with me anyway. In fact, you'll beg to sleep with me, and you'll sleep with me so many fucking times that you won't get a wink of sleep that night."

"Oh, is that so?" I roll my eyes. "Is that why you're blackmailing me because you think I'm just begging to sleep with you?"

"Me blackmailing you is me doing you a favor."

I open my mouth to protest, but he doesn't let me.

"It's me giving you a lie to hold onto. So the next day when you wake up after all the sleeping you've done, you can pretend and say you didn't like it. You can pretend that you didn't want it. You can tell yourself that you were forced into and that you didn't beg me to let you sleep with me one more time. You're a pretty fucking liar, aren't you? So I'm just speaking your language. Are there any more questions and objections you have before we begin?"

"Yes," I say. "I do actually."

"Dazzle me."

"If anyone should help me, it should be him. He's my boyfriend, not you," I point out.

"Well, your *boyfriend*"—his jaw is as hard as his tone—"is almost passed out drunk in a bar like the rest of his teammates because they're taking the night off. Against all the rules. So I'm your only option."

"Why aren't you?"

"Why aren't I what?"

"Passed out drunk like the rest of your team?" I clarify. "If it's their night off, it's your night off."

He stares at me with his usual flat look. "I never take a night off and I don't get drunk."

"Oh right, I forgot." I raise my eyebrows. "You're this extreme control freak who probably measures out his alcohol intake too."

He keeps holding his blank expression. "I don't know what they are teaching kids at school these days"—I narrow my eyes at his choice of words, but of course he's unfazed—"but getting drunk isn't cool. It makes you behave like a clown who has to stay glued to the toilet bowl the next day." A pause then, "I had a real-life model to teach me the hazards of drinking."

Oh right, his dad.

Of course I know about his dad. Who left them and was a neglectful alcoholic.

No matter what he pulled just now, I shouldn't have brought it up.

"I'm sorry. I shouldn't have—"

"Not your fault," he cuts me off.

"Your dad," I hesitantly broach the subject. "He—"

"No."

"No what?"

A muscle jumps on his cheek. "I'm not talking about my father with you."

As much as I want to know more about it, it's not something I can push him about. Again, no matter what he just did. So I ask something else that I always wanted to know. "What about smoking?"

"What about it?"

"When did you start that?"

He waits a beat to answer. "Back in college."

I so want to ask why. I so do, but I'm not going to. But then he goes ahead and explains, "People who smoked always looked peaceful. So I wanted to try it. I wanted to see what peace looked like."

I swallow, my heart squeezing. "So why only one cigarette per day?"

"Because rules are important," he says. "And because I don't deserve a lot of it."

"Don't deserve a lot of what?"

His chest moves with a breath. "A lot of peace and cigarettes."

"I don't understand."

"You don't need to understand."

I do.

I so do.

I need to. I want to.

Despite everything and myself, I want to understand him. Why he is the way he is. Although it's not a big mystery, is it? He had a shitty childhood either due to his father or circumstances out of his control. So of course he'd grow up to be someone who craved it strongly. Rules, structure, control. I don't understand why he thinks he doesn't deserve peace, though.

But again, it's not something I can push him to tell me.

"Well," I begin, sighing. "I don't know what they taught *you* at school back when dinosaurs roamed the earth"—I raise my eyebrows—"but smoking isn't all that cool either. One cigarette or not, it slowly kills you and turns your lungs black."

"Good for me then, isn't it?"

"How is it good for you?"

"Because I think black may be my color."

"Is it because you also have a black heart?"

"And a black soul to match. Like the devil."

I stare at him.

He stares at me back.

I decide I won't speak first.

He probably has decided the same thing.

Then I decide this is stupid. So I say, "You're not that old. You know that, don't you?"

He takes a few seconds to answer. Then murmurs, "I am."

"And I'm not that young," I keep informing him.

"You are."

"I'm just seven years younger than you."

"You're younger than my baby sister."

"What, is that your cut off? You can't like a girl who's younger than your sister?"

"Pretty much. I don't want to think about who was making her pigtails when I was making my sister's."

"You—"

"Or"—he pointedly looks at my T-shirt—"what cartoons she was watching when my sister was hooked on Disney."

"You're so—"

"But then again, I don't like you, remember?"

"You—"

"So are we doing this or not?"

I have two choices here: I can either hang up now and put an end to this—and I should. Or I could take his help because I *am* nervous. I am very, very nervous. I hate that he knows that. I hate how he got that information, but I can't deny that running lines with someone might help.

I also can't deny running lines with *him* is something I never even dreamed about. I dreamed about him being jealous, of him wanting me back, of him kissing me, of me dancing for him. But I never imagined I'd be sharing my passion with him. And as much of an asshole as he is, I still want to make the dream I never saw come true.

"First, I didn't have pigtails. They were too much trouble for my mother, so up until I was fourteen, my hair was really short. She wouldn't even let my nannies braid my hair"—his jaw clenches—"and second, all kids love Disney. A lot of adults love Disney too. And third, yes, we are doing this. But first, I want you to show me something."

A frown appears between his brows. "Show you what?"

"Your room."

"What?"

"Show me your room."

His frown only thickens. "You want me to show you my room."

"Yes. Show me."

"Why?"

I shrug. "Because I want to see it."

Because if I'm sharing my passion with him, I want him to share something of his. Which he won't do by himself. I'm going to have to force him. Besides, this is probably the last time we'll talk like this. After tonight, Shepard will be back and when I tell him the truth, all of this will be over, right? No late-night phone calls. No pictures. No blackmail. We will have no reason to be in contact with each other.

Like it's been for the past year.

He will go back to standing in a corner of a room and I will go back to dancing and being with Shepard. This time around, it will be for real.

Plus I want to punish him a little for what he put me through just now. And what better way than to force him to show parts of himself when he's always so adamant about staying in the shadows.

"You want to see my room," he repeats, still confused.

"Yes," I answer. "First, because you pulled such a bullshit stunt with me and mocked me. And second, every night you ask me to show you something. Every night you ask me to send you pictures. Of stupid things. Of inconsequential things. I mean, you don't even ask to see my face and I don't know if it's insulting or flattering or whatever, but it's only fair that you show me something in return. So"—I lift my chin—"turn the phone and show me your room."

He studies me for a few moments. "I don't ask to see your face because I don't need a picture to remember it. It's here"—he taps his temple with his long finger—"burned in my fucking brain. And you've got a boyfriend, remember? You don't want your face on another man's phone in case it gets into the wrong hands. In case that man's an asshole." Before I can open my mouth to say anything at all, he answers the question I never asked, "And yes, I know these things because I've got a sister your age. She's slightly older than you but still."

And then I'm not staring at his face anymore.

I'm staring at his room.

Which is a shame because it's something I've really wanted to see for a long, long time. I've really wanted to get a glimpse into his life, any glimpse. And now that I'm getting it, I can't completely focus on it because my mind's still on what he just said. My mind's still on the fact that... did he just imply that he was protecting me?

By not asking to see my face.

He did, didn't he?

How... How does he do that?

How can he be so cruel and heartless, a villain, one second and then turn around and be my tortured hero the next? How can I both hate and love him at the same time?

Maybe because hate is just love wrapped up in barbed wire. Or maybe for us, love is just hate coated in glitter.

In any case, I try to focus.

I try to take in what's in front of me because I may not get the chance after tonight. So I soak in every little detail of his hotel room. Which I have to say, at the first glance, is not all that interesting. It's a generic hotel room with a gray carpet and the bare essentials someone might need to survive: a couple of armchairs by the window that overlooks the snowy city, a chest of drawers, a closet, and a little hallway that breaks off from beside the closet where I assume the bathroom may be and the room's door.

Everything is neat and free of mess.

Very Stellan, I'd say.

Cold, smooth, and untouched.

But then there's his bed.

It's the only thing in this room that holds any life in it. The sheets are rumpled; the pillows are strewn about. The gray blanket is untucked and lies in a heap at the foot of the bed. In fact, it's not even lying there; it's *dangling* half off the bed. As striking as it is, the state of his bed, it's not the most striking thing, though.

That title goes to all the books that are scattered around on the bed.

I run my eyes all over them, trying to take in as much as I can at the first glance. Some are thick. Some are thin. Some are easy to see because they've landed on top after some kind of explosion went off. Some are hidden under the debris of other books. Some are hardbacks. Some are paperback. Some have their corners folded. Some are in pristine condition.

But all of them belong to him.

All of them seem touched and read and probably loved by him.

Swallowing, I go, "Do you..."

He turns the phone to bring his face into focus. It appears tighter than before. The lines sharp and the features honed, dark eyes careful. As if he hates giving me a peek into his extremely private world, but he's doing it nonetheless.

Because I want to see it.

Then, he asks, "Do I what?"

"Always travel with these many books?"

He watches me for a few moments, keeping silent before replying, "Yeah."

"Were you..." I ask, watching him back, "looking for something to read? Is that why they're all scattered around like that?"

"Yeah."

"Did you find something?"

"Yes."

"Are you going to read it?"

He slowly shakes his head. "No."

My heart squeezes. "Because you can't focus?"

"No."

"Because of me?"

"Yes."

My heart squeezes harder. My belly swirls.

I feel things running up and down my spine.

Then, whispering, "I'm sorry."

He exhales a short breath before rasping, "No, you're not."

This time, I shake my head slowly. "No, I'm not."

My unabashed honesty makes his lips twitch.

"Tell me your favorite book," I ask him then because I'm not letting him off the hook so easily.

He shoots me a look.

And I raise my eyebrows in response. "Look, we can either argue about it and waste time, or you could just give up and do as I say so we can move on."

He stares at me for another four seconds before sighing and then leaning forward, he reaches for something. He holds up a book he must have gotten from the scattered pile on his bed. It's one of the thicker paperback books and has the left-hand side corner of the cover folded. I see the yellow pages and the small black lettering peeking through as I read the title.

"*The Adventures of Rune*," I read out loud before looking up at him. "What's it about?"

His jaw moves back and forth as if he doesn't want to say. "Adventures of a man called Rune."

"Ha-ha. Tell me."

He moves his jaw back and forth again, and he keeps doing it for some time. Before he gives up one more time and begins to tell me the story. It's about a group of survivors who are trying to make it on a distant planet after earth has been destroyed. There are strange animals on it. There are hostiles on it. It has a purple moon and three suns and a bunch of other stuff that I don't really get.

And if I'm being honest, I drift off after a while.

Because A: I didn't think it would take a while for him to tell me the story. And B: I have other things to focus on. Like how amazing he looks right now. How his tanned skin simply shines. How his eyes glitter. There's a slight tilt to his rose lips as if he's on the verge of a slight smile. How he's talking with his hands.

I mean, when has he ever talked with his hands?

He's moved them twice now. *Twice*. While trying to explain about this acid rain that happens during the full purple moon and how it kills people.

And I realize something.

He loves it.

He loves this story. He loves this book.

He loves books period.

"You love this," I tell him, cutting him off while he was talking about a character who gets killed halfway through while he thought he could've had a good redemption arc.

"Hence the favorite," he deadpans.

"No, I mean you love books," I explain.

He shrugs. "They're okay."

I lean forward. "Are you kidding me? You carry that book around, among other books, wherever you go. I asked you one question about it and you couldn't stop talking. I mean, you. Who never says more than two words at one time, let alone a whole paragraph of words. *You*. And the way you lit up?" I shake my head. "Oh my God, Stellan, you love it. I'm sorry, but you do and..." Something occurs to me then. "Do you love soccer this much?"

I don't know why I asked that.

Except I don't think I've ever seen him light up like that for soccer.

And I should know. I've watched him a lot.

"You don't, do you?" I conclude when he holds his silence.

At my words, that silence becomes even thicker. I can see it pulsating between us. I can see it making his body tighter, more rigid.

"Is that why you..." I keep going. "Is that why you never went pro? Because you don't..."

Holy shit.

That's why, isn't it?

He doesn't like soccer.

Stellan Thorne, who everyone calls the Cold Thorn because he's known for his legendary control on the soccer field, he's known for always keeping his cool no matter what and always making the goal even under extreme pressure, doesn't like soccer all that much. That one of the Thorne brothers, soccer royalty of Bardstown, doesn't love soccer as much as his siblings do.

It feels like a dirty little secret.

A secret no one else knows. No one else could've even guessed it.

I didn't even guess it and I'm a certified Stellan Thorne stalker.

"Oh my God, is that why you wouldn't accept the promotion for the longest time? Because you—"

"I wouldn't accept the promotion"—he finally breaks his silence, his voice lashing—"because my brother needed it more than me. He deserved it more than me. He needed that job more that I ever did, all right? Now—"

"So then why do you do it?" I ask, my voice high sounding. "Why do you do this job if you don't need it? Why do you do it if you don't love it? If—"

"Because I don't have to love it," he declares.

"What?"

"Why does everything have to be about love?"

"But if you love books—"

"I don't fucking love books, all right?" he lashes out again, a muscle in his cheek jumping.

"It's a job," he tells me. "It's a fucking job and doing it well is the only thing that matters. As long as you do your job well, you don't need to wax poetic about it. You don't need to write songs about it. Love is not a requirement. *Love* is never a fucking requirement for anything. Love, like any other emotion, makes things complicated. I don't want to love anything, let alone my shitty fucking job. Is that clear? I'm not a teenage girl with delusions of grandeur or misguided notions. I'm not a *teenage fucking girl* who thinks love is the answer to all her prayers and her dreams." He stares at me, his eyes cold and harsh. "I'm not *you*. So are you finally fucking done so we can do this and I can get some sleep?"

CHAPTER 13

THE NEXT NIGHT...

"Oh my God," Tempest breathes, looking at me in the mirror. "This has to be the most beautiful thing I've ever seen."

She's referring to my *maang tikka*, an Indian wedding jewelry that you wear on the parting of your hair. You place it in the middle of your parting and secure it with a little hook. It usually has a pendant that drops down to the top of your forehead that's all sparkly and lavish. The one I'm wearing is made of gold and is studded with red stones. My *biji* helped me pick it out for the play.

"I know," Wyn breathes out as well, her eyes glued to the crescent-shaped sparkly pendant.

"Are you kidding?" I have to jump in here. "*That* is the most beautiful thing ever."

I'm referring to the sparkly princess cut diamond sitting on Wyn's finger. Because guess what, she got engaged!

Yup!

Conrad popped the question—yay—and they're getting married. I'm so, *so* happy for her. This is super exciting and of course, the happiness on my new friend's face is a sight to behold.

We take a few moments to admire her ring before Wyn goes, "But back to you. I so want that for my wedding."

Meadow is next. "I know. Me too."

"How about we go shopping for it?" I suggest from where I'm sitting on the dressing room chair.

This is the first time I've gotten a chance to actually sit down and focus on my makeup and costume. Since the play has an Indian backdrop—yup, I came up with the idea—I'm the one helping everyone. Not that I'm an expert, of course. I hardly understand Hindi, but I have a great tutor, *Biji*.

In the beginning of the semester, our professor had asked us to write a script and imagine a set we'd like to work on. Hypothetically. Because not in a million years we could've imagined putting on a show with the dismal budget we had. Anyway, of course I took inspiration from all the movies I grew up watching and wrote down a loose script based on one of my favorite movies. I detailed the kind of costumes that would go into it, the kind of stage setting, the background music I'd like and so on.

We had so much fun discussing it in class and doing a table read. And I thought that was the end of it. But then the dean managed to find some extra money in the budget and our own efforts brought in some cash, and together it was enough to be able to do one show.

And everyone unanimously picked my play.

Since then, we've been developing it—the script, the costumes, the set, everything—and since it's largely my vision. I'm the one who's been responsible for most of the elements.

Meadow's eyes are wide. "You think so?"

I turn to face her, all my jewelry tinkling. "Of course. We can hit up my *biji* and she'd totally be down with that."

Before Meadow can speak, Tempest chimes in, "I'll take you up on that offer." Her gray eyes roam over my jewelry and my red *saree*. "I would love to get a *saree* too."

"Let's make it a shopping date," Wyn suggests.

My heart feels all light and warm. "Yes, I'd like that."

Tempest beams. "Okay, now we're going to leave you alone so you can focus, and, you know, do what you actors do before you go on stage."

Honestly, I don't even know what actors do because this is my first time. And I'm so thankful that they all showed up in support. Not to mention surprised because I wasn't expecting them at all. But they all said that Shepard texted them early this morning and told them to go because he wasn't going to be there.

He *is* the world's best boyfriend, isn't he?

I can't wait to see him tomorrow.

I haven't talked to him since last night and I miss him. I so, so miss my boyfriend.

But first, I have to do this.

I have to go on stage.

After all my friends leave to go find their seats, I do last-minute lines with my cast members, and then fifteen minutes later, it's time for us to take our places on the stage. I stand on the chalked cross and close my eyes for a few seconds and open them when a bright light shines upon my face.

What happens after that, I don't remember.

I don't think I could ever be able to tell what exactly happens around me. Who moves. Who speaks. If the light is shined where it was supposed to shine. If the violins peaked where they were supposed to. If the audience laughed at the spots we predicted them to or if they gasped where we thought they should be gasping.

I don't remember any of those things.

All I remember is that I'm burning.

I'm burning because I'm fire.

I'm flowing because I'm the ocean.

I'm flying because I've grown wings.

It's transcendental. It's sublime.

It's an aphrodisiac.

It's how I feel when I'm with *him*.

I couldn't stop that thought even if I wanted to. I couldn't stop thinking about him in this moment, his gleaming eyes and his dark hair; a cigarette dangling from his rose mouth and his deep voice calling me Dora.

So when the play's over and the lights of the auditorium come on and I see him, I think I'm imagining things. Among the audience who just stood up to their feet to clap and cheer and whistle, he's standing all the way in the back, by the exit, as he always does.

But somehow, I know it's not my imagination.

Even though it's highly unlikely for him to be here, he *is* and there's no way I can look away from him. He's the center of my focus as I take the bow with the rest of the cast members. Like I'm the center of his as he claps like the rest of the people.

Actually no, not like the rest of the people.

He claps slowly. Deliberately as if.

And he claps just for me—somehow, I know that too—and not the rest of the cast.

How's he here?

What is he doing here?

Just as we finish taking our bows and the applause has started to die down, he turns around and leaves. He pushes open the door to the auditorium and walks out. And I have no choice except to run after him. We've finished with our formal bow, but people are still on the stage, waving and laughing and hugging each other, but I break away from them.

I dash off stage, push past startled people lingering, just off the curtain, and come out into the hallway. Except for a few stragglers, it's empty. For a couple of seconds, I stand frozen, thinking that maybe I did imagine him. After all, he should be with the team. There's a game tonight and he needs to be there for it. There's no way he missed his game, missed his *job*—for me, no less—even though soccer really isn't his thing.

Still, I make myself move and go in search of him even though I have absolutely no idea which direction he went in. But apparently, I picked the right one because a few steps in, I get yanked by the arm and pulled into the prop closet.

As soon as I hear the sharp thud of the door being closed, I come to stand on my tiptoes.

With anticipation.

With eagerness.

Even though for the first several seconds all there is, is darkness and silence punctuated by heavy breaths. In the back of my mind, I realize that maybe I should be screaming right now, struggling against the grip around my bicep.

What if it's not him?

But I know it is.

I recognize him from the bite of his fingers on my flesh, how sharp it is.

How hot and stinging.

I know him from the way he breathes, all thick and noisy. I know him from the *scent* of the air that leaves his lungs, smoky and spicy, marshmallow-y.

And I'm proven right when he lets me go and pulls the dangling switch to the bulb, flooding the cold and damp closet with yellow light.

Before I know it, I'm taking him in.

I'm taking in little nuances of his face after weeks and *weeks* of just long-distance phone conversations. I'm taking him in without the screen between us. I'm gorging on his face, eating up his hard cheekbones and that clean-shaven jaw; biting the center of his pouty mouth and licking the stubborn line of his nose. I'm tracing his thick eyebrows, his chocolate brown hair that's polished back. I even focus and try to count his countless forest-y eyelashes.

"What are you..." I whisper, trying to calm myself down. "What are you doing here?"

Up until I spoke, he was taking me in as well. Probably in the similar manner as I was, but at my words, he looks into my eyes. "I had to come."

His voice is deep and growly, familiar, but there's a quality to it that's foreign.

Which is when I realize that he *wasn't* looking at me like I was looking at him, no. His gaze, like his voice, has a different quality to it too. It was there when he was clapping back at the auditorium. I was so flustered at his sudden appearance that I couldn't figure it out what it was.

I know now.

It's awe.

He's looking at me with awe.

Like he can't believe I'm real.

And if I am, then he can't believe that he gets to look at me.

"B-but you have a game tonight," I remind him, my skin breaking out in goose bumps, not from the chill lingering in the closet but from his awe-filled heat.

"I had to see you."

"You have a game in an hour," I insist.

"I took the night off," he says like an afterthought.

"You took the night off? You never do that. You... The game—"

"I need you to promise me something," he cuts me off.

"What?"

"Promise me you'll never let your dream go."

My mouth parts on a breath. "What? I—"

"Just promise me," he commands urgently. "Promise me that no matter what, you'll always, fucking always, go for it. You'll always seize your destiny."

"You think this is my destiny?"

"Fuck yeah."

I look at him for a few seconds, my body overcome with all these emotions before nodding. "I will."

He lets out a breath of relief. "You were..."

When he doesn't seem to pick up the trail he left, I ask, "I was what?"

He licks his lips. "Luminous."

My heart thumps. "L-luminous."

A frown furrows his brows. It's light and it's curious. "No, you were... I don't..."

"You don't what?" I prod when he trails off again.

He shakes his head slightly. "I'm trying to think of a word to describe you, but I can't..." Another shake. "I can't find it."

My throat is going dry. "Luminous is good."

"Luminous is not enough."

"I—"

"Radiant. Dazzling. Scintillating. Resplendent. Incandescent. Luminiferous..." He licks his lips again. "I don't... I can't find words."

He looks so lost then.

So lost and God, so adorable.

A word that *I* never thought I'd use to describe him. And without volition, my hand rises up and goes to his harsh cheek. I cup his angular jaw and whisper, "It's okay. You just did. You used"—I count in my head—"seven words to describe me."

The muscle on his cheek beats under my palm. "None of them are right."

"I liked luminiferous."

"Fuck luminiferous."

"It wasn't all me, though."

"It was all you."

"No, really," I tell him. "I had help. Everyone chipped in. Everyone—"

"Fuck everyone."

I rub my thumb over the crest of his cheekbone. "You helped me."

"Fuck me too."

"You helped me run lines," I swallow, blushing. "You practiced with me."

In the beginning when we'd started, I was shy. Even though I wanted to share a piece of myself with him, I still felt some reluctance. This play, this role is so very close to my heart. But he was patient and nonjudgmental. He was encouraging even.

Not in a gushing way; of course not.

It's so very rare for him to use more than two sentences together—well, except when he talks about his books, but still—but in the way he looked at me through the screen. How his eyes lit up when I'd deliver a line and how he kept taking longer pauses between the cues, so he could stare at me.

It made my heart race. It made my breaths flutter too.

And when I went to sleep, I dreamed about him. Not that I already don't, but last night, it was so vivid. So real.

So wonderful and so painful.

That I decided to put it out of my mind. I decided to put *him* out of my mind.

But he's here now.

He came to see my play. He flew in *early* to come see me.

He *took the night off* to come see me.

"Maybe," he rasps, his eyes roving over my features, breaking into my thoughts, "but I wasn't the one making magic on the stage."

There are flowers in my heart. "You think I made magic?"

"I think that's the least of what you did, but yeah."

I smile. "That's it. That's the word."

"Yeah?"

"Magic."

"You like that?"

"Yes."

"But I don't think that's correct either."

"But—"

"Fire. Glorious, bright, hot. You were fire."

"Fire," I whisper.

"The kind that can melt the Arctic. The snow outside."

"You?"

"Me."

The way he says it, with a smoky voice and a heavy-lidded look, makes me swallow. It makes me blurt out, "I'm not going to sleep with you."

"No?"

"No."

Something flickers in his eyes, all over his features first. "Okay."

I dig the pads of my fingers on his face. "No, seriously. I won't sleep with you. I'm serious, Stellan."

"I can see that."

"I won't..." My breaths are choppy as I take in his calm expression. "He does my homework."

An indulgent look enters his eyes; that's the only way to describe how he's looking at me. With a... *fond* sort of expression. It makes me feel so young, as young as he says. Younger than his baby sister.

"Yeah?" he rasps.

Despite the blush that steals over my cheeks, my entire body, I go on. "Yes. He... He thinks that I should focus on my passion. On the things I like rather than stupid books and stuff. So he helps me. Even though he doesn't like books himself, he does my homework, Stellan."

For some reason, he's not getting the urgency in my tone. Because he still appears unfazed and *fond*. "As he should."

"Do you remember the old coach?"

"Yeah."

"He had him fired. I saw the news. He"—I take a breath, trying to calm down my heart because he did do that—"said he would and—"

"And what?"

"And he did it. For me."

"Yeah?"

I nod. "Yes. Because I told him he creeped me out and—"

"Well, he did the right thing."

And just because he's so calm about all of this, I grab his suit jacket with my other hand and try to explain it to him. "And he listens to me, okay? I tell him about my day. About practice and the play and all my dreams and... He *listens*. It's important to me. And he..." I pause to pace my breaths once again. "He texted all the girls. He asked them to come over. Because he knew I'd be alone tonight. He knew my *biji* wouldn't be able to attend. My parents would attend my play over my dead body. He knew how much that bothered me so... He *knew*."

But the thing is that *he* knew as well.

This man in front of me, who flew in early, just so he could watch me.

And so when all my friends had shown up, at first I thought it was because of him. I thought *Stellan* had texted them. And God, in my twisted mind, I still hope that it was Stellan somehow. That everything he said last night, all the bullshit he spewed about the phone, was somehow true and he invited everyone because he knew how lonely I was.

"I'm not an expert, but that's what a boyfriend is supposed to do, isn't it?" he murmurs, his eyes so pretty in this moment. "Make sure his girl doesn't get lonely."

"Yes."

"Well, then I'm glad he's taking his duties seriously."

Disappointment sags my shoulders then. Of course it was Shepard, my boyfriend. The best boyfriend in the world. Not his twin brother.

I don't know why my mind is so messed up when it comes to him.

"So I'm *not*"—I twist my hand in his jacket, press my palm on his jaw—"going to sleep with you. I *can't*. I can't do that to him. You can't make me do that to him. I can't break his heart. I can't. I won't. And I..."

"And you what?"

I step up to him, my neck craned, my body stretched taut, my calves burning from standing on my toes for so long. But I need to be close to him for some reason. I need him to understand what I'm saying, where I'm coming from.

"I love you," I declare.

And he goes rigid.

Absolutely fucking rigid.

I ignore it, though, and keep going. "I do. I love you. I've loved you since the moment I saw you and it fucking sucks." I think he goes even more rigid, but I ignore it once again in favor of the point I'm trying to make. "It fucking sucks big time. It hurts, okay? Because you can't love me back. You won't love me back. You probably don't even know how. So I... I don't want to be in love with you. What I want is..." I look into his dark, glittering eyes. "I want someone to love me. I want that, Stellan. I want... No one has ever loved me. Expect my *biji*. No one has ever accepted me for who I am, and I-I want that. Somehow, he does that. *Somehow*, he loves me and I..." I lick my lips. "And you just talked about my dream, didn't you? You're always talking about it. My passion, my acting. Well, this is my dream too. To be loved. To love. So just... let me, okay? Don't take that away from me."

His eyes drop down to my wet mouth for a second.

And then another second passes.

And another.

And *another*.

It takes him five seconds to look away from my mouth and in that time, my lips have become stung and swollen, needy, as he says, "He loves you because he can't not love you." Before I can decipher those words from him, he goes on, "Because loving you is the easiest thing in the world. Which also makes it the hardest."

"What?"

He takes in my face, his gaze molten and shiny. "You're off the hook."

I know what he's saying. I know what he means, but I... I don't know how to react. I don't know what to say, so I tighten my hold in his jacket. "Are you... Are you serious?"

"Yeah."

I didn't think it was possible to fist his jacket any more than I already am, but I find a way to crumple it even more. "But you said I tortured you. You were so hell-bent on—"

"It's not your fault that you have the kind of fire that has the power to melt me," he speaks over me. "It's my fault for trying to punish you for it. And turns out, I do."

"You do what?"

"Care about you," he admits albeit reluctantly from the look on his face. "You said that if I cared about you, I wouldn't be doing what I'm doing so"—he swallows thickly—"I do."

My heart squeezes. "You—"

"And I have already hurt you enough," he keeps going, his eyes slightly narrowed, "in ways you don't even know about."

"What does that"—I frown, tugging at his jacket—"mean?"

"It *means* that you belong to my twin brother," he says, his lips barely moving as he lets out the words, the words that I get the feeling he doesn't want to utter. "And as much as I want to cross that line, I won't."

I'm waiting for it.

The relief to come.

This is what I wanted, didn't I? I wanted him to back off. I wanted him to leave me alone, leave Shepard alone. I wanted to keep my wrongdoings a secret from my boyfriend and just move on with my life.

So then why do I still feel on edge?

Why do I feel so... miserable?

He's doing the right thing. He's being the good guy that everyone always calls him. So why do I hate that so much?

"So this..." I try to speak. "This is *really* it?"

Please say no.

Please say no.

Please, God, just say no.

"Yes."

"You're leaving?"

"It's better if I do," he says, and my grip tightens for a second. "Besides, you should go out with your friends. Celebrate. It was a good play. You wrote it, didn't you?"

Again, I blush as I reply, "Not really, no. We did the script, but it's based on one of my favorite movies."

While practicing last night, I only gave him the basics of the scene without telling him about the whole plot. Turns out, I was a little shy sharing this piece of me with him. Maybe it was self-preservation, hiding that deep part of me from my blackmailer. Whatever it was, it doesn't matter now.

I'm glad that he was here to see it.

"I wish..."

"You wish what?"

I simply shake my head in response. Because I can't tell him what I wish for.

I can't tell him that I wish I could see it with him. The movie.

It's about these two best friends in college, a girl and a boy. The girl loves the boy, but the boy loves someone else, the new girl in college. So the best friend leaves and the boy ends up marrying the new girl. Years pass, they have a daughter together, and when the new girl dies, she writes letters for her daughter. In those letters, she tells her daughter to go find the best friend. Because she always knew that the best friend loved her dad and she—the new girl—came between them. If she hadn't, their life would be different, and they'd be together now. So now that she's gone, it's time to reunite them.

I played the role of the best friend.
I wish he didn't have to go.
I wish he loved me.
I wish...

My grip twists and tugs, and I decide I won't let him go. Maybe I can come up with an excuse for him to stay. Any excuse. Any ridiculous or flimsy excuse at all. But then my hands fall away from his jacket, limp and useless.

I fall away from him too.

Because I need to stop being ridiculous and count my blessings that this is over.

Good thing there's a wall behind me, cold and damp, giving me the support I need. So I don't totally crumple on the floor like I want to do in this moment. Maybe when he leaves, I can do that but not right now.

"Except..."

CHAPTER 14

My eyes jerk up to his face. "Except what?"
God, I sound so hopelessly hopeful.
So hopelessly pathetic.
But I don't think he notices.
He's busy elsewhere.
He's busy looking at me.
Because while my eyes are on his face, his are roving all over my body. Ever since he shut us off in the closet, he hasn't looked anywhere else but at my face, but now his eyes are traveling. Observing. Surveying.

They're at my throat, taking in my lavish necklace made of gold and red beads. At my ears, taking in the jewelry that I'm wearing there as well. He's taking in my costume, the traditional Indian dress in red and gold, along with my henna tattoo, my bangles, and rings. He even goes down to my ankles that are decorated with a henna tattoo as well along with tinkling anklets on each foot.

"Except"—he picks up the thread from before, his voice sounding both thick like his eyes and edgy like this body—"this is goodbye, isn't it?"

I thought our phone call from last night was goodbye, so I should be glad it wasn't. That I got more time with him. I shouldn't be greedy.

Still, my heart squeezes. "Yes."

"Goodbyes are important," he says.

I swallow. "Yeah."

"Sometimes more important than hello," he keeps going.

I simply nod, my heart aching.

"And isn't there a thing called story coming full circle in the end," he says, a light frown between his brows, "in theater, I mean."

I think about his words for a second. "You mean like break a leg?"

"Yeah." His eyes flick back and forth between mine. "It means after a long turn of events, you end up in the same situation that you started with."

"O-kay," I say, confused as to where he's going.

"So since this is the end, doesn't it make sense that we come full circle too?"

Slowly, something is happening to my heart. I don't know what, but it's starting to beat. And it's starting to beat right. "How?"

He licks his lips. "Well, the night we met, you had a costume on."

I'm hanging on to his every word like they're diamonds. "Yeah."

"And here you are, at the end, in a costume again."

"I am."

"And while a white dress and a pair of fake wings were easy to figure out, I don't know what you're wearing tonight."

"You want to know what I'm wearing tonight?"

"Tell me."

And there it is.

The relief I've been searching for.

It's completely irrational and nonsensical. Much like the things he's just said. The things he's said don't make sense, do they?

They're just an excuse, a very flimsy one, to linger.

He wants to *linger*.

Right?

Something I wanted to come up with but couldn't. So *he* did. And I know, I *know* in my heart, that he did it for me. He came up with this excuse for *me*.

Because that's all we have, I realize.

All we have are excuses. Because he's my boyfriend's twin brother and this is the only way we can be around each other. By making weak rationalizations. At least for tonight. At least until Shepard comes back tomorrow.

So I look down at myself and whisper, "This is a *saree*."

"A *saree*."

I look up. "Yes. It's a traditional Indian dress."

"Tell me about it."

Swallowing, I blush.

"So there's a top-like thingy called a blouse"—I point to the golden straps on my shoulders and his gaze flicks to it; the blouse I'm wearing is red in color and shows a ton of my cleavage, stopping just below my breasts, leaving my midriff bare—"and then there's yards of fabric that's sort of draped around my body and tucked around my waist, which is the actual *saree*."

My *saree* is also red in color also with a golden border and a matching golden sequin sewn all over; I wave my hand at my waist to show him where I've tucked it in to hold it in place and his eyes go there, making my bare skin tingle.

Then I move on to the last part of the *saree* that's draped over my torso and slung over one of my shoulders. "And this is the loose end of the *saree* called *pallu*, that goes over my shoulder."

"And what does that do?" he asks.

I lift my eyes back to him and even though I knew where he'd be looking, it still makes me shudder. It still halts my breath to find his eyes on my chest. It still makes my breasts feel heavy, tingly.

Just like the night of the charity event.

"It's..." I try to answer him. "It's supposed to cover up..."

"Cover up what?" he asks, keeping his eyes glued to my heaving chest.

"I... It..." I try again. "Well, it goes over my shoulder as you can see and... What are you doing?"

I'm not sure why I asked because I know exactly what he's doing.

Exactly what he's *done*. He has leaned closer to me, and he has tucked his finger—long and graceful—under the edge of my *pallu*.

He has curled his finger under the fabric.

And before I can take another breath, he tugs at it and the *pallu* comes slithering down and away from my body. Where he catches it in his fist.

"Seeing," he says, his eyes on my bared skin now.

My bared and *shivering* skin.

Of my midriff, my chest.

His eyes on my tits that bounce with every broken breath I take. On my nipples that were hard before, yes, but they're so very, *very* hard now.

Painfully hard.

"W-what?" I stutter, my legs shaking.

"This is full circle, isn't it?"

"Uh-huh."

"So in order for it to be full circle, I need to *see*. Like I could in your white dress," he explains before looking up and continuing, "And now I can."

"But y-you're not supposed to do that," I blurt out.

"No?"

"No, you're not supposed to..." I swallow, pressing my palm harder on the wall. "To pull at my *pallu* like that."

"Why not?"

"Because that's... That's the point."

"What's the point?"

"That's the point of a *pallu*. It's supposed to cover my body. It's supposed to p-protect me. When a man pulls on a girl's *pallu*, it's... It means he has bad intentions."

That's what my *biji* told me once when we were watching this movie, where the guy pulls on the girl's *saree* and exposes her. I mean, I could gather that from the scene, but she told me that a *pallu* is the symbol of respect and dignity. It's a symbol of a woman's modesty and in Indian culture if a guy pulls on it or tugs it away from her body, he's not the kind of guy you want to associate with.

"Bad intentions," he repeats on a murmur.

"Yes."

Another little movement accompanies his response.

It's accompanied by him leaning forward even more, to the point where I feel the tails of his suit jacket rustling against my *saree*-covered thighs. Then he puts his fisted hand—the hand that's clutching my *pallu*—on the wall by my waist and looks down at me. "I remember someone having bad intentions that night too."

I crane my neck up at him. "The guy in the c-car?"

"The *dickhead* in the car, yeah."

"You told me not to go with him."

"I did."

"You *protected* me from him," I remind him.

Something moves through his face.

Something too grave, too heavy for the comment I just made. It wasn't exactly light, my reminder, but it wasn't this laden with things either.

As laden as he appears in this moment.

So much so that his gaze turns thick as he looks down at me. His voice turns almost guttural as he says, "And I will do that."

"What?"

"I will always protect you."

I believe him.

I totally and absolutely believe him.

And I absolutely know how ridiculous it is because of the things he's done. Yes, he took them back, but that doesn't change the fact that he did them in the first place. Not to mention, look what he's doing now. He has me partially undressed. So my belief should be ridiculous.

But I still have it and it's unshakeable.

I glance down at his hand, the one clutching the *pallu* of my *saree*, keeping me exposed to his molten eyes. Then, looking up, "I know."

His grip tightens, tugging at my *pallu* as he comes even closer. "And you do need protection because we both know what happens next, don't we?"

I do.

I absolutely do.

"Yes," I whisper with wide eyes.

"Tell me."

"I ask you to..." I hiccup. "But you can't. You can't kiss me and you definitely can't touch my..."

Something akin to torment flashes through his eyes. I can't fully read it, but whatever I can tells me it's there.

"No, I can't."

My chest shudders with my breaths, as tortured as that look in his eyes and crazily, I begin, "But it..."

"It breaks the circle, doesn't it," he completes my thought.

Swallowing thickly, I nod. "It ruins the ending."

God, this is crazy.

This is so, so crazy. It doesn't make sense. It does not make sense at all, what we're saying, what we're doing. We need to leave. We should get out of the closet. But for the life of me, I can't make my legs move.

For the life of me, I can't seem to walk away from him.

"So there's only one thing we can do, isn't there?" he rasps.

I look at him with pleading eyes. "What?"

"You do it for me."

"W-what?"

He comes ever so closer, his eyes glinting. "If I can't touch your tits, then you're going to have to touch them. For me."

"You want me to—"

"Yeah."

"But..."

"That's the only way this can happen."

I bite my lip, my heart racing like crazy. "I'm... I don't..."

"Do it," he commands, licking his lips. "Unbutton your blouse."

My chest is heaving, caving in on itself. "I... My blouse?"

"Yeah, unbutton it."

"What? I... No."

That's the right answer, isn't it?

It doesn't feel like it, but it is. And I'm proud of myself for finally saying something that makes sense. For finally acting like a rational human being instead of this lovesick, lustsick, heartsick, just sick, sick, *sick* girl.

I can't do this.

I absolutely cannot do this.

But I want to do this.

I so, *so* want to do this.

And I don't know how to make myself do it and...

My thoughts break when I notice something passing through his features at my no. Something dark and dangerous and oh so cold and yet so beautiful. That it takes my breath away. It makes my fingers tingle, itching to do what he's asking me to.

"That's the thing, though," he says, lowering his face toward me.

I inch up mine until I think we're breathing over each other. "What thing?"

"If you don't unbutton your blouse, I'm going to have to *make* you."

"You—"

"I'm going to have to force it." He licks his lips. "And you remember what will happen if I do it, don't you? I told you. That night."

He did.

He told me, the night of the charity event, what will happen if he has to force me.

"Y-yes."

"Tell me," he invites. "Tell me what will happen if I put my hands on your tiny little blouse."

"You will r-rip it," I say, my voice barely there. "You'll rip my blouse. You'll tear my buttons. You'll..."

"I'll what?"

"You'll..." God, my heart is pounding and pounding. "You'll wreck my dress and strip me naked."

"Yeah, I will," he confirms, his gaze swirling. "If I get my hands on your blouse, it won't survive the night. Your tiny little buttons will be a thing of history and all the things your *pallu* is supposed to cover will spill out in the open. For everyone to see. And of course that will piss me off. You know that, don't you? Not only because I'll be forced to ruin this sparkly dress fit for a fiery fucking princess like you, my Lolita, but also because they'll all get to see what only I have the right to."

At his words, I swear I feel my buttons strain. "But you don't—"

"So isn't it better if you just do as I tell you and both your dress and the people who may see what I don't want them to see get to live a long and a happy life?"

"Yes."

"So then why don't you do the honors?"

And I finally understand.

I finally *believe* what he told me. About his blackmail being a favor to me. Because then I could pretend I didn't want it. I didn't want that one night with him. I could lie and say that he made me do it.

But it's not true, is it?

I haven't let myself think about his one-night proposition beyond what is appropriate and proper. But I'm thinking now, and I realize that I wanted—*want*—it so badly. I wanted that one night with him so, so badly that given the first chance, I would've taken it and run to him.

I would've ruined everything before fixing it.

And then I would've blamed myself.

So he took the blame away. He took the blame on himself. He did it to protect me even when he was trying to hurt me.

He's doing the same thing here.

Because I'm dying to show him my tits.

I've been dying ever since I met him and so he's making it so that I can. Without drowning in guilt, without blaming myself.

God, I love—

No, no, no.

I don't.

I can't.

This is all there is. This one night.

I lick my lips. "But I... This is blackmail."

"I *am* a man with bad intentions."

No, he's not.

He's so not.

"If I... If I do this, you'll give me my *pallu* back?"

He stares at my lips for a moment before saying, "Cross my heart."

And then I can't stop the urgency in my hands. I want to rip my own buttons for him. For this man who's pretending to be bad for me so I could pretend to be good. I work as fast as I can and then my fronts are hanging loose. They're fluttering, grazing my skin with every heavy breath I take. With every heavy breath *he* takes as well.

That I can feel wafting over my face, my forehead.

I can hear it too.

And it wavers, his breath, before turning even noisier as I part my blouse and show him what he wants to see.

My tits.

I even go so far as to cup them and lift them up and away from my body, my back arched, offering them to him.

"Like this?" I ask.

He releases a harsh breath, his eyes glued to my mounds. "Yes."

I squeeze them slightly. "Do you... Do you like them?"

His other hand comes up and for a second, for a very, very short second, I think he's going to touch them. That he's going to cross the line and touch his twin brother's girlfriend, but he doesn't.

He smacks his other palm on the wall, by the side of my head, and rumbles, "Do I like them?"

"Yes." I squeeze them again, lifting them up. "Do you like my tits?"

His jaw clenches. "Yeah."

"I've wanted to show them to you for so long."

He leans closer, putting pressure on his arms, doing a push-up as if. "I know."

"For so, *so* long, Stellan."

"Fuck," he groans.

I squeeze them tightly, bringing them together and pulling them apart. "Thank you for making me."

His eyes are glued to my tits and my working hands. "They're so..."

"They're so what?"

"Soft," he breathes out. "They look so fucking soft. They look... I..."

He shakes his head, trailing off.

"You can't find the words?"

"Fuck no," he says, shaking his head again, his eyes still pinned on my tits.

I squeeze them again and again, bringing them together, pulling them apart as I say, "Soft is nice."

"Fuck soft."

"They're also..."

"Also what?"

"Heavy," I confess. "They feel so heavy. So swollen. And achy."

A vein pulsates on his temple. "Achy."

"Uh-huh. It's like something..." I swallow. "S-something is making them all full and tingly and stretching them out and I don't... It hurts, Stellan. It—"

"Your nipples," he says.

"What?"

"Pull them."

My hands stop. "I-I don't..."

"Tug at them. Tweak them."

"But I—"

Looking up for a second, he says, "Or I'll do it."

I shudder. "You... But won't it make me hurt more? I—"

"No," he rumbles. "It'll make you feel better."

"Playing with my nipples?"

"Yeah." He clenches his jaw. "Do it. Play with your fucking nipples, Dora."

And even though I know it's not true, even though I know we're making excuses and playing with my nipples won't make me feel better at all, I still do it.

Because he told me to.

Because I want to.

I tug at my nipple and moan, my eyes fluttering closed.

And he groans.

Opening my eyes, I notice he's back to staring at my tits, at my working hands, and I ask, "L-like this?"

"Harder."

So I do it harder. I pull at them with my forefinger and thumb as I moan, "Stellan, I—"

"Twist them," he orders next, his voice low and rough.

Dark like the rest of him.

Commanding.

And once again, I obey.

I twist my nipples and I do it so hard that I can't help but come off the wall. I can't help but arch my back and moan out his name once again, my tits jiggling with my broken breaths.

"Fuck, fuck," he growls, "*fuck*."

"Stellan, I think—"

"Distract me."

"What?"

Veins stand taut on the side of his neck as he snaps his eyes up. "Tell me what else you're wearing."

I pause. "W-why?"

"Because," he says with clenched teeth, "if it's hurting you, showing me your tits, you bet your ass it's hurting me too. If your tits feel all full and swollen, you bet your fucking ass I'm full and swollen too. I'm achy too, Dora. Because like you, I've wanted to see your tits for a long, long time as well. Like you, I've dreamed about seeing them. And I don't know much about dreams, but I do know that when they come true and when they come true in a way that's *spectac-*

ular and exceeds all your goddamn expectations, then it's very likely that it blows your mind. It's very fucking likely that in this case, I'm going to blow in my motherfucking pants. Because I'm full and swollen and goddamn hurting in my dick and aside from blowing in my pants like an unruly teenager who has zero impulse control, there's also a very high possibility of me blowing on your swollen and full tits. There's a very high possibility that I blow so much that I paint your tits with my spunk and drip down your cherry fucking nipples like milk. So before I do any of that"—he jerks his chin up, motioning toward my ear—"tell me what that is."

As soon as I get his meaning, my eyes are ready to go down, ready to see the evidence.

He's hard, isn't he? That's what he means.

But he doesn't let me.

"Don't," he orders.

"What?"

"Don't you fucking dare," he warns.

"But I—"

"You're *not* putting your hungry fucking eyes on my dick," he says with his teeth clenched. "And they're hungry, aren't they? I can see that. So no, you're not looking at my dick. You're keeping them on me and you're telling me every single thing you're wearing until my raging boner calms down and I can breathe again. I can breathe and fucking protect you, yeah?"

My breaths are rapid.

And my tits are so heavy in my hands that I can barely lift their weight. I can barely think at all, but for him, I do.

"It's called a *jhumka*," I tell him, referring to my earrings. "It means little bells in Hindi."

He breathes out loud. "It's fucking beautiful."

It doesn't sound like it from his tone but I understand that he's trying to calm himself down. Which again makes me want to look down and see, even through his pants, but again, for him, I do as he says.

I tell him about my *maang tikka* that I'm wearing on my forehead, my big and lavish necklace around my throat. My nose ring that's called *nathini* in Hindi that's usually more extravagant than a normal nose ring with studded gems. I tell him about my henna tattoo, my anklets, my little toe ring that's called *bicchiya* in Hindi and again is usually more lavish than normal toe rings.

I list every little thing I'm wearing on my body and when I'm done, I ask, "Any better?"

"What do you think?"

I look at the tight features, beads of sweat on his forehead, and go to wipe them off. But yet again, he stops me. "Don't." I open my mouth to protest, but he continues, "Don't fucking touch me right now. Put your hands back on your tits."

"But won't that—"

"Just do it."
"I think I should cover them up."
He shakes his head once. "Wouldn't make a difference."
"Why not?"
His jaw clenches. "They're fucking tattooed on my brain."
I bite my lip at his words. Then, switching gears, I ask, "Is it big?"
He waits for several beats. That I watch him count under his breath. "Do I have a big dick. Is that what you're asking me?"
I nod.
"That's not a good question right now."
I know.
But I can't stop myself.
I squeeze my tits that I'm still holding, and I begin, "Do you think..."
"Do I think what?"
"Do you think"—I squeeze my tits again—"you could fit it between my tits?"
He remains silent for a few seconds. Then his voice, somehow both threatening and tortured, asks, "Are you asking me if I can titty fuck you?"
"Uh-huh," I say.
Although what I wanted to ask him was if he could fuck me in the pussy with it and if he did, would it hurt? But I guess I have some decency left in me to not torture him like that.
So I'm asking him the second best thing.
"Yes, Dora," he says hatefully, "even though my dick is big enough to hurt you, I can still titty fuck you. I can still stick it between your heavy and full tits and fuck them until I do worse than coming on your tits and instead paint your pretty fucking face with my wad. And then I can titty fuck you a second time because my spunk would've made you all slippery and juicy, so of course my dick instead of going down will stay up. And I'm not going to take care of it by myself, am I? Not when you have a perfect pair of tits that I can ride to get rid of my hard-on. Not to mention, you also have a perfect pair of bee-stung lips that I'm going to have you part. I'm going to have you keep your mouth open and your tongue out so when I'm humping your tits like a desperate man who hasn't come in months, when we both know that I just did, so I can mouth fuck you while I'm titty fucking you. Is that enough of an explanation?"
Wordlessly, I nod.
He does another push-up-like thingy, his veins standing taut. "And in case there's any doubt, I can also pussy fuck you, yeah? Just because my dick is big enough that it'll hurt even if I simply point it in your direction, I can still fuck your pink little pussy hole. I can also fuck your asshole. But that's not what we're doing here, are we? We're finishing the story. We're coming full circle and we're doing it in a very safe and responsible way."
Suddenly, I'm overwhelmingly sad.
I'm so freaking miserable that this is goodbye.

When we never even got to say hello first.

I know I shouldn't say it. I know.

But still I blurt out, "If we're coming full circle, then after I asked you to touch my tits, I also asked you to kiss me."

I did.

And... And I think it's okay.

It's okay if he kisses me. Because it will be a goodbye kiss.

It will be a kiss to end things.

And then tomorrow when Shepard comes back, I can get a new start. A new beginning.

It makes sense, doesn't it?

"No."

"What?"

"I'm *not*. *Going*. To *kiss* you," he says slowly, enunciating every word as if I won't get it.

As if he needs me to get it.

My heart cracks and I duck my head down.

Because he rejected me again. He rejected me for the thing I shouldn't have asked him in the first place. I should have never asked him. I don't know what I was expecting or hoping or even thinking and I...

My thoughts break when he touches me.

When he cradles my face and tilts my neck up. When he looks down at me with shimmering eyes, with a face made of sharp features and even sharper regret.

He roves his eyes over my face for a second or two before taking his hands off the wall and stepping back. He takes my *pallu* with him and partially opens his fist, causing the fabric to drop down between us like a curtain of red sky and twinkling stars.

Then he raises it and drapes it over my shoulder like he's really draping me with stars.

With celestial and heavenly bodies.

And covering me up from the world.

From his eyes too.

Before I can stop him, he turns around and leaves me in the closet, all covered up and dazed.

ACT 2

The Bride-to-Be, The Love of Her Life, & The Fiancé

CHAPTER 1

THE WILDFIRE THORN

THE NEXT NIGHT...

I find him at The Horny Bard.

It's one of those seedy bars with loud music, sticky tables, and everything bathed in red neon light. It's never been my favorite place to hang out in Bardstown, but apparently is very popular among the soccer players.

Including him.

This is probably not the ideal place for me to do what I've come to do. I probably should wait until I can get him alone. But the longer I put off doing the right thing, the more time I have to do the wrong thing.

The more time I have to do something dangerous.

Because that's what I am, aren't I?

I'm dangerous.

I've always known that. I'm like my father. I'm a danger to my family.

But what I didn't know was that I'm a danger to her as well. I'm a danger to her heart, like she said. I'm a danger to her happiness. To her happily ever after.

I've always considered her a threat.

A threat to my peace. My control. My promise.

A threat because she makes me feel things. She melts the ice around my heart.

And while that may be true, I'm the one who's gone out of his way to ruin her. I'm the one who's selfishly tried to use her and abuse her.

Not her.

So she's not the problem. I am.

In fact, I realized something. I realized she's the girl who makes my heart race. But not in the way my anger does. She doesn't make the world disappear or she doesn't make my vision blurry. I don't have to look for a grounding object to get control of myself, no.

She makes the world bright. She brings the world into focus. When I'm with her, I don't feel like I'll burst out of my body. I feel like I can *feel* it for the first time. The heat on my skin. The air in my lungs. The blood in my veins.

I feel human.

I don't know why I didn't realize that before. Maybe because I was so focused on running away from her, so focused on keeping her at a distance, blaming her, being angry at her and the fact that she makes me *feel* when I don't want to, that I never focused on the *feeling* itself.

I never focused on the fact that when I focus on her, I'm grounded.

She's my grounding object.

And I have to protect her, don't I?

She's a treasure. A rare fucking treasure that I need to guard with my life.

So this is it.

This is how I do it.

He's in his usual nook in the back of the bar. It's hidden by a brick pillar and is made of plush leather couches. And as expected, they're occupied by his—*our*—high school friends. Ark Reinhardt, an ex-soccer player who went pro for a couple of years but blew out his knee and now runs a security company, The Fortress, along with a very famous boxing gym in town; Homer Davidson, another ex-soccer player, but he never chose to go pro in favor of following in his father's footsteps and taking over the family business; Byron Bradshaw, who did choose to go pro and currently plays for Seattle. He's in town because we're playing against his team the day after tomorrow.

Anytime we're all in town or are close by, they insist on getting together. While I'm not much for hanging out with people, it's one of the very few get-togethers I don't dread. However, I'm not here to meet and chat people up.

So as soon as I reach their nook, I slide the phone out of my back pocket and set it down on the table.

Right in front of Shepard.

He's been watching me approach the group—they all have been—but while they all had looked relaxed before, well, except Shepard maybe, they don't now. They read the tightness in my frame, the determination in my eyes.

"This belongs to you," I tell Shepard.

He's in the middle of taking a sip of his beer when his gaze shifts to the phone on the table. I know the instant he recognizes it as his phone. His entire body tenses, a light frown appearing between his brows. He slowly lowers the bottle, his eyes glued to it for several seconds.

Then, looking up, "That's my phone."

I shift on my feet. "It is."

His eyes are slowly getting dark.

For being identical twins, there's a tiny difference between him and me. I don't think people notice that; well, she probably does, but that's not the point. The point is that his eyes are a touch lighter than mine. So when he gets angry, you can see them getting darker and darker by the second.

While mine always remain dark.

"Where'd you get it?" he asks, slowly and softly setting his beer bottle down on the table beside it.

"I found it," I tell him truthfully. "In the locker room."

"When?"

"The night I benched you."

"That's the night I lost it."

"Yeah."

He watches me for a few seconds, his breaths still even, but like the darkness in his eyes, they're getting heavier. "So what, you had my phone this whole time?"

"I did, yeah."

"Why?"

"Because"—I take a deep breath and fist my fingers—"for the last six weeks, I've been using it behind your back. I've been using your phone to pretend that I am you. To lie." Then, "To her."

Even though I'm completely focused on my brother, I can see movement in my periphery. I can see Ark shifting; Byron straightening up from his sprawl; Homer fidgeting with his crisp tie. I can even hear them mutter things. Ark cursing; Byron whistling under his breath and Homer, being closest to me in nature, simply holding his silence, but I can sense his gaze sharpening.

The only person who hasn't moved or said anything is my twin brother.

It's coming, though.

It's going to happen.

Because unlike her, he believes me. I can see that.

I can see that he believed every word I said.

Good.

Slowly, he stands up.

Again, I see movements in my periphery; Ark's coming to his feet as well. Byron too. Ark and Byron and Shep were inseparable back in high school. All three of them were soccer gods and popular as fuck. All of them never backing down from a fight. With Ark's tatted up body and Byron's heavy muscles, no one messed with them at school. I know they're both doing it to be on the ready, to have Shepard's back. Homer stands up as well, but given that we used to be the closest to each other in the group, he's probably doing it for me.

They don't need to do that; I'm not here to fight or fight back.

Not only because I will never fight my brother, my family, but because I'm here for the exact opposite reason: surrender.

"You've been using my phone," he begins, his voice low, eyes now completely dark, "behind my back."

"Yes."

"And you've been doing that to pretend. To lie to *her* that you are me."

"Yes." I nod. "She doesn't know. She doesn't know that the guy she's been talking to these past weeks is me. That she's been talking to the wrong twin. She's got no clue and—"

He pounces on me then.

And given his reflexes, it happens in a flash.

One second, he's on the other side of the table and the next, he's upon me. He's got his hands in my collar, and he's pushed me several paces back until my back thumps against the pillar. And with him, come our three other friends, who simultaneously grab Shepard and try to pull him off me.

I address them all in general. "It's okay. You can let him go."

They don't.

But before I can insist, Shepard thumps my back against the pillar once more and gets up in my face. "You've been pretending to be *me*."

I keep my fists at my sides and reply as calmly as I can against the jarring pain in my back, "Yes."

Another shove against the pillar. "To *get* with my girl."

"She's not your girl, though," I say, again as calmly as I can.

He tightens his fist in my collar. "What'd you say to me?"

"Shep," Ark warns, his tatted hand on Shep's collar, his green eyes alert, "let him the fuck go, okay? Let your brother go."

Byron pulls at Shepard too. And given how strong Byron is in addition to rumors about his steroid use, Shep should move back, but it's the testament to my brother's hatred and anger that no one can make him budge.

In fact, he tightens his hold even more and gives me another shove. "Say that again."

I grit my teeth against the pain. "I know."

"Yeah, what'd you know?"

"About the ultimatum."

His features still for a second before rippling with rage and I can't help but envy him. I envy him for being able to display his emotions so freely. I envy him for having that freedom.

I fucking envy him.

Which is strange because I've never done that.

For all my crimes against him, I've never envied him, begrudged him his freedom. In fact, I've always been grateful that it was me and not him or any of my other siblings. Yes, Ledger has issues with anger, but they're not as big as mine. And for all the ways I'm wrong, I've always been grateful that it's me and not them.

Not my twin brother.

"I know what the world thinks isn't true," I continue. "What *I* thought isn't true."

He clenches his jaw. "You shut your fucking mouth."

"And you never corrected anyone, you never corrected any assumptions because either your ego didn't let you or because you wanted it to be true so badly that you didn't mind the deception. Either way—"

This time, his retaliation comes in the form of a punch.

A hard jab to my left jaw.

At which point all three of them try to calm him down but to no avail. They try to pull him away, but Shepard doesn't budge. His anger is too much in this moment and I can see that.

I *understand* that.

For the first time ever, I empathize with him.

I'd do the same thing if I were him. I'd beat the shit out of me too.

"Either way, you love her," I say, wiping the blood off my mouth.

"Yeah, I fucking do, you asshole," he growls.

"So—"

"And if you think you're going to take her away from me, I'll—"

"I'm not," I tell him truthfully.

"Yeah?"

Looking him in the eye, I state, "I told you before: she's yours. She'll stay yours."

"So then why the fuck did you go after her? Why the *fuck*"—he gets closer to me even more—"did you go behind my back and lie to her?"

Because I'm an asshole.

Because I'm selfish.

Because I thought it would solve all my problems, these unruly feelings that I don't know what to do with. And because what I told her the other night is true. Until I said it to her, I hadn't known. Why I pretended, why I lied. There was no reason for me to do that. There was no reason for me to carry on the deception past that first night.

And the answer is that I did want to get to know her.

I couldn't do that as Stellan. The man with hidden anger and control issues. The man always on the edge. The man who has to cage himself, leash himself tightly in order to keep the chaos inside of him in check.

The man who thought of her as a threat.

But I could do that as Shepard, her best friend. As my twin, I could assume a role, a character, and be with her even if for a little while. I could get to know the girl who's only ever been out of reach but somehow has been the center of my fucking universe since the moment I saw her.

My Lolita.

My Cherry Lips.

My flame.

Dora.

The girl who torments me and grounds me at the same time.

"It doesn't matter why," I tell him.

In response, he twists his fists in my collar for a second before laying another punch on my face. This one was harder than the first, so it takes me a moment to gather my wits. Spitting out the blood on the side, I pant, "It was wrong and I shouldn't have done it. I shouldn't have—"

Another punch.

That not only jars me but also our friends. This time, Byron manages to get Shepard to step back a little but only for a few seconds. And then my twin brother is right where he was, raging and twisting my collar in his fist.

"Yeah, you shouldn't have," he growls. "I told you, didn't I? I told you that she's mine. That if you go near her, I'll fucking declare war and guess what's coming, you asshole."

Again, I wipe the blood off my mouth. "If that's what will make you feel better, then fine. You can have your war."

He narrows his eyes at me. "I will."

"But I won't fight back."

A muscle jumps in his cheek.

I know he's always hated it.

My reluctance to engage, my refusal to rise to his bait.

And while I can't tell him why I am the way I am, I can tell him this much, "You're my brother. My twin. And I wronged you. I went behind your back. I betrayed you. You have every right to fight me. You have every right to declare war. Just know that I'll take it. I'll take whatever you dish out."

He keeps his tight grip on me for a second or two.

Then, in an expected turn of events, lets me go.

He spits on the floor, muttering, "Fucking pussy."

And turns around, ready to leave, when I call out, "Just..." He pauses but still has his back on me. "Just take care of her."

At this, he turns around. "What?"

"Just..." I breathe out, swallowing. "I lied to her. I deceived her. I hurt her. She's going to... She's going to need someone. She's going to need someone to be there for her. She's going to need someone to hold her hand, to wipe her tears, to..."

"To what?"

Pain stabs in my chest as I say, "To love her. She needs someone to love her. No one has ever loved her and it fucking blows my mind. She's..." I swallow again. "She's different. She's *rare*. She's... everything. She needs to be protected. She needs to be cherished and treasured. So just... treasure her. Give her whatever she wants."

Because I can't.

I'm not allowed to. I wouldn't even know how.

Shepard was right when he said she's bright and colorful and passionate.

And I deliberately lead a dull and colorless life. She's reckless and I need to be leashed at all times. She's untamed and I need to be tamed.

She's fire and I'm wildfire.

I'm not a good fit for her.

But Shepard is.

He keeps watching me for a few seconds, his dark eyes taking my features in. I'm not sure what he's looking for, but if it's veracity, then he should be able to find it. He should be able to see that I mean every fucking word.

I mean it and I want to set fire to it at the same time.

Because I want to be the one to give her everything.

I want to be the one to protect her.

Me, no one else.

But I'm the thing she needs protection from, so it will have to be him.

I know the exact moment he finds what he's looking for—I still don't know what exactly that was, though—as he says, "Stay away from her."

With that, he leaves, and Byron and Ark follow him.

A small crowd has gathered around the nook and I see a couple of cell phones out. Thankfully, Homer takes the responsibility of waving them away while I gather myself and get ready to leave. Before I can do that, though, he's back and the way he's staring at me, I know he has something to say.

I wait and his growled words come out. "What the hell were you thinking?"

I take in a deep breath. "I wasn't."

Homer gets his handkerchief out of his pocket and hands it to me. "He's your brother. You don't do that to your brother."

"I know," I reply, taking it and wiping off the rest of the blood.

And I'm guilty.

For going behind his back, for betraying him. But for some insane, unknown, bizarre reason, I'm also not. Because in my twisted head, I still think she belongs to me. I still think he's between us. He's the wrong twin not me.

For the millionth time, it doesn't make sense.

But I can't shake it away.

It doesn't matter, though.

It's over. It's done.

A different voice interrupts my thoughts. "What the fuck were you thinking?"

It's Byron.

With his big and broad body, Byron looks more like a football player than a soccer player. And he did play football in school, but he always gravitated toward soccer, so that's what he chose. Pair that with his dark bun and a full beard, he looks like a lumberjack football player who's a soccer player. Which is why the media calls him the Big Daddy. Byron 'Big Daddy' Bradshaw.

And right now, he looks pissed.

"You don't fucking do that to your brother." He keeps growling.

"Already covered that," Homer says, clapping a hand on his shoulder.

Byron doesn't move his eyes away from me, though. "I know you guys don't see eye to eye. Not that Shep would ever tell us why but... *Jesus*. You're supposed to be the good twin. The twin who follows all the rules. Who's so annoyingly good that I always wanted to punch you. What the fuck happened? What the fuck did you do?"

"Apparently I'm just an asshole in disguise," I say.

Byron stares at me for a few seconds. Then shakes his head. "You need to sort yourself out, you get me?"

I watch him.

I want to punch him too.

I've always wanted to punch him because he's friends with Shepard. Because Shepard trusts him more than he trusts me. As he should, but still.

I want to do the same now too. I want to break his jaw and I know he'll give back as good as he gets. But I can't. Shepard needs good people around him. So all I do is reply, "You should be with my brother. He needs you. He needs a friend."

CHAPTER 2

LATER THAT NIGHT...

I love my bedroom.
Despite being sent here to live, away from New York City, away from everything I've ever known so my mother could rein me in, it's my favorite room in the world. Because I decorated it just the way I like now that I don't live under my mother's roof.

It has a cozy queen-sized bed with the softest sheets and a blanket with a colorful Rajasthani print and golden tassels. My mom never liked this blanket. Not because it's from India but because my *biji* gave it to me. My walls have vintage posters of my favorite Bollywood movies—no mystery as to why my mother hates that—and I have a whole collection of old cassette tapes of my Bollywood music. Again, very vintage and cool.

My window with sheer white drapery overlooks the back garden. It has a perfect view of the tree under which I sometimes smoke and on other nights dance in my white dress. When it snows, I can see miles and miles of snow-covered grounds.

I'm sure my mom wasn't counting on me making it my safe haven, but I did. I made it the safest, coziest, the warmest place—not by temperature but by the vibe—I could.

So for a few seconds, I can't compute how that changed.

How my bedroom, those sheets, these pillows, my blanket, turned into something I'm having a hard time looking at. Because every time I look at those pillows, I think of how I'd propped my phone against them to dance. Every time

I look at that blanket, I think of how I'd make myself comfortable before picking up my phone. How I'd lie on those sheets for hours, texting away.

With my boyfriend.

My *fucking* boyfriend.

"Why?"

I know I said that but strangely, my voice is coming from far away, from the bottom of a well. So I'm not sure if he heard me.

But apparently, he did because he replies, "Because he's an asshole. He's a selfish prick."

I look up at him then.

Shepard is angry.

No, he's raging.

It's a rare sight. I've seen him lose his temper before, mostly when he's watching game replays or when his team loses because he always thinks he's responsible for it and could've done something to prevent it, but this is different. I've never seen him seething like this. I've never seen him vibrating with rage.

My best friend.

My boyfriend.

But he's not, is he?

Turns out, he never was. We never got there.

Never got a *chance* to get there.

Because apparently, this is the first time I'm talking to him. This is the first time I'm talking to Shepard—the *real* Shepard—ever since he went away for the season. This is the first time we're having any sort of interaction with each other.

"Jesus." He tunnels his finger through his hair, messing up the already messy strands. "I should've... I should've called you from the road. I thought I was giving you space. I thought... after the night of the party, you needed that from me. To think. To make up your mind. I don't know. I just... I should've checked up on you." He tugs at his hair. "Fuck. *Fuck*. I should've—"

"It's not your fault," I tell him.

Because it's not.

In fact, as soon as he knew, he left everything and came to me.

To tell me.

The truth.

Something that apparently, I already knew. But refused to believe.

And so my first reaction was joy.

My *very first* reaction was happiness, giddiness, *relief*.

That it was true after all. That *he* is the one I've been dancing for. That he is the one I've been telling all my woes to; I've been texting with. *He* is the world's best boyfriend.

Him. Him. *Him*.

And I've been crying for him. Since last night. Since our encounter at the theater where he left me all covered up and clothed. Where we said goodbye and brought our story full circle.

I've been mourning his loss.

But now I don't have to, I thought.

Because he's my boyfriend after all.

But then I realized that he wasn't supposed to be that. He wasn't supposed to be my boyfriend, let alone the best boyfriend.

That's when I realized that it's not a good thing.

He lied to me.

He deceived me.

And I was so foolish, so fucking stupid, that when he told me the truth, I didn't believe him. I didn't fucking believe him. That's what kills me the most.

My stupidity.

He made me stupid. His love made me stupid.

So it's not Shepard's fault. It's his.

It's mine.

"I love him," I say.

Again, my voice comes from the bottom of a deep well, but like last time, he does hear it. And he goes still. His harshly breathing chest stops moving. His features set in a hard line and in response, I turn to stone as well.

But I can't stop the words from flowing out.

I can't stop my own truth from flowing out as I stare up at the face that for all intents and purposes looks like the man I love but doesn't belong to him.

"I've loved him since the moment I saw him. On my eighteenth birthday party. I saw him under the pink magnolia tree, and I fell. Instantly. I got obsessed. *Instantly*. He was just so different from anyone else I'd ever met. Any man I'd ever met. I felt safe with him. I felt like I could be myself with him, my usual reckless and impulsive self, and he'd keep me safe. I'd never felt that around any man before. Maybe it was the fact that I was wearing that provocative white dress, and he wouldn't look at anything other than my face. Or the fact that he told me to stay away from him because he was a stranger when every other strange man I'd met has tried to get closer to me any way he could. I don't know what it was, but I wanted him to kiss me. I wanted him to want me.

"But he didn't. And I got so angry at that, so *petty*, that I came to you. I asked you to dance with me. It wasn't my dad I was trying to piss off; I remember you asking me that. It was *him*. I was trying to piss him off. I was trying to make him jealous. Which is why I kept coming back. To you. Which is why I showed up everywhere you went because I knew he'd be there. Which is why I always made sure to grab your hand, laugh with you, flirt with you, because I knew he'd be watching and...

"I didn't stop. I didn't stop, Shepard. Even when I knew your heart was getting involved, I didn't stop. I didn't tell you the truth because I... God, I didn't want to hurt you. I didn't want to make you feel what *he* made me feel. I didn't want you to ever, ever go through the pain of unrequited love because *I* was in unrequited love. You're my best friend and I... When you gave me that ultimatum, I made the decision to move on. From him. I made the decision to be with you and..."

I try to breathe, but my breaths keep getting caught up in my chest. Still somehow, I push on. "But I think it's too late. I think I'm a bad person, Shepard. I think what I did, how I used you and never told you the truth... it makes me the worst person in the whole world. Because if I could do it to you, my best friend, then I could do it to anyone. I could break anyone's trust, anyone's heart. For him, I could do anything and..."

I grip his shirt tighter.

I twist it and tug at it.

As my vision gets blurrier and blurrier.

As my knees feel weaker and weaker by the second.

"I don't want to. I don't want to be bad anymore, Shepard," I plead, my voice breaking. "I don't want to be stupid anymore. He told me the truth. The other night. He said that... He said that it was him. That it had been him all along, but I didn't believe him. I didn't... God, I'm so stupid. I'm so blind. He makes me so *blind*. And I don't want to be. P-please, I don't. I want to be good.

"I want... I want to forget him. I want to move on." I shake my head, my tears wetting my cheeks, dripping down to my throat. "I don't want to love him anymore. I don't w-want to love someone who'd do something like that. I don't want to break my heart for him. I don't want to cry for him. I don't want to want him. I don't..."

I'm not sure what happens, but the next thing I know, my face is pressed against Shepard's chest. My nose is buried in his throat and his arms are around me as I sob and sob and fucking sob.

For my broken heart.

My broken trust.

For my broken love.

But Shepard keeps holding me, giving me support, giving me shelter against the shivers that are wracking my body. He's giving me his body heat to combat the chill seeping into my bones.

The kind of chill I don't like. The kind I don't ever want to feel.

It's a chill that's colder than winter.

It's a chill like him.

"It's okay. It's okay. It's going to be okay," he soothes and rocks me like I'm a child.

Which makes me wail harder.

That he's being so good to me when I've betrayed him so badly. When I've been so awful to him.

He doesn't give up, though. He keeps stroking my hair. He keeps rocking me. He keeps whispering soothing things. "Just trust me, yeah? Just trust me. I'll take care of everything. I'll take care of you. I'll give you what you want."

"But I—"

"You love him?"

Ashamed, I nod. "I d-don't want to anymore."

"Just trust me."

So I give him all my weight.

Because he said to trust him and he's the only one I trust in this moment.

The *only* one.

I can't trust *him*. I will never ever trust him. And I certainly can't trust myself. I can't trust myself because I'm the one who fell for him. I'm the one who thought he had more to him. I'm the one who didn't believe him when he told me the fucking truth.

And I'm the one who's weeping and wailing because this is the end of our story.

The end of Stellan 'The Cold' Thorne and Isadora Agni Holmes.

~

The Next Night...

It feels like the night of the charity event.

I'm dressed up in fancy clothes, a backless dress that's held together by a couple of strings and has frills with a leaflet embroidery at the border. It's black and significant. Because black not only is my least favorite color, but it's the color you wear at the end.

Of someone's life.

Black is the color you wear to mourn death.

I'm mourning the death of me and my love.

And it's exactly the kind of dress he'll hate. Because of how free flowing it is and how there are just too many fucking strings in the back than a dress could possibly need. It also shows off the two dimples in my back and the crack of my ass. I checked in the mirror to make sure.

So I'm dressed to kill and as if someone has killed me.

I'm seated at the table with my friends, Tempest, Wyn, and Meadow. Plus their partners. Even Jupiter is here, working on the waitstaff. Like before, one of the seats at the table is empty because my *partner* is nowhere to be seen. It's okay, though; I trust him. I trust him with all my heart.

Instead of rejecting me and storming off in anger after I told him the truth last night, he held me for almost an hour as I cried in his arms. He not only held me, he took care of me. He stroked my hair; he rubbed my back; he told me he would fix everything. He said I didn't need to worry about anything anymore. That he had it. He's going to give me what I want.

So when he told me he was going to come pick me up the next day to go to this team event, I agreed. Even though I wasn't in the mood to go anywhere. I didn't even think I had the energy to go anywhere, but I somehow gathered every little piece of life I had left in me and got myself ready on time for him.

I wonder where he is, though and why he left me as soon as we got here.

Even so, I try to put on a good face for my friends. I try to focus on the conversation that's happening around me. All three of them, Tempest, Wyn, and Meadow, unanimously told me that they loved the play. That they loved the plot, the costumes. But what they loved the most was me. They would've told me all this the very same night, but I'd disappeared. They'd looked for me, but when they couldn't find me, they left. But they're so glad that we're all meeting up tonight so they could tell me in person.

For a couple of seconds when they'd started showering me with compliments, I couldn't figure out what play they were talking about. What plot. What costumes.

Then it all came rushing back.

The play I was so nervous for. That *he* helped me run lines for. And the costume that *he* was stripping off my body in the closet. *He* said the same thing, that I was luminous.

Him. Him. Him.

It feels like everything is tainted by him.

Everything is ruined by him.

I am ruined by him.

Still, I act like I'm fine and smile like I'm not dead inside.

I'm so thankful when there's commotion up front, by the makeshift stage, and their attention switches. Finally, I see my best friend up there. He's at the podium and, leaning forward, he begins, "Sorry for all the fanfare and shit, but I wanted to say a few things. Number one: we're killing it this season so, Seattle"—his eyes find the captain of Seattle's team, Byron 'Big Daddy' Bradshaw—"you better watch out. Because we're winning tomorrow."

There are both cheers and boos from the audience because in addition to New York City FC, Seattle's team is also present. Byron flips him the bird from where he's sitting, and a chuckle runs through the crowd. Even though he's smiling, I'd still be afraid of him with how big he is. How fierce-looking with his linebacker body and that full beard and man bun. He looks like a lumberjack who knows how to wield an axe like a Viking. I can imagine him tackling his opponents with his body on the soccer field as if it were football. Although from what I hear, he's extremely agile and fast for having a body like that.

"Number two: we all know how awesome I am"—again a wave of cheers and boos goes through the crowd, cheers louder this time, however—"but we all know that soccer is a team sport, so I guess I can't be awesome without you all. So thank you." Then, "For making me so awesome."

Laughter and claps reverberate throughout the room.

"And *since* you guys make me so awesome and because let's just say I couldn't be here without you and your hard work, I have an announcement to make in front of all of you."

He pauses and I can see the crowd is curious.

Despite myself, I'm curious too.

And then his eyes swing over to me as he says, "Well, more like a question to ask."

I forget to breathe.

For several moments, all I do is stare back at him.

Until he moves away from the podium and steps down from the stage, starting to head toward me. And then I can't stop breathing. I can't stop the air rushing in and out of my lungs. I can't stop myself from choking.

Because somehow, I know. I *know* what he's going to ask.

And I think the rest of the room knows as well.

Tempest's chanting, "Oh my God, oh my God. Oh my fucking *God*."

Meadow's whispering, "Is he doing it? Is he really going to do it?"

Wyn replies back to Meadow, "I think he is. I so totally think he's going to do it."

I push my chair back. I have to.

I have to get out of here.

But I can't.

Because just as I'm about to stand up, he reaches where I'm sitting. And looking into my eyes, he comes down to his knee. He picks up one of my hands that I had curled into a fist on my thighs. He opens the fingers one by one and rests it on his open palm.

"I guess by now everyone in this room knows how I feel about you. How ever since I met you, I'm a changed man. They know how crazy I am about you. So I guess I want to make it official. I want to ask you if you, Isadora Holmes, would make me the happiest man alive and marry me?"

I think the table across the room can hear my breaths.

I think they can also hear how fast my heart is beating.

And if they can hear it, I'm sure Shepard can hear it too. I'm sure he can see how badly I'm shaking. How my mouth is parted and trembling, and how wide my eyes are. How cold my hands are and again it's not the kind of cold I like.

I don't know what to do.

I don't know what to say.

I *can't* say what I want to say. I can't say no. Not here, not now.

Not in front of all these people who are watching us.

Not even if we were alone.

So I say nothing at all.

For probably too long because he whispers, only for my ears, "Do you trust me to fix it? Do you trust me to give you what you want?"

I nod, without hesitation.

"So then say yes."

His eyes have something in them I can't read. It's heavy and grave, and it begs me to do what he wants me to do. So I do it.

"Yes."

And the room breaks out in deafening applause. It breaks out in cheers and laughter and smiles and enthusiasm. Even through that, even through the chaos in the room as people rush in to congratulate us, when Shepard pulls me to his feet and hugs me tightly, whispering the same mantra to trust him, my eyes find two things.

First, Jupiter.

She's standing a little to my left and her eyes are wide.

Shocked.

In that moment, I know. That all my suspicions about her liking Shepard were true. And God, he just broke her heart.

No, not he. Me.

I just broke her heart.

But that's not the only thing I did. Because a moment after Jupiter, I find him.

He is where he always is.

In a corner, hidden away from everyone.

I knew where he was the moment I arrived at the party, and I knew he was watching me—this time I knew for sure—even though I didn't look at him once.

I look at him now, though.

I look at him over his twin brother's shoulder and find him staring at the sparkling diamond on my finger. My engagement ring. And I realize that along with breaking Jupiter's heart, I killed his.

Because this is what death looks like.

It looks like him in this moment.

CHAPTER 3

"That's a nice ring."

I jump at the voice coming from beside me.

"Mom," I murmur, going alert.

I've been standing at the bar for the past hour as people come to congratulate Shepard and me. For the most part, I've been able to respond to their enthusiasm appropriately. I've been able to match them smile for smile and laugh for laugh. But the more people come and visit, the more afraid I become. The more it starts to set in.

I'm engaged.

I'm *engaged*.

Holy fuck, I'm engaged.

To my best friend. To the man who loves me, but I don't love him back.

What if this is the wrong decision?

I mean, it has the *makings* of a wrong decision. People should be in love when they get engaged. They should be enthusiastic and happy and filled with joy.

They shouldn't be like me.

They should not be looking at their ring and wondering if—when—their fiancé is going to regret it. What if he tries to fix everything but things can't be fixed? What if *I* can't be fixed?

What if I'm doomed to love him—the wrong twin—for the rest of my life?

So in the midst of all this, I forgot that my mother was here as well. My dad too. But my dad's way of dealing with me is to let my mom deal with me, so I don't think he'll personally be approaching me. He's already engaged in a heavy discussion with Shepard and Coach Thorne.

My mother reaches out for my hand and strokes the ring. "That's a big diamond. Wonder how much he spent on it."

I try to take my hand back, but she doesn't let me go. "Thanks. I'll let him know you like it."

Still stroking the ring, she looks up. "Please also give him my condolences."

I stiffen. "I'm... I'm sorry?"

Keeping her face neutral and pleasant, she squeezes the ring into my finger. "He's marrying a girl who's going to ruin his life."

I grimace from the pain. "M-mom, you're... I'm not going to r-ruin him."

She increases the pressure, making me almost hiss with the pain. "I think you are."

I try to pull away from her. "Mom, please. I—"

"Because you're fucking his twin brother behind his back"—she mashes the ring into my finger—"aren't you?"

I'm so shocked, so fucking jolted at what she just said to me that the pain doesn't even register for a second or two.

I go numb.

"What?" I ask in a small voice.

"Does he know?"

"I..."

"I bet he doesn't."

"There's nothing—"

"Because if he did"—she keeps twisting the ring into my finger, her sharp nails digging into my skin—"he probably wouldn't have spent this much on a ring."

Pain slams back into my body and tears well up in my eyes. "I-I'm not... I haven't done anything with h-him."

Her eyes flash with hatred. "But you want to."

I shake my head, trying to break free from her grip. "N-no, I don't... I'm—"

She leans closer to me and hisses. "This is why. This is *exactly* why I wanted you to stay away from the team. I wanted you to stay away from the players. I knew you'd pull something like this. I knew it."

"I promise I'm not doing anything. I won't do anything. I—"

She tugs at my hand, pulling me closer, her eyes heated. "If you haven't, then you will. Because that's who you are. Because you're an attention whore. You crave attention. You *steal* attention. You stole it the day you were born. From me. I was lying there, barely alive and bloody, and my husband—the man I loved, the man I finally thought would love me back—was more concerned with you. He was more concerned with your cries and your freaking coos. And it only got worse from there. Every time you'd cry, he'd come running. Every time you threw a tantrum, he'd give you everything your heart desired. It took me *years* to pull him away from you, *years* to show him your true colors. To show him that we made a mistake. That we never should have had you. That I'm supposed to be the love of his life, not you. Because you're exactly like my mother. Everyone was so enamored by her too. My father *lived* for her. He loved her more than he ever loved me. My husband was supposed to be my person. He was supposed to love me the most but then you came and ruined all that. You come between people. *You* came between your father and me. And now you're going to come between brothers. You're going to ruin both their lives."

"Is that... Is that why"—I lick my lips, my voice sounding so childish—"you don't love me? Is that why Daddy won't speak to me?"

"Your daddy won't speak to you because he knows what kind of a daughter he has. And now you're going to show the entire world what kind of a slut you are."

I shake my head. "Mom, listen, I—"

"No," she snaps, her nails feeling like needles now, that ring almost fused to my skin. "You listen to me: it's done. You're engaged. To the captain of the team, no less. Do you know what that means? It *means* more press, more media. You're in the public eye, more than you ever were. And if you screw up, if you create a scandal and make a joke of our family, you're not the only one who'll regret it. I'll make sure that your lover boys regret it too."

～

J stare down at my ring.

It *is* nice.

It's platinum with delicate filigree work that circles my finger and a sparkly princess cut diamond that sits between a circle of little diamonds. I love it and as I stare down at it, I wish my mom had given me a chance to talk. If she had, I would've told her that she shouldn't worry about me coming in between anyone anymore.

It's over.

It's done.

It's dead.

I'm dead.

Sighing, I look up into the mirror above the bathroom sink and decide to freshen up my lipstick. After my run-in with my mother, I came to the bathroom to clean up the blood—apparently, she did pierce skin—and find my equilibrium. I didn't go to the one by the ballroom but found a solitary bathroom up a flight of stairs because I knew it would be empty.

Just as I'm about to leave, though, the door opens and the bathroom is not empty anymore.

It has an intruder.

I see him in the mirror.

He fills the doorway.

His shoulders spanning from one end to the next.

He has a suit jacket on, and his shirt is crisp. His hair's polished and pushed back and his boots are shiny. And in the midst of all that, there sits a bruise on his jaw and a black eye.

He looks dangerous.

Probably because he *is* dangerous.

A man with bad intentions.

I keep holding his eyes in the mirror, keep watching that sharply sculpted face. It's blank right now, dead like it was in the ballroom. Lifeless and colder than winter. I watch him trace the line of my backless dress. His gaze getting hooked on the strings and then hitting those two dimples. Followed by the tiny crack of my ass. Which is when he comes back to life and his bruised jaw clenches.

I hope it hurts him.

I hope the hurt never leaves him.

His eyes come up. "What'd she say to you? Your mother."

At his gravel-filled voice, I clutch the edge of the sink to keep myself upright. "Who are you?"

A light frown emerges between his brows. "What?"

"Yeah." I lift my chin even though I feel beginnings of a shiver rolling down my naked spine. "Who the hell are you?"

That frown thickens. "Dora, I don't—"

I clutch the sink tighter and suck my belly in. I want to shout, *stop calling me that*. But instead, I say, "What's your name? What should I call you?"

Because this is a game to him, isn't it?

It was a game to him the first night we met and then again when he pretended to be his twin.

Comprehension dawns on his face and he steps in. He closes the door behind him and stands there, straight, with a wide stance and closed fists, like a sentinel.

"People call me cold."

Even though I'm the one who brought it up, the reminder of that night has me curling my toes in my heels. It has me shuddering, but I stay strong.

I don't have any other option *but* to stay strong.

"People are right."

His eyes stay trained on mine in the mirror. "She once called me wildfire, though."

Strong, strong.

Stay strong.

"Who is she?"

"People call her Isadora," he replies.

"Well—"

"But I call her Dora."

"You—"

"She has other names too," he keeps going. "Lolita, Cherry Lips, but my favorite is Dora. And she is"—he licks his lip—"the loudest song, the brightest star, the hottest fire, and the most beautiful girl I've ever seen."

That shiver I was afraid of, the one that was going to roll through my spine, has now taken over my body. Still, I hold the fuck on. "She sounds like a fool."

Anger ripples through his bruised features. "You're not a fool. You were *fooled*, but you're not a fool."

"What's the difference?"

"The *difference* is that I played with your trust. I deliberately lied to you. I made a fool out of you. So you're not the fool, I am."

I circle my eyes over his face. I touch each bruise, his black eye, with my eyes. "And looks like you got beaten up for it."

Another clench and I hope this one hurts him as well. "Yeah."

"Did it hurt?"

"Yeah."

"Did you break something?"

"No."

"Bummer."

"Maybe next time."

"Well, a girl can hope, can't she."

His lips twitch at my response. A very slight twitch, but it's there.

I keep staring at him for a few more seconds, his dark eyes shining, intense. Penetrating.

When I feel his gaze getting through my muscles and bones and into the heart of me, I look away. I break it and put my lipstick in my clutch. I pat my finger over the corner of my mouth, rubbing away the excess. I purse my lips, take one final look at myself, and turn around.

Keeping our eyes connected, I walk up to him, my high heels clacking on the tile. The only sound in the room. When I reach him, I say, "Can you step aside, please?"

His eyes roam over my face. "What'd she say to you?"

"I need to leave," I tell him instead.

"She said something to you. What'd she say?" he insists.

"People are waiting for me."

"What the fuck did she say, Dora?"

That's when I snap.

That is when I *fucking* snap and yell, "Stop calling me that!"

In response, his jaw clenches again, and for the third fucking time I wish to God, I wish to all that's holy, that it hurts him. That it hurts the fuck out of him because it hurts me.

It hurts *me* to see him this way.

It hurts me—the fool here—to think about how much it must've hurt him to get beaten up like that. Even after every fucking thing he's done, it *hurts* me because he's hurt.

"I will if you tell me," he replies with all the calm in the world.

Which pisses me off even more. "You want to know what she said to me? Fine. She said that I'm a slut. That I'm an attention whore and that I've always been this way. Since the day I was born. Because the day I was born, my father was more occupied and attentive to me than to her. Instead of showing all his devotion and love to her, the mother of his child, he chose to shower me, the child, with it. She also told me that she was the one who convinced him to stop wasting his love on me and instead love her and only her. Which is great to hear really because I've always wondered why my father ignores me. I've always wondered why my mother ignores me too. Now the mystery's solved. Now I know. *Now* I can live my life in peace. Oh, and she also said if I pull the same shit and come between two brothers, like I tried to come between her and my dad—two brothers being you and your twin—then she's going to make you regret it. Which I can only assume means that she'll have both of you fired and ruin your careers. So I better watch out."

And since I'm on a roll, I keep going even though I think, I *think*, I see his features hardening. I see his eyes narrowing and shining with a harsh light. But I don't give a fuck if he's angry. He can go to hell and burn there for eternity for all I care.

"Do you want to know what else she did, though? She cut me." I show him my ring finger and since it's my *fuck you* finger, it all works out. "She scratched me with her long talon-like nails and squeezed the ring into my finger so hard that she broke skin. But that's not the best part. The best part is that this isn't the first time she's done something like this, no. She's been doing it for years now. It started with a little pinching here and there, little instances where she'd grab me so hard that she'd leave marks. Then they escalated. She'd smack me, mostly on the back of my head so whatever mark she left was hidden by my hair. She'd shove me and I'd hit wall and then days after that, she'd make me wear long sleeves and long skirts to hide any bruises.

"Even though these incidents got severe, they were still rare. They'd happen usually when I'd been a little rebellious. Like the time I snuck out to a party when I was thirteen and my mother found out. She shoved me into a bush of roses. Then this one time she caught me running lines up in my bedroom, so she tore up the script and smacked me so hard that for a few seconds I saw stars. Then this other time she caught me slipping my bra to the driver because I wanted to go to the movies but I was grounded. She shoved me into my closet and locked me in for over sixteen hours without food or water or bathroom breaks. My dad had thought I'd run away."

I throw him a tight smile but keep going, "In any case, they happened maybe once a month. But then that changed too. Last year. Because I started hanging around the team more and given my track record of seducing men and getting them to do bad things, she never wanted that. She wanted me to stay away from you guys. And now I'm guessing from my father too because I'm thinking about it and I've seen him more this last year than I have any year while I was living under his roof. So instead of once a month, my mother started physically abusing me once a week. So *this*"—I flip him the bird again—"is what she did this week."

He's breathing harshly now, his chest moving up and down, punching the crisp white shirt. And punching so badly that I think he's going to tear it right in the middle. He's going to tear his shirt from the force of his breathing, from the force of his bulging muscles, his little white buttons popping out and flying.

And I honestly, *honestly* wouldn't care about it.

But then I get a look at his face.

I get a look at his bruised jaw and that black eye. They seem to be pulsating, throbbing almost, on his skin that seems flushed now. So tight. So, so tight and straining, almost like his shirt. And his eyes look bloodshot.

Which is when I realize that this is not anger. This can't be anger.

It's much bigger than that, much hotter.

Hotter than fire.

Wildfire.

It scares me, the way he looks right now.

Not for myself, no.

But for him. It looks like he's going to come apart. It looks like he's not only going to tear his shirt but also himself. He's not only going to tear *himself* but everything around him, and I can't help but whisper, "Stellan?"

And his breaths escalate. His red-rimmed eyes go frantic at my voice. His bruises become even more stark and glaring.

"Your mother beats you."

His voice is a whisper, but it's a heavy whisper. A rough whisper. A whisper made of glass and gravel and something else that I don't really understand.

While I was so extremely cavalier and comfortable telling him about it just now, bragging about it for some reason—maybe that's the only way to deal with what she just told me—I'm not feeling any of those things right now.

No, I think my fear for him is increasing.

"Stellan," I say, stepping toward him. "It's not that... It's fine. I'm—"

He grabs hold of my arms then, his fingers digging into my skin. Not in a painful way but in an urgent way. In a way that makes me think that somehow, someway, I've stepped on something.

I've stepped on a live wire and I'm not sure how that happened.

I'm not even sure *what's* happening.

Why is he so heated? So hot to touch as if he has a fever.

"You're not staying here," he states.

"What?"

"You're not staying here," he declares again, his eyes skittering over my features. "Where she can get to you."

"She's... I don't live with her. I don't—"

He pulls me closer, his fingers flexing, pulsating. "Even if you don't live together, she got to you, didn't she. She fucking got to you and... It's because of me, isn't it. You started hanging around the team because of me. Because you lo..." Trailing off, he shakes his head. His breaths are both coming fast and broken somehow. "So this is my fault. This is... You're not staying here. You're coming with me."

"*What*?"

He shakes me in his grip. "You are. You're coming with me. I'm taking you away. *Right now*. You're—"

"No," I shout, stopping him.

And even though his grip is tight, I still manage to break it and step away from him. Probably because he wasn't expecting it. He wasn't expecting such a vehement denial on my part.

But then why wouldn't he?

After what he did.

After how he played me.

After how he can't even *say* the L-word. He couldn't, back there. He had to actually cut himself off before he said it.

God.

"I'm not going with you," I state, taking a couple more steps back.

He steps forward. "Dora—"

"No, stop calling me that!" Another few steps back and I would've taken more, but my spine's stuck to the wall now. "And stop coming close to me."

He comes to a screeching halt, his body almost rebounding with the force.

"Listen—"

"No," I say again. "You listen, okay? You *fucking* listen: first, it's not your fault. In case you weren't paying attention, my mother has always hated me. Second, I'm not going anywhere with you. I will never go anywhere with you. We won't even be in the same room again. We won't... You lied to me."

He goes still then.

So absolutely fucking still.

Still as death.

It's okay, though.

Now I'm the one whose chest is heaving. I'm the one whose breaths are broken. I'm the one vibrating with rage, vibrating with so much fury that I can set this world on fire.

That I can set *him* on fire.

"You fucking lied," I lash out. "Not once, not twice. Not even three times. For days. For *weeks*. For *weeks*, you lied to me. You deceived me. Every word out of your fucking mouth was a lie. Every time I picked up the phone..."

I trail off.

I have to.

My breaths are running away from me again. It's been happening ever since I found out how stupid I've been. I've gotten randomly dizzy over the course of the day. As if it's hitting me once again, what he did. What he kept *doing* for days and weeks.

Everything was right there, wasn't it? All the clues were right there. His sudden possessiveness. His sudden bossiness. The fact that he was doing my fucking homework when I knew—I *knew* for a fact—that Shepard would *never* do such a thing.

How he'd take interest in my practice, ask me questions about it. Ask me questions about *Biji*, about my favorite movies. How he'd asked me to *dance* that night.

In my white dress and fake wings.

It was him.

All along, it was him.

He was the one doing these things and oh my God, I'm so fucking stupid that I never realized. I'm so fucking stupid that I didn't realize even when he told me.

"E-every time y-you..." I try again but fail.

This time my vision is starting to get blurry too.

And the next thing I know, I'm enveloped in strong, steely arms and his face —his fucking beautiful face—is swimming in my vision. His stupid fucking bottomless voice is filling my ears. "Jesus, fuck, just breathe," he says, his voice rough. "Just breathe, Dora."

Which brings me back to life, his name for me.

And I start to push against him as I yell, "Stop fucking calling me that! Stop fucking calling me Dora. I hate it, okay? I hate that name." I push against him again some more. "I hate how you say it. I hate your voice when you say it. I hate your face when you say it. I hate your fucking eyes when you say it. I hate, hate, *hate* every single thing about you. I hate"—I keep pushing and thrashing against him—"you. I hate you so much that it hurts. You lied to me. You *lied*. You played me. You played with my feelings. You played with my trust. You played with my heart."

Now along with pushing and thrashing, I've somehow started to punch him in the chest as well. I have a very loose realization of it. A vague sense of reality as to what I'm doing. Where my hands are and the harsh things on his body that I'm hitting.

Whereas I know exactly where he's touching me. I know exactly how his arms are still bands made of steel that are wrapped around my waist, keeping me standing, keeping me grounded and glued to his body.

"Do you understand what that means? Do you have any *clue* what you've done to me? Any clue at all. How you've fucked me up." I hit his jaw, I think. I can't be sure as I keep going, "Every time I thought I was talking to him, I was talking to you. Every time I thought I'd managed to move on from you, that I thought I could do this, that I could be with him, I was getting closer and closer to you. Every time I thought I'd pulled myself away from you, I was drowning even more in you. Every time I felt guilty for talking to you behind his back was one more time the joke was on me."

I scratch the side of his neck, tug at his collar, pull at his hair. I do everything I can to get away from him while at the same time get my hands on him.

"The fucking joke was on *me* because I believed you at the theater, in that closet. When you told me you cared about me. When you let me off the hook. I *believed* you. But that's not true, is it? I believed the wrong thing. What I should've believed in was when you told me. The truth. Over the phone the other night. When you told me how you'd been lying to me, deceiving me. I should've believed you then. But I didn't. I didn't believe that you could do something like this and for me no less. And so when Shepard actually told me, do you know what my reaction was? I was happy. For a second, I thought all my dreams had come true. That what you'd said in the closet was right. You did feel something for me. You did care about me. That you *cared* about me to go to such lengths. But just like how I believed the wrong thing, that was the wrong reaction too. Because if you really *felt* something for me, you wouldn't have done this. If you really cared about me, you wouldn't have hurt me like this. You don't know how to care, do you? You don't know the right way. You don't know... You can't... You're twisted. You're a lair. You're cruel. You're harsh. You're cold. God, you're so fucking cold. You're c-colder than winter a-and... It's my f-fault. For always believing the wrong thing. For always feeling the wrong thing. For *loving* the wrong twin. For... I... Oh God, you're so *cold*. You're..."

And that's it.

That's all the words I have for him.

That's probably all the words I know right now. The rest flow down my cheeks as salty water and leave my body in hitching breaths. All through this, I am acutely aware of one thing, however, one big and broad and heated thing: him.

I'm acutely aware of how his arms are still around my body, holding me upright. Actually no, his arms have moved. Something I'm only realizing now. Before, he had both of his arms wrapped around my waist, holding me against his body. But now one arm of his has moved and my breaths freeze when I realize where his hand is.

It's cradling my drenched cheek.

His long fingers are splayed wide, spanning the side of my throat all the way up to my forehead, his digits going into my hair. And his thumb is moving, scraping over my cheek, swiping at the tears.

With the realization that he's trying to wipe my tears as fast as they are coming, comes another realization. That he's leaning over me, and he's got his forehead resting on mine and he's so close, his warm breaths fanning my tear-drenched mouth.

Which, in turn, gives me yet another realization.

I don't know why these are coming to me in pieces, maybe because I'm too emotionally overwrought, but they are and this one is that along with his breaths fanning over my wet mouth, he's also breathing out words.

Soft, raspy words as he wipes my tears and rolls his forehead over mine.

"I'm sorry," he's saying, "I'm so sorry. I'm so fucking sorry."

He's repeating it like a litany.

A chant.

A poem with soft words and repeated rhymes.

"I'll do anything, okay?" he murmurs. "Anything at all. Just, please. Please stop crying. Just stop crying, baby. Stop crying, stop crying, please stop crying, sweetheart."

And I could've taken it.

I could have.

His reverent touch. His sweet breaths. His sweeter words. But I can't take him calling me baby and sweetheart—two endearments—in one breath.

It's too much.

It makes me so achy. It makes me cry harder.

So much harder that in addition to him holding on to me, I need to hold on to him back. My arms move from his chest and fly over to his shoulders. They wind around his neck and, sobbing, I say, "It... h-hurts."

"Tell me what to do. Just tell me what to do and I'll do it."

"Y-you hurt m-me."

"I'm so sorry, baby."

"I told you about my d-day. I s-shared things with you about my..."

"I wanted to know," he says. "I just wanted to know."

"Know what?"

"Everything." He presses his forehead against mine. "I wanted to know every little thing about you. About your dreams, your passion. Your drive. Things that make you *you*. Things that make you smile, make you shine. Things that make you so fucking irresistible that I... I forget to breathe around you. I just... couldn't not know."

And God, I would've told him. I would've told every little thing about me. I would've laid myself bare, if only he had asked. If only he had been honest and he had come to me and he had said all these things to me *before*.

But he chose to lie.

He chose to pollute everything.

He chose to make a fool out of me.

"They were not yours to take, those things," I tell him, pulling at his hair. "They were mine to *give*. You understand? They were mine and you took them under false pretenses. You..."

He rolls his forehead over mine. "I know. I know, baby, and it's my fault. It's all my fault. It's—"

I pull at his hair again because I don't want him to sound apologetic. I don't want to hear regret in his voice. He doesn't get to go off the hook just by sounding like I'm killing him with my pain.

"It was you," I accuse. "*You* did my homework. You stayed up night after night, finishing up my stupid assignments."

"I wanted you to focus," he replies.

"On my play."

"Yeah."

"And it was you. You asked them to come, my friends."

"Didn't want you to be alone on your big night."

My heart squeezes and I hate him.

I really, really do.

Because I can't even enjoy these things. Things I always dreamed of. Things I *wanted* from him since the moment I saw him. His care. His warmth.

Him.

Because he tainted them with lies.

His selfishness. His assholery.

"I danced f-for you," I say next.

He swallows thickly. "Fuck, baby, please."

I pull at his hair. "You *made* me dance for you."

"I—"

"W-why did you ask me to put on that dress?"

"Because I wanted to remember that night. Wanted to torture myself with the memory of it."

I clench my eyes shut for a second at having my suspicions confirmed. "I hope you were. I hope you were fucking traumatized."

He nods, his thumb dragging up and down my cheek. "It was one of the hardest things I'd ever done, watching you dance through a screen."

"That's why you kept yourself hidden, didn't you? Because you knew."

His eyes find me through the tiny space between us. "That you'd recognize me. I knew you would and…"

I fist his hair again. "And *what*?"

"And you'd stop," he confesses, the bruise on his jaw looking especially nasty. "I knew you'd stop dancing. If you knew who you were dancing for."

That's the thing, isn't it.

I wouldn't have.

I probably would have danced harder. I probably would've danced longer.

Because he was the one I was dancing for anyway.

"I would have," I lie.

Because he doesn't deserve to know the truth.

Not after what he did.

His fingers on my face, my hair spasms. "Every time you said you'd do anything to be his, I wanted to break something."

"I did want to be his."

"Every time you said his name, I wanted you to say mine."

"I will *never* say your name again."

"Every time you did something for him, you told him something," he goes on, his voice guttural and serrated. "Every time you laughed, you smiled, you stayed up late texting him. Every time you danced, I wanted to tell you. I wanted to fucking tell you that it was me. That it's me you've been talking to. It's *me* you've been sharing your secrets with. It's *me* who's making you smile. It's *me* who's making you laugh. It's me you're staying awake for like I've stayed awake for you. It's fucking *me* you've been putting on your show for. It's me. Not him. It's finally fucking me who's taking care of you, who *gets* to take care of you. Who gets to protect you. Who gets to save you from the world, from yourself. Who gets the privilege of making you smile and laugh and fucking dance. It's *me*. Not him."

Our breaths are harsh.

They're clashing against each other.

Our fingers are tugging and pulling at things on each other's bodies. And I bet if we tried, we could listen to our hearts pounding in our chests at the same time. As if going to war against each other.

Or maybe, maybe, just beating in rhythm with each other.

At least that's what I'd always hoped.

But I'm done now.

I'm done hoping.

I'm *done* with him.

"It wasn't you," I tell him, gathering my breaths and my composure. "I did all those things for him, with him, because of him. So they're not for you. And you don't get to come in here and change the narrative that you yourself set, okay? You don't get to come here and flip my fucking reality upside down just because you *feel* like it. So I want you to let me go. I need to go. I don't want anything to do with you."

He doesn't.

God, he doesn't.

And I'm ready to lose my shit because I need him to let me go so I can go sob in a corner. So I can go break down because he chose to finally give me what I always wanted, but he broke my heart in the process.

"You don't have to," he says, his eyes brimming with something. "But I need you promise me something."

"You need *me* to promise *you* something?" I ask in disbelief.

He said the same thing in that closet too, didn't he? And while I gave him my promise freely back then, I'm not going to do the same. I'm never ever going to do the same.

He isn't deterred, however, as he states, "I want you to go on the road."

"What?"

"When the team leaves day after tomorrow for the next few weeks, I want you to come along. I'll make all the arrangements. I'll—"

"I... What? *Why*?"

"Because I want you away."

It takes me a few seconds to understand where this came from and what he's talking about. And then it hits me, and I go still.

"From m-my mother?"

Anger, pure and clear, ripples through his features as he replies back, "From your fucking mother."

My heart starts to pound then.

In a different way than before. In a way that makes my body tingle, my belly swirl.

Even though it happened only a little bit ago, it still feels like a distant memory. His face, his body, him. How he'd reacted to the news; how he'd looked when I told him about my mother. How it felt more than anger.

It felt all-consuming and scary.

Wildfire-y.

I know I was the one to call him that, but I don't think I knew what it actually meant. Not until today. Not until now.

Not until he got that way on my behalf.

For me.

I was so busy absorbing his extreme reaction that it's only now hitting me, that it was all for me. His fire. His anger. His whatever that was, it happened because of *me*. And despite myself, despite everything, his wildfire is thawing the chill. The bad kind. The kind I'd felt ever since Shepard came to me last night.

"I can handle my mother," I state firmly because I don't want to melt.

He grits his wounded jaw. "Promise me you'll go."

"My mother is none of your concern."

"Promise. Me."

"No."

"Don't do this, Dora."

God.

I push at him then. "I've asked you multiple times now, please stop calling me that."

Not that he budges. "Don't be stubborn about this."

"I'll be stubborn about whatever the fuck I want," I shoot back, pushing at him again.

"This is for your fucking safety," he growls, his arm tightening.

"If this is about my safety, then you're the last person I should listen to," I tell him. "I'm the most unsafe with you."

Again, our breaths clash and our bodies collide with each other. And again, it could also be that we're breathing in tandem. We're living in tandem. We're existing in the same space.

Then, with a sharp swallow, he says, "I will stay away. After this. I will stay so far away from you that you won't even notice me around. You won't even *know* I'm there, yeah? You don't have to look at me. You don't have to look at my face. You don't have to know that I even exist. I will erase myself from your life, if that's what it takes, all right? I will do anything you want, any-fucking-thing that you can think of. But I want you to go on the road with us. I *need* you to go, do you understand?"

He grabs my face then.

With both hands.

And like his grip from before, when he'd almost lost it at the news about my mother, it's tight and urgent. It's brimming with things I don't understand. That I don't even hope to understand in this moment.

"I *need* you to do this," he says, his eyes swirling and intense, so, so intense. "I need you to be safe. I need you to be away from her. I need you where she can't get to you. Not now. Not ever. Not fucking ever, Dora. And I'm going to make it so. I'm going to make it so that she never lays a hand on you and that's a promise. *My* fucking promise to you. I will break every other promise I've ever made in my life, every other promise that I will ever make in my entire fucking life, to keep this one, do you understand? So I need you to promise me that you'll go. I need you to do that for me. I need you to let me keep you safe. And I'll do anything you want for it. Anything at all."

"Anything?" I whisper.

"Any-fucking-thing," he promises, his hands so hot on my cheeks.

His breaths so hot.

His body all feverish once again.

I watch him for a few seconds. I watch him watch me. I watch him standing on the edge for me, waiting for my answer. I watch him hanging on to me. As if his head's on the guillotine and I'm the one with the sword.

Like I'm the one who could kill him if I wanted.

And I realize I've never felt this alive in my life.

I've never felt this powerful.

All because this man, this cold and heartless man, the man of my dreams, promised he'll give me anything I wanted.

So what *do* I want?

"I just got engaged," I whisper.

In response, he flinches, his fingers pressing into my cheeks.

"To your twin brother."

His breaths were already hot and fast. Now they're noisy too.

Now they're loud and thick.

I slide my hands out of his hair and bring them down to the bruise on his jaw. "I'm going to marry him soon." I look at my fingers touching the nasty scrape. "Then I'll be his forever."

His fist is clenching and unclenching in my hair.

"But before that happens," I whisper, still staring at his wound. "I want you to kiss me."

This time, his body doesn't go through a flinch but a whole shudder.

And I look up.

Into his eyes.

They're dark and gleaming. Molten and fiery.

I press my fingers into his bruise a little and I know it hurts him. Even though he shows no reaction to it, but I know. Because it hurts me. Because we're so entwined in this moment. We know each other's thoughts. We know each other's desires.

He knows.

He *knew* before I asked him.

I can see that.

He's not at all shocked at my request.

I'm not either.

I'm the girl who could have anything in this moment—and I know he will make it so—but this is what I chose.

Him. His kiss.

My destiny.

"You told me you wouldn't cross that line." I trace his mouth with my fingers as I keep my gaze steady on him. "In the closet. You said you wouldn't cross that line for me. You let me go. You let me go after *everything* you've done. All the lies you've told. All the games you've played. All the deception, all the pretenses. You chose to let me free. And we both know it's not because you care about me. So maybe you did it because you're such a good guy after all. Such a good brother. Such a good coach. Maybe because when push comes to shove, you could never break any rules. You could never stray off your path. You could never touch your twin brother's fiancée. You couldn't touch his girlfriend, let alone his fiancée.

"But I want you to do it now. I want you to touch me. I want you to kiss me. I want you to break your rules for me. I want you to ruin yourself for me. Destroy yourself. Wreck your morals. Cross all your stupid fucking lines. I want you to do what I did for you. How I lied and cheated. How I fucking loved you despite not being supposed to. I want you to be like me and let me be your Lolita."

I don't know what I'm expecting.

I don't even know what I just did. What I just said.

All I know is that I want him even after everything.

And I want him to hurt *because* of everything.

Can you hate someone even when you love them?

Can you love someone even when you hate them?

I wonder if hate and love coexist. If fire and ice live together.

I don't know. All I know is that I want him to say yes.

God, please say yes.

Or I'll really die. He will really have killed me.

But I guess that's what's written in the stars.

My destiny is to be killed by him and his is to kill me.

Because he says, "No."

CHAPTER 4

If someone asked, I'd say dying is painful.
Death is not peaceful. They lied.
Death hurts.

Being in love hurts. Being in love with Stellan 'The Cold' Thorne hurts even more.

I'm about to push him away and leave, and Jesus Christ, leave for the last time because I'm never coming back when he decides he wants to say more. He squeezes my cheeks even more and tilts my head up. So all I can see is him.

His face. Still beautiful.

His eyes. Still molten and fiery.

"Because I'm Stellan 'The Cold' Thorne and you're Isadora Agni Holmes. And you're the only girl, the *only* girl in this whole wide world who has the fire to melt me. And you did, remember? You're the only girl in this whole universe who has the power to make me break my rules and you did. You're the only girl I will cross lines for. The only girl I will erase them for. The only fucking girl I will wreck and destroy my morals for and I already did that, baby. I already fucking did. And it's not a good thing."

"What?"

"Me, unleashed," he bites out, his words, his look, his entire body intense. "Me, uncaged. Me, without rules and unburied under a six-foot deep layer of ice is not a good thing. It's not a good thing that you can do that to me, okay? I called you a plane crash, remember?" Slowly, I nod, trying to understand what he's telling me. "I called you a car crash, a virus, a disease. I'm that. *Me*. I'm a disease, okay? I'm a plane crash, baby. A fiery fucking plane crash. I'm that multi-car highway pileup, do you understand? I'm dangerous. Like you said. Look what I did. Look what I'm capable of. And it's not even the worst of it, okay? I can do so much worse."

My heart is pounding so hard that I'm shaking with it. I'm shaking with *him*.

God, he's shaking.

He's fucking *shaking*.

"What does that..." I grab hold of his wrists, his collar, his shoulders, everything I can possibly get to with my two hands and puny strength. "I don't know what that means."

"It means that the reason I said I won't cross that line is not because you're my twin brother's girlfriend or his fucking fiancée. The reason I said I won't kiss you isn't because I have some high morals or unbreakable rules. The reason I said I won't cross the line is for you. Because you deserve someone safe. Someone you don't need protection from. Someone who cares about you the right way. Who knows what that word means. The reason I said I won't kiss you is because I shouldn't. Because I shouldn't be your first kiss."

It's hot.

Everything is so hot and sweaty.

Everything is misty and slippery.

My cheeks. His lips. My eyes. His fingers.

His breaths. My breaths.

Everything is drenched with something. Drenched with my tears and my love and my hate. His torture and his desperation. His angst.

In the midst of all this, I whisper, "So will you..."

"Will I what?"

I look into his eyes. "Will you never kiss me?"

Something moves in them. He wipes my tears. He breathes onto my mouth before dropping his gaze down to them. "I will." My eyes go wide and he continues, "But only because for once in my fucking life, for *once* ever since I met you, I want to make your eyes smile rather than cry. I want to make you smile rather than cry. I want to pick up the pieces of your heart rather than scatter them away in the wind. And I want to do it when you *know* it's me."

"Stellan—"

And then he does.

He makes my heart smile. He picks up the pieces because he gives me my most greatest desire: his kiss.

And I'm not going to lie, I've turned into a stone.

I've gone all still.

My brain is working, though.

My brain has too many thoughts running through.

His mouth is wet and he's kissing me.

His jaw is smooth—except for the bruise—and he's kissing me.

His mouth is hot and I want to grip his hair and he's kissing me.

I want to bring him closer, and he tastes like cigarette smoke and marshmallows, and he's kissing me.

His breaths are harsh and he's kissing me.

I want to fly and I want to dance in a field with long stalks of grass *because* he's kissing me. And then I want to make snow angels because holy God, he's kissing me.

He's kissing me. He's kissing me.

He's *goddamn* kissing me.

And I'm not going to kiss him back.

Nope.

That's the thought I decide to focus on. Not the heat of his mouth. Not the taste. Not how wet it is and oh my God how fucking glorious this feels. How *out of the world* this feels. How relieving that it's finally happening. That I won't die, I won't leave this earth without knowing heaven. Or that I could write a ten-minute song, an hour-long play, and a book of poetry based on the feel of his mouth alone, his taste, his heat and I don't even like books.

No, my main focus is that I'm not going to kiss him back.

I know, I know I begged for this.

I begged *on my knees* for this. I beat on the ground. I punched the sky. I fucking lied and cheated and cajoled and cried to him for this kiss.

But that's the thing.

He made me wait. He made me wait so, so long for this.

He hurt me so much.

So I'm just returning the favor.

I'm just going to stand here, locked within his embrace, frozen and unmoved.

Cold.

Colder than winter.

He can envelop my mouth into his all he wants—the very first thing he does when he puts his mouth on me—and he can suck on me like he's sucking on a piece of fruit. I'm not going to budge. He can suck on me like I'm a peach from down south or a strawberry from up north. He can suck on me like I'm a slice of watermelon sprinkled with sugar. I'm not going to move my mouth against his.

Not even a little bit.

Not even when he frames my face exactly like he would hold a slice of watermelon to his mouth. He actually cradles my cheeks in his big hands and tilts my head back. He stretches the muscles and the tendons of my throat until I'm craned up all the way and oh God, the roughness of his hands, the calluses from probably picking up too many soccer balls in his life, feels so wonderful against my satin skin.

And that tongue.

Oh my God, he's lapping at me with his tongue.

And he's sucking on my bottom lip at the same time.

I mean, how can he do that?

How can he do both things at the same time and how is it that I'm feeling it not on my mouth but also in strange places of my body. Like my inner elbows and the back of my neck and holy shit, in my belly button. All the things he asked photos of.

And while I'm trying to figure out the mystery of why his kiss on my mouth also feels like a kiss on other places of my body, he's hard at work up there. He's kissing and kissing and *worrying* my mouth, making it all swollen and puffy. Making it all tingly and hot. All red too, I'm sure.

In the back of my mind, I think that maybe touching up my lipstick was a waste of time. Not only because he ate it all but also because if this is how he kisses, I probably won't need any lipstick ever. He can just kiss me and make my lips look pouty and pink.

In fact, I don't think I will ever need another stitch of makeup either.

Because I'm pretty sure he can be the blush on my cheeks and the shine in my eyes and make beauty marks on my body with his teeth.

Which is exactly what he's doing right now.

After sucking on me like a piece of fruit, he's nipping at my lips.

I also think, I *think*, he's not only kissing me with his mouth. He's also kissing me with his fingers.

He's *eating* me with his fingers.

Not only is he rubbing his rough palms over my smooth cheeks, but when he knows I won't move and will hold my stretched-out position, he moves those fingers of his into my hair. He tunnels them deep and fists the strands. He fists and unfists them. He twists the strands, tugs at them. As if he doesn't know what to do so he's doing everything all at once.

Not to mention, his body.

He's kissing me with his body too.

His heaving chest that keeps pushing into mine. His moving ribs that keep dragging across my breasts that feel overfull and swollen. Just like back in that closet. My nipples feel plump and sore like he's sucking on them instead of my mouth, but I shouldn't be surprised because didn't I already mention that I feel this kiss in every part of my body?

So maybe, *maybe* if I move my mouth a little, it would be okay.

If I part my tingling and sore lips, it wouldn't be such a big deal. Because how many kisses would feel like that? How many kisses consume your entire being like that?

This kiss is one of its kind.

A kiss of cold.

A kiss of fire.

Besides, let's not forget this is my very first kiss, so I guess it's okay. And just because I'm grabbing hold of his strong, massive, sculpted shoulders—shoulders I used to dream about—doesn't mean I've forgiven him. Just because I'm fisting the collar of his suit jacket—the jacket that I also used to dream about and have one in my closet right now that I wear over my sleep pajamas some nights because I miss him—doesn't mean I've forgotten everything he's done.

I don't have to love him to kiss him back.

Or at least I think so.

In any case, my thoughts that I was so focused on have taken a major dive in the last five seconds. Ever since I opened my mouth and he snaked his tongue inside. Or rather *thrust* his tongue inside and took over my mouth.

He took it and invaded it and conquered it. As he tastes me from the inside. As he curls and swipes his tongue. As he touches the roof of my mouth, tangles his tongue with mine. He even swipes it along the sharp edges of my teeth.

He goes for every corner and every cranny and he's not gentle about it.

Why would he be?

Assholes are not gentle. And he's an asshole in disguise.

Assholes are plunderers and conquerors and oh my God, so fucking masculine and dominating, and I just want to smack him and fist his hair and eat his lips back.

Especially when the moment I do all those things—I punch his shoulder and pull his hair and bite him back—he emits a war cry.

Or in this case his groan.

This needy and tortured sound he makes in the depths of his gut.

His chest. His throat.

All of which vibrates against my body.

All of which makes me moan in response.

And my moan is needy and tortured as well.

My moan is fucking horny.

Because God, I am horny.

And I just kiss him.

And kiss him.

And kiss him.

And keep kissing him until he remembers that we have to breathe too. We have to break the kiss and he has to rip his mouth away from me, and instead of heat and warmth and cigarette smoke and marshmallows, I taste... stupid air.

I drag a lungful of it as I say, "I... I'm s-still angry."

His fingers on my waist tighten and flex—I don't even know when he put his hands there because last time I checked, they were on my face—and he pants, "I know."

"This d-doesn't mean anything," I tell him again.

He fists my hair with his other hand. "I know that too."

"You're not a plane crash," I say next because I cannot, absolutely cannot, let him think that about himself even though he hurt me.

I don't even know why he thinks that, but I can't let him do it.

He huffs out a breath. "I am."

"Or a highway accident."

"I am that too."

"I don't believe that," I say vehemently, automatically.

"You should start believing the things I say," he says back.

Maybe I should.

Maybe I should grow up and stop believing in fairy tales.

He's shown me enough times that he's cold and cruel. He's callous and calculating. He's unpredictable like the fire.

Like me.

I flick my eyes over his face then.

His flushed cheekbones. His kiss-blown eyes, made even darker and more dangerous by that black mark around it. His rose mouth, all swollen and red and ruined probably as much as mine. And that pulsating bruise on his jaw that squeezes my heart.

I bring my hand down to his forehead and flick the strands that have fallen over his brows. "I ruined your hair."

His own fingers swirl in my hair. "Fuck my hair."

I look at the wrinkled collar and creased lapels. "I also ruined your jacket."

"Fuck my jacket." He waves away the comment, roving his eyes over my face. "Never like wearing them anyway."

"So then..."

I trail off when I find the answer for the question I was going to ask. Instead, I fist his lapels again. "You do it for me. You wear your jackets for me."

"Yeah."

"Was it your jacket?" I ask then. "The one Shepard put on me that one time."

His jaw tics. "Yeah."

My heart clenches.

There are so many things, so many, *many* things he did and said that I hadn't known until now. So many little pearls and gems hidden under the treasures of things he said to me these past weeks. That I know I'm going to keep finding for days to come.

"Is that when you started wearing your jackets?" I ask. "Because you didn't have one on the first night I met you."

"Yeah."

"Because my dresses are always short?"

"Because their eyes are always filthy."

"I wore this dress for you," I confess.

"I know."

"To hurt you."

He looks into my eyes. "I know that."

"It shows off those two dimples and my mole."

The pads of his fingers dig into my bare flesh. "Along with the crack of your bouncy little ass."

I moan lowly. "I checked to make sure."

"Which is why"—he kneads my flesh—"you're going to wear my jacket when you leave here."

I want to say no. I want to stomp my foot and act all diva-like.

But I decide to let it go for now.

Just for now.

It doesn't mean I'm still not angry with him, just for the record.

"Okay," I give in.

"Good."

"But let me tell you that you're not my bodyguard."

"Don't really give a fuck about labels."

"No bodyguard behaves like this," I point out.

"Yeah, so then what am I?"

"The way you behave?" I raise my eyebrows. "My daddy."

My eyes go wide at what I just blurted out.

And his flash.

Then, squeezing my waist and fisting my hair, "So then that's what I'll be. I'll be your bodyguard, your protector, your fucking daddy"—I shiver at that word—"if it means you will be on that bus the day after tomorrow."

Oh, that.

I completely forgot about that.

"I—"

"Promise me, Dora," he asks, all serious.

"It's not really that bad. I—"

"Fucking promise me," he seethes.

And so I give in to that too. I give in to him because he looks so intense. He looks as if he'll lose it if I say no. "Okay."

A look of satisfaction comes over him.

It's crystal and it's clear.

Along with a look I've never seen before on anyone, let alone on him. It makes his features all sharp and cutting. His cheekbones even higher and his bruised jaw even more square.

Almost animalistic.

Possessiveness.

It's possessiveness.

It says that I'm his. I belong to him. For now and forever.

Which also reminds me that that's not true.

I'm *not* his for now and forever.

I'm someone else's. His brother's.

And the fact that I forgot that fact—the very fact because of which we kissed in the first place—is so fucking jolting to me. It's so fucking jarring that I kissed another man because I got engaged and then forgot about the fucking engagement is...

Oh God.

Oh God.

Oh *God*.

I kissed another man. I kissed *him*.

"I'm..." I whisper, my left hand, the hand with the ring, unfurling on his chest. "I'm engaged, Stellan."

I say the same thing that started it all, but my tone is different.

My tone is scared. My tone is small but full of guilt.

He notices that. He notices the change and for some strange reason, his possessiveness only increases. His grip on me increases too. His fists in my hair tighten. His chest ripples as if he thinks I'll fly away but he won't let me go.

"You—"

"I'm engaged. I'm..." I snatch my hand away from his chest and bring it up to my tingling, swollen mouth. "And I... You... My mom's right, isn't she? She's right. She... I'm a slut. I'm..."

I have to be.

For doing what I did.

It's not a surprise, but I also didn't know I was capable of something like this. I have committed so many heinous crimes in the past. I've hurt Shepard so badly and out of the goodness of his heart, out of love, he decided to fix me and this is what I do the first chance I get.

"Hey." He grabs my face, squeezing my cheeks. "Hey, Dora."

"I'm—"

He squeezes them harder. "No, not one word. Not one fucking word in favor of that fucking bitch, all right?" My mouth parts, but he keeps going, "Not one *fucking* word. Or I swear to God, I'm going to go out there and I'm going to fucking choke her to death. I will suffocate the life out of her. Do you understand what I'm saying to you? I will end her godforsaken life for hurting you, for making you think you're anything other than perfect. So not one fucking word or I will lose it."

He will. I can see that.

So gripping his wrists again, I whisper, "But she said she'll... She'll do something, something bad to you and to him if I—"

"I'd like to see her try," he growls.

I grip his wrists harder. "He's... He's not going to like what we just did. He's doing this to help me. He's doing this because I told him I want to move on. I want to move on from you. From... He's—"

"And he will. He will help you. He will fucking help you. And for that"—he grabs me tightly—"I want to tear him apart. I want to beat the shit out of him but the fact that he loves you is his only saving grace. But that's it. That's all I can give him. He's going to have to deal with the rest," he says firmly. "He's going to have to fucking deal with the fact that I stole a few moments of heaven with you because he's getting you for the rest of his life."

Is he?

Because look what I'm doing.

Look at what we're both doing.

This isn't the way to start a forever relationship. And while I still want to move on from this man in front of me, I don't know if what Shepard is thinking is a good idea. I don't know if *marrying* him is the way for me to get over this toxic love.

So at last I say, "I'm scared."

Anger ripples through his features and he holds me tightly. "I will never, not ever, let anything happen to you. I promise you that, okay? I will take care of you. No one will hurt you. No one, including me and including your monster of a mother."

He will protect me.

The guy who hurt me is going to keep me safe.

And I...

Why do I want to believe him?

I don't want to think about that, though. Not right now.

So I reach up and put my mouth on him once again. I know it's wrong. I know it's not what I'm supposed to do, but I do it anyway. I kiss him and this time my only focus is his mouth. My only focus is kissing him back when he takes over.

My only focus is tasting him, touching him, feeling his hair, testing the strength of his shoulders. My only focus is climbing his body like a tree and I guess his only focus is making me climb it, *helping* me climb it because he does that.

He lifts me off the ground with his hands on my ass and wraps me around his body. My thighs go around his waist and my arms wind around his neck, and then I'm plastered against the wall. I'm plastered in between him and the wall.

All his hard parts are pressing into my soft ones.

And like the dancer I am—the dancer he'd called me either as Shepard or as himself, I don't remember; all I remember is that I'm his dancer in the moment—I dance against him. Because he's the thing I want to dance against. He's the one I want to dance for.

And I can't get enough.

I want more.

I rip my mouth away to pant. "I want..."

But trail off because kissing him is better. So I go back to that.

Until he snatches his mouth away from mine and growls, "I know what you want."

To emphasize it, he fists the cheeks of my ass and *makes* me go up and down his hard abdomen. He *makes* me dance. He *makes* my pussy jolt and spasm.

"I don't... This can't be right," I tell him even though I haven't stopped my movements.

"It is," he argues as he doesn't let me stop them.

"You..." I fist his hair, planning to pull him away but only managing to bring him closer. "You s-should stop. We should—"

He presses a hard kiss on my mouth. "Can't."

I plant a hard kiss back. "But, Stellan—"

He fists my hair, dragging my head back and going for my jugular and sucking on it. "I made a promise."

I arch my back, tilting my head to the side, giving him all the access. "What promise?"

"To take care of you."

"But he said that too. He—"

He licks the side of my neck and bites my earlobe. "Fuck him."

I push at his shoulders again and again, only managing to writhe against him some more. "No, Stellan. He's your brother. He's... It's his job. He's my—"

He looks up, his fingers flexing on my ass. "It isn't."

I'm panting as my heart pounds and pounds. "Stellan, please."

He licks his lips. "No."

My pussy clenches so hard at his refusal. "But, Stellan, that's... I... I'm engaged. You just said that he's the guy who—"

"But you're not married yet, are you?"

I shake my head. "But that's really crossing a line and—"

"It's mine to cross."

"No, it's mine too. I'm doing it too. I'm—"

"No," he growls, something flickering in his eyes, something dangerous. "I'm making you do it."

I freeze. "W-what?"

"Aren't I?" he goes on. "I'm giving you no choice."

No.

No, no, no.

He's doing that again.

I won't let him do it. I won't let him make the same excuse.

I clutch his shoulders. "Stellan, don't do this."

He leans closer, pressing against my center. "I have to."

"No, you don't. Don't make yourself the bad guy here. Don't—"

"But I am the bad guy. I followed you in here, didn't I?"

I shake my head. "Stellan—"

"I followed you in here, knowing you'd be alone. Knowing I could lock the door, lock you inside with me."

"This isn't right," I tell him urgently even though I was the one who started this. "This is... You can't take the blame. We can't do this at all. It would really make me a slut and—"

He squeezes my ass so hard that I have to finish on a moan, on a deep arch of my back. And then he squeezes it again, not that hard, but it still smarts, for good measure. Then, growling, "If you're going to call yourself a slut, then you'd better change it to *my* slut."

I go still. "What?"

He nails me with his gaze, his jaw hard. "Because I'm making you, aren't I? I'm *making* you my slut."

My entire body clenches with his words and I have to fist his shirt and curl my toes. I have to stop breathing for a second to let his words sink in.

"I'm *making* you my baby. I'm *making* you my fucking sweetheart," he continues. "And I dare them to say otherwise. I dare the world to question me. I fucking dare them to tear us apart."

Maybe it's crazy, but I wanted to be his slut.

I wanted to be reckless and impulsive and insane for him.

"Yours," I whisper.

"Mine," he agrees on a growl.

"And are you mine?"

Something big passes through his features. "If I could be anyone's, I'd be yours."

My heart squeezes so hard that my eyes sting. "I always wanted you to be the one to keep me safe. I wanted you to be the one who puts a leash on me, who protects me. I wanted you to be my bodyguard, my daddy."

But you hurt me...

His nostrils flare with possessiveness as he declares, as if he heard me, "And I will make it up to you. Until he gets you, you're mine. Until you're married, you're under my protection, aren't you?"

"Yes."

"Good." His chest breathes out with relief like he needed me to accept that; that I'm his until I become his brother's. "So tell me what you'll tell them."

"I didn't want it," I whisper.

And oh my God, oh my fucking God, I think I come.

I think I come just by saying those words.

Just by looking at his face when I say them.

All dark and flushed. All possessive and determined.

All cold and cruel.

So beautiful.

"Exactly," he whispers back, bringing his hand away from my face and gripping my thighs.

My bare thighs and I jump.

I don't even know when he got his hand under my dress because up until now, everything was covered down there. But suddenly, it's not. My dress has ridden up and it's gotten right there.

Right up where my aching pussy is.

I can see his dusky fingers over my honey thighs, gripping them roughly.

Tenderly.

Because even though he's doing this to me, I also want him to do this.

"My daddy did this," I say, fisting his collar.

"Yeah, he couldn't stop himself," he says gutturally.

"Why not?"

"Because"—he digs his fingers harder—"you got engaged tonight, didn't you?"

"Yeah."

"Someone, a motherfucking asshole, put his ring on your finger."

I jerk and writhe against him. "But he's a... He's a good guy. He's—"

"Everyone who wants you is an asshole," he growls. "And he gets to have you, so he's the biggest asshole on this planet."

I shake my head. "But—"

"So he *had* to follow you, didn't he, your daddy," he goes on, cutting me off. "I had to follow you in here because I got jealous. Because your daddy needed to lay his claim on you. *Because*"—his eyes ripple with authority, with possessiveness—"you were his before you were someone else's."

God, yes.

Yes, I'm his.

My hands pull at his collar then as I twist my hips against his torso. "But I told him to get out."

"He didn't listen though, did he?"

"No."

"That's because"—he fists my dress tightly—"he saw how easy it was going to be. How *easy* it was going to be to get to that pussy."

"Easy."

"Uh-huh. Because you're not wearing any panties, are you?"

My breath hitches. "I... This dress doesn't really a-allow for them."

A puff of breath escapes him, and he digs his fingers into my flesh for a second before stepping back and lowering my shaking legs to the ground.

He doesn't let me go, though.

Keeping his hands on my thighs, he keeps my balance. He keeps me stuck to the wall and lowers himself on the floor. He goes down on his knees and slides the hem of my dress up.

"What..." I breathe out. "What are you doing?"

"Getting what I came for."

And I have to grip his shoulders for extra protection because the more skin he reveals, the harder it becomes to keep standing. The more his hands, his large and scrape-y hands ride up my skin, the harder it becomes to breathe. And God, they are large. They are so, so large and dusky and strong looking against the backdrop of my soft skin.

"But I—"

"He got on his knees for you, didn't he? So it's my turn now. He got to put his ring on your finger, so now it's my turn to put my mouth on you. And believe me when I say, baby"—his eyes are pinned on his hands as they move over my thighs, pushing my dress up and up—"your daddy's hungry."

He's watching as he goes up and up.

Until he's right there.

Right where my pussy is, all sloppy and wet.

"And this dress"—he fists the hem—"this dress that you wore for him. You did, didn't you?"

"Uh-huh."

"This dress is making him hungrier." Looking up, he rasps, "It's almost like an invitation, see? *Come and get it, Daddy. Come and get my pretty pink pussy.*"

I want to move. I want to writhe.

I want to hump the air, but he won't let me.

He keeps my hips pinned to the wall and I curl my toes and clench my eyes shut against the wave of arousal. "But I... I didn't mean it. I didn't know. It's just a dress."

He hums and goose bumps rise up on my skin.

"So let this be a lesson," he says, his thumb making circles on my thigh, still keeping my dress just a micro-inch away from where I'm aching. "Let this be a lesson that this is what happens to girls if they wear a dress like that in public. This is what happens when they show off their tight ass to anyone other than their daddy. This is what happens when they leave their juicy little pussy out, for all the world to see." Leaning forward, he takes a whiff of my pussy but through my dress. "Let this be a lesson, baby, that this is what happens when you wear another man's ring instead of Daddy's."

I jerk again or want to.

But I can't because he won't let me go.

So I tug at his collar, my body shaking, my voice shaking. "But I... Please, don't—"

"Don't what?" he asks.

"I..." I swallow, all delirious with lust. "I want to be a vir—"

I don't know why I said that.

I don't know why it even came into my brain.

We weren't even going there, were we? He wasn't even going to go there. But maybe I wanted him to. Maybe that's where *I* wanted to go and oh God, no.

No, no, no.

That can never happen. That's not going to happen.

Even if we play pretend like this.

Even if we make excuses to linger.

His chest shakes with a large exhale. His jaw clenches and it does it so hard that I feel like he will bust his jaw again, all by himself.

"A virgin."

My belly is clenching, shuddering much like my whole body. "Please, Stellan. I... I'll do anything. Just don't—"

"Don't worry," he says, his tone harsh and his face angry. "I'm not going to put my big fucking cock in your tiny little pussy tonight. You know how big it is, don't you? You know it will hurt. You know your cherry will drip down the length of my meat and leave a blood red ring at the base of it. So I'm not going to fuck you where I can't take care of you after. Where I can't wrap you up in silk and soothe the pain with the softest cloth that I can find. Although I have to say that you're always so hot for it, aren't you? You always want more than what you get. You're always so desperate, so fucking needy. Such a fucking slut. And the only reason I don't mind is because the only man you're a whore for is me, isn't it?"

"Yes. For you."

"So for that very reason alone, I'll go easy on you tonight." His fingers still straddle the line of keeping me covered and exposing me any second. "For that reason alone, I'm going to kiss your sweetheart pussy like I kissed your lips. All I'm going to do is eat you, drink from your cherry snatch. But I won't breach her. Nothing will get into your wet fuck hole tonight, not even my tongue. For that very reason, Cherry Lips, your daddy will leave you a virgin for the wedding night."

With that, he pushes the dress up then and exposes my pussy, so wet and sloppy and throbbing that my inner thighs are smeared and takes his first lick.

CHAPTER 5

My *biji* thinks all of this is a bad idea.

First the engagement. Although she definitely thinks that the ring is amazing.

"*Chalo, uss khote de puttar ke bhai ke pass toh thodi akal hai,*" she mutters when I show her the ring. Followed by, "*Haye rabba, anguthi toh dekh lo. Hamari kudi vargi haigi. Ek dum*, first class."

Resting my head on her shoulder, I roll my eyes. "*Biji*, translation please."

She looks to the side and grabs my face.

Planting a big kiss on my forehead, she says, "I love the ring. It's pretty. Just like you and I don't know how those two could be related, let alone twins. When one clearly has excellent taste while the other still can't get his head out of his ass."

It takes me a few seconds to gather my wits about me and whisper, "Thank you."

She waves my compliment away. "But are you sure, *meri bacchi*?"

I swallow. "Yes."

"Because all of this is too soon. Being his girlfriend is one thing, but getting engaged is..." she trails off, shaking her head.

"It's going to be fine. This is the right decision."

It is.

I've thought about it and my decision to say yes *is* the right decision. My decision to trust Shepard is the right decision. Because what made me trust him in the first place still stands true: I can't be trusted because my heart still belongs to the one who doesn't know what to do with it. And if Shepard can fix it, fix me, then I should let him.

Besides, minus a few road bumps, the plan is the same.

To be the best fiancée to him.

Taking a bite out of her Pop-Tart, she says, "I still don't like that you're going on the road."

Pop-Tarts are her favorites, so I bring them with me almost every visit. Along with *kulfi*, an Indian ice cream and *gulab jamun*, an Indian dessert. Usually, we watch movies, but today, we're simply lounging on her bed, eating Pop-Tarts and shooting the shit. While her admirers go in and out, bringing her roses.

I twirl one in my hand. "Why not?"

Roses are my favorite flower.

I know, I know. I dream about the pink magnolias enough, but they're my second favorites.

My top favorite will always be roses. They're pretty and pink and velvety. Plus, they also remind me of a certain someone and his mouth. So ever since I've met him, I've taken to stealing some from my *biji*.

It's pathetic, I know.

But no one has ever given me roses, so my options are kind of limited. I could go out and just buy them, but I think that's more pathetic than never receiving one.

So stealing it is.

She looks back at me. "Because he's going to be there."

I squirm, hugging the rose to my chest. "It's okay. It's fine. I'm engaged now." I show her my ring again. "It's all good. I'm moving on from him. And this time I really mean it."

Aside from what happened in the bathroom yesterday, that is.

Okay, I know what I did was bad. No matter how much he tried to absolve me of it. And I also know it can't happen again. I *won't* let it happen again. My only excuse for this one time is that I have no excuse.

I did it willingly and with my complete volition.

I betrayed my fiancé.

And the only thing I can do now is that I never do it again.

"Well, maybe this will help him get his head out of his ass. Seeing another man's ring on your finger."

"That's not what I'm trying to do here, *Biji*," I tell her one more time. "You know that. I was never trying to do that."

She huffs and looks away.

With that thought, I say goodbye to *Biji* and go home to pack. My mother, of course, isn't happy about me going on the road with the team. But since I'm engaged now and Shep was extremely happy when he heard about me joining him, she couldn't stay no. She did say she'd regularly check up on me though.

It takes me a day to get my affairs in order: taking a leave of absence at college for the next few weeks, which my dean wasn't happy about, but since I'm a rich, spoiled girl and he knows my dad, he let me go with the condition that I turn in my assignments and complete my homework on time.

I also let my drama professor know that I'm going away. This one hurt me a little bit because right after the play, he had told me about this great drama camp opportunity. He said that I should apply for it and that he'd help me. He said I have a gift and that he'd be honored to help me reach my goals. I just about broke down crying. Anyway, at my news of going on the road, he was a bit disappointed, but he assured me that we could discuss my application over Zoom calls. Not to mention, I could join the classes via Zoom.

Shepard picks me up for the bus the next day. I'm cautiously positive about the days to come, but then the first thing I see when I board the bus is *him*.

It's one those big buses with rows of seats up front, which are all full, and a couple of private rooms in the back in addition to the bathroom. There are a couple of booth-type thingies too, all the way in the back, just off the private rooms with a table in the middle, which is where he sits, tucked away in a corner with a clipboard.

It's not as if I wasn't expecting to see him, but for a few seconds, I can't take my eyes off him.

I've of course seen him in his athletic T-shirts that show off every single bulge of his sculpted muscles, every single flex as he moves and breathes, and those gray sweatpants that he wears with them. But this is the first time I'm seeing him *after* that night.

After what happened.

After how he...

And as if he hears my thoughts, he looks up.

His eyes landing on me.

Like he knew I was standing there all along and maybe he did. He flicks his gaze over my features and he licks his lips.

All rapidly. All quickly.

As though he was doing it as an afterthought before going back to his clipboard. But I'm the one who has to suffer the consequences. I'm the one whose steps falter to the point that my *fiancé* has to grip my hand, steady me, and ask, "You okay?"

I press my hand in his. "Y-yes."

He looks me over before saying, "Come on."

After that, I keep my head down and decide that it's best if I don't look at him at all. No good can come of this. But then I realize we aren't stopping. As in we keep going down the aisle until we reach the last couple of seats. Just before that booth-like thingy where *he* is sitting. And before I can protest—although I'm not sure what I'll do to protest; the rest of the seats are filled anyway—Shepard is stepping aside so I can slide in and he's taking a seat beside me.

Which is how I come to spend the next three hours, all tight and rigid in my seat, all squirmy and hyperaware, my body tingling and that ache in my pussy. So I'm relieved when we reach our destination and check into a hotel. But as it turns out, even that poses a problem for two reasons.

Number one: when we go to the reception, it occurs to me that I may have to share a room with my fiancé. The fact that I'm balking at that should be indication enough that I'm not the best fiancée in the world and Shep is better off without me. But then he says that we have two separate rooms.

"Yeah, since you were a last-minute add-on," he explains with a shrug, "and my room isn't that big to begin with, it's just better if you have your own space. Plus, on the road, I need to focus, yeah? I need to focus on my game, on the plays and whatnot. You'd just be in the way. So it's really for the best, babe."

I'm not going to lie, I'm a little... hurt. I didn't know he thought that I was in his way. Not as his fiancée but as his best friend. But I wave it all away and grab the keycard that he then gives me before dropping me off at my room two floors down from his room.

And then comes problem number two: my room happens to be on the same floor as *his*. Something Shep casually mentions as he's dropping me off. I start to freak out at the news and feel a certain type of excitement that again does not bode well if I want to move on.

But it is what it is, and I'll have to deal with it. Besides, it's not as if we're going to run into each other or anything. He'll be at practice and I'll just hang out in my room. I'm on the bed, doing just that when I hear a knock at my door. And just by the two authoritative thuds on the wood, I know who it is. With a pounding heart, I jump off the bed and open the door to reveal him.

With a thick frown and super angry-looking.

"Hey," I breathe out.

His still-bruised jaw tenses. "What the fuck are you doing here?"

At the sight of him, all my good sense vanishes and I'm just... needy. Still, I keep my wits about me and say, my words coming out as a question, "Uh, this is my room."

His jaw tenses harder and his chest punches out with a large breath. "*Why* is this your room?"

I swallow and then blurt out, "I'm not going to do it with you."

"What?"

Oh God.

Why did I have to say that? Why the fuck did I have to say anything regarding that?

I shake my head. "Nothing."

He studies me for a second. "If by *it* you mean fucking, then you can relax. I'm not here for that."

My thighs clench at his *fucking*. "Right. Of course I didn't—"

"Although it's curious that that's the very first thing you thought of."

"I'm..." I blush. "I mean, can you blame me after what happened? It was a mistake and—"

"What happened," he says, his eyes glinting, "was not a mistake."

My heart's pounding. "But it can never happen again."

He watches me for a second before saying, "Was this your idea? Staying in two different rooms?"

I'm a little thrown off by his change of topic and how he didn't agree with me about it not happening again, but I let it slide. Because I didn't even want to talk about it in the first place. Me and my stupid mouth.

"No, it wasn't. It was his." Then, "He said that rooms were booked separately and he needed his space to focus."

"What?" he bites out.

"Yes, that's what he said and—"

He breathes out sharply, stepping back. "I'm going to go have a talk with him."

"What?" I step forward, grabbing the sleeve of his T-shirt. "No. You're not."

He's not looking at me, though. His face is dipped, and his eyes are on my hand fisting his T-shirt. The heat of his dark gaze is enough to let me move it, but I stand firm.

And call out, "Stellan?"

He lifts his eyes. "What?"

I want to say other things, other important things, but I end up asking, "Is that what you really want? Me sharing a room with... him?"

I shouldn't have asked him that. It's none of his business.

But God, I...

I couldn't help myself.

His chest moves again. Not only that, though. I see the vein on the side of his neck pulsating as well with how tight he's holding himself.

"No."

"So then—"

"What I want doesn't matter, does it?"

I let a few beats pass before I say, "Well, this is what *I* want. I want a separate room and I want space, so."

He does the same, letting a few beats pass before speaking. "You're all alone here."

I let go of his sleeve and fold my arms across my chest. "So? I live in a house all alone."

"That's because your parents are dickheads."

"No, they know that I can handle myself," I tell him. "That is to say I *can* handle myself, thank you very much."

He grits his teeth. "You're not fucking welcome because you can't. Because what the fuck are you going to do if someone sneaks into your room in the middle of the night? Dance him to death?"

"For your information, there's a thing called hotel security, okay?" I raise my eyebrows. "They have that here. And secondly, there's another thing called a lock. This thing here"—I point to the knob—"you turn it a certain way and it locks the door. From the *inside*, okay? So you can rest easy."

And I give myself credit for not stumbling my way through that speech because all through my explanation, he doesn't move his eyes away from me. He doesn't look anywhere else, least of all the knob I was pointing at. And gosh, he can be scary like this.

All authoritative and commanding.

Then he flicks his eyes downward, taking in the fluttering pulse on the side of my neck, my trembling chest, my bare arms, my night pajamas as a whole. Making me realize they're skimpy. Spaghetti-sleeved top with a wide neck and short shorts. All lacy and baby pink.

I curl my toes on the carpet as he takes his time perusing my body.

And I bite my lip when he reaches my feet and takes in my curled toes.

Then, bringing his gaze up, "If someone wants to sneak into your room in the middle of the night, trust me when I say, no amount of security or locks guarding your door is going to stop him. A firing squad even couldn't stop him. He'll bust through your door as he's taking bullets after bullets just so he gets to look at your face before he takes his last breath, yeah?"

My heart is racing.

My breaths are messy.

And gosh, that ache in my tummy has traveled down to my pussy now.

"Y-you would," I whisper.

"What?"

I lick my trembling lips. "You would stop him." His nostrils flare and I keep going, "Your room's on the same floor, isn't it? Shep told me when he was bringing me up. So *you* could guard my door, if you're so worried about someone getting in. You're my self-appointed bodyguard anyway."

Things flash in his eyes then.

Dark things.

Fiery things. Molten things.

Possessive things.

"We both know that's not what I am," he rasps. "Because that's not what you *need*."

"You think I..." I clutch the doorknob tightly, shifting on my feet, trying to get rid of the hurt. "I need a daddy?"

"I think you need someone to take care of you and keep you safe twenty-four seven," he growls.

I blush, shifting on my feet again, and he notices my movements.

I know he noticed them before, but this time, he takes a whiff, a visible whiff of the air as if smelling me. Like he did the other night and holy God, I melt.

I melt right there on the floor at his feet.

Somehow, I try to put words together. "Fine then. The job's already yours. Can I please go to sleep now?"

Because this is too much.

His proximity. His authority.

His care.

No, Isadora. He does not care about you. Not really.

Not how you want him to.

The fact that I just want to kiss him and kiss him. I even taste him on my tongue and we're standing six feet apart.

He looks me over one last time before stepping back again. "Lock your door."

I roll my eyes before sing-songing, "Yes, Daddy."

The last thing I see before I shut the door in his face is his flared eyes and tight fists.

So yeah, that's just day one.

Over the next few days, we develop a routine. Lots of bus travel where Shep and I sit in the same seat and *he* sits right behind us. I'm not going to say that my awareness of him has lessened. Oh gosh no. I still feel his gaze, and I still tingle and hurt everywhere, but I will say that I think I've learned to handle it better.

Besides, I have homework.

Ew.

Which I have to do *myself*.

Double ew.

So I spend the long hours on the bus, trying to do what God only intended I have someone else do for me. Until one particularly frustrating day I get a text:

WILDFIRE THORN

Is it history?

I stiffen at his message and first go to hide it from Shepard. But then I remember that he's up front, shooting the shit with some of the guys: Ledger, Riot, Isiah. Actually, he's been doing that a lot. As in, we sit together for a little while and then he gets up to go talk to the guys, leaving me alone with the only person sitting in the corner, his twin brother. He's uber popular, plus the captain of the team, so I totally get it. I do miss my best friend, though; I'm not going to lie, but again, I won't complain. I have no right to.

I will simply trust him and the process.

Looking down at the phone, I tap out a reply.

ISADORA

No. Math.

WILDFIRE THORN

Ah, that's why you look like your dog died.

I roll my eyes at the phone.

ISADORA

I wouldn't have a dog. If anything, I'd have a cat.

With long, sharp claws. 🗡 🗡 🗡 Who'd look at everyone with disdain including me and especially you.

And second, how do you know what I look like when you're soooo busy with whatever's on that clipboard?

> **WILDFIRE THORN**
> It's hard to be busy with my clipboard when you sigh every five seconds and disturb me.

> **ISADORA**
> Oh, I'm sorry, I didn't know the sound of my breathing was so objectionable to you. 😊😊😊

> **WILDFIRE THORN**
> And why don't you sheath your kitty's claws and tell me what your assignment is about?

I sit up straight then.
I so, *so* want to look behind me.
God.
I so want to look at his face.
Just once.
Because he's asking to do my homework, isn't he?
But I can't.

Not only is Shepard up ahead, in my line of vision, but also because if I do look at his face, I may spontaneously combust. With a pounding heart, I type out:

> **ISADORA**
> So you can do my homework for me?

> **WILDFIRE THORN**
> So that in turn I can focus on my work, yes.

I breathe out loudly.
Just to annoy him.
And I swear I hear a deep but low chuckle from behind me.
It settles in my belly as a warm, sticky puddle of something sweet.

> **ISADORA**
> You don't have to be so mean about it. Math is hard. 😊😊 😊😊

> **WILDFIRE THORN**
> Not for me, it isn't.

> **ISADORA**
> That's because you're weird. 😊😊😊

> **WILDFIRE THORN**
> I'm also the guy who's going to get you a passing grade on your homework.
>
> So how about we wrap up this chitchat and you let me help you.

I don't.
I will *not* stop chitchatting with him.

> **ISADORA**
> I have no clue how your baby sister hasn't killed you yet.
> If this is how you treat people her age, I don't want to have anything to do with you.

> **WILDFIRE THORN**
> If she had, you'd be failing every class right now. So you should really thank her.
> And second, you're younger than my baby sister. There's a difference.

> **ISADORA**
> Yeah? What's the difference?

> **WILDFIRE THORN**
> The difference is that you call me by a name that gives me the right to take care of you in all the fucking ways. So stop arguing with me and let me do my job.

I groan loudly, throwing my head back.

Again, I hear a chuckle, low and deep, and again it settles like a gooey puddle of something sweet.

> **ISADORA**
> Fine, you win! 😭😭😭

And then I email him the assignment and shut my stupid laptop.

> **WILDFIRE THORN**
> You should save that response for the future.

> **ISADORA**
> Yeah, why?

> **WILDFIRE THORN**
> Because you've got a habit of arguing with me and I have a habit of winning them.

So from then on, he does my homework and writes my assignments.

Which again cannot be good for the cause—me moving on from him—but he won't budge. I don't even know how he has the time to do any of it, but his response is always, *you're on the road because of me, so it's my responsibility.*

Which he is super big on, of course.
Being responsible.
Doing the work.

Doing his job.

As days pass, I notice that that's all he does, though.

He *works*.

He sits in a corner either busy on his clipboard or watching game replays while discussing strategies with Coach Thorne. But he never, not ever, gets involved with the guys. He hardly ever talks to them outside of work talk. Even Coach Thorne does that and I still maintain that he's so scary.

Which leads me to conclude what I already knew: he's alone.

He's lonely.

Despite having siblings, he's still the outsider. And then there's the fact that he believes he's dangerous, a shitty brother, which I don't understand.

So I decide that I have a responsibility too.

Despite what he did and what my cause is, I'm going to draw him out of his hard, icy shell. I'll somehow make it so that he isn't as lonely. Especially when so many people are around and especially when they're so nice.

I have to say that all the guys have been very respectful toward me. Maybe because I'm the boss's daughter or because I'm the captain's fiancée. Whatever it is, they don't treat me like a pariah. I'm extremely thankful for that, especially because I was a little afraid they may keep their distance because of all the nasty rumors about me.

Since we're all traveling together, I've managed to form some nice friendships. I particularly like Isiah—he's hilarious; I also like Christopher; his mom makes the best baklava in the whole world and is very particular about parceling it no matter where he goes. Something that the team's nutritionist isn't very happy about. Ledger is cool too even though he more grunts than talks and is always on FaceTime with Tempest and their twins. Not to mention, Riot is one of the good ones as well. Even though he too is always FaceTiming Sophie, his three-year-old daughter, and Meadow.

So when the guys play poker to kill time, I join them and try to have *him* join us too. Not too blatantly but in subtle ways. Like laughing too hard with them so he takes notice. Or playing the damsel in distress who doesn't understand a thing about poker and is losing. That is true, though; I don't. And Shepard is so competitive that when we play teams, he won't pick me or stop to explain the rules—which is surprising if I do say so myself because in the past when we've played games like this, he always made sure to stop and explain the rules to me, much to everyone else's dismay—but it's fine. It works to my advantage.

Or it should.

But so far, I've had no luck in drawing him out whatsoever. Even when the noise gets super loud, he keeps his head down and continues working.

God, the focus on this man.

The world would be burning down around him, and he wouldn't let go of that stupid clipboard.

So then I try something different.

It's my personal mission to introduce Bollywood movies to as many people as I can. Usually, they all watch game replays on this big TV up front or some other sports channels or even the news. But one day, I break the norm and make them watch one of my favorites.

It's about this guy, a journalist who's traveling to cover an event for his show. And on the way over, he meets a mysterious girl at a train station and falls in love with her. But turns out that mysterious girl belongs to a group of terrorists who are planning an attack on the capital on Independence Day.

It's a tragic love story and I love it.

And I'm both happy and surprised to say that most of these macho, athletic men think so too. But since they're 'men,' they show their frustration by cursing at the TV or by booing or throwing tantrums and stalking off. Isiah did that twice but came back both times. Riot kept grumbling, *fuck this shit*. Ledger simply walked away before the climax, saying, *he doesn't need this shit before the game*. And Shepard glared at me several times during the movie. I even caught a few sniffles here and there.

Although throughout all this, *he* didn't say a word.

He probably didn't even look up from his clipboard even when this famous song came on. When the hero, since he's the hero and since this is a movie, *dances* on the top of a moving train. From what *Biji* tells me, this song is one of the most iconic moments of Indian cinema and is so ingrained in the Indian pop culture that people talk about it to this freaking day.

I mean, it sparked a fucking debate among the guys.

It *did*. I'm not even lying.

They all wanted to chip in and argue if this could be done in real life. And I thought maybe now, *now* he'd say something. Just to dismiss the whole concept and quote physics and common sense that hey, this is foolish. But he didn't.

So frustrated and bored because I had no interest in hearing the debate if he wasn't going to chip in, I threw my hands up and said, "Okay, stop. I don't care what you guys think. If a guy does that for me, if a guy dances on the top of a train for me, I'm his. For life. I'm giving up my freaking life to be his. End of discussion."

Of course it wasn't the end of discussion.

Because then the catcalling began and all the ridiculous comments about how Shepard needs to find a way to make this stunt happen to impress me.

Ugh.

In any case, all my ideas to draw him out have majorly flopped and at the end of the movie day, I'm not feeling very enthusiastic about things. So when we reach our hotel, I have an early dinner with Isiah, Riot, Ledger, and Shep at the restaurant downstairs before saying goodbye and going up to my room. They're still back at the table, winding down, but I'm tired and miffed, and I just want a long shower before I hit the bed.

And just to mention, I'm still not rooming with my fiancé. Not that I expected to since what he said about needing his space during the season was pretty definitive but still. My room, as it has been for the past couple of weeks, on a different floor than his and on the same floor as *his*. Again, I'm not sure who's booking these rooms, but somehow, they have a very uncanny and uncomfortable knack of putting me with the wrong twin.

But as soon as I step on the elevator, which is crowded and almost full, all my thoughts about hitting the bed vanish.

Because *he's* there.

CHAPTER 6

He stands in the corner.

All tall and broad and God, so handsome. His eyes lock with mine and I have to remind myself to get on before the doors close.

I find a spot just by the buttons, all the way in the front while he's all the way in the back. Still, though, it feels like he's close. It feels like there's no one between us. It feels like the air's running out of my body and my legs are about to give in.

Because he's looking at me.

I know he is.

I can feel his gaze.

It's like the flame of a candle, the match, his cigarette that he's holding too close to my body, making me heat up. My skin. My belly. The place between my thighs that only he knows what it tastes like.

The elevator stops on every floor almost and slowly people disappear.

Until there's only the two of us.

And then I have to, *have* to, grab hold of the steel bar so I don't fall. Because this is the first time we've been alone like this since the night he came to my room, all angry about my accommodations, a week ago. So all the life's gone out of my legs and I have no energy left to support myself.

Actually no, I'm lying.

I do have the energy. I *do*. And I realize that when he closes the distance between us. Up until now, we were standing on the opposite sides of the elevator, but now that we're alone, he steps up to me, crowding my back, and that's when all my energy flows out of me and I sag.

I sag against him.

My back hitting his massive chest.

Massive and hard and solid and heaving chest.

Or maybe he makes it so. I don't know. Maybe he *pulls* me toward him until our bodies touch with only a graze of his finger. By only tracing the column of my neck with his rough digit from behind.

"What..." I swallow, my hands fisted, the spot where he's touching me tingling. "What are you doing?"

His words waft over my skin like a warm breath. "Trying to figure out something."

"F-figure out what?"

"If it's just me or if you're," he rasps, his finger now just below my ear, swirling, "really as soft and smooth as I remember."

I have to clench my eyes shut then, my belly tightening. "Stellan, you—"

I think he comes closer then.

I feel his body shifting against mine and then his plump mouth at my ear, whispering, "It's not just me."

Biting my lip hard, I say, "I-I don't think this is appropriate."

"Hmm."

"Can you—"

This time, he stops my words by stopping the elevator.

Yeah, he does that.

Much to my shock, he reaches from behind me and very calmly presses the emergency stop button, bringing us to a screeching halt. I try to turn around to face him, but he's still crowding me from behind and won't give me the space to do so.

Still, I whisper, "Why did you... Why did you do that?"

"Because I want to do..." He pauses a second, bringing his hand back, and now, from what I can feel, rubbing the strands of my hair. "*It* with you."

My whole body freezes and explodes at the same time. Both no and yes are at the tip of my tongue at the same time. Which is why I stumble and stutter out words, "You... It... I don't think w-we—"

"Relax." He tugs a strand of my hair. "I'm just here to ask a question."

I wish I could say that I do relax.

Or rather that's all I do.

But I don't.

I do let out a relieved breath, but there's also a pit of disappointment in my belly. Ignoring all that, though, I ask, "What question?"

"If it really does it for you," he goes on, sifting through my hair, his breath on the side of my neck. "Dancing on the top of a moving train."

I fist my dress. "You were l-listening?"

"Hard not to," he replies, moving on to the right strap of my dress, tracing it with his thumb. "When you were making such a ruckus."

"I wasn't—"

"You know it's a stupid thing to do, don't you?"

"I knew you'd say that."

"Not to mention, dangerous."

"I knew you'd say that too."

"In conclusion, only an idiot with no common sense would do something like that."

Despite everything, I laugh. "God, you're so grumpy."

He tucks his thumb under my little strap and pulls at it. "That and I hate dancing."

The strap slides off my shoulder and drops down my arm, making my breath catch in my throat. "I could... I could help you."

Now that my strap is gone, he trails his fingers in circles on my strapless shoulder. "Help me with what?"

I fist and fist my dress, my skin shivering, my thoughts scattering in the wind at his touch. "I could... I could teach you."

"To dance."

"Yes."

"No, I think I'm okay."

I don't know why, but I keep at it. "I mean, you could l-learn to like it."

"No."

"It's really fun, though, I promise."

"I'm allergic to fun."

Right.

I know that. I mean, if I don't know that by this point, then I don't know what the fuck I'm doing with my life anymore. But then again, I think I *do* know. I do know what I'm doing, what I'm talking about.

I'm not talking about dancing at all, am I?

I'm talking about... love. I'm talking about how I could teach him to love and maybe he could learn to love... *me*. And if that happens, then maybe we could live happily ever after.

There are a lot of ifs here, though. Plus the little fact that I'm engaged to his twin brother and I'm supposed to be moving on from him. Oh and he lied to me and broke my heart, and I'm angry at him.

But Jesus Christ, it's so hard.

"So are you going to stop?" he asks then, his fingers still working on my skin.

"S-stop what?"

"Trying to get my attention."

"I'm not trying—"

"If you've got something to say," he goes on, "now's your chance."

I breathe out and bite my lip. "Why don't you ever talk to the guys?"

"I talk to the guys."

"No, as in like why don't you ever have fun with them?"

"Because I just said I'm allergic to fun and that's not my job."

"But you're always doing your job," I protest.

"That's what they pay me for."

I turn my face to the side, trying to catch the sight of his face in my periphery. But maybe he's too tall for me to do that or he has angled himself in a way that all I manage to get is the cut of his bruised jaw. Either way, I don't get to look at him more than that.

Oh, and his maddening finger, playing with my strap, my skin, my hair.

"But you don't even like your job," I remind him.

"I don't have to like it to do it well," he reminds me back.

"But, Stellan," I say exasperated. "You don't take nights off. You don't like parties. You don't drink and I understand why, but... I think you're lonely and you need friends. I think you take everything super seriously. You need to relax a little. You need..."

"I need what?"

I sigh. "A life. You need a life."

He exhales a long breath as well. "You worried about my life?"

"Yes."

I'm worried about my life too, but that's not the point right now.

"Well, there's a way to fix it," he shares.

I perk up. "What?"

"It involves a thing called *it*," he growls lowly, "that unfortunately we're not going to do. Because you're engaged to my brother, and you think it's inappropriate."

I don't know how I manage to put together words, but I somehow do. "You don't think that it's inappropriate?"

"No," he growls, sending shivers down my spine. "Because all I can think about is you. And what you taste like and what you feel like on my tongue. All I can think about is getting to taste you, taste her, again. *Because* all I can think about, Dora, is how much better it'll feel and how much better she'll taste if I manage to get inside. If somehow, some-fucking-way, I manage to get into that cherry-flavored pussy."

Oh God.

I think I'm... I think I just came. Or if not then, I'm so close to coming.

"But I can't do any of that, can I? Because you insist on staying a virgin. And you should. You should save it. You should give it to someone who'll make love to you," he seethes, his voice thick and angry and a little tortured.

"And y-you won't?"

"No," he rasps. "I'll fuck you."

"What's"—I have to catch my breath here—"the difference?"

"The difference is that I want to stretch your pink little pussy out and mold it to the shape of my dick. So that only I get to fuck it. I want to rip that cherry from you and wear it on my dick like a badge of honor. The *difference* is that I don't just want to pop that fresh cherry and fuck it out of you. I want to fuck you every day. Every night. I want to fuck you until I don't want to fuck you anymore. I want to use you to get off and get you off and then leave. Like I wanted to do when I was blackmailing you. So yeah, you should stay a virgin," he growls. "For that asshole. As if he already doesn't have everything because he gets to spend his godforsaken life with you. But I don't have to like it. I don't have to like the fact that he gets you while I don't. So again, no. I don't think it's inappropriate because I don't have any space left in my brain to think about that when all of it is taken up by my personal fucking Lolita."

I am that.

I am his Lolita.

And he wants me. He wants me so badly.

Sometimes I think he wants me more than I want him. And that's saying something because all I've done is want him since the moment I saw him. All I've done is live lifetimes in the year that I've wanted him.

So why can't I have him? Why can't he have me?

What's stopping us again?

"So you're going to stop flirting with the guys," he continues. "Or making them watch shitty fucking movies, is that clear? I'm already walking on broken glass every fucking minute of every fucking day that I have to see you with him. I will not sit there and watch you be the ray of sunshine that you are that other guys fight to bask in, is that clear? I will not be subjected to it and I will not allow it. Or trust me when I say each one of those guys will be running drills until the end of time."

"Okay," I agree hastily. "I-I won't."

He breathes for a few seconds.

Then, in response, he tucks his thumb under my strap again and pulls it up, sliding it back into place on my shoulder. Reaching forward, he presses that button again and gets the elevator going. When it reaches our floor, I'm the first to alight and walk down the hallway. I feel him behind me, but I don't look back, and when I get into my room, I shut the door and press my back against it before sliding down to the floor and hiding my face in my knees.

Wondering once again, what the fuck is stopping us.

The answer to that—among other things—is my mother.

Who, as she promised, calls me every day.

Mostly to remind me of her threat. Sometimes she berates me for my dress choices. Sometimes she tells me that I was standing a little too close to another player on the team during the press conference or sometimes she simply tells me off for no reason other than the fact that she loves to tear me down.

But no matter what she says, I am acutely aware of the fact that I need to toe the line.

Which is fine because I have no intention of doing anything inappropriate.

∼

Over the last couple of weeks, I've been to enough victory parties on the road that I know what to expect. Large crowds, loud music, lots of booze—I don't think players drink a lot, though, because they're all on a strict regimen, but still—and adrenaline. I also know that, like the players, I won't be touching a drop of that booze. Thanks to my self-appointed bodyguard who frowns upon everything fun.

Including dancing.

I haven't tried doing that, though. Mostly because in my heart of hearts, the only person I want to dance with is the one who hates dancing. And even though I know he'll let me dance with my fiancé if I wanted to, I just don't want to put him through that.

Which, again if we're being honest, has to the most twisted thing ever.

That I won't dance with my fiancé because I don't want to make his twin brother jealous. I won't even flirt with my fiancé or laugh with him like I used to. I won't hold hands with him or indulge in any public displays of affection with him. All because I know his twin brother won't like it.

And my fiancé has tried to get me to do all that too.

Despite staying on two different floors and always being too busy to spend any one-on-one time with me, Shepard has tried to be openly affectionate with me. He has tried to hold hands or include me in jokes. He's tried to be goofy with me, but I've more or less pulled back each time.

Mostly because he does it when *he's* around.

Like on the bus or at parties like these.

Which sometimes makes me think whether he's trying to do what I used to do: make him jealous. I had my reasons and I guess he has his. He's probably still angry at Stellan for pulling what he did.

And there's their rocky relationship.

Anyway, as soon as we arrive at *this* victory party, I feel like it's going to end in disaster. Maybe because it's in a bar that's too crowded for my liking. Or the fact that everyone's a little too drunk by the time we get there. Or it could be that this is the home base for the team that lost so the crowd is angry at us, the intruders.

Whatever it is, I know it's not going to be a good time.

Sure enough, ten minutes into our arrival, a fight breaks out between a few of the bar patrons and some guys on the team. When that's settled, there's some catcalling and booing. We get a reprieve for about twenty minutes, when a group of cheerleaders approach the guys on the team.

Before I take a little bathroom break, I watch them disappear in the crowd one by one. As I'm coming back, I'm waylaid by a couple of drunk guys. They try to chat me up and flirt with me. One of them offers me a drink, which I politely decline. When I tell them that I need to go, they try to get into my space and touch me.

While I have plenty of experience with dealing with pushy men, I still get a little scared about how loud and brash they're being. I try to catch Shep's eyes over their shoulders, maybe call out to him even though I don't think he'll hear me over the din, when I find him flirting with a couple of those cheerleaders.

For a second, I can't figure out why I'm frozen by this. I mean, I don't mind

—I really do not—that he's flirting with other girls. That's not the reason for my immobility. And then it occurs to me.

I'm frozen because I *don't* mind. I'm not at all uncomfortable by this. Or jealous by him choosing to flirt with other girls. In fact, I'm relieved. That his attention is occupied elsewhere, and he probably won't be flirting with me, thereby torturing his twin brother.

It's the same thing I felt—the relief—when Shepard decided to have two different rooms. And while back then I thought it would pass and I'd grow more comfortable with us being engaged, now I don't think so.

I haven't grown comfortable at all.

In fact, I've grown even more restless over the last couple of weeks. I've grown even more antsy and unhappy and downright miserable that the man I'm in love with is tormented and I can't be with him. I can't do anything to ease his misery, to soothe him.

So I can't do this, can I?

I can't.

I can't be engaged to Shepard. I know he's trying to help me. He's trying to fix things. But I have to fix things myself. I can't use him as a crutch anymore. I can't *use* him period; he's my friend and this is *my* life.

Coming back to the moment, I try to break away from the guys. I try to go to Shepard and ask him if he could talk to me. Now that I know I can't wait a second longer. But these guys won't give me an opening and my fear ratchets up. I'm about to really make a run for it when I see a hand appear on one of the guys' chests.

It's large and dusky, and it's splayed wide with long fingers.

And it's accompanied by a growled, "Back away."

It comes from behind me, that growl, and the guy it's addressed to goes wide-eyed at *his* arrival. I know who it is, of course.

As if I wouldn't know.

They could take away my vision and I'd still know who it was just by the sound of his voice. They could take away my hearing too and I'd still know who it was just by the scent of his skin.

I'd know him anywhere.

He's the man I'm in love with and no matter what I do, I can't stop. No matter how much it hurts, I can't stop.

He's like a drug, see.

He's like that cigarette he smokes. And while he can pace himself and indulge in only one per day, I can't. While he can control his bad habit, I'm a full-blown addict. While he knows how to handle the poison in his veins, my blood is downright toxic by now.

I can't pace myself. I don't know how.

I don't know how to measure my love or who to give it to or how *not* to give it to the one who doesn't know what to do with it. All I know is to love.

I'm fire, aren't I?

All I know is to burn.

I don't even notice when those guys skitter away. I'm too busy basking in his heat, his wildfire. I'm too busy leaning against his chest like I had done in the elevator.

Or at least I try to.

He stops me at the last minute, wrapping his fingers around my bicep. Flexing his grip, he growls in my ear, much like in the elevator. "You're coming with me."

I nod.

Without hesitation. Without preservation.

And then, he's dragging me out of the bar, his fingers threaded with mine, tight and braided as if for life. I look down at our entwined fingers as he keeps dragging me and how *right* it feels. How destined. And meant to be.

Destiny, my brain supplies on a whisper.

If he's meant to hurt me, I can't stop him. If he's meant to break my heart, I can't do anything but hope that it's easy for him to break.

In fact, I want to live with a broken heart and a tragic fate.

I want to die at the end of this story.

All through the ride back home in the cab, he's quiet and seething, and I'm quiet and introspective. We reach the hotel, and he ushers me inside. We ride the elevator in pin drop silence and when he walks me to my door, again we don't say a word to each other. He takes the keycard from my hand, slides it in the door, and opens it for me. I step inside, but before he can leave me there, I spin around and decide to finally break the silence.

I'm not sure what I'm going to say, but I have to say *something*.

"Stellan, I—"

"Lock the fucking door," he growls.

And slams the door shut.

CHAPTER 7

I lock the door like he said.
And then stand there.
I stand there and I watch the door — *my* door — that he's essentially shut in *my* face.
I count the seconds.
I wonder how much time is long enough to open it and run after him. But then I think that's the point, isn't it? That's the *whole* point that I don't have to wait anymore.
I don't have to fucking wait.
I can run after him now. I can chase him, be with him. I can be free. I can fly. I can take away his pain now. He doesn't have to walk on broken glass. I'm his.
Nothing is holding me back anymore.
So I throw open my door and...
Well, I come to a stop.
Because the man I was going to run to is right there.
He hasn't left.
He's standing in the middle of the hallway, his legs braced apart and his fists tight.
His eyes on my door.
"Y-you didn't..." I whisper, my eyes wide. "You didn't leave."
"I was trying to figure out something," he says, roughly, his chest heaving.
His repeated words from the elevator yesterday make my heart pound. "Figure out what?"
"How long," he growls, "should I wait before busting through your door?"
"You couldn't bust through my door," I say uselessly, arguing my point from the first night.

"No?"

"No, it was locked."

He studies me and licks his lips. "One day I'm going to sit you down, really gently, and explain to you in a way that will get through your pretty head that when a man's desperate enough to get to you, as desperate as I am right now, no amount of locked doors will stop him from getting inside."

"You would," I remind him.

His chest jerks with a particularly harsh breath. "I would, yeah."

"So problem solved."

"But then who would stop me?"

I look at his agitated features, his towering body, that dark hair and those bruises that have almost completely faded. I look at the man I fell in love with at first sight. And I say the only thing I *can* say.

The truth.

"See, the thing is, Stellan"—I swallow—"that if you're on the other side of the door, I'll unlock it myself and run to you."

Which is exactly what I do.

I run to him and jump into his arms.

And because he's so strong and protective and everything that I've ever wanted and needed, he catches me. He heaves me up, wraps his arms around me and before my next breath, kisses me.

Or more like attacks my mouth.

Which is fine really because I'm doing the same thing.

I'm attacking his mouth and he's attacking mine and I don't even care that maybe we're bruising each other. I don't care if I pull his hair too hard or if he bites me a little brutally. I don't care if his fingers are squeezing my ass in a way that I know he'll leave his fingerprints behind as if my body is a crime scene. Or if I scratch the side of his neck in a way that I think I draw blood.

It all sounds okay to me.

It all sounds like it was supposed to happen. We were supposed to crash like this. Our kiss was supposed to be more like a war than peace.

I mean, we had to wait so long to do it again.

If I'm being honest, it was easier the first time around. That year that I waited—that he waited too; now I know—was easier to survive somehow. But these two weeks were hard. They were probably the longest and hardest two weeks of both our lives.

Maybe because now we know what it feels like.

The taste, the feel, the heat of our mouths.

So I'm glad that when he begins to walk, he doesn't break it. He keeps our lips fused. I hear the thud of the door closing and yet we're still kissing each other, thank God. Although I will say that I'm a little miffed when my back connects with something—a wall, maybe—and he pulls away.

But I guess it's okay. I'll allow it.

Because there are things that need to be said. Things that need to be cleared up so when he gives me a chance to breathe, I pant, adjusting my thighs around him. "Thanks f-for saving me from those guys."

He comes to settle between the cradle of my thighs, pushing our lower bodies together. Then his hands that have come up to my face tighten as he growls, "Because somehow you always need saving, don't you?"

I wrap my arms around his neck and thrust my fingers in his hair. "I'm glad I have y-you."

His features ripple with anger as he fists my hair too. "Yeah, well it makes one of us."

"But I'm safe now. You don't have to be angry."

"I'm always angry," he corrects me, pushing into me some more, making me arch my back. "And the fact that I left you where you shouldn't need to be saved in the first place is what's making me want to put my fist through the wall."

"What?"

"He was supposed to look out for you," he keeps growling, his words hot, his breaths hotter. "He was supposed to not fucking let you go off on your own. What he wasn't supposed to do"—he tugs at my hair—"was chat up a bunch of girls who aren't his fucking fiancée."

"I don't care," I say truthfully, tightening my thighs around his waist. "Stellan, I don't care. I—"

"I'm going to fuck him up," he promises, cutting me off.

"What?"

"I have to fuck him up. I have to teach him a lesson. I have to teach him how to fucking do his job right. How to fucking watch you and look after you and—"

"No," I tell him, digging my heels in the backs of his thighs. "You're not doing anything. You're not saying anything. You're not fucking him up, okay?"

"He needs to—"

"No, Stellan, promise me. *Promise* you'll stay out of this."

I need to handle it.

Me.

No one else.

I need to tell Shepard that this isn't working. That I know he was trying to help me and I *know* that he loves me, but I... I don't. I can't. All my love is already taken. I also know it's going to hurt him. And God, I'd do anything to avoid it. But I already did that before and look where we all ended up. So no, this time I'm going to be truthful and I'm going to come clean.

I'm going to break off the engagement.

But it will be *me* who does that, not him.

So when he still doesn't say anything, his eyes promising punishment and retribution for his twin brother, I insist, "Stellan, I need you to promise me that you won't say anything. And neither will you mess with him. Like you did before. No messing with his game, Stellan."

He growls low in his chest, his eyes flashing.

His jerks my head back a little. Then, leaning even closer to me, his heavily breathing chest dragging across my breasts, he goes, "You know this doesn't bode well for him, don't you?"

"W-what?"

"You," he seethes, "*begging* me to leave him alone. *Pleading* with me to spare the man you're going to marry. That's exactly the kind of thing that'll earn him extra laps around the field tomorrow and every day for the rest of his fucking life. Or until his legs give up, whichever comes first."

"Stellan, you—"

"And this is what he does. He slacks off on the job. He never puts his mind to anything other than his precious fucking soccer. So then I have to come in and pick up his slack," he says. "And I do it because that's the only way I can make up for not being there, for not being his shitty brother. That's the only I can make up for all of it and—"

"Why can't you be there for him?"

Because I want to know.

I *need* to know. I need to know why he thinks the way he thinks. There has to be a reason.

He looks at me like he's only now remembering that I'm here and he's been saying these things. Then, swallowing, "Because I can't."

"I don't –"

"And it doesn't fucking matter right now. Because he's about to be schooled in how to treat you right. How to fucking watch you –"

"I'm not a wayward little girl, okay?"

He pushes his body into mine. "You're *my* girl."

A breath escapes me. "But –"

"And he needs to learn how to fucking treasure you."

I know we're speaking over each other, attacking each other's words like we did our mouths. But I don't want to fight with him. I don't want to argue. I just want him, however I can get him.

I hike my thighs up his waist. "Please, stop. Just… You don't need to do any of those things. You don't —"

"I do though," he insists, his eyes glinting, his breaths still hard. "Because that's not the only thing he's fucking up. That's not the only thing he's not delivering on."

"What are you talking about?"

"What I'm talking about is his fucking promise. The *promise* he made about fixing things."

"About… About fixing my broken h-heart?"

He moves his jaw back and forth for a few moments. "Yeah. About you moving on."

"But I don't think that –"

"You haven't, have you?"

My breath hitches. "N-no."

His nostrils flare and I *think* I see a hint of relief on his face. As if he's glad that I'm still stuck on him. He's glad I haven't moved on.

"You still love me," he rasps, licking his lips.

I caress his harsh jaw. "Yes."

This time, his entire body moves and flares with a breath—a relieved breath; I know for sure—and rubs across mine, making me whimper. And that's how I know that this is the right decision. That being with him, giving him my love, is the right decision.

I mean, look at the way he's all wrapped around me right now. Look at the way the tension has left him. The way he's almost giving me all his weight like whatever burden he's been carrying on his shoulders has been lifted.

I know I've been saying it to my *biji* a lot. Telling her how everything that I've done so far is the right decision. But I never once felt it to be. It never gave me any happiness.

This, I feel in my bones though. This, I feel in my soul.

This is what I'm supposed to do: Love him.

This is where I'm supposed to be: *with* him.

With this complicated, hot and cold, fire and ice, heartless and protective man. Who sets both my heart and body on fire.

"It's not a good thing, baby," he says, coming to rest his forehead over mine. "Loving me is not a good thing."

I crane my neck up and whisper against his lips, "I can't stop."

Another shudder goes through his body and his eyes flutter almost closed. Then, "I'm going to hurt you."

My heart clenches and in response to it, I clench my entire body around him. My thighs squeeze his slim hips and my arms wind even tighter around his neck. "I believe you."

He tenses for a second. "Yeah?"

"Yes. I believe everything you've said." I lick my lips as I take him in. "I believe you're dangerous. I believe you'll hurt me. But I also believe you'll try to protect me from that hurt. You'll try to keep me safe. I also believe you care about me. I believe all the good things and all the bad things about you, Stellan. I know you don't see that. I know you don't see any good in you at all, but there is. There are good things in you, trust me. So many, many good things. So I believe it all. And I still want you."

"We can't have that, though," he says, his eyes swimming with a thousand emotions.

"So what are we going to do?" I whisper.

He keeps our gazes locked. "I'm going to be the one to have to fix you. I'm going to be the one who has to help you move on from me. Who has to make you fall out of love with me."

"Yes," I agree even though I feel tightness in my chest.

"No one else can do the job right."

"No."

"Besides, it's fitting, isn't it?"

"Uh-huh."

"Yeah," he rumbles, pulling my head back even more, nosing the side of my throat. "Until you're married, you're under my protection. So I'm going to protect you from me."

My heart squeezes again and again, in response, I tighten my body around him. "I am."

But I'm not getting married.

I add silently.

Because if I tell him, I know, I *know* he'll lose his shit. And while I'm aware of the consequences of what happens when I lie to him or hide things from him, I'm going to keep this little fact under wraps at least tonight. Or at least until I actually break things off with Shepard.

"In fact, I should've done that right from the start. I never should've trusted someone else when it comes to you. When it comes to someone as precious as you. So it's all really my fault, isn't it?" he goes on, his mouth skimming the slope of my shoulder.

"Yes"—I look to the ceiling, my eyes starting to get lazy—"all of this is your fault."

The fact that I love him.

The fact that he won't love me back.

"I fucked up," he rasps against my skin.

"So then how are you going to make it up to me?" I ask.

And he stills.

He looks up, his eyes dark and drugged.

And I continue, repeating what he said to me the night I found out that I had, indeed, done what I'd set out to do. Melt him and eat his words.

"How are you going to make it up for a year worth of torture? How are you going to make up for making me watch you and watch you from afar? For making me wait and hope and cry and for what? For one kiss. One kiss, Stellan. It was just a kiss. And you wouldn't even give it to me. You refused to give it to me. How are you going to make up for that? For making me chase you, run after you, lie for you, cheat for you. All because you wouldn't kiss me. I *danced* with another man for you. I *flirted* with another man for you. I used him because I loved you so much." My breaths are shallow and rapid, my eyes are stinging. "I love you so much, Stellan. How are you going to make up for making me fall in love with you?"

He rubs the apple of my cheek with his rough thumb as he cradles my face so tenderly, with such reverence that I want to weep.

I want to kiss him.

Then I want to dance for him and flirt with him and love him. All the things that I wanted to do but he wouldn't let me.

"It's a long list, isn't it," he says, his eyes flicking back and forth between mine. "The crimes I've committed against you."

I fist his collar. "Yes."

"So I'm going to start with the latest one."

"What's your latest crime?"

In response, he moves me, he hikes my thighs up, and adjusts himself in a way that his hard abdomen is pressing right there.

Where I'm all achy and swollen.

Where I've been all achy and swollen since... I don't even know when. All I know is that I don't remember the last time I wasn't aching. I don't remember the last time I wasn't hurting.

He presses against that tender, pulsating part of me and says, "Standing outside your door."

I arch my back and rub my swollen core against him. "What?"

"Every fucking night."

My hands are fisted in his collar and tug at it as I ask, "W-what?"

"You told me to guard your door, didn't you?"

"Yes."

"So that's what I've been doing."

"You..." I tug harder at his collar. "You've been... standing outside my d-door every night?"

He moves his jaw back and forth, his fingers flexing in my hair. "Yeah. Sometimes I pace. Sometimes I stand at the end of whatever hallway we're in, far away from it. Sometimes I stand against the opposite wall. But sometimes"—he licks his lips—"I stand right there. Against your door and listen."

"You l-listen?"

"Yeah. To you."

"Me?

Again, his jaw moves as if he's mulling the words, measuring how much to say. So I bring my fingers down from his hair to his face and cradle his cheek. I cup his hard jaw, hoping that my soft touch will let him know that it's okay.

It's okay to tell me whatever it is he want to tell me.

He can tell me all his secrets, all his aches and pains and fears and desires. And I will keep them in my pocket and cherish them like little stars.

"Sometimes you're just moving around," he says, his voice rough and low. "I hear your little feet rustling on the carpet. Sometimes you're humming. Actually, you're always humming. Softly, sweetly. Like there's always a song stuck in your head. Sometimes you talk to yourself. But you do it so low that I can't always catch it. But sometimes I can. Especially when you're doing lines, rehearsing, and then you stop and I hear a scratching sound as if you're writing something on the paper, making little notes. Sometimes the TV's on and you're watching something. You're shouting at the TV. Sometimes you burst out laughing and it becomes really hard."

I rub my thumb on his cheek. "What becomes hard?"

He looks up. So far, he's been studying my face. Staring at my throat when he talked about humming. Staring at my lips when he mentioned laughing.

But now he looks into my eyes. "To stay on the other side."

I want to tell him that he shouldn't have.

That he should've just knocked, and I would've let him in.

I know I was concerned about all of this being appropriate or not, but if he'd asked for me to let him into my world, I would have. That is all I've ever wanted anyway.

"But that's nothing compared to how hard it becomes," he goes on, his fingers flexing on my face. "When I hear you."

"Hear me what?"

"Moan."

I go still. "What?"

"You do that, don't you?" he rumbles, his hips shifting between my thighs, rubbing up against that part. "You moan. When you touch yourself."

"I... You..."

"You also whimper and sob."

"I don't... I'm—"

"But the one that gets me every single time"—he moves again, rubbing against my core and holy God, I moan; I have to I can't stop—"is your whine. Did you know you do that?"

"N-no," I say because I've got no clue what else to say.

"You do," he tells me, moving against me once again, rubbing up, pressing down. "You do it when you're close. When you're right there, your needy moans become impatient whines. You sound like a whiny little princess who wants to come but can't wait for it. And then when you do come, you call out for God. Did you know that too? You call out for Him and that gets me too."

"Why?"

"That gets me mad, see, because it's not God that made you come. It's not God who's standing at your door, listening to your cries, memorizing the way you breathe, the way they hitch when you like something. When you've hit the spot. It's not God who strains His ears, trying to catch the slurping sounds of your pussy. It's not God's dick that gets hard the moment He hears the rustling of sheets. Because He knows, He fucking *knows*, that He's about to get lucky. He's about to hear you come because you're probably getting down to business. And since you've forbidden Him to touch you or get to you or make you come Himself, He has to content Himself with *hearing* you come. Imagining what you look like right that moment.

"It's not God's dick that throbs in His pants. It isn't His dick, baby, that fucking leaks when you make a ruckus like a needy little slut. So yeah, it gets me mad. It makes me angry that God gets all the credit, that God gets all your prayers when we both know it isn't His name you cry out when you come."

"I—"

"Whose name do you call out then?"

"Y-yours."

"And who's standing at your door with his hard dick in his pants that he needs to keep squeezing every two seconds because once again, he's ready to blow in his pants, while you're being a whiny little whore for him on other side?"

"You."

"Me. Not God. It's me."

I knew it was coming.

The last part about me calling out his name.

Because I *do* do that.

I do touch myself almost every single day and whenever I do, I call out his name. Because he's the one I'm thinking of. He's the one I'm imagining when I'm horny. And I'm horny all the time. Because he's around all the time.

On the bus, at games, at parties, in the hotel.

Just the thought that his room is only a few doors down no matter where we go is enough to get me wet. And it's not a new phenomenon. I've been imagining him and touching myself ever since I saw him.

But the fact that he knows, that he heard, is...

"I'm not that loud," I say at last.

A breath puffs out of him, all hot and misty, all tasting like smoke and marshmallows. "You are. And even if you weren't I'd still hear you. I'd hear you from my room, from the reception downstairs. I'd hear you from another town. And you know why?"

I swallow. "Why?"

"Because as always, everything you do, you do it for me," he says possessively, his chest pushing into mine with a large wave of breath. "You get horny for me. You moan for me. You call out my name. So I'd hear you from across this goddamn world because you lie down on your back, your thighs spread and open, your finger playing with your sweetheart snatch for *me*."

I nod, slipping our mouths together. "Yes."

Grasping my throat with both of his hands and pressing both of his thumbs on the triangle, he says, "So that's what I'll do then. That's where I'll start. Atoning my sins. Paying for my crimes. I'll start with my mouth on your pussy and then I'll feed her my dick. I'll fuck her with my dick. I'll fuck myself out of your system, baby. I won't let you suffer any longer."

I know he's trying to atone for his sins, but the truth is that we're both sinners. We're both criminals. We've both done awful things, desperate things for each other.

We've both hurt each other, tortured each other.

Which makes me think that for all our differences, maybe we're not that different at all.

We're the same.

The fabric of our souls is the same. We share the same veins in our hearts. We share the same chambers. So I'm done fighting with him. I'm done making him pay or paying my dues. I just want to be with him.

I squeeze my thighs around his waist. "You don't—"

"But we have to get our story straight, okay?" he begins, looking at me meaningfully. "We can't have the world blaming you when it's my fault."

I know what he's referring to, and I almost tell him that we don't need a story. We don't need to pretend that he's making me do anything. We don't need flimsy excuses. I'm not marrying his brother anymore. I'm his and his alone.

But I can't.

Not yet.

Not until I tell Shepard.

So I do as he says. I follow his lead and let him take the burden for now.

"Okay," I agree on a whisper.

"Tell me what happened tonight," he whispers.

I give him a peck on his mouth. Then, "I went to a party where my daddy saved me."

He gives me a peck back. "Because your fucking fiancé was fucking around on the job, wasn't he? He was fucking slacking and—"

I give him a peck again. "It's okay though. I don't care because I'm safe."

The double necklace of his fingers around my neck tightens. "You are, aren't you?"

I roam my eyes around his features as I reply, "Thanks to my daddy."

I shiver at the dark look in his eyes. At how vulnerable of a position I'm in. With his big body lodged between my thighs and his strong and rough hands wrapped around my throat. He could so easily do anything to me, keep me pinned forever, choke me with his fingers and oh my God, use that... hard thing on me.

I can feel it, see.

This is the first time I'm feeling it.

He's kept it away from me so far.

He wouldn't even let me look at it back at the theater.

But now I can feel it on my tummy, all hard and throbbing.

His chest shakes. "So now I want what's mine. What's my due."

And I can't help but move against it and whisper, "But I... You know that I'm getting married soon and I..."

He shudders, a low growl escaping him. "You're saving it."

I shudder too and rub up against him. "I am."

"But the thing is that he doesn't deserve what you're saving," he says, his fingers squeezing my throat, his hips moving, making me arch my back and push back. "He left you alone at the bar. He leaves you alone on the bus. He leaves you alone where I can get to you. Where if I get hungry," he rumbles all the while making me go crazy with his rocking, making me go insane, "I can so very easily get to my sweetheart's pussy. I can so very easily kneel before you and flip your flimsy dress up. I can spread your legs and stick my head between your thighs and eat you. I can so very easily suck on you and drink you down. And if he finally gets a clue and comes to stop me, I can end him. So very, very easily. So you tell me, who deserves this pussy first: me or him. Your fiancé who doesn't have a clue how to guard the treasure between your legs or me, your daddy, who's hungry and thirsty and has been that way for ages, just waiting for his turn."

I look at his feverish face. His drugged eyes. I flex my throat under his grip. I clench my thighs around his hips. I fist his hair. I breathe his air.

Digging my heels, I whisper against his mouth, "You. You get it. But you have to wait."

He stills. "What?"

"Because I have to do something first."

He presses into my body. "There's nothing you have to do."

"There is, though."

"Dora, I—"

"I have to do something for *you*."

"What?"

I place a soft kiss on his parted lips again. "It's your turn, isn't it? And you've only ever seen me dance with other men. And you've only ever seen me dance from far away and from the shadows. And I've only ever danced for you in my dreams or in the middle of the night, under the pink magnolia tree where we met for the first time, imagining you standing there, watching me. So now that you're finally here, in my room, and you won't let me go no matter how much I ask you to, I need to dance for you."

I place a tender kiss on his mouth again. "So can I? Can I dance for you, Daddy?"

For several moments after that, there's silence. I don't even think he's breathing as he stares down at me. When I think I can't take it anymore, he speaks and he does it commandingly. He does it with a thick growl and a possessive tone.

"You'll dance, but you'll do it without his ring on your finger."

And then he proceeds to take my engagement ring away leaving me bare.

CHAPTER 8

I don't know why I'm so nervous.
    I've done this before. I've danced for him multiple times. Either to make him jealous or when he was pretending to be Shepard.
    But this is the first time I'm dancing when I know it's him and I'm doing it for his pleasure. I'm doing it without any ulterior motives or agendas. I'm doing it because I want to do it and he wants to see me do it.
    So of course the dress I choose to wear is that same white dress and those fake wings that he saw me in that first night. That I brought them with me on this trip should've been indication enough—again—that my engagement should never have happened, but it did and I'll deal with it later.
    Right now, I need to go out there—I'm in the bathroom—and dance for him.
    I press a hand on my stomach—for some reason, my bare finger feels heavier and throbby—and blow out a breath. Then I open the door and step into the room. Which is bathed in a yellow light. I realize he's turned out all the lights except the lamp on one of the nightstands.
    I stare at that lamp for several seconds.
    Because for some reason, I can't look at him yet. For some reason, I'm shy. I know he's there. He's on the bed, propped up on the pillows. That much I could gather as soon as I stepped out, but actually looking at him is proving to be harder than I thought.
    Closing the door behind me and keeping my eyes on my feet, I walk in farther. As if on stage, I come to stand in the center of the room, a few feet away from the foot of the bed. I should probably look up now. But still, I keep my eyes on my red-polished nails and wipe my sweaty palms down my thighs.
    "Eyes on me."

My heart is beating so loud that I don't know how I heard him over the din. But I did and before I can give it any conscious thought, I look up.

And oh my God.

Oh my God, oh my God, he's *naked*.

He's...

Well, no.

He's not naked. I spoke too quickly. Because he does have his jeans on. They're dark blue bordering on black, just for the record, and they're still there, molded over his legs. One bent at the knee, the other straight out.

His feet are large, and he's got pretty toes. Just, again, for the record.

He also has his shirt on. It's a light gray button-down and the sleeves are folded back up to his elbows.

But.

But. But. *But.*

The buttons of that button-down are open. And not just the top two or three like when we were on that video call the night before my play, no. They're all open. All of them. Every last one of them, meaning I can see his chest.

I can see all of his torso.

And Jesus, *Jesus*.

I think... I think I'm about to drool.

Well, I think I'm already drooling and my mouth is drying out at the same time. So I have to lick my lips as I take him in.

I start with his throat. I know it's innocuous. But I wanted to start with something I've seen before and wouldn't completely make me thoughtless. Because I have so many other things to discover.

So I look at the deep triangle of his throat. Those shapely but dense collarbones that mold into the globes of his shoulders that I can't see right now but I know are there. I also know they are heavy and solid and full of strength. Not only because he carries so much on his shoulders, so many things that I don't know about. But also, they've carried me. I've used them to heave myself up on his body. I've used them to keep my balance.

I love his shoulders. I love them so much.

After that, we enter a dangerous territory because I reach his chest and as suspected through his countless button-down shirts and the coats he wears that he doesn't even like, it's massive.

It's sculpted and densely packed with muscles.

In fact, his pecs look like slabs of stone.

They look like his shoulders. That they can carry all the weight in the world and I decide to make them my pillow as soon as we're done here. His chest is where I'm going to sleep tonight and all the other nights to come.

And then I lose all my train of thought, all the promises that I'm making myself because abs.

He's got them.

That legendary six-pack men have. Those muscles neatly arranged in a tight, ridged ladder that I'm assuming all the girls want to put their dainty feet on and climb. That all the girls want to lick and squeeze and bite. All the girls want to kiss and leave lipstick marks on.

I'm not going to lie, just the thought of girls getting to do that to him makes me mad. It makes me want to find all those girls and scratch their eyes out. It makes me want to tell the world that he's mine.

Mine and mine only.

And I will kill anyone who dares to look at him. I will—

"If you're plotting a murder in your head, I suggest you do that on your own time."

I jerk and look up. "What?"

Now that I'm not distracted by his bare chest—that's tanned and lightly dusted with hair; I just want to put it out there—I take him in as a whole. And I realize that I was right. All those nights I danced for him, I always imagined him sitting sprawled on the bed, propped up against stark white hotel pillows. I always imagined his thighs wide and his body taking up the maximum space in the bed, him all authoritative and dominating. Like he's my king and I'm his slave girl.

While all that's true, I completely missed one thing.

I thought he'd be all lazy and laid-back as I entertained him. But those words do not apply to him at all.

I mean, he *should* look all casual with his one hand resting on his bent knee and the other simply settled on his thigh. But they're both fisted and they're fisted so tightly that his knuckles are jutted out and leached of color.

"I'm waiting," he tells me in a low voice, his chin dipped, his dark eyes glinting.

"It's just..." I finally manage to say, fisting my dress. "You're so handsome."

"Am I?"

"Yes"—I swallow—"and I was thinking that maybe I should kill all the girls out there who think the same thing."

I think amusement flickers through his features. But it's dark and edgy and fucking possessive. Like he likes that. The fact that I'm ready to kill for him. And if this is what he likes, I think he's going to love me.

Because I will do it.

In a heartbeat.

"And I'll hand you the knife," he says, his bare chest moving with an impatient breath, "when I'm done killing all the men out there who think you're beautiful and want you for themselves."

"But I only want—"

"That's not the point, though, is it?" He flexes his fist again, twisting it as if antsy and itching to fight. "The point is that it's been a thousand years and I'm still waiting."

And I'm done making him wait.

So another deep breath later, I go to my phone sitting on the coffee table to my right that's all ready to go and hit play. Music fills the air and there it is: his turn.

I chose the song that requires me to spin a lot. That requires me to move my hips in ways I know he likes. He likes it when I writhe for him. When I move them in a figure eight. When it looks like I'm dancing against something.

A pole maybe.

But mostly against something that's much hotter and I bet, thicker.

And throbbing and alive.

And maybe I'm not dancing against it but with it inside of me.

So I try to emulate that. I try to emulate how I'd rock my hips and twist them and arch my back as if I were riding his dick. I have zero experience of course, but I give it my best shot. I give it all I have. Because I'm dancing for the love of my life and I can't let him down.

Although I do have to, a couple of minutes into it.

Because during one of my turns, I notice something. Him, getting even more on edge. As he sits up straight, away from all the pillows, his shoulders and spine rigid. His bare chest heaving with the large breaths he's taking, his rose mouth parted. His bare skin that's bathed in yellow light is all shiny with sweat.

But that's not what gives me pause.

What gives me pause is the fact that he's got his hand.

Right *there*.

In between his large, muscled legs.

And he's got it exactly like he had described before. While he talked about standing at my door with his dick hard.

He's got his hand kneading his dick.

Massaging it, pressing it like you press on a wound that's painful and throbbing.

And big and thick and hard.

And I know his dick is all of those things because I can *see* it. Again, not all of it, no. Because why would he be so merciful as to give me a glimpse of everything that he is and everything he has. All I can see is that he has his zipper open, probably to let it breathe, and I can see the ruddy head of it peeking through the waistband of his pants.

And oh *Lord*, it's shiny.

That head.

It's juicy and angry and all red and oh my God, I fall. At the tiny glimpse of his dick, I stumble on my feet and come crashing down. My palms break my fall and I'm panting so hard and so loud that I think he was right.

That they can all hear me.

They can hear me all over this building, all over this town.

But I don't care about that because I think they can hear him first. They can hear his loud breaths better than they do mine. Because his are noisier and growly and much faster than mine.

As fast as he probably is himself because as soon as I fall, he's there.

While I'm still coming to grips with the fact that I *actually* fell, he's already out of the bed and standing over me, his masculine feet, and pretty toes in my line of vision.

I look up just as he bends down to pick me up. But I don't want to be picked up.

I want to be here, kneeling at his feet.

I want to be where his dick is. Where it's close to my mouth.

And it's so close. God, it's so, *so* close like this and I can still see the slippery head of it. I also see dark curly hair through the slight opening of his zipper and holy fuck, I've never wanted anything more.

I'm going to go so far as to say that I haven't even wanted him to kiss me this bad.

As bad as I want his dick right now.

So I grab his thigh, getting even closer to my promise land as I breathe out, "Did you like my dance?"

He's still bent over me and at my words, he reaches out and grabs my hair. He pulls my head back and growls, "Did I like your dance?"

"Yes."

"Does the fact that my dick is throbbing like a motherfucker and dripping down on the floor like a fucking faucet answer your question? So stop looking at it with hungry eyes and get away before I paint your face with my fucking spunk."

He can pull me back from his dick all he wants, but I'm not letting go of his hard thigh. I'm not even looking away from it. How can I when it jerks at my next words? "I want to suck it."

I hear him breathe out and his fingers tighten in my hair. "No."

"But I—"

"You're not sucking my dick."

I frown, hugging his thigh with both arms. "Why not? I'm good at it."

"No, you're not."

At this, I have to look at it. "That's—"

His face is as flushed as his dick, sweat beading his forehead. And I do feel bad for him. I can see he's on edge. I can see he wants me badly. But at the same time, I want his dick just as badly and ladies first, right?

"Because you've never sucked a dick before. So get the fuck up," he rumbles, his eyes promising retribution if I don't listen to him.

My belly clenches at his rough authority. "But you got to taste me."

"Yeah, and you taste fucking divine."

I blush. "Please. I know men like that."

His cock jerks and his breath is loud. "And you know a lot about men, huh."

I flex my arms around his thigh. "I—"

He leans down further while at the same time pulls me up. Then, looming over my mouth, he says, "You remember the deal, don't you?" He shakes his fist in my hair a little, making me gasp and moan. "And trust me, I've got no problem in dragging you to bed by your hair, kicking and screaming about how you want to suck me off first." He pulls me up further that I have to let go of his thigh and hold on to the tails of his shirt. "I've got *no problem* in forcing your dancing legs open and eating that tasty cunt of yours while you're bitching about how unfair I am for getting to taste you while you still haven't gotten to taste me. So the choice is yours: you could either be a greedy little brat right now or you could quietly let me stick my dick in that sweet little snatch and let me make you my good little whore later. Either way, baby," he growls, his eyes slitted and full of lust, "I'm getting in that virgin pussy tonight and making it bleed. And it's going to bleed for me, trust me, because if there isn't a ring of red around the base of my dick, then it didn't happen. And it's happening, yeah? I'm getting in there first because finally, *fucking finally*, it's my turn. So what is it going to be: my greedy little brat or my good little whore."

Both.

I want to say both.

Because God, I'm selfish.

But I gather whatever good sense I have and whisper, "The s-second one."

Satisfaction crosses his features that he won this round but only for a second. Because it soon vanishes, intense possessiveness replacing it. Intense authority and hunger. And as he yanks me up and then makes me climb his body, I wonder if he's so possessive and dominating right now, what's going to happen when he's done claiming me.

And why am I so, so looking forward to that?

As soon as our mouths touch, he starts eating me. And then two steps later, we're on the bed. I feel the hot sheets—warmed up from his body—on my back and I realize that I still have my wings on. I completely forgot about the wings. While I'm absorbing that fact, I realize he's pushing my white dress up and then he's dragging my panties down.

And I guess I'm wet—I'm super-duper wet—because the level of it can be measured by when he throws them over his shoulders and they land somewhere with a thwack.

At which point I realize that I should probably stop staring at the ceiling and heave myself up on my elbows. I should probably *watch* him do all these things rather than just feel them by the tugs of my dress and the roughness of his fingers. By the groan he emits when he's uncovered my pussy and by the way the bed dips when he settles himself on it, with his face between my thighs.

But just as soon as I make that decision, he starts eating me.

Like in the bathroom that night, he starts with my inner thighs. Sucking and lapping at my skin, slurping in all the juice. Again, it reminds me of a fruit or when you eat an ice cream cone. How you first go for the dripping ice cream, licking it with the tip of your tongue, letting the sweetness spread, savoring it before going for the real prize.

Or maybe he does that because I'm always so over full and so overflowing that he can't help but clean me off in the places where I have dripped down before going for my pussy.

Which is messy, I'm not going to lie.

It's so messy and slippery and swollen.

How did I not know how swollen it was?

It's throbbing right now, all engorged and lusty. Like a second heart but instead of love, all I have is lust beating through it. And he loves the taste of my lust. I mean, I already knew that; he did just say that I taste divine. But still, I am shocked when he goes for my whole pussy right off the bat.

In the bathroom, he started slow. He started with my clit. He took it in his mouth and sucked on it like a little pearl and when I dripped because of his ministrations, that's when he brought out the big guns and lapped at me.

But he's got no such problem right now.

As he viciously sucks on my clit and pulls at the lips of my pussy. As he nips those lips and groans while doing so.

And honestly, I've got no problem either.

I don't mind his tongue or his teeth or all the sounds he's making. All groans and grunts and slurps.

I think that's what does it for me.

That's what makes me hornier and grip his hair and bear down on his mouth. That's what makes me arch my back and moan loudly. As loudly as he said I do. Maybe even more because my pillow doesn't have lips like that. My pillow isn't hot and wet and oh so fucking good at eating me out. And when the damn bursts inside of me I arch so sharply that I touch the sky. I see stars and galaxies.

I scream.

And then I hear a rip through my own mayhem. But before I can figure out what that was, I feel that magic mouth of his on my tits. I feel him sucking my tits, vacuuming them in his mouth, drinking from them and, well... I think it was the sound of my dress ripping, but who cares.

He's sucking on my tits with the mouth that's all wet and slippery from my juices, and all is right in the world.

All is horny.

Him, me. His mouth on my nipple, my fingers in his hair.

His hot chest breathing over me, my shaking thighs wrapped around his hips.

Everything feels dipped in honey, sticky and sweaty. Everything feels dipped in glitter and bathed in red neon light, dark but shiny.

And I think he makes me come again.

With just his mouth on my tits.

I think this time when I do come, I'm rubbing my juices on his bare stomach. I'm rubbing my lust on his skin. Not that he needs it. He's plenty lustful on his own. Because as soon as I come the second time and I'm blinking my eyes open, he moves away. He gets off the bed and I know what he's doing. I know it's here.

His turn at having me.

So I simply lie here, with my legs all sprawled, my dress hiked up around the waist and torn down the middle. While I'm watching his face, how dark and flushed it looks and how red his mouth appears, red and wet from the sucking.

He's watching the state of me as he takes his shirt off, revealing those gorgeous globes of his biceps and shoulders. I was right—they could carry the weight of the world. They could carry me. And pair that with his broad chest and steely abs. I could make a home for myself on his body and would never need a roof over my head.

When his eyes reach the center of me, I whisper, "I look like a disaster, don't I?"

He looks up, his eyes black. "You look like an angel."

To prove his point, he glances at my wings.

Which makes me blush even more because on top of my torn dress and open legs, I've got wings flanking my body, making a mockery of me. "A fallen angel."

His hands are on his jeans now and I stop my breaths—I wish I could stop my heart too—so I don't miss anything. So I don't miss the thing I so wanted to suck on but am going to have to wait because he's taking his turn.

And when it comes into view, I squeak.

Now I know why I could see it through his waistband.

Because it's big. Which is an understatement, but I'm not a writer. I only know how to feel and act and I'm feeling a deep clench in my belly. A deep spasm in my already fluttering pussy. Not only because it's so big that it touches his belly button but also because it's so thick that I know I will have to pop my jaw to get him inside.

I don't even know how it can be contained within the confines of his jeans. There is no way it can be. Maybe he needs special pants for his special dick.

Plus, look at how dark it is.

As dark as the rest of his lust-flushed skin. And slippery. Thanks to all the pre-cum, I think. Even now I see a pearl of it oozing out of the head and dripping down the side, tracing that thick vein.

That I want to trace with my tongue.

And... oh my God, no.

He's covering it.

He's produced a condom from somewhere—probably from his jeans pocket or something—and he's tearing the packet with his teeth and rolling the rubber down his length. That sexy teeth move aside, I absolutely do not like that he's covering his cock up with latex before going inside of me. Because I don't want anything between us.

Before I can protest, he grabs my ankles, pulls them to the sides, spreading my legs even more, and gets on the bed. His dick bobs and I imagine a drop of pre-cum oozing out but getting caught up in the stupid condom instead of plopping onto my trembling belly as he comes to situate himself between my thighs. Which wrap around his hips while I rub my heels on the hairs of his bare thighs.

"A pretty angel," he says as he hovers over me, picking up the thread where we left it before I got distracted by his dick.

Resting my hands on his sculpted sides, I glare at him a little. "I can't believe you put a condom on."

He frames my face with his hands. "And a reckless angel."

I scratch him in response. "I can't believe I don't get to suck your dick."

His lips twitch. "A greedy angel too."

I scratch him again and just because I'm angry, I say, "I can't believe it took you this long to just fuck me when I would've let you do it a long time ago."

He chuckles. "Yeah, you would have because you're my angel."

And I stop doing what I'm doing because I have to see this. Out of all the sights tonight, this one's the most important, the most memorable.

Him chuckling.

Him looking so handsome and adorable while doing so.

Him looking like my dream come true.

All my anger melts away and I bring my hands up to his face, pressing my thumbs to the curve of his mouth. "You…"

His eyes go grave. "I know."

"What?"

His fingers flex around my face. "I'll be careful."

"Careful?"

"I swear on my life, Dora," he promises. "I'll make it good for you."

Oh.

That.

Virginity and all that.

Honestly, we've come so far and we've waited so long that it doesn't even matter. That's the last thing on my mind. In fact, the very first thing that's on my mind right now is the opposite of that.

Which is what I was going to say before.

So I say it now, "I want you to make it hurt."

He frowns. "What?"

"I want you to rip it. Like you ripped my dress." Something passes through his face that looks a lot like regret and to stop it, I insist, "I want to bleed for you. Because if I don't bleed, it didn't happen, right? And I want it to." All games aside, this is the truth and I want him to know that for sure. "I want it to happen. I want to lose it to you. I always did. You're the one I've been saving it for and you deserve it the most. You deserve everything from me, Stellan. Everything that I am. Everything that I will be and—"

He stops me with a kiss.

I know why. I know I got a little too emotional for him. A little too expressive and lovey-dovey. Especially when he's trying to fix things. When he's trying to make me fall out of love with him.

But again, I'm tired of pacing. I'm tired of not being who and what I am: a hopeless girl completely and irrevocably and undeniably in love with him.

So if he can't handle that, then he's free to break my heart and move on. He's going to do that anyway no matter what I do. So I might as well be myself. I might as well be clingy and annoying and shower him with all my love.

Because he needs that.

This lonely, complex man needs my love.

All my thoughts of love, or any thoughts for that matter, vanish, though, when he moves and adjusts himself. And then a second later, enters me in one go.

He rips into me like I asked him to.

But I know not because of *why* I asked him to.

He didn't do it to make me bleed more, no. He did it because it's better this way. It's better to do it in one go rather than prolonging the torture. And he knows a lot about it, doesn't he? Torture. Suffering through it and doling it out.

And I know that because as soon as he slams his way in, he stops. He hugs me. He hugs me oh so tightly. He hugs me like I'm really an angel and he's the devil who made me fall from grace.

He hugs me like he will never let my dead body go.

He hugs me like he will never let *me* go.

And years later, I won't even remember the pain. I won't remember the blinding flash of it and how I jerked under him. I won't remember how I scratched his sides or how I moaned so loud that I almost broke the windowpanes and let the winter in.

This is what I'll remember, him hugging me with concern and despair.

And something that feels a lot like the thing he can't feel: love.

I will remember how he called me baby and sweetheart over and over and told me that it's going to be okay. That he's sorry but he'll make it all better now.

And he does too; I'll remember that.

He gives me time to adjust to his size, his invasion, and when I have, he starts to move. It's very slow and gentle. They're tender, his movements. And for all my talk of him ripping into me and making it hurt and bleed, I'm glad he does it that way.

Because holy shit, he *is* big.

And sex hurts, man.

The first time, it really does.

So I'm glad it's with a man who's so careful. Who knows exactly what I need in this moment. And who despite wanting to move faster, goes really slowly for me. And I know that he does because of how insanely he's vibrating right now. How everything in his body is so clenched, how every muscle is standing in stark relief.

Yes, I'm glad it's with him.

Like I always wanted.

And then when I want him to move faster, he does that too. When my pussy is all adjusted to his size and turns needy once again, his strokes fasten. They become deeper and faster and oh so hotter. They become so hot that I'm sweating with the pounding he's giving me.

I'm shaking and shuddering.

My wings all fluttery at my back.

I'm all swollen and slippery.

And so, so in love.

With my Wildfire Thorn.

Seriously, though, people who call him cold are crazy. He's as hot as wildfire.

And now I feel him in my stomach. I feel his cock thicken inside of me, his skin turning darker and even more heated, and I know he's about to come. I know what those bunched up muscles mean and just touching him and kneading those hard muscles of his, I come.

I explode around him and he explodes inside of me at the same time.

But mostly, what I'll remember about our first time is that through all of this, through a slow fuck and a hard pounding, through my orgasm that overcomes me and then triggers his own, he never once stopped kissing me.

CHAPTER 9

LATER THAT NIGHT...

"Isn't this amazing?" I chirp, looking up at the night sky.

"If by amazing," he rumbles, "you mean insane, then yes, it is amazing."

I tilt my head where it's resting on his hard chest and look up at him. "You think this is insane?"

Snowflakes land on his face, in his hair. Even in his eyelashes. They're super tiny and disappear as soon as they touch his hot skin but leave him all shiny and sparkly. So fucking beautiful. And in the midst of all that, there's smoke wafting out of his mouth as he takes a drag in.

Then, still looking up, "It's cold out."

"So?"

He takes another drag. "So we're lying on the ground."

"But—"

"*While* it's snowing."

"But—"

"In the middle of the night."

"I know but—"

"In a fucking park that you wanted to walk to," he keeps going, smoking. "Instead of staying at the hotel room with a perfectly nice bed we could be sleeping in right now. So yeah, it's pretty fucking insane."

I'm done with his complaining—which believe it or not, he has done a lot of ever since I said that we're going out—so I reach out and put a finger on his smoking lips, causing him to finally dip his chin and glance my way.

"First, this *is* amazing, no doubt about it. Second, lying in the snow *while* it's snowing is the only way to enjoy the snow. Think of it as like tanning, only we're doing it in winter. Third, we didn't walk here after all because you wouldn't let us, remember? You *insisted* that we take a cab. I mean, that's not how you have a midnight adventure. Especially when you call yourself colder than winter. And you even brought a coat with you and wouldn't shut up about a winter weather advisory. So I don't know what you're talking about."

He stares at me for a few moments, his mouth all soft and hot under my cold finger. When he opens it to say something, I smush my finger on his lips. "Oh, and fourth, I'm not sleepy at all. I'm weirdly very energetic right now. So tough luck, big guy, you're going to have to stay here."

I smile sweetly and remove my finger before rubbing my cheek on his hard and cozy chest and go back to staring at the frosty moon and pretty snowflakes. I even catch a few in the palm of my hands, watching them melt and sighing.

The arm that's tucked around me moves and goes up. He buries his fingers in my hair and, fisting it, he pulls my head back and then instead of the cold snow, I'm staring at his heated face.

"First, the reason we took a cab was because walking here would've taken us more than forty-five minutes and by then no matter how much you love winter, you would've frozen to death, putting a tragic end to your midnight adventure. Second, I *am* colder than winter. The coat's for your benefit because again no matter how much you love winter, it'll still give you frostbite. And third, there's nothing weird about you being energetic. It's called endorphins. Aka happy hormones. Aka that happens after sex. Biology 101."

I open my mouth to say something, but like I did before, he stops me. Not with his finger, though, but with his mouth, pressing a kiss before he says, "Oh, and I can leave whenever I want to."

No, he can't.

Because I know about the coat.

I was just messing with him. I knew he wore it for me—it's a long overcoat—and I know that's the reason I'm wrapped up in it.

So he's not going anywhere.

Besides, let's not forget that we're cuddling.

Yup.

And it was his idea too.

I mean, I did want to use him as a pillow and cuddle with him, ever since I saw his chest revealed in its full glory anyway. I mean, his chest is made to rest my head on.

But he got there first.

As soon as we lay on the ground, he was the one who reached for me and hauled me up against his side and put his large palm on the back of my head and made me do what I already wanted to: rest my head on his chest, tuck it under his jaw, and lie here for an eternity. And then he wrapped me in his coat, keeping me plastered to his side.

Twenty minutes later, he's still doing that.

I cup his cold, harsh cheek. "No, you can't."

"No?"

"Because if you leave, who's going to keep an eye on me?"

He clenches his jaw in response.

"*Or* cuddle me to keep me warm."

"This is not cuddling."

"This is absolutely cuddling."

"I don't cuddle."

"You cuddle me, though."

"You—"

"Oh, and if we're talking about hormones and chemicals and stuff, shouldn't it be Chemistry 101?"

"I—"

"And doesn't that mean we have insane chemistry?" I repeat my words from long ago.

His lips twitch, his eyes roving over my features. "I thought the words were *In. Sane*, not insane. And it also means that I want to sit you down at a desk and make you write over and over, 'Isadora Agni Holmes should not annoy Stellan Thorne.'"

I smirk and rub my thumb over his jaw that's stubbled after a long day. "How about you *bend* me over a desk instead and I write, Stellan Thorne only pretends to hate when Isadora Holmes annoys him. Secretly, he wants to be annoyed all the time."

And then to annoy him further, I reach up, wanting to place a sweet kiss on his lips. But he stops me a hair's breadth away from his mouth and growls, "If I bend you over a desk, Dora, you won't be able to spell your name, let alone write those two sentences over and over." Then, "Actually, you won't be able to sit at a desk for at least a week, let alone put pen to paper."

After delivering that threat that sounded more like a promise, he finally bridges the gap himself and gives me a hot, wet kiss, tasting me and letting me savor his smoky, marshmallow-y taste.

When he lets me come up for air, I whisper, "You taste like marshmallows."

He glances down at my lips. "You taste like cherries."

"Did you really want to do that," I ask shyly, referring to what he told me about wanting to eat me out on the bus, "to me? On the bus?"

Amusement flickers through his features. "I made a pros and cons list."

"You did not."

"Uh-huh. I got to ten pros. Pro number one: I get to eat your pussy. Pro number two: I get to make you my whiny little whore. Pro number three: I get to eat your pussy. Pro number four: Everyone on the bus, on the fucking highway, would know that you belong to me and that I'm giving it to you good. Because you're so loud, aren't you? Pro number five: I get to eat your pussy. Pro number six and seven and eight and nine and fucking ten: I get to eat your goddamn pussy."

"W-what stopped you?"

"The fact that there's a chance they could get a peek at your sloppy snatch and that's not something I can allow, can I?"

"No."

And I wouldn't want to show them either. Only he gets to see it.

He comes down for another kiss.

When he breaks it, I look at his face, his mouth as I murmur, "I thought you'd taste like a rose, though."

"A rose."

"Uh-huh." I trace the curve of his mouth with my fingers. "Because the first time I saw you, I thought your mouth looks like a rose, all plush and soft."

"Hmm. If that's your way of complimenting me, I suggest you try again."

I look into his eyes. "Roses are my favorite flowers."

"Yeah, no."

"And you were smoking, so I thought a rose set on fire," I share. "So up until my mom sent me away to Bardstown, I'd stand under that pink magnolia tree and smoke a cigarette thinking about you."

He goes rigid. "You smoke a cigarette."

Oops. Should not have told him that.

"I—"

"No," he declares.

I wrinkle my nose. "How did I know you'd say that?"

"Because as reckless as you are, courting death like this, you still have some sense left in your head to tell you that I'm not going to be happy about it."

"You know, you smoke and—"

"Yeah? Well, I can do whatever the fuck I want."

"That's double standards."

His eyes narrow. "Are you going to stop doing it?"

I glare up at him. "You know, you're taking this daddy thing a little too far."

He narrows his eyes. "You wanted a daddy, remember?"

"I changed my mind."

"You can't. Not with me."

Stubbornly, I make him wait.

"Dora," he warns.

I sigh. "Fine, I will."

He sighs too. "Good."

I huff. "I'm not happy about this."

"I don't give a fuck."

Mad, I go to look away from him, but he doesn't let me. He goes for another kiss and I refrain for about five seconds before I give in and kiss him back. Maybe I should hold onto my anger at how bossy he was but when he's sucking on my mouth like he's sucking in air, I can't be.

Breaking the kiss, he rasps against my wet mouth, "I won't let you ruin yourself for me. You've done that enough."

I fist his hair. "But I—"

"How do you feel?" he asks then.

I blush because I know what he's asking. "Was that the second reason you didn't let us walk here?"

His pretty features ripple with something akin to remorse. "It was bad."

I put both of my hands on his cheek then. "It wasn't."

"I could've been more careful."

"You were careful," I insist. "It was exactly what I wanted."

"You—"

"No, it was," I cut him off. "I told you. I wanted to bleed for you, and I did. And I liked it."

"That's—"

"And"—I squeeze his cheeks—"you insisted on cleaning me up down there with a hot towel on top of drawing me a bath for my sore muscles. Even though I didn't say a single word to you. But"—I place a soft kiss on his lips—"I'm thankful nonetheless. And I'm fine, I promise. So end of discussion."

Even though I'm lying a little bit.

There is some soreness between my legs and my inner thighs throb when I move too quickly. But other than that, I'm truly fine and itching for a round two. Which I forgot to add up there, he denied on account of 'my pussy being too trashed for another fucking.'

His words, not mine.

Pressing a hard kiss on my mouth as if every time I kiss him now, he has to kiss me back, he growls, "You didn't have to. Your pussy looked plenty beaten up on her own." Then, muttering to himself as if, "That was the least I could do after how I hurt her."

At this point, I have to do it.

I have to pull him even closer.

I have to pull him over my body and have him settle into the cradle of my thighs, right where my sore pussy is that he so tenderly massaged with that hot towel and wrap my thighs around his strong hips.

So I do that.

I pull on the collar of his shirt and make him come over me. When he's exactly where I want, I arch my back under him and line my core up with where I know his dick is. "Are we done discussing how your dick's a beast and my pussy is a beauty that he kidnapped and then violated in his library that contains like thousands of books?" Then it occurs to me. "Which your room has, by the way. Oh my God, we're like the beauty and the beast!"

His lips twitch. "First, not God, me. And second, I don't think that's what Gabrielle-Suzanne Barbot de Villeneuve had in mind when he came up with *Beauty and the Beast*."

I frown. "Who is that?"

"A French novelist," he tells me, framing my face with one hand and taking a drag of his cigarette with the other. Letting the smoke out away from me, he finishes, "Who wrote *Beauty and the Beast*, the original version, back in 1740."

I blink up at him for a few seconds. "It's not Disney that came up with *Beauty and the Beast*?"

He stares at me unblinking for a second. "No, Dora. It's not Disney."

I narrow my eyes at his condescension.

And he emits a very low chuckle.

God, I hate him.

I hate how much I love him. I hate how happy his chuckle makes me.

No, actually, I'm lying. I just love it.

"Anyway." I wave all of this away. "That's not the point."

"I can't wait to hear the point," he quips as he takes another drag.

I roll my eyes. "The point is that I read the books you told me about."

That gets his attention, and he stubs the cigarette in the snow and looks down at me. "You read the books."

"Uh-huh. *The Adventures of Rune*."

He keeps staring at me for a moment or two before asking, "How many pages?"

Damn it.

I squirm under him. "Like twenty..."

His lips twitch again. "So basically one chapter."

I push at his shoulder. "Hey, it's a really long book and there are like, eight in the series. I bought them all but stacked together they looked even taller than me. So I kinda watched the movies."

I did.

I bought the books after my play.

The very next day.

Because I was under the impression that I'd never get to be with him again. That that night was goodbye and we'd go back to being strangers like we essentially had been this past year. And God, I was so heartbroken about it. So sad and miserable and so fucking devastated. So I went out and bought those books that he was talking about, that he could not *stop* talking about, all determined to get to know the world he loves so much.

Thank God there were movies, though.

Which were really, really good, actually. I can see why he loves these books.

Which is why we're having this conversation in the first place.

He pulls a face. "Movies are shit."

I roll my eyes again. Of course he'd think that. Books are always better than movies, but since I hate reading, movies are my only choice.

In any case, I stick with the point. "So anyway, I got to talking to one of the girls in my drama class. And she really loves those books too and she said they inspired her to pursue her career path today. You know, acting. But get this"—I play with the collar of his shirt under his coat, looking at his throat—"her family wasn't all that into it. They're all lawyers and doctors and stuff, you know? And she's the first, uh, actor. Or any arts person for that matter. And she told me it was scary, telling them about her interests and that this is what she wants to pursue. Which, as I said, is completely different from everything she's ever known. So"—I clear my throat again—"yeah, she did it and she's really happy today. Isn't that amazing?"

I kinda think I didn't really think it through.

In my head, this story sounded very convincing and believable. Pair that with my acting skills—because there isn't a friend, and therefore, I had no conversation with anyone—and this would've been a home run.

I don't think it was.

I think it sounded very long-winded and phony, and I don't think my point was all that obvious. Which could be my only saving grace here.

"You think I'm not pursuing a different career path," he begins, dashing my hopes immediately. "Something to do with books because my whole family is in soccer and so I'm pressured into it."

I whip my eyes up and, fisting his shirt at his chest, I ask, "*How* did you figure that out?"

His features are at war with each other. Half of them amused and the other half annoyed. His jaw, on the annoyed team, clenches. "Because it isn't that hard to figure out. Because I've already dropped the ball with you once when you fooled me into thinking that you were dating my twin. And *because* I know how your twisted little mind works."

I fist his shirt harder. "You really need to let that dating thing go, okay?" His jaw clenches again, but I keep going, "I fooled you. Deal with it. You fooled me too. We're even. And second, aren't you?"

"Aren't I what?"

"Into soccer because your brothers are?"

"I'm into soccer because it comes easy to me."

"But you don't even like soccer," I say urgently.

"So?"

"So you could be doing something else. You could be doing something with the books and—"

"No."

"But—"

"No."

"But, Stellan—"

"Fuck no."

I glare up at him, breathing harshly. "I don't get it."

He's breathing harshly too. "You don't need to get it."

"I do," I tell him.

"Yeah, why?"

"Because..." I try to shake him, but he's so strong and solid that all I manage to do is pull him even closer until we're breathing against each other, our breaths fighting. "Because I love you, you idiot. I care about you. I want you to be happy and soccer doesn't make you happy."

A particularly hard gust of air escapes him at my words.

Like I gave him wings with my words and then brought him back down to the ground.

By saying those three words.

Which is so ironic because they make me want to fly.

He grabs my face then, tightly, tilting my head back. "You want me to be happy, yeah?"

I nod.

"So then I want you to stop with the love bullshit and get a clue," he growls, his body pressing down on me. "This isn't a good thing, Dora. Loving me is not a good thing. I have said this to you a million times. You need to smarten up and move on from a man like me. That's what we are trying to do here before you go marry my fucking brother, all right? We're not trying to fall in love, we're trying to make you fall out of it. So if you want me to be happy, you will stop messing with things you don't understand and let it the fuck happen."

Let it happen, is it?

He wants me to fall out of love with him. When every time I say it or allude to it, it looks like I've given him the world. It looks like I've made him the most relieved and satisfied and the happiest man alive.

"By you fucking me?"

"Love is a drug," he tells me. "It's an addiction. The best way to break an addiction is to indulge in it so much that you get sick of it. Or you overdose and they take you to the hospital and pump it out of you, whichever comes first. So yeah, by fucking you. And fucking you so much you either get sick of me or stroke out and realize I'm fucking toxic."

But you know what, fuck him.

I'm so mad I could bite him.

"Give me my ring back," I order.

A thundering expression crosses his face. "No."

"Give it to me."

"No."

I smack his chest. "If you want me to marry your twin brother, then give me my ring back."

Coming closer, he pushes his nose against mine. "You will get a ring when you marry him. You don't need this one."

I smack his chest again. "I need it to keep men like you away."

His fingers flex around my face. "You have a man like me to keep men like me away."

I scratch his jaw then. "What's so bad about you, huh? Other than the fact that you are an asshole and a liar."

"Everything," he growls, tugging on my hair. "Everything is bad about me."

I can see he believes that.

He absolutely believes it.

And you know what, I believe him too.

I believe there's something bad in him. Something that makes him think he's a bad brother, a bad man. But more than that I believe that whatever it is, it's more harmful to him than it can ever be to me.

So when I see the self-loathing so thick on his features, my heart squeezes and I fuse our mouths together. When I should be leaving, I hold on to him so tightly with my entire body that our edges blur and mesh together.

And even though he wants me to leave him, he holds on to me just as tightly. Tighter, in fact. So much so that he's crushing me into the snowy ground while at the same time, keeping me plastered to his chest. And our kiss feels so desperate.

As desperate as the kiss of two people in love who are afraid to lose each other.

～

The next morning, I'm walking down the hotel parking lot to get to the bus so we can head out while thinking about when to tell Shepard.

It has to be today, though. I just need to figure out when exactly.

I'm aware that it will stress him out and maybe I should wait until the season is over so he can focus on the game. But I've already hid the truth from him before and it didn't turn out that well. Plus, the championship game—which I'm sure they'll get to play—is still a few weeks away and I'm *not* waiting that long to tell my fiancé that this isn't working out. As in he can't fix things. He can't help me move on.

I'm very firmly—even more firmly—stuck on his twin brother.

And that I *slept* with the said twin brother last night.

Twice.

Well, he fucked me just once but then in the park, he ate me out while I lay there on the cold grass, all heated by his body and his mouth on my sore pussy, and tasted snow on my tongue every time I gasped.

For the record, I told Stellan that it was really unfair that he keeps getting to eat my pussy while I still haven't gotten to taste his cock. And his words were: "Yeah, but see, I'm an asshole with double standards. I don't really give a fuck about what you want right now. As long as I get to bury my face in your cherry-flavored cunt and make it dance on my tongue like you danced for me. And keep doing that until sometime next week. So instead of arguing with me, why don't you relax like Daddy's good whore and let him spread your legs and get some pussy, yeah?"

Actually, if we're counting the number of times he ate me out yesterday as sleeping with him, then I think the count is up to three times or four...

I'm almost at the bus now while pondering such dilemmas, which is when it happens. I slip on the patch of ice and bump my forehead on the side of the open door.

"Ow," I whine.

"Shit. You okay?"

Did I mention that I've been thinking about telling my fiancé that I had sex with his twin brother *while* walking with said fiancé?

Yes, that's exactly the scenario I've found myself in.

And I think it's karma. I betrayed Shepard last night—although if we're being honest, I've been betraying him ever since I've known him—and now the universe is biting me in the ass. In any case, he looks concerned as he climbs down the steps of the bus to come check on me, which makes me feel even guiltier.

I rub my forehead that's slightly throbbing. "Yeah, I guess I just wasn't looking."

He removes my hand gently from the spot to replace it with his. "Hmm. Doesn't look too bad." He presses the spot and I hiss. "Ah, it got you, huh. But—"

"What happened?"

A loud and very familiar voice cuts Shep off and his jaw clenches. He glances over my shoulders, and I know he's watching his twin brother arrive. I also know that his brother is getting closer fast because with every second, Shepard's jaw gets harder and his eyes harsher.

Shit.

This isn't going to be good, is it?

He gets really upset when something hurts me—as evidenced by his ministrations last night and countless other things that he's done over the past year—and after what happened at the bar when he had to come to my rescue, this is going to be really, really bad.

I spin around just as he reaches us, and I realize I was right.

It is going to be bad.

He's dressed as he usually does, in a workout T-shirt that emphasizes his dense muscles and low-slung sweatpants with his hair pushed back and polished as always. But the rest of him has agitation written all over it. His tight face, his heavy breaths and his dark, frantic eyes that land on me.

I open my mouth to tell him that it's okay, but he gets to speak first. "What the fuck happened?"

I wince at his lashing voice. Not because I'm scared of it or him, but because he's worrying over nothing. Taking a step toward him, I soothe, "Nothing. It's just... I wasn't watching where I was going and I literally walked into a door. It was so stupid. And so embarrassing but..."

I trail off.

Because for some reason, my explanation—that I thought would put him at ease—is kinda making things worse. His eyes are darkening, which I didn't think was possible, and his face, which was already very angled, looks even more angular now.

And then there's his voice.

It isn't lashing anymore, but I don't think it's a good thing. Because it's low and rough and it shivers down my spine as he says, "You walked into a door."

I want to say yes. I want to once again put his mind at ease.

But for some reason, I can't speak. My heart's pounding something fierce now and I can't think over how loud it's being.

Or at least I can't think of anything other than this one thing: I've seen him do this or be like this before. Very recently, in fact. On the night of my engagement when I told him about my mom.

When I was being all casual about it—while not feeling casual on the inside, though; on the inside, I was downright miserable and hurt—and he stood there both still and vibrating. He stood there both hot skin and cold eyes.

He looks exactly like that right now.

His posture may be rigid and carved out of stone. But the vein on the side of his neck is pulsating intensely, making me think of his heart beneath layers and layers of ice, beating and pulsing like it's going to beat out of his chest.

"Stellan? I..." I take another step. "It's fine. I'm—"

His eyes move over my shoulders and his jaw hardens further. Much like Shepard's had but on him, it looks severe, much more dangerous. "Where were you?"

"What?" Shepard says.

"What the fuck were you doing?" he asks, again in that low, vibrating, *shaking* voice.

"What?" Shepard goes in disbelief. "What is your problem? I—"

Finally, something breaks in Stellan, I think.

Because he moves toward Shepard, advances on him really and his voice booms, "What the fuck is my problem? What the fuck is your problem? Where were you, huh? Where the fuck were you when she was getting her head bumped? Why weren't you looking after her? Why weren't you—"

Even though my eyes are pinned on Stellan, I know Shepard has come closer as well. I can hear his feet shuffling behind me, his voice getting angrier, "Hey, listen, you asshole, I'm not her babysitter. I'm not—"

"No, you're not," Stellan bites out, his teeth clenched. "You're her fucking fiancé. You're supposed to look out for her. You're supposed to—"

"If you've got a problem with how I treat my fiancée, I don't give a fuck, all right. I—"

Stellan goes to advance on Shepard, and I decide to stop being frozen and absolutely horrified at what's happening and how it even came about and stop him. I thrust my body between him and Shepard, and say, "Stellan, stop. It's okay. I'm okay."

He's still staring at Shepard, his eyes promising murder, his chest displaying all the mayhem inside of him. "You can't drop the ball here, do you understand? You cannot drop the fucking ball with her. It's *her*. It's—"

"Stellan, stop," I plead, my voice thick with tears. "Please, stop. It's fine."

But I don't think he's listening to me.

I don't think he can listen.

Not over the chaos in his own body, over his own loud breaths and his heartbeat. And I probably shouldn't do it. I probably should not get even closer to him because for some reason, I'm very aware of the fact that I slept with him last night.

I'm very aware of the fact that only a few hours ago, we were tangled up with each other and watching the snow. Before he dropped me off at my room and told me to lock the door like he always does.

And when I did but promptly unlocked it to throw it open, I found him standing in the exact same spot. Looking exactly like he had the first time I'd found him standing there.

So I jumped into his arms once again and we made out like two people with *In. Sane* chemistry just inside my door. After which, he finally left, and I fell on my bed and spent the next hours dreaming about him.

So again, now that I've grown closer to him, I shouldn't do this either. I shouldn't put my hand on his chest, which feels feverish to the touch.

But I do it.

Because I don't think I have any other choice. I don't think he'll hear me otherwise.

"Stellan," I say, pressing my hand right where his heart is. And God, it's going. It's really, really going and that's what keeps me firmly in my place. "Stellan, please. Look at me."

When he still doesn't, I increase the pressure and get so close that we're touching in a way that I don't think I *should* be touching my fiancé's twin brother, not out in public at least where my fiancé can see it.

But I decide to put that out of my head and focus my energy on saving Shepard because from the looks of it, Stellan may murder him.

"Stellan," I try again, fisting his T-shirt. "Look at me, please. Just *look at me*."

Finally, my urgency gets through to him and he jerks his eyes away from Shepard. They come to settle or more like crash against me and God, they're so intense, so penetrating, so full of things that look like urgency and anger and restlessness and... is that fear? I don't even know anymore, what his gaze is made up of.

There are a thousand different emotions in them and fuck everything else.

Fuck the world.

I have to put my other hand on his chest. I have to get even closer to him.

I have to soothe him, put him at ease about something that I don't even understand. All I know is that he's burning, and I have to save him.

"I'm fine," I whisper loud enough so that only he can hear me, so that he thinks we're in a safe bubble and not part of this world or whatever it is that's happening to him. "Nothing happened, I promise. You can see for yourself. I'm really fine. It's okay, Stellan. You can—"

"What the fuck's happening?"

I snatch my hands back and move away as the third lashing voice enters the scene. I don't have to look to know who it is. It's Coach Thorne and he looks angry. At which point I also realize that there's a crowd gathered around us. Mostly they're all on the bus, crowded around the windows as they witness what's happening.

And I take a few more steps back.

And two things happen at once: My back collides with Shepard's chest and he takes the opportunity to wrap his arm around me and Jesus, pin my spine to his chest. As if staking his claim.

In front of his twin brother.

And second, his brother absolutely notices it, his eyes glancing down to Shepard's arm around my chest, his fingers curled over my shoulder. And his stance gets wider, that chaos in his eyes getting crazier. Although right now the dominating emotion happens to be anger.

It happens to be retribution and mayhem.

Then Shepard speaks and I think all hell is going to break loose. "Stellan here thinks that I'm not doing my job well."

This is addressed to Conrad, but I'm watching Stellan getting this close to losing it. I wish he'd look at me instead of Shepard's arm on me.

Conrad speaks. "Shepard, on the bus. Right now." Then, to Stellan, "You and me, we need to talk."

No one moves for the next few seconds.

Which prompts Conrad to repeat his command to Shepard and thankfully move his arm from around me. I breathe out a sigh of relief as Stellan looks into my eyes. I give him a shaky smile, just to reassure him that I'm fine. That there's no need for this, but he grits his jaw before commanding, "Go."

Swallowing, I nod and follow Shepard into the bus.

I want to look out so badly. So fucking badly and see what Conrad and Stellan are talking about, but I don't dare move my eyes away from my feet. I hold myself tightly too, lest I break down and run back to him to give him the biggest and tightest hug he's ever gotten in his life.

And then climb his body and kiss him and kiss him until the end of time.

I think by the time I reach my seat—Shepard has gotten waylaid somewhere to chat with a couple of his teammates—I have gotten my urges under control. But then I see a simple, unassuming white gift bag on my seat with a rose peeking out of it and I lose it.

A tear falls down my cheek as I pick it up with trembling hands. My knees give out and I plop down on my seat when I stick my hand inside and feel what it is.

My white dress.

The one he tore.

I pull it out and notice that the bodice is mended. It's as good as new. Did he... Did he sew the dress for me? I clutch the rose to my chest as I also discover a note inside it.

And it says,

Sorry. For the dress and for setting your favorite flower on fire.

CHAPTER 10

THE WILDFIRE THORN

*T*oday is going to be a bad day.
I knew that as soon as I woke up.
I didn't get a lot of sleep last night, but when I did manage to find some, I saw my mother in my dreams. Not the first time and probably won't be the last either. I usually don't remember any specifics of dreams like this except her face. She looks like how she always looked: tired but loving, her blonde hair fluttering around her face, her blue eyes looking at each of us with endless patience even though she should've lost it a long time ago.

And in the midst of all that, there was a bruise on the side of her head.

She would have a lot of them from what I remember. But she always had excuses for them too. Excuses that no five-year-old would ever doubt, no matter how transparent they seemed.

I did, though.

I always did.

Because I knew the truth. It's a burden to know it, isn't it? The one who knows the truth is always the one whose shoulders are the heaviest.

Anyway, I knew right away as soon as I woke up that today was going to be one of those days when I needed to distance myself from everyone.

"What the fuck was all that?" my brother Conrad snaps.

This is not distancing, though.

I look at him from where I'm standing just inside the door to one of the back rooms on the bus. We're on our way to our next game and this was the only place we could've talked. Set up like an office with a tiny desk and a chair, this isn't a huge space, but it affords privacy. And it's better than standing in the middle of the parking lot and having words with onlookers, which is what my brother wanted.

If it were up to me, we wouldn't be having this conversation at all.

Standing on the other side of the desk, he doesn't give me a chance to reply as he continues, "I cannot believe I'm having this conversation with you: but what's going on with you? What's happening? You're benching players, arguing with them. You're acting like you're pissed off at the world, more than usual. Is it because—"

"Mom would say that," I say softly, causing him to stop and look at me with a frown.

"What?"

I lean against the door only because my knees are shaking. "She'd say she walked into a door."

Conrad is watching me carefully. "What are you talking about?"

I look into his eyes. "When he beat her."

Conrad blinks.

That's the only reaction he gives me. But that doesn't mean he isn't affected. Our oldest brother is the most controlled, disciplined, self-sacrificing man I've ever known. He gave up his dreams, his career, his happiness for the sake of us. And he would've kept doing it if he hadn't found the girl of his dreams and if she hadn't pulled him out of his still life.

He's the best man I know.

People compare me to him. My own siblings say I'm Conrad 2.0. Good, controlled, quiet, responsible. They can depend on me. They know I'll show up. They know I'll get the job done.

But I know the truth, don't I?

I know I'm nothing like Conrad.

I know I'm not good.

All of this is a way to keep me leashed. It's a way to keep them safe from me. It's a way that I don't become the man who birthed us.

"You..." he begins but trails off. "When he beat her."

"I know," I tell him.

His jaw clenches for a second. "What do you know?"

I swallow, pressing my spine against the door, looking for something in the room that I can use to ground myself. Because the world is slowly disappearing. And then I remember.

Her touch.

From only a few minutes ago.

It was soft, feathery at first and then became tight and hot. Strong. Stronger than I could've guessed for a girl so tiny.

I use that.

I use the memory of her touch in the middle of all the chaos and take a deep breath. "That on top of being an alcoholic with anger issues and a fucking manwhore who fucked around on Mom, Dad was also abusive. He hit her. Smacked her around when anger got too much."

"You—"

"And I know you know that. Of course you know that. You've seen it. You grew up with it more than any of us did. Which is why I also know that you've kept it from us."

His fists are clenched and that tight control that's his forte is straining at the edges. I can see he's shocked that I knew. But also angry that there was something to know in the first place. And then his protective instinct kicks in like always and he asks, "Does anyone else—"

"No." Then, "Not beside you and me. And more recently Ledger."

Ledger had to be told because of his own anger issues.

Conrad's still cautious. "So Callie doesn't know?"

"Absolutely not," I assure him.

I'd die before I'd let Callie find out. Even though she's married now—to the guy we all hated once upon a time, by the way—with a baby girl and another on the way, she's still our baby sister. And nothing touches her. Least of all our piece of shit father who left as soon as she was born, quoting her birth to be the reason for his abandonment.

"And Shepard?"

I think of how small her hand looked on my heavily breathing chest only minutes before and take another deep breath at my twin brother's mention. "No."

Not that it gives Conrad any relief because he asks in the same tight voice, "How do you know?"

Sometimes I forget that I'm one of his brothers. That he cares about me as well. Not because he hasn't shown it over the years but because it's hard for me to imagine, after all that I am and all that's inside of me, that he'd find me worthy of his care.

But then again, he doesn't know the truth about me, does he?

"He told me," I answer him.

"Dad told you," he asks in a flat voice, but I know the question is there.

"Yeah," I say, thinking about her sitting out there, by the window, her eyes on the passing scenery like she wants to be out there rather than cooped up in a bus with a bunch of Neanderthals who can't stop salivating over her. "I think I was about five. I found him crying in the backyard. He said he'd done something bad. And when I asked what, he told me. He said he'd never done this before and that he wouldn't, after this."

I'm fisting and unfisting my fingers.

I'm trying to keep her face in my mind. Her unique metallic gray eyes; her pouty lips; the way she looked when she caught the snowflakes in her hands last night.

"Fucking liar," Conrad mutters.

"What?"

Conrad looks at me a beat as if he doesn't know if he should say it. But then decides to and shares, "Wasn't the first time."

I go still.

"He got his start long before that."

He says more, my brother. I can see his mouth moving, but I can't hear him. And in a few seconds, I know that I won't be able to see him either. He'll disappear right alongside the world that's already getting blurry by the second.

I'm trying to imagine the feel of her hand on my body. I'm trying to imagine her laughter, her voice. I'm trying to imagine the way she looked when I made her come, wings flanking her, black hair sprawled over the pillow, all flushed and hot, dewy with sweat, so beautiful that if my heart wasn't buried under six feet of ice, it would've broken at the sheer beauty of her.

I'm trying to *fucking* imagine.

But nothing is helping me slow down the race of my heartbeats. The rush of my blood.

"I am like him."

Maybe it's just me, but I think the world has gone quiet. There's a pin drop silence both on the outside of my body and on the inside.

And I can breathe.

I can see.

Aside from the obvious advantages, I don't know why I said that. What made me blurt out the biggest secret of my life. The secret I wanted to take to my grave.

Maybe it's the fact that it's suddenly gotten harder now.

Much, much harder to keep it.

To carry this secret around.

Not from the world, no. The world can go fuck itself.

From *her*.

After last night.

After how she looked at me with her gemstone eyes. Like I'm her hero. Like even though I have something bad in me, I still have something good too. I'm worthy of redemption.

Of her forgiveness.

Sometimes I think that pretending to be my twin brother and deceiving her were the least of my crimes. Because this is a bigger deception, playing this role of a good guy.

In reality, I'm an unhinged, unstable grenade who couldn't even look at her without going into a mad panic. The feeling of hopelessness and helplessness that used to overcome me whenever Mom used to make excuses for her bruises.

In reality, I'm an emotionally paralyzed man who couldn't even take her joke. She was joking about the door, wasn't she? I could see that. I could see she was trying to put me at ease, but like a moron, I couldn't take it.

I didn't even ask her if she was okay.

I didn't even have the decency to make sure *she* was okay.

So maybe I blurted the truth out because I had to. I had no other choice. Because if I can't tell her—I'm not going to fucking scare her; she's already been plenty traumatized by me—then maybe I could tell someone else.

And fuck, it's relieving.

It's a fucking relief. The soothing feeling under my skin is relief, isn't it?

Although I have no right to feel it because I confessed my crime to the last person I should have: my big brother. Who's had to take all our shit for so long so he doesn't need mine.

Who also doesn't believe me. "You're like who?"

I know he heard me, *and* he understood me. But he's confirming, so I give him what he wants. "Dad."

Again, he chooses to watch me impassively for a few seconds. "Sit."

"I'm not—"

"Sit the fuck down."

My brother doesn't know the danger he is in. He truly does not or he wouldn't have asked me to move from my spot. I had deliberately kept myself glued to it, my feet firmly rooted on the floor and my back firmly plastered on the wooden door.

Because I know if I moved, I wouldn't be able to stop myself or pull myself back from the things I don't want to do. It's like you're afraid of going too fast so you stand still.

But I do it.

I very carefully place one foot in front of the other as if I'm carrying explosives in the pit of my stomach and take a seat.

Conrad does the same.

"Explain to me how you're like him."

I've never done this before.

Never *imagined* doing this.

I don't know how to start. What to say. So I pick the most obvious one, to me at least. "I get angry."

A few moments of silence before, "The whole world gets angry."

"I'm a little different than the world."

"In what way?"

"In the way that I want to burn it down."

He moves his jaw back and forth. "Are you saying... that you're like Ledger?"

Ledger, our youngest brother, has issues with anger. He's always had issues with it. Growing up, he'd get into fights at school, at the playground. He'd be constantly suspended, threatened to be expelled. It was always either me or Conrad who had to go and clean up his mess.

Every time I was called in for the duty, I wanted to tell him. I wanted to share that I am like him. That maybe we could deal with it together; I could teach him like I'd taught myself. But something always held me back.

Something like the fact that we weren't—aren't—the same.

I'm worse than him.

So I did what I could. Without blurting my secret out. Even last season when he was suspended from the games, I tried to reach out to him, explain to him how important it is that he gets help. We even forced him into going to anger management classes, which drove a wedge between us, but still.

"No," I tell Conrad. "I'm not like him."

"I don't—"

"I'm worse than him," I state.

"You're worse."

"Yes, the guy he punched last season, for which he got benched," I explain, my eyes locked with my brother's. "I would've put him in a coma."

I would have.

It was a guy from a rival team and Ledger had punched him during a live game because he was spewing bullshit about Ledger and the fact that he comes from soccer royalty, shocking everyone and earning him severe displeasure from the team and higher-ups on the board.

I was one of them, the people who were displeased.

Not because I am this good guy who doesn't believe in violence—I absolutely believe in it; I just don't give in to it—but because I knew how it must have felt and I wish I were there to help him through it.

So the displeasure was for myself.

Not for my younger brother.

"All this time... I..." He shakes his head. "You ..."

Conrad is one of those men who measures his words and speaks only when there's an absolute need to. In this way, yes, we are alike. Although I guess his inclination for keeping quiet is natural while mine is fabricated to keep me under leash, like everything else in my life.

In any case, he may be quiet, but I've never seen him speechless.

It doesn't feel good that I'm responsible for it.

"I never saw it," he says simply.

"No one did," I begin. "Because I kept a lid on it. I kept a very tight fucking lid on my anger, my issues." Then, "And I never told anyone about them because I didn't want to burden anyone. You, specifically. We already had a father who was a monster, who'd beat his wife. Who'd beat his son." Conrad goes still. "Yeah, I saw him hit you one time, when you were protecting Mom. It made me so angry. So fucking angry and I wanted to..." I grit my teeth. "I wanted to do something... bad. I wanted to hit him back even though I was just a kid. I wanted to hit and smack and fucking punch everything and everyone I could find. So I did the opposite. I *always* did the opposite. I pushed it down and focused elsewhere. I did chores. I did homework. I followed all the rules, every rule, all the time. I ran all the errands. I played soccer. I ran track. I was in the swim club. I was in the math club, science club, all the fucking clubs. I did everything I could to push my anger down because I did not want to be like him. I didn't want to do the things he did.

"And then there was Ledger, his anger, his reckless behavior. So we already had two people in our family who were similar on top of every other thing that went wrong with us. Dad's leaving, Mom's sickness. You did everything you could for us. You left your career, your dreams, the girl you loved, to deal with us. I didn't want to be one of the things you had to deal with as well."

Yeah, there was a girl he loved.

Back when he was in high school. I never liked her, and she never made him happy; I could see that. But I wanted him to come to that conclusion by himself rather than fucking fate taking that choice away from him and causing them to break up because of Mom's illness and his increased responsibilities.

"So I was taking care of it myself," I finish.

And I was.

I *am*.

I've read books. I've done research. That's how I know what a grounding object is. I know all the breathing exercises and tips to recognizing your triggers. Staying away from those triggers. Distancing yourself from them.

Which is why again, today is not a good day.

Besides I didn't think I deserved any help. Not after what I am.

"Do you call that taking care of it?" Conrad asks after a while. "What happened out there?"

I stiffen in my seat. "That was different."

He watches me with shrewd eyes. "Are you saying that you didn't want to beat the shit out of your twin brother?" Then, "Because I've seen you with him. I know he tests your patience. He tests everybody's patience. It was nothing different. But somehow you were. Somehow I've never seen you this close to breaking."

My fists clench. "He's not doing it right."

"Doing what right?"

"Taking care of her."

It's true, isn't it?

What the fuck was he doing last night when she needed his help? Why *the fuck* was he flirting with those girls when he should've been there for her? Why the fuck was he flirting in the first place when he has a fucking fiancée?

How in the world can he look at someone else when he has her to look at?

How in the *fucking world* does he look away from her in the first place?

How the fuck is he engaged to her in the first place?

When I asked him to take care of her, I didn't mean fucking marry her. I didn't mean that he fucking make her *his wife*.

His...

I tighten my fists. Just the thought makes me want to get up, grab her from him, and fucking run away somewhere. I wouldn't even waste time beating him up as long as I have her with me.

As long as I get to protect her.

Cherish her, fucking worship her like he should be doing right now.

Rather than letting her almost get attacked by other men and bump her fucking head on the door.

I mean, fucking *Christ*.

He should be beside her, at all times.

He should be holding her hand, steering her away from danger. He should be laying out fucking flowers and stars and clouds in her path. Actually, no, he should be carrying her everywhere she goes because there's a chance she might slip on a cloud or get her heel caught up in the petals of a flower.

"So then"—Conrad shifts in the chair—"are you saying that you know how to take care of her?"

"No," I say instantly.

Because I can't give her what she wants from me: love. Even if I set aside the fact that I have this giant fucking beast inside of me that demands my absolute control every second of every day, I wouldn't even know how to love her.

I never learned.

In fact, I've spent my entire life unlearning any emotions, burying them deep inside of me. Besides, she said that I didn't know how to care for her the right way and she's right. Even if she's forgotten her anger at me, I haven't. I *remember*.

"You know they're engaged, don't you? You know that means they're going to get married." Then, leaning forward, "You know that I told you that you should get away. Do you remember that?"

I do.

In one of my weakest moments, I confessed my feelings to Conrad. He himself was going through a crisis of his own—relating to Wyn, his now fiancée—and I ended up telling him about my crisis to make him feel better. He told me to get away from them. To get away from all the misery that was in store for me.

Of course I didn't.

I couldn't have, now that I think about it.

Even if there was a slightest chance to see her, to be near her, I would've taken it.

"She loves me," I tell him.

"What?" he bites out.

"I'm fixing it."

"You're fixing it."

"Yes."

He shifts in his seat again. "Explain to me one more time what you mean by that."

"It means"—I take a deep breath—"she'll marry Shepard. Because Shepard is the right guy for her. They both suit each other."

You'd think that after saying this same set of words so many times, I'd be more used to it, and it wouldn't taste bitter. You'd think that days after that fucking engagement, I wouldn't want to simultaneously obliterate my twin and vomit my guts out at the thought of them tied together for the rest of their lives.

But I do.

These words taste bitter.

In fact, after days of watching them together, days of watching her wear his ring, they taste like poison now.

Poison that burns, that gives third degree burns.

The only thing, the only fucking thing, that gives me relief right now, as hollow as it might be, is the fact that I have that ring in my pocket. It's sitting heavy and hot, but at least it's not on her finger.

"And what of the little fact that she loves you?"

I thrust my hand down my pocket and fist the ring. "As I just said, I'm fixing it. I'm helping her move on."

"From you."

I press my thumb against the diamond. "Yes."

"You do know how insane that sounds, don't you?"

I realize that.

To an outsider, it does sound insane. To an outsider, it looks like I'm stealing my twin brother's bride-to-be. But the world doesn't know what we have.

The world doesn't know what this is all about.

I'm trying to make her happy. I'm trying to give her what she wants—love—the only way I can. By getting her to move on from me and marry the man who loves her.

When she sees that I'm not the man she thinks I am; when she realizes the things she wants from me, vulnerability, intimacy, emotions are not something I'm capable of giving, she'll lose interest.

She'll move on.

It'll hurt, but she'll be better for it in the long run.

But I'd be lying if I said I'm doing this solely for selfless reasons, no. I'm also doing this for me. I'm doing this because while she's falling out of love with a man like me, I could get to be with a girl like her.

Even if for a little while.

Because I may not be her destiny, but she is mine.

Taking a deep breath, I look at my brother to find him steadily watching me. "Are you"—I swallow, my chest tight—"disappointed?"

"With what?"

"With the fact that I'm like the man we hate the most."

Conrad takes his time answering the question and in the seconds that pass, I regret asking it. I regret telling him the truth about me. No matter how strangely relieved I feel at having shared the burden, it still wasn't a very good idea.

"We do hate him the most," he says finally. "He was a deadbeat dad. He fucked around on Mom; he beat her, abused her. He left us when we needed him the most, when Callie needed him the most and she didn't even know it. So yeah, he deserves to be hated. But you're not like him."

CHAPTER 11

I always wanted to see his room.

And even though I got a peek of it through the phone screen that one night, it still wasn't as satisfying as actually being in his room in person. So it makes me happy. Although how I got in here isn't something that's going to make him happy all that much. I stole the master keycard from the housekeeping cart. But only for a minute and I didn't even have to flirt with anyone in order to do so.

So maybe he should take that as a win and move on.

When I tell him, I mean.

I haven't yet; because he's not here.

I don't know where he is, which is why I've had to take such drastic measures as stealing and sneaking into his room to wait for him to get back from wherever he went off to. Which happened as soon as we reached our next destination.

After his long talk with Conrad in one of those back rooms, he came out looking grim. So severely grim and rigid that I almost sprang out of my seat and went after him. I almost forgot that my fiancé was sitting right next to me. And today was the day he decided to spend his entire time sitting beside me. Maybe because today was also the day that *he* decided to sit up front and away from his usual spot.

And as the time passed, his grimness didn't go away.

He hardly looked at anyone. In fact, I'm sure in the entire four hours of our journey, his eyes were firmly planted on his clipboard and his laptop screen.

In any case, I didn't get a chance to talk to him at all. Not even through texts because I couldn't text him on the bus, but then when we did reach it and I could, he wouldn't reply back.

And since all else has failed, this is what I've chosen to do.

I stand in the middle of his room, but it doesn't look like his room yet. As in, all his stuff is packed and sitting in a corner and every other object, furniture, the little armchairs and the desk, in the room is untouched. While I know that much of his room is probably going to stay that way, I know at some point he's going to have to make use of the empty closet and of course bring out his books.

That he isn't going to be able to read.

Because of me.

Because of how much I disturb his peace.

Which at one point made me happy when I resigned myself to the fact that what people thought about him was right: he is cold. But now it makes me sad when I *know* I was right all along: he's as hot as wildfire.

I mean look at the way he reacted to my little accident. That, if not for his such an intense reaction, I wouldn't even remember right now.

Which gives me an idea.

It's terrible. I am terrible for thinking it, but I can beat myself up about it later. Right now, I need to do things. I need to know what his secret is because I'm starting to think that there is one. There is a freaking secret, which is why he thinks he's so bad: a bad brother, a bad man.

I flit about his room, dragging his luggage from where it's sitting in that corner by the door and opening it to look through his things. One by one, I dig through his clothes and since I'm already unpacking, I also hang his clothes in the closet. See? I can be nice. I also arrange his shoes and put his T-shirts and things away in the chest. At one point, I take my own clothes off and put on one of his coats just because being here has made me miss him more and he's always putting me in his coats, isn't he? I guess I'll just save him a step and wear it myself.

His books are packed in a different suitcase—have to be for how many there are—and I bring them out as well and arrange them on the bed, like I saw them that one night, before picking out what looks the most interesting to me so I can give it to him to read and promise that I won't distract him.

When I've unpacked every single thing he owns, everything very normal and run of the mill, I once again stand in the middle of his room, both relieved and disappointed. I don't know what I was hoping to find, but I didn't find it and I don't know if it's a good thing or a bad thing.

Sighing, I crawl into his bed, among the scattered books, and lie down. I decide to watch some TV to stay awake until he gets here.

And the next thing I know, I hear the shower running in the bathroom and I'm jerking upright in the bed. In the process of that, I realize that my legs get tangled up in something: a blanket.

I'm covered in a blanket.

I wasn't covered in a blanket when I got into bed.

My eyes snap over to the bathroom. The door to it is ajar and steam wafts through it and...

He's here, isn't he?

He's back.

Just as the thought occurs to me, the shower shuts off and a few seconds later, the man of my dreams is standing at the threshold, rendering me speechless.

Rendering me frozen and breathless.

Because all I can do is stare at him. At his gorgeous, magnificent, breathtaking body that's draped in only a simple white towel. That I think makes his tanned skin, in contrast, look even darker and more delicious, shinier. Or it could be the fact that his muscles—holy *God*, his muscles—are still damp from the shower.

They're actually wet if we go by the droplets, several of them, sluicing down the hills of his chest and the rugged terrain of his abs. I think it's his hair; it's wet, falling over his forehead and he hasn't really toweled the water off. So the droplets are cascading down the side of his neck, tracing his veins, and his shoulders, bumping onto his sculpted collarbone, and *oh my God*, he has to be the sexiest man alive.

He has to be.

Even that light dusting of his chest hair is sexy.

"I love your chest hair," I blurt out and then immediately both blush and cringe.

I don't think that was very cool of me, just blurting things out like that without context. On the other hand, though, he does know my obsessive tendencies, so what the hell.

In any case, I can't really tell what he's thinking because his features are all blank, his eyes cool. "You should put some clothes on."

I fist the blanket. "What?"

He walks farther into the room and goes straight to the chest. While getting his drawstring pants out, he says, "And I'll bring you back to your room."

I dig my heels on his bed as if planting them even more firmly. "I'm not going back to my room. Where..."

I had more to say, I swear. But then he drops his towel on the floor, and I forget all the words in the world. Because I get to see his ass for the first time and... I guess what they say about being able to bounce a quarter off an ass is actually a real thing.

It's reality.

I could bounce a quarter off of Stellan Thorne's ass because Stellan Thorne's ass is a work of art. It's tight as a drum and round. And he actually has these dips on the sides that means that just like his chest and abs and arms and thighs, every inch of his butt is made of tight, sculpted muscles.

And I want to bite it.

I do.

How come I didn't get to bite his ass last night? How come he's keeping himself away from me like this?

Once he's put his pants on, he turns and commands, "Let's go."

I keep my fingers fisted around the blanket and my heels digging into the mattress. "Where were you?"

His chest moves with a large breath as he repeats, much closer this time, "Let's go."

I jump out of bed then, my heart racing. "I texted you. But you never got back to me."

Another breath, but this time it's accompanied by his gaze flicking up and down my body. Very quickly and almost impassively. "I was busy."

I take a step toward him. "With what?"

He doesn't like my question as evidenced by his sharp exhale. "Can you just put some clothes on so we can go? I'd like to get some sleep tonight."

"No," I state.

This he definitely does not like because his sharp exhales are followed by a muscle on his cheek jumping. "No?"

"No, I won't put any clothes on."

"You—"

"Because I already have clothes on." I wave my hand down my body. "Your coat."

"That's—"

"So if you're so eager to make me leave, you're going to have to drag me out of here, kicking and screaming, wearing just your coat and nothing else underneath," I declare.

He looks down at me and I realize I started this conversation when I was by the side of the bed, but I'm finishing it only a few feet away from him. Meaning, I've been walking toward him all this time and somehow I have no recollection of it.

Somehow my body already knew what to do, my legs already knew what direction to walk in.

His.

And now that I'm here, it's harder to maintain this minuscule of a distance.

It feels cruel that I don't get to touch him when I'm so close to him.

"And what about him?" he asks, his voice growly.

"What about who?"

"Your fucking fiancé."

Oh, right.

I have a fiancé.

Still.

I didn't get to talk to Shepard either today. Even though we spent all four hours sitting side by side—me pretending to be busy with reading for my drama class and him playing games on his phone—I never brought up the subject of our engagement. I mean, I wasn't going to bring it up with the entire soccer team present, including the coaches. Including *him*.

And when we reached the hotel, he disappeared as well. I take full responsibility for the fact that I was busier trying to track down the love of my life than my fiancé, though.

Guilt sits heavy in my stomach, but for now, I'm going to ignore it and focus on this asshole in front of me. Who's not *really* an asshole but likes to act like one sometimes.

"How do you think he's going to feel if I drag you out of here, kicking and screaming, wearing only my coat?"

"My fiancé is your twin brother. So maybe, *just maybe*," I say, looking up at him, "you could answer my questions instead of fighting with me. And we could avoid this whole hallway drama and be respectful to him."

He advances on me then, his eyes narrowed, flashing with threatening things. "You think I want to be respectful to him?"

Swallowing, I start stepping back. "He's your brother."

"Yeah," he rumbles, his face dipped as he keeps gaining on me. "And he put his fucking ring on your finger."

My heart's racing. "The ring that you won't give back."

"Because why should he get everything, huh? Why *the fuck*," he bites out, leaning down farther, "should he get every fucking thing in this world?"

"But—"

"He gets to fucking marry you, doesn't he?" he cuts me off. "He gets to make all your childish dreams of love come true. He can live without you wearing his fucking ring on your finger for a few fucking weeks."

"Love is not childish," I say, my heart twisting.

"It's a fucking nuisance, though." He leans closer. "A nuisance I don't fucking need right now. Like you."

A second later, my back collides with the wall and I say, my breaths harsh, "You know you sound completely irrational right now, don't you?"

His jaw tics for a few seconds. "Yes."

"So—"

"But you're still not getting the ring back."

I look up, my fingers pulling and twisting the hem of his coat. "What am I supposed to tell him?"

"Tell him you lost it."

"He's doing this for me, okay? He put this ring on my finger because he's helping me and—"

"He'll live."

"You're being completely—"

"Irrational, I know."

"You..." I shake my head. "I don't even know how we got here. I didn't come here for the ring."

Although it occurs to me that I should have.

That I may have to think of something to get it back from Stellan. So I can give it back to Shepard when I break things off.

"So then why in the fuck did you come here?" he growls.

"Because I wanted to talk to you, okay? I was worried about you. We didn't get to talk all day. You wouldn't return my texts. You wouldn't even look at me on the bus. You..." I shake my head, searching his face for some clue as to what even happened this morning. "You looked so... horrified this morning. So angry, so agitated, so *worried*, so... I don't even have a word for it. What... You were about to beat him up, weren't you? Shepard."

His chest flares with another breath. For a second, it looks like he won't answer. But then, roughly, "He didn't save you."

"From bumping my head against the door?"

Things ripple through his features. Some reminiscent of this morning, some new that I don't recognize at all. "Yes. Among other things."

I let go of his coat and put my hands on his chest, damp and hot, so strong as I say, "Listen, what happened at the bus was an accident." I press my hands on his chest like I did this morning, to soothe him, to get him to hear me. "It was an accident, Stellan. There was no way anyone could've saved me from it, okay, let alone him. Plus, nothing even happened. Look." I point to the spot where I hit my head. "Nothing. Not one little scratch. As I told you this morning, I'm fine. It was embarrassing, but that was the worst of it."

"I would have," he rasps.

"You would have what?"

"Saved you from the accident."

My heart races. "You... That's impossible. That's—"

His eyes swivel over to the spot I pointed out. Then, reaching up, he presses his thumb on it like Shepard had, but his fingers are extremely gentle, careful. As if handling a piece of fine china or the velvet petal of a rose.

"Or died trying," he finishes both his thought and his perusal, taking his hand away.

I dig my fingers on his chest then. "Please don't hate him because of me. Please, Stellan."

"I don't hate him," he says.

"So why does he hate you?"

In response, his jaw tenses.

Still, I press, "Why can't you be there for him? You said that last night." Last night that feels like forever ago right now. "What does that mean? What does that—"

He steps back. "You need to leave."

I shake my head, keeping at it. "What did Coach Thorne say to you? Back on the bus. Why did you look like that when you came out of the room? So... So grim. So rigid and—"

"You need to fucking leave," he growls angrily.

"No." I put my foot down. "I'm not leaving. I'm not—"

"Look," he says loudly, with a biting tone, and then proceeds to pinch the bridge of his nose. "This is not a good time, all right? This is a bad fucking time. Wrong fucking time. When I say you need to leave, you need to listen to me. You need to fucking listen to what I *say*. I can't... I can't be trusted right now. I'm not fucking safe. I'm not... Now"—a deep, *deep* breath expands his chest and hollows out his stomach, twitching his muscles—"I've had a very long day that I'd like to put an end to. So why don't you grab your clothes from over there"—he motions with his jaw—"put them the fuck on and let me walk you to your room."

I look in the direction he said my clothes are. I see the light pink dress I wore here, on one of the armchairs, along with my white panties and bra that I'd also taken off when I donned his coat. I look at my clothes, on top of each other, and what strikes me the most is that they're so neatly folded. All their edges are clean and smoothed like he had all the time in the world to do that after a very long day that he wanted to put an end to.

Like how he had all the time in the world last night when he sewed my dress together. After he dropped me off at my room at four in the morning.

Taking a deep breath of my own, I smooth my hands down his coat and reply primly, "No."

He breathes out so forcefully, so impatiently at that, it's a wonder that I don't blow away from the strength of it. "Jesus, fuck. You—"

And then I shut him up.

Because I've had it with him. I'm not going anywhere. He can't make me. By arguing about it, he's just wasting my time now. So I lower myself down on my knees, the coarse carpet scraping against my skin, and look up at his shocked face.

"You say that word a lot," I tell him, looking into his dark eyes. "Bad."

His chest shakes. "You—"

"But I'm not going to argue with you," I continue. "Because you just said you've had a long day."

"Dora, I—"

"So I've decided that I'm going to make you feel better."

"What?"

I nod, folding my hands in my lap, looking like the picture of patience. "I think I'll give you a little blow job first and then you can fuck me."

He opens his mouth to say something and I'm ready for it. Whatever it is. Whatever obstacle he's going to throw in my path.

But all that comes out is a puff of air at first.

Followed by a disbelieving, "You think you'll give me a little blow job and then I can fuck you."

"Yes," I confirm, nodding. "I figure that should make you feel better."

"You figure that should make me feel better."

"You know, repeating everything I say is not going to change my mind. I'm sucking your dick one way or another."

He clenches his jaw as he stares down at me and into my defiant eyes.

He clenches his jaw again when I lift my chin to show him how determined I am. And I would've kept doing that, kept being all determined and stuff, but he decides to bend down in a flash and fist my hair, tugging my head back.

Then, his harsh face fills my vision as he growls, "Does the fact that the dick you're dying to suck is a ten-incher change your mind?"

I grip his waist. "No."

His fist flexes in my hair. "You've seen me, haven't you? You know I'm not kidding. You know how much I made you bleed. What do you think is going to happen when I stick it in your mouth?"

"I don't care."

His nostrils flare. "If I stick it in your mouth, I'm going in your throat. And if I'm going in your throat, I'm fucking the fuck out of it."

I raise myself up on my knees. "You can."

"I can, huh. I can throat fuck you. Like I fucked your little pussy last night. Like I want to fuck your tiny little asshole one day. And if you thought your sweetheart pussy hurt with my daddy cock, then I'm going to fucking wreck your sweetheart asshole. You're going to cry like you've never cried before and you're going to whine so loud that they'll call the cops on me. How about that? Does that change your mind about making me feel better?"

I raise myself up even higher, my pussy waking up just by the mention of it in his growly voice. "No, because I'll tell the cops that you're my daddy and I wanted you to fuck my asshole. That I begged you to fuck my asshole. I wore short skirts. I went without panties. I fucking bent down every chance I got. All because I wanted you to stick your dick in my ass. I'll tell them that I wanted you to fuck my pussy too and I wanted your cock in my mouth. I'll tell everyone that. Which I don't think you want me to do. Because you want everyone to blame you, don't you? You want everyone to think you're making me do things, that you're forcing me, which is not true at all. So I don't care. I don't care what you do. You can do whatever you want to me as long as it makes you feel better. Because the thing is, Stellan, you always know how to make me feel better. How to be there for me even when it looks like you're not. So let me do the same. Please, let me do the same."

It's true, though, isn't it?

He always knows. At the bar last night when he came to my rescue; then again when he took my virginity and I was so hell-bent on him being rough, but he was so careful. The night we met when he warned me against getting in that strange man's car.

He always does that.

He *always* knows what I need and that I need to slow down when I want to speed up.

He *knows*.

So it's only fair that I get to know him too.

"Please, Stellan. You can't love me, can you? You can't even share parts of yourself with me for some reason. So give me this. Let me do this for you. Share *this* with me. Or I'll stay here until my knees are bleeding and I collapse."

He won't say yes, will he?

He'll never say yes.

He'll never give me any part of himself.

That's why he's letting go of my hair, isn't he? That's why he's stepping back from me. Even though he keeps our gazes locked and connected, he's moving back, his features impassive.

And then he hammers the last nail in the coffin when he breaks that connection too, when he turns back and away from me, walking to the chest of drawers as if I wasn't in the room.

I wasn't kneeling at his feet.

Ready to skin my knees and bleed for him.

He opens the drawer and gets something out. It takes me a moment to figure out what it is: a black leather belt. I think I've seen him wear it or one like it on several occasions. He lets it unravel first, the loose circle of it, before slowly, very slowly and deliberately looping it around his fist.

I don't know why he's doing that.

I don't know what it means.

But my heart is pounding something fierce.

When the belt is all snaked around his fist and forearm, with only the tail end hanging, he walks to his left and sits in one of those armchairs, his thighs sprawled, his abs bunched up and looking even stronger that way. He goes for the cigarette pack that sits on the side table, something I hadn't seen until now. The Zippo lighter is right next to it, and after getting a stick out, he lights it with quick movements.

Once lit, he takes a long drag and releases a thick cloud of smoke.

Taking the cigarette out of his mouth and keeping it pinched between the fingers of his belted fist, he says, "Lose the coat."

It's softly spoken, but it's a command. I can hear it.

Eager and shaken and excited and nervous, I do as he says.

Then, finally, *finally* looking at me and taking another drag, he says, "Crawl to me."

CHAPTER 12

My pussy clenches at his words.

I can feel my juices sliding down. I can feel them smearing my thighs, making their way on to the coarse carpet where I was going to keep kneeling till the end of time.

Waiting for his call.

And it has come, hasn't it?

So I should go.

Only I have never crawled for anyone before. So yes, I'm nervous. But I asked for this. I asked him to let me make him feel better and if me crawling across the room to him, all naked no less, is what he wants, then I'll do it.

Slowly I come down on all fours and begin.

My long hair forms a curtain around my face, my tits are dangling with every step I take and my knees rub against the rough carpet, my skin getting chafed. The closer I get to him, the more heated I feel.

And I think it's because of the fiery heat that he's emanating.

From his naked chest, from his dark eyes.

The way he's watching me like he wants to eat me alive. That's the only way to describe it. Intense and blazing hunger.

I also think some of this heat may be my own doing as well. It's coming from my slippery pussy. From the lust that's flowing thick in my veins and sitting heavy in my tummy. From the fire that he stokes in me.

Which makes me think that it takes me an eternity to get to him.

An eternity to reach his spread thighs. To enter the cloud of his smoke and scent and come to kneel before him. He's so tall and broad that when he leans over me it feels like the room has gotten darker.

It feels like I'm really in a shadowed, moonless alley and in the clutches of danger.

Keeping the burning cigarette in his mouth, he reaches forward and goes for my hair. He hefts the majority of my long tresses in his belted fist and brings it to the front, over my shoulder. Then he goes for more and keeps doing it until all my hair's in the front, hanging down my chest, fluttering over my painfully swollen tit and a turgid nipple and tickling my belly.

And then he proceeds to sift the strands through his long fingers, a frown of concentration between his brows.

I lick my dried lips. "W-what are you doing?"

"Braiding your hair," he says, his eyes on his task, his cigarette still clenched between his teeth.

Before I can confirm that he said what he said, he begins to do just that. Very carefully and tenderly, he parts my hair in three thick ropes and starts looping one through the other. First under, then over.

Until a lattice forms.

Goose bumps break out on my skin as I watch his dusky fingers working expertly as he makes his way down my long, thick hair, braiding it in loose pleats.

"Where did you learn to do that?" I ask even though I think I know the answer.

"For my sister."

"So you'd braid her hair?"

"None of the others could. Ledger was too young to learn; Shep was too impatient; Con had other responsibilities. So I volunteered."

My heart squeezes for the boy he was.

I wonder what he was like back then. Probably just as serious and controlled as he is as a man. And it makes me so sad for him. For the childhood he probably never had. For all the smiles he never smiled and all the laughs he never laughed.

For all the carefree memories he probably didn't get to make.

Fisting my hands at my sides, I ask, "Why are you doing it to me?"

He's almost at the end of it. "Because I want it out of the way."

"Out of the way for what?"

He doesn't answer. Instead, he finishes his task, takes another drag of his cigarette, and lets the smoke out as he plays with the tail of my newly formed braid. "Sometimes, in a crowded room, I can recognize you from your hair. From the color of it. How it's got a polished sheen to it. How it's wavy but not too wavy. How it's so thick and yet"—he tugs at my braid—"so soft."

"I..." I swallow, watching his thumb flick the ends of my braid. "It's because of my mom. She's from India and you know, they have really thick hair over there. And mostly jet-black and—"

He tugs my hair again. "She at least did one thing right."

"You—"

"And sometimes I see the honeyed flush of your skin and know it's you. Just a flash of it is enough. Maybe your bare shoulder or the nape of your neck," he says, his eyes still focused on the hair. "One time, I recognized you from just your fingers. You were reaching for a glass at the bar, at a crowded party, and I saw your small hand peeking through the bodies between us and I knew. I knew it was you."

I swallow again, gulp really, something occurring to me. "Is that why... back then. You asked for photos of all those things? Of me."

"I asked for all those photos of you for... *after*."

"After the one night you wanted?" I ask even though I think I know.

He throws a short nod.

"What did you do with them?"

He looks me in the eyes. "There's still going to be an after, isn't it?"

Right.

Because he thinks I'm marrying his twin brother. And even if I wasn't, he can't give me what I want. He can't give me my dream of being loved. So this, whatever we have, is doomed either way. And I have to say I've never hated my desire to be loved as much as I do right now.

"It's my mom again," I say, not knowing what else to say right now. "My skin, it—"

"It's you," he says, looking up, his eyes dark, his cigarette between his teeth. "All of it is you. You make my heart race a certain way. You make it beat in a way I thought was the same but..."

"But what... What does it mean? What—"

Taking another drag, he jerks his chin at me. "Hands behind your back."

"I-I'm sorry?"

The cigarette goes back in his mouth, and he begins to unloop the belt from around his fist. He comes closer, oh so closer, leaning over me. I watch the burning end of the cigarette almost, *almost* touching my skin, the side of my face, but he stops and looks me in the eyes. "You wanted this."

For a second, I think he's talking about burning me.

That he wants to use his cigarette to brand my skin.

A love bite. A love burn.

Made out of one controlled addiction on another.

Something that will hurt me in the beginning but will stay with me for the rest of my life. Something bigger than a tattoo. Like a blood oath, only our oath is going to be done with fire.

Me, Agni. Him, the wildfire.

But then I realize what he's saying. What he's asking me to do.

And he's right.

I did want this.

So staring back at the darkness that's his eyes, I bring my arms back, my chest thrusting forward, the braid that he's made out of my hair swishing against my tits, my nipples, making my breaths hitch.

I thread my fingers together as he loops the belt around my wrists, the leather grazing my skin. It's soft but scary. It's loose but binding. And the whole time he's working back there, I watch the sharp angle of his jaw.

I watch the muscle of his cheek standing taut because of that cigarette clenched between his lips.

"Why are you tying my hands?" I whisper to his side profile.

"Because they'll be in the way."

"I won't..." I begin and then trail off because my breath gets caught up in the jangle of nerves that's my body right now. "I won't try to push you away or anything when I, you know, do that."

He's finally done, and he swings his eyes over to me. "Do what?"

"S-suck your dick."

That's why he's doing all this, isn't he?

Braiding my hair. Binding my hands behind my back. Preparing me for sucking his dick. Preparing if I try to balk if he goes too deep.

He moves away from me then and settles back in his armchair. Smoking, he rasps, "You think you're going to suck my dick?"

He looks so relaxed right now and someone who didn't know him better might think he really is that way. But he isn't.

I know. I can see.

He's strung taut like a tightrope.

His muscles are pulled tight. As if lying in wait. Like a trap. One wrong move on my part and he'll snap me up.

"Aren't I?" I ask, twisting my wrists, testing the tightness of the belt.

"No."

"But—"

"You are not going to suck my dick, Dora, because I'm going to fuck your throat."

I clench my thighs together, my pussy spasming. "What's... What's the difference?"

He circles his eyes over my face, my parted lips, my heated cheeks. He studies his own handiwork: the braid that's slung over my shoulder. He takes in my heaving chest, my fat nipples. He even studies the trembles that shake my belly. The shiny evidence of my arousal painting my inner thighs.

Then, coming back up to my face, "For someone who claims to know so much about men, you don't know the important things, do you?"

"Maybe"—I lick my lips, twisting my wrists again—"you could teach me."

He chuckles lowly, smoke wafting from his lips. "Oh, I'm going to teach you." Then, "Because I'm sure your daddy didn't take the time to do that, did he?"

I clench my thighs again. "No."

"I bet your daddy never taught you," he begins, pinching the cigarette between his fingers, leaning over a bit to tap the end on the ashtray sitting on the side table, "not to sneak into a man's room in the middle of the night, did he?"

I swallow. "No."

"And not just any man but the man who's had his last nut"—with his free hand, he grabs his thick arousal over his sweatpants and squeezes—"in a fucking condom instead of your pretty pink pussy."

"Y-you could come in my pussy anytime you like," I whisper, clenching my core.

"Yeah?"

"Yes," I say eagerly. "I told you I didn't like the condom."

I hated how it separated us from each other.

After being apart from him for ages, I didn't want anything between us.

He cocks his head to the side. "Tell me your daddy at least taught you what happens when a man nuts inside a warm, cozy, *fucking fertile* pussy like yours."

I fist my fingers, struggling against the grip of the belt again and lie, "I'm on the pill."

He watches me through the smoke for a few beats. Then putting the stick away on the ashtray, he leans forward and in a flash, he's got his fingers wrapped around the back of my neck. He's pulling me toward him, making me lose my balance but catching me at the last second before I go crashing against him.

Then, flexing his grip on me, "I see he didn't teach you then. That's because he's an asshole, your daddy. That's lesson number one. Here's your lesson number two: Don't be a dick-thirsty whore and lie to your new daddy. Because he's a bigger asshole than your first, yeah?"

"I—"

"Which is why I won't just teach you with words," he goes on. "We'll use actions tonight. *Examples* so the lesson sinks in. And tonight's lesson is: what happens when a reckless girl like you offers up her cock-sucking lips to a man like me. How that innocent little offer can turn into a vicious throat fucking where she leaves with a sore jaw and her tight tummy swollen with a big load of daddy cum, okay? I'll teach you what happens when you walk into a room, all excited and eager, eyes full of hearts and rainbows, thinking that you'll get to suck your first cock, but you leave it all wrecked and ruined and used like a perfect little cum dumpster." His jaw tics. "*My* perfect little cum dumpster."

I press my thighs so hard that I have to whimper. "I want to."

"Is that so."

"As long as I get to taste you, I'll do whatever you want. I'll *be* whatever you need me to be."

I go to kiss him then.

Seal my words with a kiss, but he stops me. Then with features rippling with heavy, intense things, he growls, "Open your fucking mouth and stick your tongue out."

I look at him for a few seconds, my breaths heavy and my heart racing.

Then I do as he says.

I open my mouth and stick my tongue out.

But he isn't happy with that, so he commands, "Wider."

I obey and open my mouth more.

Again, it doesn't seem to satisfy him. "Fucking wider. You're trying to fit my dick, not a fucking lollipop that they teach girls like you in the movies and romance novels. You know the kind of heat I'm packing. So open your fucking mouth until your jaw pops and stick your tongue out far enough so I can see the back of your throat. That's going to fucking swell up like the shape of my cock. Is that clear?"

I think my nerves are malfunctioning. They're firing off and buzzing at random times. They're electrocuting me and making my pussy flutter haphazardly.

Or maybe it's all the things he's saying to me.

All the filthy things that both shock me and make me go crazy.

So crazy that I do what he's asking me to do before he's even finished his command. I open my mouth wide enough and stick my tongue out far enough that I can fit him in.

Something akin to arousal and amusement, both dark and possessive, flash through his features and he shifts in his seat. Clutching that sexy cigarette back in his mouth, he lowers the waistband of his pants and takes his cock out. He leaves the waistband just under his heavy sac, making everything, his dick and his balls so tight and swollen and so fucking sexy like that.

But then the sight of his erect rod itself distracts me, hard and flush, ruddy and gosh, just as slippery as it was last night.

Pre-cum oozing out of the head.

Before I even know what I'm doing, I lean forward and I do it with such force that I almost topple, but his hand on the back of my neck saves me at the last minute.

Which is when I realize its true purpose.

The hand that's gripping me.

It's there to give me balance. Because my own hands are tied and I can't do it for myself. And I see that. I see it when concern breaks through his anger and flares into his eyes. Then, "You don't learn, do you? You don't fucking learn." He digs his fingers around my neck. "You don't suck me off, I fuck your mouth. Stop acting like a greedy whore who's obsessed with my dick and be fucking careful before you hurt yourself."

"I-I'm sorry."

"Now, one more time," he states patiently, "open your mouth and stick your tongue out like my good little bitch in heat. So I can put you on my cock. And no, not to lick. If you think I'm going to let you use your tongue to do something as tame as lick me, then you have another think coming.

"You're going to use your tempting little tongue to slobber over me, do you understand? You're going to drool over my fat cock that you've been making hard since the year I met you. You're going to make a puddle in my lap with your drool like the one you've made at my feet with your pussy. You have, haven't you?"

I nod, unable to speak with my mouth open.

"Yeah, you have. So you're going to grease my cock, lube it up, make it all shiny and slippery, like it would be if I stuck it into your whore of a pussy right now. And when I'm all drenched from your mouth and ready, I'm going to push into that mouth of yours. I'm going to push past those pouty lips and get into your throat and do what I've been dreaming about doing again since the year I met you."

I blink and ask him what with my eyes.

And it's a testament of us being so in sync that he understands and answers, "To take your breath away."

My chest heaves.

He leans even closer. "To make you breathe for me. To make you breathe when I want to, how I want to. To make you live for me. Because that's what I've been doing ever since I met you, haven't I? I've been living for you. I've been breathing for you. Either to stay away from you or to stay close. Either to forget about you or in the process remember every single thing about you twice. Either to hurt you or save you. Either to fuck you out of my system or fuck you into my bloodstream. I've been a slave to you since the second I met you, Dora, so you're going to be a slave to me. To my dick. You're going to gag on my dick. You're going to fucking choke on it and if you do it hard enough, if you do it where you see stars behind your closed eyes, I may just give you what you've been begging for ever since I met you too: my life-giving cum."

I break his rule then.

The rule where he said to stay silent and moan out his name. To plead, "God, Stellan I—"

But he doesn't let me.

Because he puts me on his dick.

And I think he's angry because he doesn't give me a chance to lube him up at all. He doesn't give me a chance to slobber all over his cock like he just said, to get him ready to push into my throat. To drool over him, make a puddle in his lap.

He simply pushes in.

His big, fat dick simply invades my mouth like it invaded my pussy last night and I have no choice but to let him. I have no choice but to open my mouth even wider than what he was first satisfied with. Even though I did pop my jaw doing it.

Taking the real thing is much harder.

It not only pops my jaw but causes me to clench my eyes shut and stop breathing for a second. Like he wanted me to.

And I feel so proud.

God, I've never felt such pride in anything I've done.

Including my stage debut.

I feel so accomplished that I gave him what he wanted. That I gave him my breaths that I can't help but get even hornier, even more desperate about this whole thing.

Not to mention, I get to learn his taste. Finally. He feels heavy on my tongue, hot, so much hotter down here than anywhere else. His marshmallow taste is also thicker down here, muskier.

More potent.

Like a drug uncut and crystal clean.

One hit of it and I'm addicted. I'm hooked.

I am a slave.

Again, like he wanted me to be.

I'm a slave to his taste. To his length, his thickness. I'm a slave to his velvet skin stretched over the strongest steel. I'm a slave to that pulsing vein running along the base of his dick. I'm a slave to his rough hands that are now framing my face, his fingers buried in my hair to keep my head in place so he can push in and out, set a pace without my interference.

My permission even.

Although that's not true.

He has my consent. He always did and he always will.

Consent to make me gag and choke and steal the rest of my breaths away.

Because I realize I'm doing the same to him.

I'm stealing his breaths too. I'm taking them away with my moans and giving them back with my gags. I'm making them faster when I move my tongue against that vein of his. And slowing them down when I open my throat more and more to have him inch down.

And it's making me buzz. It's making go lax and loose. So much so that he switches his technique. So far, he was keeping me still and bent over him, my mouth choking with his cock as he moved up and down.

But now he goes still and *uses* my mouth to jack himself off.

I don't know what's better.

Being still or being used as a blow-up doll.

I think I'm leaning toward the blow-up doll option because this way, he's able to go deeper. This way, he's finally conquering my throat like he wanted to. Not to mention this way I'm making a puddle in his lap. I'm making a puddle on my chest, drooling and slobbering all over his cock and myself.

So with this, I've given him my mouth, my drool, my breaths, my complete surrender.

I think I've become his perfect cum dumpster.

So now I can die happy.

Maybe that's what I'm doing. Maybe that's why my body is so loose. I'm so dizzy. My throat is so sore, along with my jaw and I'm seeing stars behind my closed eyelids... hey, another thing that he wanted from me.

He wanted me to see stars.

He said he'd give me his cum if I did that. So does that mean I...

Suddenly, air slams back into my lungs and I lose him.

CHAPTER 13

I detect movements behind my back.

I feel tugs and pulls at my arms and my shoulders and my head seems to be cradled on something smooth and hard. I want to look up and see what's going on, but I'm too weak right now and kinda pissed too about the interruption, so all my energy is going into that. I realize I'm being picked up and taken somewhere. There are strong arms wrapped around me, his, and I can feel my side pressed to his harshly breathing chest.

Then I'm being moved again, and I feel a mattress at my back. Finally, my eyes blink open and his flushed and sweaty and harsh and beautiful face fills my vision. He's concerned. I can see that. His hands are shaking as he grasps my face.

"You... Are you okay? Are you—"

I go to touch his face myself and when I realize that I can, my arms fly with eagerness and relief, landing on his hard jaw. "D-did it help?"

He frowns, his fingers twitching around my face. "What?"

"With y-your day," I clarify, wiping the sweat off his brows. When all he does is remain silent, I begin, "You... s-said that—"

He stops me with a kiss.

He fuses our mouths together and kisses and kisses and fucking kisses me. In the back of my mind, I'm thinking that he's kissing me like I am, all messed up and drool-y, my lips swollen and trashed. But he doesn't seem to mind.

I think he likes it.

Because his kiss is messy as well. His kiss is so wet and hot and dripp-y and sticky like sugar. We rub our mouths together, our lips slipping over each other. And it gives me life. It makes me horny and in turn angry that he's not doing what I want him to do. He's not fucking me or giving me his cum like he promised.

So I wrap my thighs around his waist and lift myself up from the bed, almost hanging off his lower half. So I can press our hips together. So I can rub my messy pussy up against his ridged stomach. And even though I love his kisses—I *do*—I fist his hair and break it.

Then, panting against his mouth, "Fuck me."

His hands are still framing my face, his thumbs digging into my cheeks possessively. "Baby, you—"

Glaring, I arch under him. "No, no arguments. I don't even care what you think right now or how w-we shouldn't do this or whatever. I'm horny, okay? That was the hottest thing ever and I-I need you. I need you to make it better for me l-like I did for you, and you promised." I fist his hair. "You fucking promised. You said that if I saw stars, you'd give me your cum. And I did see stars, but where's your cum? I don't have it. Where is it? And on top of that, I'm horny and you don't even have the decency to fix it. You don't—"

*A*gain, as much as I love his kisses, I don't like it when he uses them to shut me up. Well, I do, yes. But not right now. Not when I haven't even gotten to the main part yet.

So again, I yank at his hair and break it.

This time, his frown is thicker. His displeasure is evident on his face, but I don't care and before he can express it, I pant against his mouth, "And no condoms."

I swear I feel him jerk over me. I swear I feel him shudder. His voice at least sounds thicker and rougher than usual. "Dora, that's—"

"Irresponsible, I know," I tell him, squeezing my thighs around his torso. "But then I *am* irresponsible. I *am* reckless. You're the one with all the control in the world, aren't you? You're the one who's supposed to save me. So save me then." I look into his dark, lust-blown eyes. "Figure out a way to give me what I want while keeping me safe at the same time."

I don't know why this is so important to me, but it is.

It's important to somehow show him I can take him however he comes. It doesn't matter if he's having a bad day or a good day. If this is a good time or a bad time. I'll always trust him. I'll always take whatever he gives me.

Because I know now.

I know he's both good and bad.

I know he's the good guy and the asshole at the same time.

I *know*.

So when he doesn't act fast enough for my liking, I go to fight with him some more. I'll keep fighting him until he surrenders.

But he upends my reality again.

He jerks back from me, unlocking himself from the cage of my thighs and arms. I see his dick bob between us, all hard and throbbing, all wet and dripping with his cum and from my mouth. Before I can get him to stop or pull him back, he's turning me around.

So now instead of my back, my knees and arms hit the mattress. Instead of him being pressed up against my front, his chest is at my back and his jaw is at my neck.

I turn my face to the side. "What are you... What are you doing?"

He sucks on the side of my neck, giving me a hickey, I think. "Showing you decency and fixing it."

"But I—"

He jerks at my arms and pulls me upright until I'm just on my knees, my spine plastered against his massive chest. He grips my throat—still all sticky and drenched with my own drool—with one hand while the other goes to my hip.

Squeezing his fingers on my body, he growls, "But you're taking it how I give it to you." I feel him move, our sweaty skin sliding against each other. "You're taking it like the reckless, thoughtless, cum-stealing slut you are. From behind."

With that, he thrusts into me and oh my God, it's so forceful, that first stroke of his cock. It's so delicious and divine and yes, painful as well. Probably because I'm still not used to taking him in my pussy. I'm still more or less a virgin and he's still so big that he touches all things inside of me, all at once.

Whatever it is, his first thrust is overwhelming.

It's everything and more.

And inevitably, words fall out of me as my back arches to take him in deeper. "Oh, thank God."

Which of course pisses him off.

I realize that later. As his fingers around my neck tighten to the point where I think he's *this* close to controlling my breaths again. And his hand at my hip makes fists out of my flesh, pulling and tugging, branding me with just his grip.

Followed by his growl in my ear, "What'd you say?"

"I—"

He shuts me up with his thrust.

Actually, no. He makes all the words spill out of me as I moan. "Oh God, please. I—"

Again, he squeezes my throat, branding my hip with his fingers. "God, huh. You think"—another thrust—"God's doing this to you?"

My own hands jerk and go to cover his on my body. "I'm... I don't..."

One more thrust, this one leaving behind a slapping sound of his hips hitting my ass. "You think God's fucking you, baby? God's fucking that tight as all fuck pussy."

I swallow under his grip. "No. I—"

Yet another thrust. This one harder than the last and I swear the last one was the hardest ever, even compared to last night, and I feel him clear to my stomach with this. "You what?"

I swallow again, turning my head to the side, pleading with him. "It's h-hard."

He turns his head too and I feel his words on the side of my face. "What's hard?"

I flex my fingers over his grip. "N-not saying... His name. You're—"

This time his thrust jerks my whole body. It jangles my nerves and jars my bones. It makes me spill out His name in a litany, in a prayer. Although I'm not sure what I'm praying for: do I want him to stop, this devious, torturing man, the love of my life who's deliberately making me break his rule.

Or do I want him to keep going?

Do I want him to keep pushing into me like this, all forcefully and urgently. Like if he doesn't, he won't survive the next second. Because that's what it feels like right now with the way he's fucking me, with the way he's holding me as well. Giving me a hug from behind as he strokes in and out of me, all violently and oh so deeply.

"I'm what?" he rasps in my ear, his breaths hot and misty.

Much like his body behind me, all around me. "You're making me s-say it."

"Yeah?" He squeezes my throat again, making me arch it back and rest my head on his strong shoulder. "What an unfair asshole am I, huh. Making you do things that are hard."

"Stellan—"

"But that's not hard, baby. I'm afraid to burst your bubble." Another jangling, smacking thrust. "But that's nothing."

"I—"

"You want to know what's hard? You want to know what's fucking hard? *This*." He rotates his hips, making me feel his cock everywhere. Making me feel his cock down to the tips of my toes. Making me feel every ridge and every inch of that vein that I was stroking with my tongue and I moan again.

God, will I ever stop moaning, in pain, in ecstasy, in love?

And in the wake of my moan, he continues, "This dick I'm fucking you with, that's hard. It's so fucking hard that it hurts. It *hurts* to fucking fuck you right now."

I dig my nails into the backs of his hands. "Stellan—"

"And it's only going to get harder, isn't it?" he cuts me off. "It's only going to get much, much harder because now I have to figure out a way not to come inside this pussy." As if to emphasize, he jerks his hips hard into me. "I have to figure out a way not to lose my nut inside your tight fucking snatch like I'm losing my mind right now. I'm losing my mind over how tight this cunt is, how warm and wet it is. Wet like a fucking river. Swollen as always like a ripe fruit. But instead of enjoying this fruity pussy, I have to figure out a way to pull out and *protect* you, isn't it?"

I roll my head on his shoulder. "P-please, you—"

"Protect your womb from my cum," he goes on, pounding into me, his fingers pulling and squeezing. "When that's not what I want to do right now. That's not what I want to do at all."

He pauses here and for the next several seconds simply fucks me.

Thank God—I mean, *thank you, Stellan*.

I don't even want to break his rule in my thoughts. Because I have a feeling he can read them. He can read my thoughts, hear my heartbeats.

He can feel my soul calling out for him.

Maybe that's why he says what he says next:

"What I want to do right now," he begins, his words a rough whisper in my ear and his cock a rough, pulsating invasion in my pussy, "is push so far in, so fucking far up your fertile little cunt that you feel me in your womb. That instead of your pussy, I fuck your womb. I fuck the very thing I'm trying to protect. And then when it's time to come, I come so much, so fucking much, that your womb swells up. Your womb fucking *hurts* with my cum. As much as I'm hurting right now. And then every time you walk, baby, you feel a little bit of me drip out of you. You feel a little bit of my cum sliding down your juicy thighs. And not just for days, for weeks. For fucking *weeks*, I want my jizz to slip out of you, reminding you of the hurt. Of how much you're hurting me right now. How *hard* it is to pull out right now."

At this, I bring my hands away from his and go up.

I push them in his damp hair—damp from the shower earlier and damp from the sweat—and arch my back even more. I press my face to the side of his neck and whisper, "I-I'm sorry."

He huffs out a breath, sliding his arm around my tummy, pressing the thumb of his other hand on my pulse. "No, baby, you're not sorry yet. You will be, though. One day."

"H-how?"

"Because one day"—he presses me into his body hard while at the same time pushing into me with his cock—"you're going to realize you've missed it. You've missed your period, yeah? One day, you're going to remember what happened tonight. What you made me do. How much you made me fucking hurt and lose my mind that I came inside of you. And you know what happens when a man comes inside of a pussy as fertile and as ripe as yours, don't you? You get pregnant. So you'll be sorry then, won't you? You'll be sorry that you made me put a baby in your belly and breed the fuck out of you. Maybe then, you'll know what's hard.

"If I leave behind a little surprise for you. A little surprise you'll want to hide, but you can't. Because it's the kind of surprise that'll grow over the next nine months, won't it? It'll stretch your body, your little belly, make it swollen. It'll stretch your tits, make them all ripe and juicy with milk. It'll stretch your cherry nipples too. Make them just as hard and swollen and juicy, and even more tempting than they are right now."

I moan when he goes up and grips my tits. When he pulls and twists my nipples as if he's imagining it right now.

"But that's not the worst part, is it?" he keeps going, driving me crazy and yes, making things hard for me, making everything so fucking hard and swollen and sweaty and lusty; probably just as much as I'm making things for him. "The worst part is that you're engaged. To my twin brother. And so on the day of your wedding, you'll walk down the aisle like that. You'll walk down the aisle, all swollen and ripe with my baby. On the day of your wedding, your tits will drip with milk, your nipples will hurt, your belly will hurt. And you're going to have to let me drain them, won't you? You're going to have to let me suck on your tits, like you always, always wanted, and feed me before saying *I do*. And from what I hear, it's the kind of thing a groom frowns upon, his bride getting titty-fucked before she pledges her life to him. And you're getting titty-fucked if I'm getting anywhere near those milky tits. Not to mention, you'll be late for the wedding too. Because if I'm sucking your tits and fucking them, I'm also getting a ride in your pregnant pussy. And again, that's not something a groom is going to approve of. So maybe then, *fucking then*, you'll learn the meaning of hard."

"S-Stellan, I think I-I'm going to…"

"Then you'll learn to say my name with every breath you take. How every *word* out of your fucking mouth should be nothing but my name," he growls, his hips working and working, smacking against my butt, his dick stroking in and out of me. "Then you'll learn how hard you make it to protect you. How hard you make my job. How hard you make it to not go crazy and lose it. How hard you make every-fucking-thing in my already fucked life."

And then I think he's run out of words.

He's said all he could and now all that's left is fucking me and fucking me hard.

I have the same problem of not being able to say anything. But that doesn't mean I can't show him. That I can't show how sorry I am for everything and how much I want to love him and soothe him. So I grab his cheek, turn his face, and touch my lips to his.

The moment I do, he groans and sighs at the same time as if this is it. This is what he was looking for, the taste of my lips, the love of my kiss. And so at his obvious relief, I come around him. My pussy spasms and gushes. Which is what makes him come too. I know because he groans again. Although this time it's louder and as if in pain. As if he really is so hard that he can't bear it.

But even so, even as hard as he is and as hard as this task is, he pulls out.

He pulls out of me in a jerk and God, *God* he…

He notches the head of his dick against that tight hole that's even tinier than my pussy. The hole he was talking about while scaring me away from sucking him off. He pushes his fat head just inside my asshole and comes in there. I feel the stretch, the sharp burn of it before it gets replaced by the heat of his lashing cum. And I know why he did that: I wanted his cum and he gave it to me. He *found a way* to give me what I want while keeping me safe. So I tighten my arms around his neck, his face; I tighten my fingers in his hair and deepen our kiss to show him my gratitude, to show him my love. As he jerks and groans, his forehead dropping on my shoulder and his arms spasming, holding me tightly.

Almost painfully.

But I bear the pain because he bore it for me.

We did it.

And I can't help but smile up at the ceiling. I can't help but sag against him in relief and laziness. But he comes through for me even now. He turns me around until I'm facing him and gently lowers me on the bed.

He settles himself between my thighs, his body all delicious and panting over mine, and once again frames my face with his fingers. Then, urgently, "You okay?"

I study his flush-darkened features and rub the frown between his brows lightly, smiling lazily. "I think I'm more than okay. I think I'm fabulous."

Even with my words, he has to go ahead and take stock of my features. He has to study my features with his own pretty eyes to make sure I really am okay. And when he sees that I am, a large breath escapes him and he finally, *finally* sags against me.

Oh, and he hugs me.

He brings his arms around and under my body and presses my curves against his hard planes, tucking his face in the nape of my neck. And my smile widens because I think along with being a cuddler, he's a hugger too. In fact, I think he's a major hugger. Remember how he wouldn't let me go last night even during sex? And tonight too. The entire time we were plastered against each other, every part of me was touching every part of him.

Grinning, I squeeze him to me. "I think you're a hugger too."

He mumbles in my neck, "This is not a hug."

"This is absolutely a hug."

"I don't hug."

"You hug me, though."

He grunts in response.

I play with the sweaty ends of his hair. "Thanks for sewing my dress."

Another grunt.

"Did you learn how to sew for your sister?"

He nods.

"Because no one else would learn it?"

He nods again.

I squeeze my arms around him once again tightly. As tightly as my heart is squeezing right now. Then, tilting my head to the side and rubbing my cheek on his heated forehead, "Thanks for the rose."

He hums.

"I ate it."

He finally looks up, hair falling over his forehead. "You ate it?"

"Uh-huh." When he keeps looking at me like I'm crazy, I explain, "That's why they're my favorite flowers because you can eat them. Or else pink magnolia would have the top spot." When he still looks at me like I'm crazy, I explain further, "Hey, it's better than letting them perish or sticking them in the pages of a book like a lovesick fool. This way those roses are a part of me, my blood."

Now he looks at me with a different light in his eyes. A fond, indulgent light.

And I blush as I continue, "And if you think I'm crazy for eating a rose, you're even crazier for giving it to me."

"Yeah, how's that?"

"Because you gave it to me based on a very fanciful and imaginary incident," I tell him, sliding my fingers up and down his sweaty back. "You know that, don't you? You didn't actually set a rose on fire. It was all in my head."

"So I guess I'm crazier than you."

"I guess so."

"They're still your favorite flowers, though, aren't they?"

"Yes."

"So then you should get one every day," he says conclusively before going back to tucking his face in my neck. "And if that gets me the top spot at being crazy then so be it."

I smile again—because God, he is crazier than me and I love him so, so much—and rub my cheek in his hair. "I unpacked your things."

He huffs out a breath. "I saw."

"I think we had sex on your books," I share next.

Although at no point did I feel anything digging into me or rustling or getting crunched beneath me. So I think his books are safe. But he doesn't seem to share my worries because all he does is shrug in response.

I bite my lip. "I have to confess something."

"What?"

"I only unpacked your things because I was snooping."

Then, cringing my face, I wait for him to get angry. I even expect him to lay into me when he once again untucks his face and looks down at me. "Snooping."

"Yes." I nod. "Only because I think you have a deep, dark secret that you won't tell me about. And so I had to take matters into my own hands."

And again, I expect him to go tight and angry over my body. Instead, something like amusement flashes through his features. "Good thing I don't hide it in my suitcase, huh."

I flicker my eyes over his features. "You're not mad?"

His chest moves with a breath. "The thing is, Dora, that with you, I think I'm going to have to pick my battles. And I'm dead tired tonight."

Slowly, I grin and squeeze my limbs around him. "Excellent choice! I totally think you should save this response. Because there are going to be a lot of battles for you in the future."

His lips twitch. "Are you done?"

"With what?"

"With pillow talk."

I raise my eyebrows. "Why?"

His eyes flick back and forth between mine. "Because I'd like to give you a bath before finally fucking going to bed."

"A bath?"

"I may be an asshole who broke your dreams of a romantic blow job and instead fucked your throat into submission, but I'm an asshole with manners. It's called aftercare."

"And that includes a bath?"

"And ginger and honey tea for your throat."

I smile again. "A cuddler, a hugger, and a tea maker with a deep, dark secret. You sure you're real? Because I think you live in a romance novel. That I will finally break my no-reading rule for."

He takes me in for a final time before, he says, "Yeah, you're done."

And then he picks me up from the bed and carries me to the bathtub for the aftercare part as I burrow in his chest and laugh, and when I do that, I swear I hear him chuckle.

CHAPTER 14

THE NEXT NIGHT...

I've misplaced my fiancé.

Or at least that's what it feels like. Because I don't know where he is. I haven't seen him in over twenty-four hours.

I know he's been busy with practice, so I understand why we couldn't meet up all day yesterday and when he must've come back from it, I was with... his twin brother. And today has been all about getting prepped for the game, so again I understand our non-communication. *But* I was at the game tonight. I waited for him through all his interviews and press conferences and all the other formalities that he's had to go through. And *yet* he managed to slip through me.

I even texted him and called him, left a voicemail and nothing.

God, it's annoying.

But I'm not leaving this city without getting to talk to him. I need to tell him that it's over. As hard as it might be, I need to tell him the truth. I'm not going to betray him like I did before.

That's why I'm here.

At this stupid party.

It's a victory party, but it's not happening at a bar like all the other parties I've gone to. From what I understand—I had to text Isiah to get the info on the party—this is someone's house. Someone from the other team and it's crowded. Plus super loud. I'm not sure how I'm going to find Shepard here because everyone looks drunk and stoned, but I have to try.

Because I do not have much time.

I need to get back before *he* finds out that I'm at a strange party.

OH, YOU'RE SO COLD

I don't like lying to him or hiding things from him either. Not again, not anymore. But if I told him what I was doing, he'd lose his shit. He'll think I did it for him—which I kinda did—but not because I expect him to love me back or something similar. But because I can't keep lying to myself or to Shepard. It's not fair to either of us.

So I'll figure out a way to tell him after I've actually broken things off. But for now, I have to do this and the fact that Stellan's in a meeting with Coach Thorne right now—I checked—works in my favor.

As I navigate the crowd, I try to find a familiar face so I can ask them about Shepard. But so far, I've had no luck, not downstairs at least. So I make my way upstairs and look through all the open doors. When I can't find anyone here either, I start looking behind closed doors.

By the third door, I'm losing hope and I'm about to close it when I detect movement on the balcony. In the shadows, I see two people and they're extremely close together. I see them moving, rocking and... Oh.

Oh shit.

I think I've stumbled upon people making out.

Yikes.

Very uncomfortable and I'm about to close the door when either they hear me or need a break anyway, so they come apart and turn my way.

And holy shit.

My search is over.

Because it's Shepard. And he's making out with a girl.

I'm about to apologize and then I'm about to close the door and give them privacy. But then I realize he's my fiancé. My *fiancé* is making out with another girl. And I... Well, I still want to apologize and give them their privacy so they can continue.

And yes again, it is the most twisted thing in the world that I want to do that. That when he whispers something in the girl's ear and she makes her way to the door, which means me because that's where I'm standing, I want to call out to Shepard, *good choice*. Because she's pretty with dark hair and porcelain skin. She also gives me a sweet smile, which makes me like her even more that she's not being catty at my interruption.

Taking a deep breath, I turn to Shepard, who's entered the bedroom as well. And then there are a few seconds of awkward silence between us, which I hate.

Then grimacing, he begins, "You weren't supposed to... You weren't supposed to see that."

I shake my head. "It's... I—"

He rakes his fingers through his hair. "Look, I can explain. I can—"

"No."

"Isadora, you—"

"No, seriously." I thrust my hand out. "You..." I swallow. "You don't have to." He opens his mouth to say something, but I keep going. "I know you think you need to explain because we're engaged, but I... I—"

"We are not," he says and finally breathes.

I can see that.

His chest moves up and down with a long breath.

"What?"

"Well, technically, we are," he corrects, again grimacing. "But we aren't, not really."

"I don't... What?"

He studies me for a few moments, his features grave, his eyes heavy and penetrating. And for a second, he looks so similar to his twin brother that I lose my breath. He looks identical and I know technically they are but still.

I've never seen him look this grim.

Not even on the night he came to me with the truth. He was angry then, yes, but not like this. He wasn't carved out from stone.

"It was fake," he says.

"What was fake?"

"Our engagement."

I blink. "Our engagement was fake."

Again, he studies me for a few seconds with those dark, penetrating eyes of his. "You said you loved him."

Something slams in my chest and does it hard. And I have to take a step back before answering, "Yes."

He grits his jaw. "You haven't stopped, have you?"

Biting my lip, I shake my head. "No."

"Not even after what he did."

I swallow again. "No."

Again, his first response is to take me in as if to make sure that what I'm telling is the truth. And when he's made sure, he gives me a slow nod. "So I was trying to give you want you want."

"What?"

Sighing, he thrusts his hands down his pockets. "He told me to."

"I-I'm sorry?"

"That night," he explains. "When he came to the bar to tell me. What he did. He told me to take care of you. He told me to give you whatever you wanted. To make you happy. So that's what I was trying to do. You wanted him, you want him, so I was trying to give him to you."

A tear rolls down my cheek. "He asked you to give me anything I wanted."

"He was pretty adamant about it," he shares.

He was, wasn't he?

Because that's who he is.

That's what he does.

He told me that every breath he takes is about me, didn't he? And here's proof. Every breath he takes is for me. Every thought he has is about me. Every beat of his wildfire heart has my name on it.

If only he loved me too.

If only he *believed* that he could love me and that it could be a good thing. Not some childish emotion put on this earth to torment him.

I'll even take that, you see.

Just his belief that we belong together. Like *I* believe. In his goodness and his darkness. In all the things that makes him *him*.

"How would..." I swallow again, still unable to understand. "How would asking me to marry you would... give me that?"

He sighs. "I thought asking you to marry me would give him the push to ask you himself." Then, "Look, I could see that he wanted you, okay? I hate to admit it. It fucking *kills* me to admit that he wants you too. He... *feels* something for you. Which is very novel for my brother. He doesn't feel anything for anyone. He's cold as ice. Well, except somehow when it comes to you. But I would've still let him suffer. I would've let him fucking burn in hell. But then..." He shakes his head. "Then I saw you. I saw your face. I... I saw how heartbroken you were over what he did, over how he hurt you. And I"—he shrugs—"had to step back. I had to step away. Not for him. But for you."

I want to cry.

I want to break down and start sobbing.

For everything. For everything I did. Everything Shepard went through, that I put him through. Every hurt, every second of his torment because of me.

Despite all that, he still chose to put me above him.

He still chose to not only remain my friend but actually work toward giving me what I want.

But I hold on because I've already done that. I've already broken down once and leaned on his strength. It's his turn now. He needs the strength from me. He needs someone to lean on too.

So that's what I do.

I walk up to him and wrap my arms around his body, around my best friend. "I'm sorry. You have no idea, Shepard, how sorry I am."

His arms come around my body as well and he squeezes me to him. "Yeah, me too."

I want to lose the battle with my tears then. But again, I hold on and say, "I wish... I wish I could take it all back, you know? I wish I could... I never meant to hurt you. I never meant to do what I did."

"I know." Then, "But if you hadn't done what you did, we never would've met. We never would've danced together. I wouldn't have my best friend."

Best friend.

Yeah, he's that.

He's the very best friend anyone could ever ask for.

The very best friend that I don't even deserve.

Clenching my eyes shut, I squeeze my arms around him again. "I can't believe you did that. I can't believe you... asked me to marry you just because..."

"Well, I'm known to do reckless things."

Something occurs to me then. "Is that why you wouldn't let me stay with you in your room? And you haven't been hanging out as much?"

He smiles sadly, his thumb coming to rest on the side of my eye, wiping the tear that managed to squeeze out despite all my efforts. "If I was hanging out with you all the time, he wouldn't have time to hang out with you, now would he?"

"He—"

"And he has, hasn't he?"

I stiffen in his embrace. "Shepard, I—"

"And I noticed that you're not wearing my ring."

Thank God my hands are behind his back or I would be hiding them from sight right about now. "No, it's not that. It's—"

"He took it, didn't he?"

My eyes go wide. "I... How—"

"I would've done the same thing."

"Shepard, I'm sorry. I—"

"It's okay. I know." His jaw tenses for a second, but he keeps going. "I set the whole thing up, so yeah, I'm aware."

Still guilt crushes my chest. "I should've come to you right away. The night you proposed to me. I knew I was... I don't know, taking advantage of you, leaning on you too much and I... I should've told you that it wasn't a good idea. I should've told you. I should've said that even though you were giving me what I wanted, I would never be able to do the same and I'm just so sorry about that. So fucking sorry."

His dark eyes, similar to the man I love, rove over my features. "If you had, then I probably wouldn't have been able to witness a miracle."

"What miracle?"

"My twin brother pissed as fuck." He chuckles. "I honestly thought he was going to kick my fucking teeth in the other day in the parking lot."

My heart clenches at the memory.

Of how pissed he looked. How agitated and *worried* for just a little thing.

And I swat Shepard's chest. "It's not funny. He really would have."

"Yeah, I would've liked to see him try."

"I'm serious, Shep," I tell him, looking him in the eyes. "He's... He's complicated."

"Is he, now?"

"He is," I insist. "There's... There's something in there. There's something more. Something deep inside of him that I don't know. That no one knows."

"Well, what's deep inside of him is ten feet of ice." He scoffs. "I've known him my entire life and trust me when I say there's nothing inside of him. Except a fucking winter wasteland."

My heart aches for him then.

That his own twin thinks that about him, that he has nothing to offer.

My heart aches for Shep too. Because I think he wants there to be something inside of Stellan, something to show that they have a bond, isn't it? Maybe that's why he keeps provoking Stellan. To get a reaction out of him. To see if he cares. If that's the truth, then I understand that. I did the same thing for over a year.

Only to find out that yes, Stellan Thorne is not cold as ice or cold as winter. He's hot as wildfire.

"You just said that he feels something for me," I remind him.

He grows serious. "And for your sake, I hope it's enough to make him realize what a lucky son of a bitch he is."

Overwhelmed, I bring my hand up to his jaw. "I don't deserve you."

Again, he throws me a lopsided smile.

Although this one is more like his usual smile. Arrogant and mischievous. "Yeah, you do. It's him who doesn't deserve you."

"That's not—"

"Which is why," he says, "you aren't going to tell him."

"What?"

"That this is fake."

I pull away from him. "Shepard, no. I can't do that. I... *We* can't do that."

"We need to do it," he points out. "You want him, don't you? This is the only way to get him. If he thinks he's going to lose you to someone else, to *me* no less, he'll probably pull his head out of his ass and see what he has."

Oh my God, he sounds like my *biji*.

"But, Shepard." I shake my head. "Not like this. Not like... I can't deceive him. I can't lie to him anymore." He goes to say something, but I keep going, "Listen, I did that, okay? I already did that and it was a disaster. He hated that I lied to him about dating you. He's going to actually lose his shit if—"

"Well, that's exactly what you want, don't you? For him to lose his shit enough that you finally get to be with him."

"But—"

"Besides, you fooled me too, remember?"

I go still in his arms.

"You played me as well. So you owe me this."

I move away from him. "Shepard, please, okay? I'll do anything else. I'll give you anything else at all. Just—"

"This is what I want," he states stubbornly.

"Why?"

"Because now that I know what your answer would've been to the ultimatum, I want him to suffer like I'm suffering. Even if for a little bit."

CHAPTER 15

I cannot believe that I'm lying to him again.
    Even after learning my lesson – and this lesson I promise I learned – I'm still making the same mistake. Actually, I'm back to where I was when all of this began, one twin blackmailing me to hurt the other. Although Shepard isn't exactly blackmailing me but still. I can't *not* do what he wants me to do and let him down. I've already done that.

It's just a lot harder than the first time when I lied to Stellan.

Because now I know the consequences. I know how painful it is for him and I don't want to hurt him that way. I don't want to torture him and play with his emotions.

God, I want the opposite.

I want to keep him safe.

I want to *protect* his emotions, the ones he clearly doesn't want to have but does.

And second, all this just goes to show even more that these two need an intervention. They need to sit down and talk it the fuck out. Shepard needs to apologize for always provoking Stellan to get his attention. And Stellan needs to apologize for not giving enough attention to his own twin brother.

Or fight it out.

Whatever helps solve the problem.

The issue is that they need to reach out to each other, and freaking have a conversation about their long-standing but clearly not buried feelings.

Which I realize is such a hard ask when it comes to men.

I mean they won't even engage in a conversation about the symbolism of it all.

The ring, in this case.

"Give me my ring back," I tell him one night, playing with the damp ends of his hair.

Like a few days ago, he's sprawled on me, all lazy and languid, so deliciously relaxed that I want to eat him. Or lick the muscles of his back that flutter with every breath he takes, the side of his neck. His chest too. His hard jaw. His cheek. The roll of his biceps.

Basically, I just want to lick him everywhere.

And I did all of that, not five minutes ago.

I even sucked him off.

Or rather he fucked my face. After which, he made me dance in his lap with his dick inside of me and I don't know what's my favorite: getting fucked in the throat or in my pussy and riding him like a pole while doing it.

I guess it's all my favorite.

He's my favorite.

The only difference is that we're in a new city and instead of his room, we're in mine. Because he wouldn't let me walk – two doors down – to his. *Because* he thinks it's unsafe.

Because he clearly has the top spot for crazy.

And maybe that's why I love him so much and keep falling in love every second of every day. If this is his way of fixing things and getting me to fall out of love with him, then he's not doing a very good job of it.

Anyway, back to the conversation at hand.

To which he replies, mumbling into my neck, "No."

"Just give it to me," I insist, fisting his hair.

He looks up, his eyes hooded. "Why?"

I try not to get too lost in his dark gaze.

But apparently, don't succeed and reply, "Because..."

"You want to wear it?" he asks belligerently.

My heart clenches in fear. "I'm... It's just –"

"Because last time I checked you were in love with me."

Now my heart clenches more but for a different reason. A reason that makes me wind my arms and my thighs around his body even more tightly. And in response, he slides his arms up my back and tunnels his fingers in my sex-tangled hair.

Then, "That still true?"

I squeeze him with my limbs. "Y-yes."

He's taken to doing that.

Asking me if I still love him. I don't know what the purpose is – because hello? Allergic to emotions over here – but I know that as soon as I say yes, he stops breathing for a second like he can't believe it and then breathes out a long breath as if relieved.

So there's no way I can stop telling him the truth.

No way I can stop controlling his breaths like he controls mine.

No way I can stop giving him relief.

"So then, no. You'll wear his ring when you're not in love with me anymore."

After delivering that decree, he goes back to tucking his face in my neck.

God, this man.

I pull at his hair again. "Just give it back, Stellan. As a sign of respect to your brother."

Because that's what it is.

Now that I've broken things off with Shepard, it's not as if I'm going to wear it. I'm going to give it back to him. He should have it. It's *his*. It's not a token of rivalry between them, or a competition. It's also not a symbol of jealousy because there's nothing to be jealous about.

Although I can't really say that to him.

Hate you, Shepard.

Hate you for making me keep secrets from Stellan.

Even though, clearly, he has secrets of his own.

"Not interested in respecting him, remember?" he murmurs, breaking into my thoughts.

Okay, this is it.

This is my opening.

Sighing, I blink up at the ceiling. "I think there's clearly, *clearly*, something between you two. Some sort of a tension. And I think you need to talk to him about it."

He hums.

I frown. "I'm serious, Stellan."

"Hmm."

I turn my face to the side. "Are you listening to me? I know you think you're a shitty brother and I know you have a secret. You don't have to tell me, even though I'm dying to know it. But maybe you can tell *him*." This idea occurred to me only recently, that if he can't tell me for some reason, maybe he can tell Shepard. "Maybe whatever it is that's keeping you both apart can be solved. It can be fixed if only you opened up and –" I feel him, getting heavier on me and I push at his shoulders. "Stellan? Are you falling asleep on me?"

Then, with an alert, a very awake voice, he replies back, "If you insist on talking about things that don't interest me, then yes."

"Ugh. You're impossible. You're –"

"And I don't want to fall asleep just yet."

I dig my chin in his hair. But the joke is on me because I don't think he felt anything because of his hard head and I'm the one who ends up with a throbbing chin.

"Why not?"

"Because I still have to draw you a bath."

This is not fair.

I don't think this is fair.

Him being so sweet after shutting me down like that. How am I supposed to stay firm and push him to do the right thing when he makes my heart race the way he does?

Then, biting my lip, "With lavender bath salts?"

His chest grazes my sore nipples – sore from all the sucking he's done – as he breathes, and I squirm under him. "Yes, with lavender bath salts."

"And a rose scented candle?"

He looks up then and takes me in, my heated cheeks, my spread-out hair on his pillow. "At the risk of smelling like a fucking flower bouquet, yes with a rose scented candle."

"Hey, you're the one who insists on getting me a rose every day."

"Still your favorite flower, yeah?"

"Yes," I whisper.

"So then," he whispers back.

Every single morning since he found out that roses are my favorite flower, there's a rose waiting for me on my pillow. And like I did with the first rose, I eat it. Not alone though; I share it with him. He thinks it's nuts but he never denies me when I pluck a petal and urge him to open his mouth. He never shies away from it when I place it on his tongue like we're both sharing a drug and getting high together.

On roses.

And so again, I don't know what's my favorite: finding a rose on my pillow every morning or getting to see his face as soon as I wake up.

Because he insists on us sleeping together.

He insists on cuddling with me all night – and yes, he's a total cuddler – with his strong and heavy arm tucked into the dip of my waist and my butt fitting against his lower abs and of course, his dick.

Which I have to say never ever goes down all the way.

He's always semi-hard and heated and I love wiggling against it to wake him up.

What can I say, I love his dick.

I love it even more when he puts me on his cock and asks me to give him a lap dance first thing in the morning.

I love *him*.

So I slide my arms down from his neck and cradle his stubbled cheek. Looking into his shimmering eyes, I say, "I'm ready for my bath now."

He circles his eyes over my features before muttering, "Thank fucking God."

And then he carries me to the bathroom where he gives me a bath fit for a princess. Well, he slides in as well so he can massage all my sore muscles, untangle the long strands of my hair with such gentleness that I always want to weep. But instead, I turn around and make out with him. Which helps because along with making me want to weep, he makes me go breathless with his tenderness. So this way, he gets to revive me with his breaths and his kisses.

Once that's done, he towels both of us off and rubs my strawberry scented lotion on me. Again, something he insists on doing even though it makes him question my chaotic scent choices: lavender scented bath salts, strawberry scented lotion, rose scented shampoo, and gardenia scented face moisturizer. Sometimes while putting the lotion on me, he'll get waylaid and eat my pussy. Sometimes he'll just play with it with the fingers of his one hand while asking me to stay still so he can finish rubbing the cream on me with the other.

Either way, I always come after the bath.

When that's done as well, he carries me back to bed and proceeds to make me ginger and honey tea because he very hungrily and lovingly fucked my throat.

But that's not the best part.

The best part is that he does it naked.

While I get to watch.

His gorgeous body on display.

The broad muscles of his back fluttering with the movements of his arms; those two dips on the side of his ass flexing when he shifts on his feet. When he's done, I get to watch him, and his glorious naked chest and those ridged abs bring me the tea he made.

"I seriously cannot get over how fucking amazing your body is," I say as he hands me my tea.

With his lips twitching, he slides in with his own, chamomile. And I have to say that I find very adorable that Stellan 'The Cold' Thorne loves drinking chamomile tea before going to bed.

"Well, ditto."

I settle against him, using him as a pillow and take a sip of my soothing tea. "And your chest hair." Then, looking up, "Is that crazy?"

I feel him shrug. "But you *are* crazy."

I look up. "Not as crazy as you though. You still hold the top spot."

"How's that?"

"You love that thing about me."

"What thing?"

I give him wide eyes. "The *thing*."

His lips tip up slightly in a lopsided smile. "Your tasty fucking asshole?"

I gasp, almost spilling my tea. "Not that, you perv!"

Although he does love it.

Love licking it, eating it, putting his finger in it.

His tongue too.

Oh my *God*.

It's... embarrassing.

And he does it all urgently and enthusiastically. Like he can't get enough of it. Like he loves it as much as he loves eating my pussy.

He chuckles in response.

And I narrow my eyes at him. "The other thing. My sixth toe."

Oh, did I mention that I have an extra toe on my left foot?

I do.

I don't like to think about it. I don't like to acknowledge it. Growing up, it was a great source of contention for me. Especially because my mother didn't like it. She'd think it was another one of my ploys to steal attention. Because I'd come back from school, crying over how kids would make fun of me. How they'd point at it and laugh. Not to mention, since both my feet were of different width, we had to have special shoes made for me to wear. Maybe that's why I love flip flops and open-toed sandals so much. Even though they show off my toes.

But the story is entirely different for Stellan.

He loves it.

He hadn't noticed right away, thank God, because they all blend so well together. But one night while he was propped up on the pillows, waiting for me to pick out a movie to watch, and I was on my tummy, facing away from him and swinging my legs, he saw it for the first time. When I told him that I didn't want to talk about it, he insisted, and we all know what that means: I *had* to tell him.

Since then, he makes sure to kiss all eleven of my toes to tell me how much he loves them all.

And for the third time, I don't know what's my favorite: him leaving roses for me or kissing my extra toe.

I feel him sigh and then shift. He goes for my tea and takes it from my hand even though I protest with, *hey, I was drinking that*, and sets it aside. He sets his mug aside too before sliding out and moving to kneel in front of me. Grabbing my ankles, he yanks at them, causing me to go flat on my back.

Then keeping my legs raised, he nuzzles his nose against my left calf. "I want you to count, okay?"

Frowning, I go to protest, "Stellan, you –"

Keeping our gazes locked, he brings my left foot to his lips. He blows lightly on the arch and I squeal because holy God, that's my ticklish spot. "That's n-not... fair."

He tsks, blowing on my foot again. "So then you should do what I say."

I squeal in response again and struggle against his grip. "This is b-blackmail."

He hums, nuzzling my ankle again. "I tend to enjoy that."

"I h-hate you."

"No, you don't," he says, blowing another little puff of air.

I squeal and arch and twist and struggle. Then, "Okay, okay. I'll do it."

He smirks, a triumphant glint in his eyes.

That asshole.

And then he proceeds to kiss all of my toes as I count them one by one. When he reaches my extra pinkie toe, he makes sure to look at me as he kisses it not once but twice, making me blush and squirm. When I reach the end of the count – eleven for eleven toes – he comes down at me.

My thighs wrap around his naked hips as he rumbles, "Eleven."

Panting, I whisper back, "Eleven."

He shifts over me, his hard dick rubbing over my pussy lips. "And what's eleven?"

I arch up against it. "S-Stellan's favorite number."

"Stellan's favorite number," he approves.

"You –"

"And what else is Stellan's favorite?" he asks, nudging my wet hole with his dick.

"All three of my p-pinkie toes."

"All three of your pinkie toes." Then, "What else?"

"And my t-tits."

"Fuck yeah, your tits." Then, rasping, "Keep going."

He slides in but only a little bit, making me moan in response.

When I forget to answer him, he prods, "What else, baby?"

My fingers dig in his shoulders. "M-My pussy."

Humming, he slides further in. "Your sweetheart pussy, yeah."

"Stellan, I –"

"There's more."

"My mouth."

"Your sweetheart mouth."

"Stellan, you need to –"

"You forgot the last one."

"My a-ass."

Finally, he's all the way in and we both take a second to absorb that. I writhe under him and he grunts over me. Then, "And your sweetheart asshole." Then, "But what's my most favorite of all?"

My heart races and my skin breaks out in goosebumps. "D-Dora."

"Yeah, Dora," he says both roughly and warmly. "My sweetheart is my favorite of all."

After that, all bets are off.

He pounds my pussy until I shatter around him causing him to come as well. And as always, he pulls out and sticks just the tip in my asshole and comes in my ass.

To give me what I want – his bare cock – but also to protect me.

Which makes me fall in love with him even more.

But the day is not done yet.

Which means I have more occasions to fall in love with him.

Despite this little detour and cleaning me up, we continue with our nightly ritual. Where he sits propped up on the pillows while I go back to using his chest as a pillow for *me*. And then I sip my tea – he rewarmed it, including his own – as he reads to me from his favorite series. I'm not going to lie, I'm really enjoying it. I've never been a reader before but I could listen to him read me all day long. And that's how I go to sleep every night, with his heat on my skin and his voice in my ears.

It's all very peaceful except we both have secrets and I'd like that to stop.

While I can't do anything about his, I get to share mine after the championship game.

Because that's the deadline.

When Shep insisted that I keep our fake engagement a secret, I gave him until the championship game. That's when I'm going to tell Stellan the truth.

Not that I know exactly what I'll say to him.

He'll be pissed, that's for sure.

He'll be *crazy* pissed.

But then again, there's always this hope that he'll fall madly in love with me by then so he'll laugh it all away and forgive me for playing with his emotions again.

Ha!

What an absolute joke.

Even if he did fall in love with me – which is not going to happen because he's so adamant at making me fall out of it and because he just plain doesn't want to – he's going to get over it pretty quickly when he finds out the truth. So all I can do is make the most of the time that we have right now and be with him until it all blows up in my face.

Which is why I hate that we have to keep this a secret.

For all intents and purposes, I'm still engaged to the captain of the team. Which means I can't be caught sneaking around with anyone let alone the head coach, his twin brother.

Not to mention, my own mother.

She still calls me and checks up on me every single day, reminding me of the rules and her threat. And I'm sure she's keeping an eye on the media about any gossip about me, waiting for me to slip up. Not that I'm going to. Even though I've broken all her rules and even though Stellan doesn't fear her, I do. I absolutely am scared of her and what she's capable of.

So it's imperative that we keep this under wraps until everything comes to an end at the last game.

But apparently Stellan has other plans.

Because now at parties, he blatantly stares at me.

Without any regard to anyone else around.

He follows me with his eyes no matter where I go or what I do or who I'm with.

When Isiah makes me laugh at his silliness, Stellan looks like he's going to break something on Isiah's body. And the next day he punishes Isiah by giving him extra laps to run. When this other guy on the team started chatting up with me – about his girlfriend no less – the next day I find out that Stellan rode him extra hard at practice and the guy was almost limping back from practice.

On top of all this, Shepard has upped his flirting game.

Even though I told him very specifically, along with giving him a deadline, that if I'm to keep our fake engagement a secret, he can absolutely under no circumstances flirt with me or use me to provoke Stellan.

But as I'm coming to find out, he didn't listen.

So he goes ahead and throws his arm around my neck whenever he wants.

He goes ahead and *kisses* me whenever he wants, but thankfully only on my cheek or in my hair. He insists that I have dinner with him every night. He insists on holding hands and being all lovey dovey and couple-y when before he'd just leave me alone.

And he simply *insists* on dancing with me at every victory party.

Like the one we're at right now.

"Shepard, you need to chill out," I tell him while twirling in his arms.

Because it's not as if I can say no to him – my stupid fiancé – in front of everyone.

He smirks. "Why, is he going to finally lose it?"

I keep my mouth shut.

Because I do have a feeling that Stellan is reaching his breaking point.

It's going to happen any day now.

He already looks like he's *this* close to breaking the neck of his beer bottle. While also turning his own teeth to dust from how hard he's gritting his teeth.

I throw him a small smile.

That only makes all the gritting and that pulsing muscle on his cheek worse.

So I look away and focus on Shepard who's still smirking. "It's not funny."

"It's a little funny."

"He's your twin brother."

"Unfortunately."

How is it that their expression, their tone, their entire freaking demeanor become exactly the same – identical; a word I never use for them – when I talk to one about the other? How is it that they can't see there's a severe lack and need for a discourse between them?

I shake my head as he twists me in his arms so my back is pressed to his chest. Then, "I'm not even going to get into how dysfunctional your relationship is with each other. But have a little compassion, will you? You're torturing him. *We're* torturing him." Then, "Let me tell him, please."

"No."

Before I can protest, he spins me back around so we're face to face, our chests colliding. I glare at him for pinning me close and he keeps smirking.

Then, "He'll live. But most importantly, do you really want to be with a guy who goes apeshit just because you're looking at another guy? He's fucking crazy with his jealousy. Not to mention,"—he looks me up and down—"I wouldn't do that. I'd never be this crazy or this jealous. I'll let you be free."

I realize – not for the first time – that yes, Shepard isn't like that. He doesn't get jealous. He doesn't burn. He doesn't go crazy. And I should've realized that right away and called Stellan out on his deception when his jealousy was spilling out in the text messages.

"But I *am* free," I tell Shepard as we sway in each other's arms. "He makes me feel free. He makes me feel like I can be myself. I can dance in the middle of a crowded bar where guys are all wanting a piece of me because I know he won't let them take it. I can jump off a high building because I know he'll either jump with me with a parachute or stand on the ground with a safety net. I know he'll always save me. I know he'll always be there. And I..." I lick my lips. "I want that, Shepard. I want him. I want his safety. I want his warmth, his heated glares, his anger, his jealousy. I even want the way he hurts me because I hurt him too. I want everything that makes him *him*. Because sometimes I think I'm the way I am because he's the way he is. We're different but we're the same."

Only I want him to love me.

But he doesn't.

And sometimes I think – again not for the first time – that if I remove this love condition of mine, maybe we can stay together, Stellan and I.

"Well," Shepard murmurs, breaking into my thoughts, "that was very poetic."

I feel a sting in my heart. "I didn't..."

"Hey," he throws me a lopsided smile, "I can take it. I'm a big boy."

I swallow. "You will –"

"If you're going to say that I'll find someone like that," he says with his jaw tensed, "then I'll ask you to just not."

I *was* going to say that, yes.

But after this all I say is, "It's not a bad thing. To want that for you."

"To go as feral crazy for a girl as my lovely twin brother who, let me remind you, is known as the Cold Thorn?" He pulls a face. "Nah, I'm okay. I'd much rather see him suffer than suffer myself."

I keep silent but I do hope, in my heart, that he meets someone who makes him feel the way his brother makes *me* feel. I know it's not all good but I wouldn't know the good without knowing the bad.

So I'll take it.

I'll take every single emotion that he's made me feel ever since I clapped my eyes on him under that pink magnolia tree. Every single torturous emotion just so I can experience the wonderful ones too.

Maybe that's why love is a drug.

And people get addicted to it despite the heartbreak.

They get addicted to the highs despite the torturous lows.

Despite knowing that there's a chance they wouldn't get the same devotion back.

So when the dance is done, I look his way again. He's still as a statue but I feel his gaze blazing. Keeping my eyes on him, I excuse myself from Shepard. I watch as he sets down his beer bottle on the nearby table as well and pushes off the wall.

And then keeping our gazes locked I walk toward him.

With every step that I take, he grows even tighter, even heated.

So much so that I can feel the heat of him all the way over here.

I wonder how the world isn't melting off from it.

I wonder what he'll do to me when he gets his hands on me. And since he can't touch me where people can see, I veer off the path and make a beeline for the exit. And I know he's following me because I can feel that heat of his at my back. In fact, I think he's crowding because as soon as I get out in the winter, he's right there.

He's right there to grip my elbow and spin me around.

To pin me against the brick wall and surround me in his heat as he comes over me, looms and leans and hovers over me like a dark shadow, blocking the moon.

"What was he saying?" he growls lowly.

I grip his face. "It doesn't matter."

"He was touching you."

"Stellan, it doesn't matter, okay? It doesn't –"

"Why was he touching you?" He keeps growling, his face a collection of sharp angles and angry lines. "You're not married yet."

"It doesn't –"

"You don't even have his ring on your finger."

"Just –"

"Because you're still in fucking love with me."

At 'me,' he borderline punches his own chest and I wince. But before I can say anything, he goes on, "Tell him to keep his hands off you. Or I will."

"Stellan, no."

"And I will make it hurt." I keep shaking my head as he continues, "You know what I did to Isiah the other day, don't you? I can do it to him. I could do much *worse* to him."

When he still won't stop, I come off the wall and inch closer myself. I tip my face up, my fingers still on his hard and dense jaw. "Stellan, baby, stop, okay? Come back to me." I press my lips to his throat because he's so freaking tall that I can't get to his lips. So I skim my lips over his skin as if calming a beast as I whisper, "Just come back. Come back, please. I'm here. I'm with you. I'm not with him. It doesn't matter if he touched me. You're the only one I want. Your touch is the only touch I crave, please. Don't be mad. Don't –"

He fists my hair then and yanking my head back, he kisses me. And as much as I like his kisses, I realize this is belt day.

The day he uses his belt on me.

I call them belt days but he refers to them as bad days. Days where he's more restless than usual, where he wants to withdraw into himself. Where he's angry and agitated. I don't know what causes them. Sometimes he wakes up that way; sometimes things will happen at practice that may make him that way.

Either way I think I've come to at least recognize the signs, if not the triggers.

Although in this case, I know what triggered his bad mood.

Shepard and his shenanigans.

Again I wish there was a way for me to fix this between brothers but I can't. All I can do is give him my wrists to bind and my throat to fuck.

Which is what I do.

I go down on my knees and go for his belt. He gets my intention and helps me. He ties my hands behind my back and I offer him my mouth. Which he takes and fucks and makes me moan. When I feel like he's close, his length is pulsing and has gotten bigger and heavier – he pulls me up and attacks my mouth.

He kisses me as I am.

All sloppy and pretty for him.

Then, ripping his mouth away, "You're my fucking baby, you know that. You're my fucking sweetheart, my treasure. You're every beat of my racing heart."

Before I can respond, he comes down on the ground.

He flips my dress up, gets his head between my thighs so he can get at my pussy. He eats the fuck out of my pussy as I whine and moan and shatter on his tongue. And while I'm still pulsating from my first orgasm, he emerges, his mouth all plump and red, wet from my juices, and spins me around. He yanks my hips out and kicks my feet apart. And before I know it, he's thrusting into my still fluttering pussy, making me cry out his name.

He fucks me against the wall, filling me, pounding me, making me lose my mind. He's leaving bruises on my skin, my hips where he's got ahold of me. And I'm probably drawing blood from his skin where I'm scratching the side of his neck, his face even.

He yanks my dress down and gets my tits out. He pulls on my nipples, making them all sore and swollen. And in response, I draw blood on his skin and strangle his dick from how tight I'm clenching my pussy.

And I'm so dazed by all of this that I don't realize we're not alone anymore.

That there's someone here.

The only thing that alerts me of their presence is the fact that he speaks.

Growls really.

"Look away."

I gasp, my eyes blinking open; I never knew I'd closed them. Panting and horrified, I turn my head to the side, which had come down to rest on his chest, to look at the intruders. This was the worst idea, wasn't it? We weren't supposed to do this here. We weren't supposed to look at each other lest someone finds out our secret let alone do what we're doing.

But thankfully, it's the two guys that I don't recognize.

My relief is still short-lived because of what they inadvertently stumbled upon.

And it's not their fault either really.

It's not as if we're hiding or anything. We're doing this right by the exit doors of the bar and we're not even on the other side of the big dumpsters that line the wall, no. So we're in their direct line of sight.

They can see us.

They can see what's happening.

And so Stellan should stop, shouldn't he?

I'm not going to lie, I kinda hate it. We have only so much time together and now we have to break apart because of these morons.

But he doesn't.

Oh my God, he doesn't stop.

Instead he growls, while still moving inside of me at the same pace, "Look the fuck away if you want to live."

They don't listen.

So then I have to force myself to think about what we actually look like.

Although I have very little idea of it.

I don't even know if my dress is all the way up, exposing my lower half, my ass and my pussy to the world. I don't even know if his jeans are all the way down or just open enough to get his dick inside of me.

All I know is that he's hugging me to his body like he always does, his heat and his fingers overwhelming in the best way.

"Listen, you fuckfaces," he growls again, his fingers on my hips tightening. "I'm about to come, yeah? And I need to switch holes to do that. I can't come in my girl's hot as fuck pussy because she's not on the pill and I can't breed her. Even though," he thrusts really hard, making me moan and close my eyes again, "I'd like nothing more. I'd like nothing more than to put a baby in her belly so fuckfaces like you, including his fiancé, know exactly who she belongs to. Me, her daddy."

I moan crazy loud at that and rake my fingers down his jaw.

"And from the sound of it, my girl would like that too. My girl, here," he smacks my ass under my dress, making me jerk and whine, "would love a baby in her belly. She'd love for me to breed her. She'd do anything to steal the cum out of me. She'd fucking poke holes in a condom if she could." He smacks me again and this time when I whine, I also nod. Because it's true. In my recklessness, I'd do anything to keep him tied to me.

"But I'm her daddy so I need to be responsible. I can't be fucking reckless like she is," he smacks my ass again to emphasize his point, "I can't let her run around with a big load of my cum in her fertile cunt. She's getting married soon and I can't ruin her life like that, by tying her to me. And that alone is pissing me the fuck off, that I can't have what I want, her swollen belly and milky tits. That I have to control myself and pull out of her sweetheart snatch so I don't accidentally get her pregnant. So to make myself feel better and to keep her happy, I come in her asshole. Which I'm going to do in about two point five seconds. And if, in the process, you get a flash of her tight asshole or God forbid her sweet pussy hole that I'm fucking right now, that'll be the last thing you see. You already got an eyeful of her tits before I covered them up so if you want to save your life," he punctuates that with a harsh pound, "look the fuck away from my girl and let me fuck her in peace."

Of course.

Of course they can't see anything.

As in, they can see he's fucking me but they can't see anything on my body.

Because he's protecting me. I bet he pushed my dress down which is now fluttering around mid-thighs and he wrapped his arm over my swollen, jiggling tits, hiding them from their eyes.

Good.

Even though I don't care that they're looking, I still don't want them to actually get a look at what only belongs to him. And just because they're still frozen, I moan, "Please, please go away. Or my daddy won't come inside of me. And I want him to come inside of me. I want my daddy's cum. I want my daddy. *Please.*"

Which is very ironic because that's the moment I come.

I clench around his hard pounding length and writhe against him. And through my own moans and whines, I hear the shuffling of feet and muttered, *did you hear that? Was he really her daddy...*

But everything once again fades out because he chooses that very moment to pull out of me and push into my asshole – just the tip of his dick – and give me his cum.

And again, I wonder what if I tell him he doesn't have to love me back?

What if when I tell him my secret after the championship game, I also tell him that I'll take him however he comes. I don't even want to know his secret if he doesn't want to tell me.

All I want is him.

CHAPTER 16

THE WILDFIRE THORN

THREE WEEKS LATER...

The things that provoke you to react are often called triggers.

The list of my triggers has always been long. So long that I've them put in two separate categories. The one that's I'm facing right now is number five on the high concern list: losing focus.

My queen is trapped.

I don't think I can save her. I could, two moves ago, but now all hope is lost. And it's because I wasn't paying attention.

These days I often find myself in a position like this.

I forget meeting notes. I find myself staring out the window instead of paying attention to the plays. Sometimes I'll start a sentence and then completely forget where I was going with it. The other day I overfilled my water bottle at the water fountain *twice* before giving up and grabbing a soda from the vending machine. I run into people while walking as if I've forgotten how to walk.

And whenever something like this would happen, I used to panic.

I used to withdraw into myself.

I used to think that the world was going to end.

That I was going to do something to make it end.

These days though, I think about her.

My grounding object.

Her shiny hair on the pillow. Her skin when the sun hits her. Her small fingers when she tries to catch the snow in her hands. My jackets on her body that always tend to drown her. Those two dimples on her back that I've licked countless times, that mole, the crack of her gorgeous ass.

Her languid eyes when I've made her come. Her eyes when she sees the rose on her pillow. Her eyes when she feeds it to me, all joyful and lusty. Her eyes when she laughs at something I've said that's completely not funny like, *can you shut the fuck up and let me suck your tits?*

Her excited voice when she talks about her plays, her characters. The way she brings her character to life when we run lines. The way her features shine when she makes me watch her favorite movies.

Her excitement when I read to her.

The nape of her neck when I bathe her. The feel of her hair when I braid it. The feel of her mouth when I kiss it, when I fuck it. The feel of her pussy when she comes around my dick.

Fuck.

Fucking fuck, the feel of her sweetheart pussy when she flutters around my cock.

I could live in her pussy.

In fact, I do live in her pussy all night. I sleep with my dick in her.

It's just something that I have to do.

It's a need I can't explain.

A need to not be separated from her.

Not yet.

And that's the problem.

"Are you going to take your turn?"

I get pulled out of my thoughts by Homer's voice and remember where I am: at The Horny Bard in Bardstown. One of my least favorite hang outs. Homer's too actually so we've found ourselves a quiet spot, away from the crowd, and have a chess board between us.

I think we both like it because it requires minimum talking and structured thinking.

"Sorry," I say, rubbing my temples.

"Worried about the game tomorrow?" Homer asks, settling back in the chair.

We arrived back in New York a few days ago because this is it.

We made it.

We're playing the championship game and this year, it's happening in New York. The last few days have been grueling with practice and meetings and strategies and brainstorming late into the night. But today we've got a day off because tomorrow's the big day and we all need it to decompress.

"No," I reply.

Because that has always been the goal.

To not worry. To not stress or get involved.

Which is why I stayed in soccer despite not caring for it.

Homer eyes me curiously but accepts my answer with a nod. "Okay."

I sigh again and confess, "I don't really like soccer all that much."

I expect the whole bar to stop talking.

I expect them to stare at me in disbelief.

I know it's all very dramatic but what I've revealed is also pretty dramatic: the fact that me, a Thorne, isn't really interested in something that's our legacy. Something that I trained for my entire life. Something I chose to do for the rest of my life as well.

But it is what it is, and it is the truth.

Much like I confessed my biggest secret to Conrad, this one brings me relief as well. Just for the record, Conrad hasn't looked at me differently since I told him about my issues. He treats me like he always did, like his brother, his right hand, a man that he can trust. I don't understand how he could do that after knowing what I am.

Anyway, I don't know if I should've sprung it on one of my good friends out of nowhere though. While it's not a random confession for me—something about keeping secrets from *her* is taking its toll on me now—it may seem like to him.

This time Homer keeps eyeing me for a long time. Then, "Well, it's not everyone's cup of tea."

I give him a look. "Is that all you're going to say to me?"

"What else do you want me to say?"

I settle against the back of the chair as well. "I don't know, how about, what the fuck or this is unbelievable or how the fuck do you not like soccer when you've dedicated your entire life to it."

Homer settles himself further in the seat, sprawling his thighs, smoothing his suit jacket. "You can absolutely *not* like things that you've dedicated your entire life to. I don't like my job, my company that I was groomed my entire life to take over either."

That gives me pause.

Because I thought he did.

Because that's what he'd talk about back in high school. He'd talk about going to business school, taking over his father's company one day. He was pretty fucking jazzed about it. He quit soccer for it too.

"You," I begin carefully, "don't like working for your company."

He shakes his head slowly. "No."

"So why do you do it?" I ask.

"Why are you in soccer if you hate it?" he asks back.

Because I've got a shitty father with anger and addiction issues who used to beat our mom and often times our big brother. Because I got that gene from him and I don't want to be. So I try to lead a life away from all stimulation and excitement lest I can't handle them. I try to lead a life of safety and control lest I succumb to temptation and become like him.

And because soccer was the only way to stay close to my family. The family that I couldn't stay close to any other way.

Anyway, since I can't say any of these things, I simply stare at him.
And he stares back.
And a look of mutual understanding passes between us.
I guess we both have our secrets.
Then, he goes, "So where's your head at, if not on the game?"
"On her."

Again, I don't think I should've sprung it on him like this. Especially after how he witnessed my fight with my brother. But it's also something I've been wanting to say for the past few weeks.

Because I hate the fact that I have to hide it.

I hate the fact that I have to sneak around with her. That I can't hold her hand in public. That I can't make her smile in public or make her laugh. I can't even look at her in public. Although I've broken that rule many times but yeah.

I fucking hate it.

I fucking hate that I can't go up to her and ask for her hand to dance. Although I know nothing about dancing. I fucking hate that I can't go up to her and bend down on one knee and offer my ring.

"Your brother's girlfriend." Then, raising his palm, "His fiancée now, I hear."

The ring that sits in my pocket makes itself known.

As fucked up as it is, I always carry it around. Probably because I don't want it to end up in the wrong hands. Or wrong fingers.

Wrong fingers being her.

As I said, I know it's fucked up. She's going to wear his ring sooner or later. I *want* her to wear his ring sooner or later. I want her to get everything that she wants. I want her to be happy. I want all her dreams to come true including the one about love. But I can't bring myself to give it back to her without doing some serious damage to someone.

To my twin brother specifically.

Who sits at the top of my trigger list.

While it still looks like I can handle most of my triggers, he's the only one who makes me angry. The thought of him with her is the only one that makes me agitated enough to bring on my bad days. The thought of her wearing his ring is the only thought that seems threatening enough to send me on a warpath.

So I've taken to keeping it on me at all times. It's better this way.

I'm under control.

My brother is safe.

The fucking ring is off her finger.

"She loves me," I tell him.

Yet another confession and the one I've wanted to make the most.

It's also the one that gives me the biggest relief.

"She," Homer begins, shifting in his chair, "loves *you*."

"I'm fixing it."

"You're *fixing* it?"

Yes.

I am.

And I mean it now more than ever.

More than when I'd said the same thing to Conrad a few weeks back.

Because not only is she my grounding object, she's also the one who's given me a chance to see a different life, hasn't she?

A chance to *live* it for the past few weeks.

With her.

Even though we live that life behind closed doors and in the darkness of the night, it's still a life that I hadn't seen before. A life that I never thought would be possible for someone like me: fucking, taking a bath, reading, talking, *laughing*. Watching her favorite movies, drinking tea. Eating roses, catching snow.

I've laughed more with her than I've done my entire life.

I've read more with her too.

And therein lies the fucking problem, doesn't it?

That I'm starting to believe that this temporary life could be real.

That maybe I could *really* live a life like that *with her*.

I'm starting to *believe*.

That everything will be okay. Despite my demons; despite the fact that I can't give her all the things she wants and needs, I'm starting to believe that I could have it all.

Even though I don't deserve it.

Turns out I haven't changed at all, have I? Because like before – when I was blackmailing her and was ready to ruin her happiness just for my selfish need – I still want to do the same.

I'm *still* dangerous to her.

"Yes," I reply back to Homer who's once again looking at me with curiosity.

"Why?"

My chest feels tight. "Because she deserves the best."

"And you're not that?"

"No."

"Shouldn't she get to decide that for herself though?"

"She should," I say gravely, my chest feeling tighter by the second. "Just not this."

And that's why the time has come to finally have a talk with my brother.

Time has come to finally sit him the fuck down and have a proper conversation with him about his intentions toward her. A girl doesn't just become your fiancée if you put a ring on her finger, no. You need to be there for her. You need to care for her. You need to actually fucking love her like he claims to.

Which, for all intents and purposes, I haven't seen.

So after the championship game, we're going to have a fucking talk and he's going to get his fucking act together.

Homer hums. "Not sure if that's the right move though. Girls generally don't like to be told what to do."

I raise my eyebrows. "And you have a lot experience with girls."

He shrugs. "It's just what I hear."

"Is that why you're stalling," I give him a pointed look, "your own wedding? Because from what *I* hear, the bride-to-be seems pretty eager for it."

That was kind of a low blow, I admit.

Because it's one of the things he doesn't like to talk about. In fact for as long as I've known him, he hasn't wanted to talk about how his father – before his death – had arranged his marriage with one of his friends' daughters. Maple Mayflower, I think her name is. He was fourteen and she was barely out of kindergarten but their families thought it was okay to decide their future without their say so.

I'm also aware that now that they're both of age and should be married, he's the one who's putting it off. Although like his dislike of his job – something that I found out today – I don't know the reason for it. I mean it could be he's pissed at his father for dictating his future in this way.

But I think there's more.

I have a feeling.

I also have a feeling that he doesn't dislike Maple or is unaffected by her like he wants everyone to believe. Maybe because I'm good at reading people but I know that every time Maple's name was mentioned, back when we were in high school, he'd get a look in his eyes. A look that said that there was something that he felt.

In any case, it's none of my business.

And I shouldn't have brought it up.

"Touché," he says, once again choosing to keep his secrets to himself like me.

Sighing, I admit, "Sorry for dragging you out here but I'm not feeling like chess anymore."

He nods. "Me neither."

"You headed home?"

"Office." He shrugs. "Got some paperwork to do."

"My sympathies," I quip.

His lips twitch. "You off to watch some more game tapes?"

"Yes."

"Well, mine too then."

With that, he gets up from his chair and leaves. And I do the same.

I shouldn't be in Bardstown at all.

The reason I came was because this was the one night I had off and I wanted to be in the same town as her. And the reason I chose The Horny Bard was because she's always telling me to get a life, to go hang out with the guys, my twin brother, and he's here. Not that I'm going to actually mingle with them or that she'll ever know I'm doing something that she wants me to do, even if the bare minimum of it but still.

It somehow makes me feel close to her.

And that's the only way I'll let myself feel close to her.

Because I've already put the plan – of finally giving her what she deserves – into motion. Ever since we came back, I've started to withdraw from her. I have to be in New York for the team and she had to come back to Bardstown because of her classes. So we already are in different places.

We touch base every night though. But only because I made a promise to her.

On the night of her engagement when I found out about her mother's abuse.

I have to take a breath and think about her twinkling laughter over something I read to her the other night in order to calm myself. In order to not hunt that woman down and choke the life out of her.

Every night I call her around the same time, and I make sure that she's okay. I make sure that her monster of a mother hasn't gotten to her.

So far she hasn't and she's not going to either.

Because when I talk to Shepard after the game, I'm going to tell him about her mom and we're going to figure out a permanent solution to keep her away from her mother.

I'm almost out at my car in the bar's parking lot when I see something that sucker punches me in the center of my gut.

My twin brother.

With a girl.

A girls that's not her.

He's at a random truck and he's got a girl pushed up against the door. He's bent over her and no, they're not engaged in anything illicit but from the looks of it, they want to.

Or at least *he* wants to.

He's awfully close to her, looming over as if he wants to engulf her. Looking at her as if he wants to eat her alive.

I know. I can understand.

Because I look at *her* the same way.

I look at his fiancée the same fucking way.

The fiancée he is clearly *not* doing any of these things with.

The fiancée he claims to *love*.

Even though I understand what's happening, it still takes me a couple of seconds to find my bearings. It takes me a couple of seconds to recognize the roar in my ears, the tightening in my gut. The heat on my skin.

It's been some time since I've felt that.

Since I've felt the dissociation from the world like this.

Where everything is disappearing and turning foggy except this rage inside of me.

Where my heart races and races like a hurtling train and I don't recognize myself or anything else around me except the thing I want to destroy.

"What the fuck," I growl.

They break apart at my voice.

My brother looks annoyed like he wasn't expecting the interruption. But once he realizes who it is, his face clears of that emotion and I watch as shock and a tiny amount of guilt flashes through his face.

It lasts a second, that expression, until he goes back to being his cocky self.

As he steps forward and situates the girl behind his body. Somehow, I'm able to tear my eyes away from him to glance at her. Only because I want to know who the fuck is she.

Who the fuck is he fucking around on his fiancée with.

Only to realize that I know her.

She's one of our sister's friends, the redhead. I've seen her around at family get-togethers. She also sometimes works on the waitstaff for the team events. Although I can't remember her name.

"Look, you need to –" Shep begins.

My gaze snaps back to him and my fists curl. "You fucking around with our sister's friend?"

His jaw clenches. "It's not what it looks like. It's –"

That gets me.

His casual statement.

The statement that people make when they know it is *exactly* what it looks like.

Before I'm aware of it or think about it, I'm on him.

I grab the collar of his jacket and fucking shove him back against the truck. I hear the redhead scream with alarm. I can also hear her voice in the background, agitated, scared but that's as far as I can be conscious of things.

Right now, it's me and him and this fucking wildfire in my veins.

Despite being in a chokehold, Shepard turns his head to the side and commands, "Go."

"But you... He –"

"Jupiter," he says gravely. "Leave. *Now.*"

I don't wait to find out if she obeyed him or not. I pull at his collar, causing him to jerk his eyes back to me. "Does she know you're engaged?"

"She's none of your business. She –"

"You know, of all the things that I thought would finally make me break," I say, twisting and twisting his collar, my body feeling too hot to exist right now, "Of all the things that I thought would finally make me snap and beat the shit out of you, I didn't think it would be this. You with a random girl like you always are."

Finally, he gives up all pretenses too and goes for my fists on his jacket. He grips my hands, trying to get out of my hold. "You keep her out of your fucking mouth, or I will break it."

I want to laugh.

I'm not a person who sees humor in things, but this is hilarious.

The fact that my twin thinks that he can break something on my body.

But then again to be fair, he doesn't know the depths of my dark need. He doesn't know exactly how long I've kept myself under leash. He doesn't how long I've pushed and pushed this anger down.

"I almost want to warn you," I say, pressing his spine harder against the truck, watching pain flash through his features. "I almost want to tell you exactly what you've gotten yourself into. But I'm not going to. I think it'll be more fun if you find out the hard way. What happens when you fuck around on your fiancée that you claim to fucking love."

Again anger flashes across his features. "I think we both know who's fucking around here."

"You –"

"I know, all right," he declares, his hands still on mine. "I know you're fucking her behind my back."

His words make me go still.

They bring the roar in my ears to a screeching halt. It subsides the burn, the heat in my body. It brings the world into focus a bit. I watch Shepard struggle against my hold almost dispassionately. I watch him wanting to get free but I don't let go.

Instead I ask, "How long?"

He pauses, panting. "Always. Since day one."

"It didn't…"

"It didn't what?" he asks, taunting me. "Didn't mean anything? It wasn't what it looked like?"

"No," I say. "It meant *everything*. And it was exactly what it looked like. But it didn't…" I take a breath and confess truthfully, "It didn't feel wrong."

He watches me for a few seconds. Then, in a low voice as if he almost doesn't want to, "This, what you saw, doesn't feel wrong either." I tighten my hold on his collar and he goes, "So can you let me go now and fucking get off your high horse."

Is that what he thinks this is?

That I'm on a high horse. That I have any morality left in me.

Even if I ever did possess a trait like that, which I don't think I did, this isn't about that. This isn't about morals or rules or boundaries or fucking right and wrong.

This is about *her*.

This is about him betraying her. This is about him going behind her back, breaking her trust, breaking her dream.

This is about him breaking her fucking heart.

And no one gets to break her heart.

No one gets to hurt her.

"You fucking asshole," I thump his back against the truck. "She trusted you. She trusts you. She thinks you're her best friend. She thinks you can mend her heart. You can help her move on. She's been beating herself up for everything she's done to you. She's –"

"Stellan, stop!"

For a few seconds I think I'm imagining her voice.

I think I've conjured her up in my head to ground myself. So I don't do what I always want to do. So I don't break my promise that I made to myself years and years ago.

But then I hear footsteps.

Running, urgent.

Followed by another plea. "Stellan, no. Don't do it. Stop!"

And I notice Shepard's focus switching to something over to the side, just off my shoulders. "Isadora, no."

"But you –"

"Don't come any closer," he warns, shaking his head.

I keep watching him. I keep watching his face.

The concern in his eyes. The lines of worry around his mouth.

Is he...

Is he trying to protect her?

Her.

From *me?*

And the fact that he's right to do that. The fact that I'm so fucking dangerous to her pisses me off even more and I jerk at his collar, demanding his attention back at me. I don't want him looking at her like that.

Only *I* get to look at her like that.

With concern. With worry.

Like she's my entire fucking universe.

Gritting my teeth, I get ready to lay one into him when I hear her again. "Stellan? Look at me."

I don't know why I'm not.

Maybe because as soon as I see her, I know, I *know*, my anger will vanish. If not vanish then it will take a backseat. My blazing fire will simmer down. My hurtling heart will race but in another way. In a way that's safe, that gives me both comfort and excitement. She's always telling me how I keep her safe but she's the one who saves me just by existing.

And that's the very reason I can't let it go, see. I can't spare him.

Not after what he did.

Not after how he hurt her.

He needs to learn that this isn't how you treat the girl you love.

This isn't how you treat *my* girl.

"Please," she pleads again.

And fuck, *fuck*.

I can't deny her.

I can't deny her anything.

I still keep a firm hold on Shepard though as I turn my eyes toward her, and it happens. What I was afraid of, it comes to pass.

I almost come down on my knees, my body feeling weak at the sight of her.

She looks like a fever dream.

A hallucination.

Standing under the flood of yellow light from the pole, she looks like I made her up in my head. Her jet-black hair framing her face, going down her back. Her satin skin flushed from the cold. Her gray eyes luminous as she stares at me. And that dress, all white and all pretty.

She's the most beautiful girl I've ever seen.

My girl.

My baby. My sweetheart.

Dora.

Do. *Ra.*

And Jesus Christ, she's not wearing a coat again. It's fucking cold out. It's going to snow soon and she needs more than that flimsy dress she's got on. Why doesn't she get that even if she loves the cold, it will still give her frostbite?

Why doesn't she get that she needs to be kept safe?

From winter.

From me.

From anything and everything that can ever hurt her.

"It's fake," she declares.

And I wake up from the trance that her sight always puts me in.

I frown in confusion.

Which she understands and taking a hiccupping breath, she explains, "The engagement. It's fake, Stellan. Shepard's not.... We're not engaged."

In the background, I feel Shepard struggling against me but I subdue him easily. He also says something, but I can't make out his words.

I don't want to make out the words.

All I want to hear is her voice. All I want to see is her.

So that's what I do.

Wordlessly.

Frozen.

She swallows, her eyes glistening. "It's not real. It never was. He was... He was trying to help me. He was trying to provoke you into being with me. He was trying to make you jealous and... It's not real. He was lying. *I* was lying. I've been lying to you all this time and I know..." She shakes her head, swallowing again. "I know that I shouldn't have. Not after the last time. Not after how much I hurt you. How much I tormented you and made you suffer. After how petty and immature I was. I... I know I shouldn't have done it but I did it anyway. And I... I'm sorry, Stellan. I –"

Again, Shepard tries to say something, something about it being his fault I think but again I tune him out and keep him pinned to the truck.

And keep my absolute focus on her.

I keep my absolute attention on the girl who's looking at me like I'm her world.

"It doesn't matter whose fault it was though," she continues, keeping our gazes locked. "Because the thing is that even if the engagement was real, I would've broken it. I would've broken the engagement myself, Stellan, and that's because I love you. I love you so much. I..." She fists her hands and widens her stance as if she's preparing to fight. "And I've tried, okay? I've tried *so* hard to not. I've tried so hard to move on from you. Mostly because of how I acted because of it. How painful it has been to know that you don't love me back. How you've hurt me and lied to me and just... broke my heart over and over. And because I always thought that if someone's your destiny, they aren't supposed to hurt you. They aren't supposed to make you cry or torment you or make you pine or make you long. For them. I always thought if someone's your destiny, they're supposed to be perfect.

"But I realize now that that's not true. The very reason you are *able* to hurt me and make me cry and make me long and pine for you is *because* you're my destiny. It's because what I feel for you is unmatched and unparalleled. What I feel for you, I've never felt that for anyone. And I know that I'll never feel it for anyone either. And the very reason I'm able to hurt you and torture you is because I'm *your* destiny. And I also realize that we're not perfect. God, we're both so far from perfect that..." She chuckles, her eyes shining like heartbroken diamonds. "And that's okay. Because you're perfect for me and I'm perfect for you. Because the flaws you have match the flaws that I have. Because the things that make you good are the things that make *me* good. We're a match, Stellan. I'm fire and you're wildfire. We're the same."

A tear rolls down her cheek.

A lonely tear.

A tear that stokes the fire burning in my gut.

"And I know you think you have to give me every desire of my heart. I know you have to give me every dream that I've ever dreamed but... I don't want that, okay? I don't want it. I don't want love. It's okay if I don't have it if I have you. I can live without love. I've done it my entire life. But I can't live without you. I don't know why you've pulled back from me this past week and I..."

She sighs again. "Maybe it has to do with the fact that you think Shepard's the right guy for me but he's not. You are the right guy for me. *You*. And I know you have a secret, okay? I know. I *know* there's something inside of you that torments you. That gives you pain. That makes you have bad days and I know you have bad days even though you've never outright told me. I can read the signs. I know you think that the thing inside you makes you dangerous. It makes you unfit and wrong. But it doesn't. God, Stellan, it does not, okay? Whatever it is, whatever secret you have, whatever it is you think is wrong with you, I can handle it. I can face it. I can deal with it. And I'll do it with you, see. I'll hold your hand and we'll deal with it together. So let me, please. Let me be there for you. Let me be with you. Let me just love you, Stellan. And you don't have to do anything in return. If you think love is childish or if love is a threat to your control or whatever it is that's holding you back, just... just let it go. Just let me love you, okay? Because I will always love you. No matter what. Just let me love you."

She's crying.

Tears are streaming down her face as she stares at me with pleading eyes. As she stares at me like her life depends on it.

On me letting her love me.

And when I don't say anything, when I stand there like a paralyzed moron, she goes, "God, Stellan, say something. Just... if you're mad at me for lying to you, just say it. Just get it over with, okay? Just... So we can move on. So we can," she licks her lips, "*talk* about this. Just let Shepard go."

And I want to.

I really do.

I don't even care what he did. I don't care about his lies, his provocation. I don't care that that's what he's done his entire life. Suddenly it seizes to matter.

Especially in the face of something else.

The fact that she lied too. And it makes perfect sense that she'd do that.

She's in love, isn't she?

She just told me.

She's been telling me for weeks now.

Love makes you lie.

Love makes you do crazy things.

Things that you'd never thought you'd do in a million fucking years.

Like when a girl flirts with the twin brother of the man she wants to make jealous. When she lies about the whole relationship with the said twin brother.

Like when a man deceives that girl for weeks on end, pretending to be his twin because that's the only way he can bring himself to get to know her. When he blackmails her all because he wants to touch her once. And when he realizes that he can't hurt her that way, he makes up excuses to touch her anyway under the guise of helping her move on.

It makes perfect fucking sense.

Because I have done the same.

Because I'm in love with her too.

Holy fuck.

I love her.

I've always loved her.

Since the moment I saw her.

She's right. That's why it hurt so much, seeing them together. That's why it tortured me and tormented me. And I've denied it. I've ran away from it. I've hidden away from it.

But it's here.

Standing in front of me: my reality.

I'm in love with Isadora Agni Holmes. The girl with the kind of fire to melt me. To make me forget my rules, my morality.

My Lolita.

Who just said that she can handle my secret.

Except she has no clue what my secret actually is.

And she should, shouldn't she? She should know the man she's in love with. She should know the man she's so ready to give up everything for, her happiness, her dreams.

Because as I said, no one gets to hurt her.

Not even me.

And if this is the way to keep her safe, then so be it.

So I turn away from her and look at my brother. I think he's been staring at me this whole time, his eyes grave, his features graver.

But there's something there.

Something akin to resignation.

As if he knows what's coming and he's accepted his fate. As if he knows why I have to do this: for her.

Good.

That'll make it easier.

Twisting my fists in his collar, I say, "I'm sorry."

He clenches his jaw and shakes his head once.

Before I lay my first of many and many more punches.

ACT 3

Him, Her, and The Fire Between Them

CHAPTER 1

THE WILDFIRE THORN

He's signing autographs.

This is his fifth since I arrived at his room at the hospital. There's a long line of people – women – coming out of his room and snaking down the hallway, all waiting to meet him and get him to sign things.

All of them eye me with trepidation. Some because they saw the security being called and nurses getting upset when I initially came. And I'm guessing there are others who heard the news of what happened only a few hours ago at The Horny Bard.

Of how I beat my own twin brother up.

And how I attracted a crowd and had to be pulled away from him. Someone called 911. And while he had to be rushed to the hospital, I was holed up at the police station for the last however many hours. While doctors were taking care of his injuries – injuries that I visited upon him, knowing full and well what I was doing – the cops were interrogating me. And while I accepted my guilt, he refused to press charges and wave it off as a little tiff between brothers. I'm not sure how he was able to convince them of that but he did.

And here I am.

I know he knows I'm standing at the door, waiting for him – he was the one to call off security and calm the nurses down when I first showed up – and I know he's deliberately making me wait.

As he should.

He has every right to make me pay for what I've done. He has every right to string me along, jerk me around. He has every right to refuse to see me. In fact he should. I don't deserve an audience with him but I'm still hoping that he'll give me one.

Because I'm only now coming to find out that that's how my brother is. Loyal.

So I settle in for a long wait until it's my turn to see him but surprisingly, after that fifth autograph, he dismisses everyone.

"Sorry, guys," he calls out, his eyes landing on me. "As much as I love spending time with you all and appreciate how you're all here to cheer me up about missing the championship game, I need a little break. As you can see, I'm kinda *indisposed*." He looks at me pointedly. "But thank you so much for showing up. Or I don't know what I would've done, how I would've coped during this difficult time."

His fans gush and cluck around him like mother hens before shuffling out of the room, again eyeing me either with open hostility and suspicion.

When we're alone, he says, "Should I run for the hills now that you're here?"

I stare at him a beat. "You could always call security again."

He settles against his pillows and goes for a cookie on the side table. "That's a better option because A, I can't run. Not right now. Something about sprained ribs. And B, I don't want to leave my cookies here."

To emphasize his point, he pops the one he picked up in his mouth.

I take in his bruised features for a moment. Then, "May I come in?"

"I don't know. Are you going to want to share my cookies?" he says, popping another one in his mouth.

My eyes land on all the flowers that fill his room. There's balloons and get well soon cards on the window, on the carts. Along with a big tray of cupcakes and a big box of cookies sitting on the table by his bed.

I enter the room as I ask, jerking my chin at the cookies, "Callie?"

"Yup. And the cupcakes."

Our baby sister loves to bake and growing up, Shepard and Ledger were always the ones who'd trick her into baking things for them. I'd always envy them, envy their shenanigans, their pranks, the demands they made because I didn't have the luxury to make them. But I'm glad that Callie took the time – even though she's pregnant and shouldn't be stressing herself out – to bake Shep's favorite things.

"I have come to talk to you," I tell him.

He pops another cookie in his mouth. "Is that so?"

"Yes."

"Because from what I recall you're not a big fan of talking."

"I've come here to rectify that."

"Big fan of using your fists though."

My gut tightens in response. But otherwise, I remain silent.

"Kinda took me by surprise," he continues. "*Good* surprise. Because I'm not going to lie, I always thought you were kind of a pussy."

I stare at him for a few seconds. Then, "I deserved that."

"You think so?"

"After breaking your nose, spraining four of your ribs, giving you that black eye and a mild concussion for which they kept you under observation overnight, yes." I clench my jaw. "Not to mention, you won't be playing the championship game. So yeah, I more than deserve it."

His jaw tenses too. "Yeah, *that* I'm pissed about."

"As you should be," I agree.

Of all the injuries that I gave him, that's the one I regret the most. Causing him to miss out on the championship game. The very thing he'd been working toward all season. The very thing the entire team had been working toward all season. I caused them to lose their captain when they need him the most. So as it turns out, I'm not that good at my job as I always thought.

"So?" he prods, staring into my eyes. "Are you going to enlighten me? Shed some light on why instead of being in the locker room, I'm in a hospital room right now? And why you spent the entire night in an interrogation room where, from what I can see, they did a very shoddy job of patching you up."

Well, they didn't patch me up at all.

I don't think they much care about potential suspect's injuries. I do have a couple of band-aids here and there but that's Conrad's doing. When he came to pick me up at the station, he insisted that I at least clean my surface wounds: a split lip, a black eye, a couple of bruises on my jaw. Other than that, I think I've got a couple of sprained ribs and if I had a concussion, it never got detected.

Because for every punch that I landed on my brother, he landed one back.

I'm very proud of that.

I'm so very fucking proud that he didn't take it lying down. He beat the shit out of me like I beat the shit out of him. Maybe that's one consolation in of all this. My mom, she was defenseless. Conrad, when he was young, he was defenseless too.

At least my victim gave as good as he got.

"He used to beat her up," I say finally.

And Shepard goes alert. "What?"

It isn't something that I wanted to tell him.

Ever.

It's not a burden that I ever wanted to give my twin brother. It's not a burden anyone should ever have to bear. But I've somehow made it so that he needs to hear the truth and I hate myself for it.

It further proves that I'm a shitty brother.

But he should know.

He should know the truth. He should know who I am.

"*Him*. Our father. He used to," I swallow thickly, "beat Mom up." I watch him go rigid at my words, but I keep going, "Not where people would notice or she'd have to miss work or anything like that. But where she'd have random bruises on her body, the side of her temple, on her arms, sometimes her neck, stuff like that. Stuff like where she'd have to limp or she'd have trouble sitting down. Stuff that young kids, *us*, wouldn't be able to take notice. Well except, me and Conrad, who knew.

"There were times where she'd cry herself to sleep. I mean there were a lot of times like that. A lot. Especially when he'd stay out all night or when he'd come back drunk. Or when he bragged about his conquests, his cheating. But there were nights where she'd cry... in a different way. It was both a cry of pain and a cry of misery. And whenever I'd hear that, I'd sneak out of our room and go to her. I'd hug her in the bed, but not real tight because I knew. I knew she was in pain. I'd just put my arm around her and stay close to her. Just to let her know that she was safe. That no one would get to her while I was there.

"She always appreciated that but," I scoff then. "What a joke, right? I mean I was, what, five, at the time. There was no way that I could fight back on her behalf. There was no way that I could keep her safe and I wanted to, believe me. I wanted to beat the shit out of that monster. I had this rage inside of me. This anger. This fucking fire to fight him, you know? To push him into a wall like he did our mom. To kick him, to punch him, to fucking *end* him. To make him pay for all his crimes but I... *didn't*. I never did. I never even tried to fight him. Not because I was little or I was afraid of him or something. I didn't do anything because," I keep my eyes locked with his as I confess my biggest secret. "I'm like him. I'm like our father."

It takes him a long moment to speak and when he does his lips are so pinched, just like his features, that they barely move. "You're like him."

Shame, pure and undiluted, runs through my body.

Shame and guilt and so much regret that I could possibly drown in it.

As I nod, still keeping my eyes locked with his. "I have issues."

"What kind of issues?"

"Anger issues."

He keeps staring at me for a few moments. Then, "I'm guessing these anger issues are worse than Ledger's."

If I could smile in this moment, I would.

Because for all our differences and the deliberate distance between us, we are twins after all. I didn't have to tell him what I had to specify to Conrad.

"Yeah," I confirm.

"And the proof's in the pudding, huh," he goes on.

"Are you the pudding?"

"Apparently."

I eye his bruised face for a few seconds. Then, throwing him a curt nod, "Yeah, I'm worse than Ledger. I've always been worse than Ledger. My anger is bigger, more vicious. And I've always known that. Even when I was little. So when one night Dad, in his drunken stupor, confessed about beating Mom and told me I was like him, I made a promise to myself. To suppress it. To bury my anger so deep that no one would ever find out. I made a promise to myself that I'd never become like him. That I'd never raise a hand to my family. I'd never hurt my siblings. Con and Ledger and Callie and you. I made a promise that I'd keep you all safe. I couldn't keep Mom safe, could I? I couldn't stop what was happening to her. So when Dad left and I became the monster of the family, I told myself it was up to me. It was up to me to leash myself. To keep myself chained and hidden from the world, from all of you. It was up to me to take care of you all.

"So I started keeping a list of my triggers. I started keeping track of what made me angry, what made me upset, what irritated me, stuff like that. I started keeping my distance from those things. Things that could excite me, upset me, make me lose control. I wouldn't go to parties, not that they ever interested me but I wouldn't say yes to get-togethers and things. I'd leave the room when you and Ledger would argue or get into fights. I'd stay away from all the pranks, how you guys would tease and trick Callie, how you'd poke fun at Conrad. I chose soccer because of this very reason. Because it never excited me, never gave me any pleasure. It was easy. It was predictable. It was something I knew well. Something that was safe. Besides I didn't think I deserved it. I didn't think I deserved to have anything fun or good or exciting. Because of who I was. And I wouldn't let myself get close to you."

Again, I keep my gaze steady on his. "Because on that list of triggers, you are at the top. You're my biggest trigger, Shepard. Always have been. Maybe it's because we're so different. We always have been. Ever since we were little. You were loud; I was quiet. You'd run around the house; I'd sit in a corner and read. You'd play pranks, get into fights, provoke people; I followed all the rules, kept my head down. And more often than not, I was the victim. Of your pranks, your taunts, your provocation. And I used to get so angry. You made me so angry, Shepard. So fucking angry. And while we did fight when we were little, we did beat each other up, after I found out about Dad, about myself, I... stopped. And trust me, it was hard. It was so fucking hard.

"There were so many times when I wanted to retaliate; when I wanted to just shut you up; when I wanted to make you stop; when I just wanted to... show you who I was, what kind of a danger you're in. Sarah Ann?" I look at him pointedly. "I don't even remember her face now but I remember how it made me feel when you showed up with her at the house. I had to leave the room. I had to leave the house. So I didn't punch you in the face. So I didn't break your bones. So I didn't do..." I take a deep breath. "What I did last night."

A force grips my throat but somehow I keep talking, "So I always thought it was for the best. Keeping my distance from you. I always thought it was the only way to keep myself under control. To keep myself *contained*. And I know you hate me for that. You've always hated me for it. For being aloof and cold and... I don't blame you. I never *blamed* you. It's not your fault the way I am."

I grit my teeth against the pain of my words. "People say that a twin is supposed to be your counterpart. A twin is supposed to be the closest to you, but you got stuck with me. That's what you always say. It's true. You got stuck with a twin with issues. Who was so wrapped up in his own shit that he could never be there for you. I could never be your brother. I didn't know how to be your brother because I'm a fucking time bomb. Who could explode any second. Who *did* explode on you last night. And... I know it's not enough, nothing could ever be enough but I'm so fucking sorry about that, Shepard. I'm so fucking sorry for who I am. For the way that I am. I'm so fucking sorry for a lifetime of mistakes with you. A lifetime of being a shitty brother. I'm just so fucking sorry."

My chest feels heavy.

Tight.

As if a crushing force is sitting on it.

I've always known that I'm the worst brother a person could ask for. But after last night I think I became worse than the worst. Because in exchange of what he did, the only thing I had to give him was a beating.

And what he did was... *help* me.

With his lies, his deception about the fake engagement.

I hadn't been able to focus on it when I'd just found out last night because so many other things were happening but I thought about it a lot at the police station while they were questioning me and when my twin brother wouldn't press charges.

Despite our differences, our animosity, he tried to make me see the light.

Maybe he didn't do it for me or maybe his method was not all that honorable. But it was still very much him and I... I've spent so much time trying to run away from him, trying to be so careful and cautious around him, trying to keep my distance that I never got to appreciate who he is as a person.

Yes, he's a prankster. Yes, he's cocky and irreverent and arrogant. And yes, he's completely opposite of me.

But he's loyal.

He's generous. He's pure-hearted.

He doesn't have secrets like I do.

I mean I always knew he was a better man than me but after last night, he has only grown in my eyes.

"Why did you blow up on me last night?" he asks, breaking into my thoughts. "You already knew the engagement was fake. You knew I wasn't doing what you thought I was doing. So why did you beat me up?"

I didn't know it was possible for my chest to feel even tighter but it does. "For her."

"For her," he repeats with a knowing look in his eyes as if he already figured.

"To show her."

"Show her what?"

Again I think he knows the answer; it's on his face but I still tell him, "The kind of man I am. The kind of man she loves."

And I don't regret that.

I thought the day I broke my promise, I'd probably also end myself.

I thought if I ever—ever—raised a hand on my family, siblings, Shepard, I'd cut these hands off. I'd break them. I'd break every bone in my body myself.

I would choke on regret.

And while I hate that I beat up my brother, I can't regret *why* I did it.

I did it for her.

I broke my promise for her.

If I was ever going to break it and become the man that I never wanted to be, doing that for her seems like poetic justice.

It seems... right.

Just like everything else with her.

"Like the piece of shit who made us," he finishes for me.

I clench my fists. "Yes." Then, I widen my stance and take a deep breath and say, "And so I'm here to ask you a favor."

"What favor?"

The force that's crushing my chest increases but I ignore it.

I thrust my hand down my pocket—I'm still wearing last night's clothes so I never got a chance to put it away, not that I ever put this thing away but still—and fish it out. His eyes flick down to the object I'm holding in my hand before looking back up to me.

"I want you to give this to her," I say with difficulty. "For real this time."

"Why?"

I set the ring down on a nearby cart with the flowers. "Because you're the right man for her."

"How's that?"

"You love her."

"And you don't?"

I press a palm on my chest.

On the left side where my heart is. I have to. Because my heart's racing fiercely.

And I wish I could punch my hand in and feel it.

For real.

The way she makes my heart race. It feels like music, something she could dance to, rather than something threatening, something dangerous.

Then, "I do."

I love her.

I've only come to find out a few hours ago and since then I've said it to myself one hundred and eight times. And yes, I've counted because now that I know I'm never going to stop saying it.

I'm going to fill the entire sky with my *I love you*s as if they were stars. As if they were flakes of snow. And they say you can't count stars, don't they?

I'm going to prove them wrong.

For her.

"But?"

And *for her*, I say, "But she deserves someone better. She deserves someone less damaged. Someone without issues. Someone who knows how to handle his emotions. Someone uncomplicated, someone who doesn't hurt her. Like I keep doing."

"In short," he concludes, cocking his head to the side, "she deserves someone who isn't our father."

I press my chest again.

Exactly.

Even though I love her, even though I will spend my entire goddamn life loving her, she deserves better than me. She deserves better than someone like our father.

Someone who doesn't constantly battle with his demons. Who can be there for her one hundred percent. I mean I couldn't be there for my own family, my own siblings, my own twin brother because I was so wrapped up in my own shit.

How can I guarantee that I can be there for her?

I want to though.

I fucking want to.

There's nothing I want more.

To be that man.

To be *her* man.

To make her happy.

To live that life with her. The temporary, dream life that we'd been living. To make it real, to make it permanent. To be able to call her mine. To be able to protect her, keep her safe, make her laugh.

There's nothing I want more than to love her, to *show* her how much I love her.

Nothing. More.

But the only way I can do that is by asking my brother to step in.

So again as much as it fucking kills me, guts the *fuck* out of me, I nod. "Yes."

"No."

"What?"

"I'm not giving her the ring back."

I clench and clench my jaw as I stare at his unforgiving features. "Look, I –"

"No, you've talked, and you've talked a lot. Now you're going to listen to me," he cuts me off, anger palpable and clear on his features now. "You're right. I always thought that I got stuck with you. I got stuck with a twin brother who's got no clue how to feel things. Who doesn't feel anything for anyone let alone me. And it pissed me off. It would piss me off so much that I'd deliberately try to provoke you. I'd deliberately try to egg you on, make you angry, make you upset. So you'd fight back. So I could see that you felt something, that you *cared* about me. But there was nothing. No sign of emotions. No sign of life. Not ever. And yes, I've hated you for that. For *years*.

"For years I thought it was you. You took it away from me. You took away the twin brother that I used to play with, that I used to fight with, argue with, the brother who I used to love. Who cared about me. Who cared about things. Who had some life in him. Who wasn't a fucking winter wasteland. *Years*, Stel-

Ian." He pauses to swallow thickly. "But it wasn't you, was it? It was him. He did that."

This time when he pauses, it's to grit his teeth.

It's to deal with the flickering emotions that I can clearly see on his face.

"I've always hated him. Not a big surprise there. We've all hated him, despised him for his drinking, his neglect, the way he'd disappear for days, couldn't hold a job. The way everything fell to Mom. To Con. And now I..." He swallows again. "I can't even begin to fathom, to fucking *comprehend* what she went through and it... It fucking pisses me off. It *pisses* me off that I didn't know. But what pisses me off the most, what makes me hate him the most right now is what he did to *you*."

"What?"

He studies my face, my features that I'm sure appear confused. Then, shaking his head, "God, you have no clue, do you? You've got no fucking clue. Okay, first: if we're placing blame on each other, calling each other shitty then I think I deserve some credit too."

"You don't—"

"Twins are supposed to be so close, aren't they? They're supposed to be each other's counterparts. So then why didn't I figure it out myself? Why didn't I get even an *inkling* that something was going on with you? That there was a reason why you were the way you were. Instead of being pissed at you and provoking you, throwing tantrums like a little bitch, stealing your girl, why didn't I dig deeper? If we're supposed to have this bond, the lack of which I always blamed you for, then what the fuck was I doing? Why the fuck did I spend *years* being pissed off at the wrong person?"

"But I never told you. You didn't know. You—"

"And you don't know either," he says.

"I don't know what?"

"That you're *not* like that piece of shit who created us," he lashes out.

I step back.

It's not because of what he said. Because I remember, very vividly, that Conrad had said the same thing the day I confessed my secret. But I move back and feel sucker punched for the second time within twenty-four hours, because of *how* Shepard said it.

With such belief, such determination and faith.

"I see you haven't put two and two together yet," he says, scoffing, his eyes so much like mine dripping venom. But I think this venom might be for our father not for me. "You're not like him. You're nothing like him. He chose to hurt us. He chose to leave us. He chose to get drunk, to sleep around, to hit Mom, *Jesus Christ*..."

He grits his teeth as if the knowledge of it is physically hurtful and I get it because it is and once again I feel guilty that I had to tell him.

"He chose to neglect every single responsibility a decent parent, a decent human being has. He *chose*. Do you understand? He chose to do all those things.

And what did you choose to do? You chose *us*. You chose to protect us. You chose to keep us safe. You gave up every single thing that you thought was a trigger. You sacrificed *every single thing* you thought could make you a threat. You chose to build a life around us, around our safety, around our protection. You chose to build a life for us. You chose to punish yourself for the things that he did to all of us but you never did. And the reason you did break your promise and lay a hand on me was again to protect the girl you love from yourself. So tell me," he says, his voice still rough and lashing, "*how*, in what universe, are you similar to the man who always chose to put himself first while you always chose to put yourself last?"

"I..." My breaths are difficult, thick, getting jammed up in my throat. "You... I don't... But I have t-this thing inside of me that's like him and –"

"Ledger has this thing inside of him too," he reminds me. "Are you saying our little brother is like him?"

"Fuck no," I reply back, my tone abhorrent.

"Are you saying that he doesn't deserve the family he has now," he keeps at it. "He doesn't deserve his wife, his two babies."

"No. God, no. I never –"

"Because that's what this is about, isn't it?" he observes. "About what you do or don't deserve. What she does or doesn't deserve. She doesn't deserve someone like our father and you're right. But you're not like our father, are you? You're the opposite. You're the absolute fucking opposite of him. What you wanted, what you promised to yourself when you were five, you did it. You're not like him at all. You're not an abuser, Stellan. You're a protector. And you're the only one who needs to understand that and fucking stop keeping yourself from the things that you want."

A protector.

Holy fuck, I'm...

I'm not like him.

I'm not...

I'm the *opposite* of him.

I'm the fucking opposite.

I'm the...

Holy *fucking fuck*.

All this time... All this time it never occurred to me. It never...

"Didn't figure that one out, did you," he says, watching me.

I slowly shake my head. "No."

He sighs, something akin to amusement flickering through his features. "For all your books and all your reading, you're not that smart after all."

I take a breath.

It comes easy.

Probably the easiest breath I've taken since I was five.

And say, "I guess not."

He's right.

I'm not smart at all. I'm pretty fucking dumb.

I'm pretty fucking slow.

But then again maybe I shouldn't be surprised. It took me ages to finally understand that I'm in love. That I've loved a girl since the moment she flew into my life wearing a white dress and fake wings.

So why should this be any different?

"Still want me to give her the ring?" he asks then.

"Absolutely fucking not," I say immediately.

His lips twitch. "So this is it, huh. She's it. She's the thing you'll fight me for."

"She's the thing I'll go to war with you for," I correct him.

He stares at me for a beat. "Good for you then. That I'm prepared to surrender. Because," he tips his chin, "I've got a mean hook."

The bruise on my jaw throbs.

Not that I care.

I have no intention of tending to these. I deserve them.

I may have not deserved the other countless things I punished myself – something that's going to take a while for me to get used to – these ones I deserve.

"I shouldn't have hit you," I say.

"You had to though."

"I shouldn't have gone behind your back," I say next. "With her."

"You had to though."

I had to, yes.

Nothing could've stopped me from going for her. I see that now.

From getting with his girl.

But then again, she was never his girl.

She was mine. Since the beginning. Since the very first moment.

"I promised her that I'd help her move on from me," I confess to him.

"And?"

"And I think I did it. Last night."

Ironically.

When I showed her who I was. Or rather who I thought I was.

It was in her eyes.

It was in the way she looked at me. Like she couldn't believe that it was me.

She couldn't believe that the man she loved was doing those things. These heinous, terrifying things. Things she thought that she could *handle*.

"Are you going to let that stop you?" he asks.

I shake my head slowly. "No."

Because I'm not that person as I've just found out.

I'm not saying that I'm suddenly perfect. I'm not saying that I'm not damaged or my demons have suddenly gone away. But I understand them better now. I understand that I'm not like my father, never was.

I'm free.

To live. To love. To want.

To go to her.

To finally, fucking finally, make her mine.

Or at least die trying.

I'm *fucking free*.

And it's all thanks to my brother.

"Do you know why I started playing soccer?" I ask.

He's a little taken aback from my change of topic but rolls with it still. "Why?"

"Because of you."

A light frown appears between his brows. "What?"

Sighing, I nod. "It was you. I knew you liked it. You followed Con around, begging him to teach you. You'd always be outside kicking the ball. I never got it of course. I was more interested in reading and books and stuff like that. But I also remember that we'd fight with each other. A lot. You'd steal my books, I'd chase after you. You'd play pranks on me, I'd fight with you. Even back then I was so angry." I shake my head. "But anyway, I picked it up because of you. Because I wanted to have something in common with you. I wanted to try to get close to you. So we didn't have to fight all the time and I kept playing because of you. Because those were the only times when it felt like we weren't against each other but on the same team. That it came easy to me is a different story. That it became safe, something I could control, something I could do with my life, is something else. But you were the one. Who got me into it. So in many ways you gave me a lifeline. Some direction of what I could do with my life. And it all started because I wanted to spend time with you. Anyway all this to say that you're my twin brother. I care about you. I don't know how to show it but I do and... Thanks for... Just thanks."

He keeps watching me too, his features impassive.

Then, "I think you should stop. Because you're going to make me cry, Stella."

And I chuckle lightly. "And we can't have that. Not with all your fans hanging around."

"Fuck no," he says, chuckling as well. "I'm the Wrecking Thorn. It's bad for my reputation."

"Noted."

"And if you're so desperate to spend time with me, maybe I can let you buy me a drink some time."

I keep smiling. "I'd like that."

I would.

I spent my entire life keeping him at a distance and now I will spend the rest of my life trying to be there for him. Being as loyal to him as he is to me.

I turn to leave when something occurs to me. "Hey, what were doing with that redhead? Callie's friend."

All traces of humor vanish from his face and his features get hard. "Nothing."

I study him suspiciously. "Are you hooking up with her?"

"Fuck no," he bursts out as if disgusted.

"So then…" Something occurs to me. "Is she the one? Is she your fucking stalker?"

He breathes out sharply. "Don't you have somewhere to be? Don't you have a girl to go and get?"

I study him again. "She is, isn't she? So what, she has a crush on you. Is she dangerous?"

"Get the fuck gone, okay?" he bursts out again. "Just get lost."

Still I take my time and then, "Do you need my help? With her, I mean."

Words sound foreign on my tongue.

I can't remember a time when I would've asked him this. I've of course helped him out where I could but I don't think I've ever *offered* my help to him. As in I've never showed him my concern like a good brother should have.

He probably realizes that and some of the tension leaches out of his frame. As he shakes his head and replies, "No. This one's all mine. I'll handle her."

Exhaling a long breath, I nod in acceptance and finally leave.

To go to New York.

To her parents' house.

When they took me away last night, I knew she'd be in trouble. People would hear about it, meaning her mother would hear about it. And instead of taking it out on the actual culprit – me – she'll take it out on her. Which is why when they first took me to the police station, I was agitated. I was uncooperative. I wouldn't answer any of their questions until I got a phone call.

Which I did and I called Conrad, telling him everything.

What I did. What happened and about her mother. I made him promise me that he'd take care of it, keep an eye on her, make sure that she was okay.

Like always, he came through.

He called her father and told him about her mother's abuse. From what Conrad told me, her father had no idea about it and when he found out, he was angry. He assured Conrad that nothing would touch her, least of all her mother.

But I don't trust her father.

I don't trust anyone with her safety but myself.

And even though there's every chance that she must hate me right now, I'm going to somehow convince her to… let me.

Just let me.

Protect her.

Love her.

Keep her.

CHAPTER 2

"Batman."

"What?"

"Your secret," I said to him one night. "That's what it is, isn't it? You're Batman."

It was midnight and as usual, we were together. I can't remember the city we were in because I've never traveled this much in my life and I can't say what the hotel room looked like. But I do remember that this one had a balcony.

Not a huge one but big enough that I wanted to go out on it.

Because it was snowing.

And because I was only wearing my favorite Minnie Mouse boyfriend t-shirt, he insisted that I wear a coat. When I denied and said that he should come with me to keep me warm, he agreed and came out in *only* his drawstring pants. Hello? Where was his t-shirt or a coat?

Looking to his side and back, he flexed his grip on my thighs that were wound around his hips. "No."

In response, I flexed my arms around his chest and shoulders. "Spiderman?"

He chuckled lowly. "No." Then, flexing his grip again and looking back, "You could be a spider monkey though." A pause followed by an explanation, "Although they're both two very different things that only share the term spider."

I dropped a kiss on his bare shoulder and licked a snowflake from his skin. "Oh, Stellan. My poor, clueless baby. You scare me sometimes." Another kiss. "Only you would poke fun at me and then worry about explaining it right. Besides," another kiss and a lick "the correct term is piggyback. See how I'm wrapped around your back and shoulder? It's called piggyback. So I guess I'm a piggyback monkey if anything."

I finished it with another kiss but this one on his cold hard cheek.
And I was.
Wrapped around his back and shoulder I mean.
Because I wanted to.
Because he looked so warm and strong and I wanted to see the snow, the stars perched on his back. Plus of course I wanted my front pressed against those dense muscles.

Before we could get back to the topic at hand though – figuring out his secret – in a very powerful display of athleticism and grace, he both got me off his back *and* wrapped around his front in not only less than ten seconds, but also without me having to put my feet down on the balcony.

Then, with one arm around my waist and using the other to take the cigarette out of his rose mouth, he said, "Now you're just my pretty Dora."

I brought my face close to his and parted my lips, drinking his smoke in.

Which thankfully he made no objection to.

It took me days to convince him, but he at least agreed to let me drink in his smoke from his mouth aka shotgunning. Which worked out because I didn't care about the smoking. I only cared about him.

"I love it when you call me your pretty Dora," I whispered after inhaling those toxic fumes. It always felt like I was inhaling him.

"Yeah?"

"Uh-huh." I nod. "I can't decide between baby, sweetheart, Cherry Lips, Lolita. They're all my favorite. But 'my pretty Dora' is most favorit*est*."

He hummed. "Not a word, baby."

"Most*est* favorit*est*," I said, teasing him.

"Well, that was the wrongest thing I've ever heard," he exhaled a puff of smoke again, "but I'll let it slide."

I inhaled again. Then, "I love when you get crazy with me. Oh," I widen my eyes, "maybe that's your secret. Being as crazy as me."

He ran his eyes over my face. "Hmm. Again not a secret, baby. Plus I'm crazier than you."

"Okay." I tapped a finger on my chin. "How about manhandling me like this?"

His lips twitched. "It's called working out every single day and bench pressing thrice your weight."

My lips parted. "You do *not* bench press thrice my weight."

He ignored it as if my comment was beneath him. "And my secret is *knowing* things."

"What things?"

"Things like you're very, *very*," he dragged me up and down his abs with just one arm; so maybe he did bench press thrice my weight, "wet right now."

I rubbed our noses together, while rubbing my bare pussy on his abs once again, spreading my juices on his skin. "I'm always wet when I'm around you. *In. Sane.* Chemistry, remember?"

Even though we'd just had sex and done our whole bath and cleaning up ritual.

He smirked. "And that three things are going to happen in the next ten minutes."

"What three things?"

"One," he slowly slid me down on the floor and turned me around, "you're about to get your pussy licked on a thirteenth-floor balcony, overlooking this city." He dropped down to his haunches as I grabbed the wonderfully cold railing. "Two, people down below are about to get a free live sex show because the moment I start eating your sweetheart pussy, you're going to start whining like my desperate little whore." He flipped my Minnie Mouse t-shirt up, exposing my ass to his eyes. "And *three*, when I lick your kitty down here, that Minnie sitting up on your tits is going to get very jealous. So Daddy's going to make up for it by making you come from just sucking on your gorgeous cherry tits."

I wanted to say something to him.

I wanted to say that it was impossible for me to come just by getting my tits licked. But then he swiped his tongue on my core and I forgot everything. Well, except the fact that he did know things. Because all three things he predicted did come to pass.

So there.

That could've been his secret, being omniscient.

But it's not.

I know now.

I know what his secret is and the fact that I'm thinking about him doing filthy things to me because of it, because of *him*, when my head's on my *biji's* lap and we're sitting in my bed up in my childhood bedroom is making me even madder.

Because I'm mad.

I'm so fucking mad.

"Calm down," my *biji* says, patting my shoulder.

"I am calm."

"No, you're not," she says, sifting her fingers through my hair. "You're breathing like a dragon."

I look up at her. "How would you know how a dragon breathes?"

"It breathes like you," she quips.

I glare at her before turning away to stare at the TV. Which I have been doing for the past hour without really seeing anything. I know what's happening though; I've seen this movie multiple times. It's one of my favorites; that's why *Biji* put it on.

"He did the right thing," my *biji* says probably for the tenth time since last night.

I curl my fingers in a fist but otherwise stay silent.

"In fact, this is the first time I feel like he hasn't behaved like a *khhote da puttar*," she continues. "*Sach kahun toh mera toh vishvas hi utth raha tha usse.*

Are koi itni bhi der lagata hai samjhane mein ki main iss kudi se pyaar karta hoon?! Chalo finally, ye toh pata lag gaya ki haan, maine pyaar kiya." And then she chuckles. "See, what I did there? I actually used the title of the movie."

The title of the movie that we're watching is: *Maine Pyaar Kiya.*

Which exactly translates to I've loved. And loosely means, I'm in love.

I breathe out sharply. "*Biji*, you... You know what, forget it. I don't want you to translate anything you just said. I don't care. I'm not going to like it anyway."

But of course, she's my *biji*.

She's like me.

Or I'm like her, whatever.

She is going to do the exact opposite of what I want her to do.

"I said I was starting to lose hope," she begins. "Because he was taking too long to realize the truth. He was taking too long to realize that he loves you." Then, lowering her voice and softly stroking my hair, "And you know that he does, don't you? That's why he did what he did. For you. To show you. To protect you."

My eyes well up with tears.

Again.

And I was doing so well. I hadn't shed a single tear in the last twenty-five minutes. I held on to my anger. I held on to my promise that I wouldn't cry for him anymore.

I wouldn't give him my single tear.

Because he's already taken too many of them.

He's already taken too much from me.

He's already broken my heart too many times for me to cry over him. And that's the thing, isn't it, he breaks my heart but he does it in a way that hurts *more* than a broken heart should. He does it in a way that all the pieces of my heart come apart and scatter in the wind. Except one small piece.

That remains.

And that little piece, bloody and still clinging to life, beats and beats.

With hope.

With longing. With pining.

It beats because yes, I know he did what he did because he loves me.

He beat up his own twin brother because he was trying to show me. He was trying to protect me.

From him.

From his secret.

That he thinks I can't handle.

That he thinks makes him dangerous.

That's why he kept calling himself bad, didn't he? He kept calling himself a shitty brother. It was all there. All the puzzle pieces: the way he kept away from everyone, the way he kept himself in the shadows, his crazy jealousy, his possessiveness, his irrational need for control and rules and that stupid one cigarette per day.

It's because he's got issues.

Issues with anger.

Like his brother Ledger.

I put it all together and I did it before the cops came and took him away. And when they did, I wanted to stop them. I wanted to tell them that it was me. He did it for me. That he wasn't a criminal or a threat. He was just trying, in his twisted way, to protect me. He didn't need to be handcuffed and hauled to a police station in a cop car.

But of course I couldn't go.

There were all these people. All this commotion.

There was Jupiter who was so scared and crying over Shep's barely conscious body. I don't even know what she was doing there; probably to see Shepard. So I went to the hospital with them. I stayed there for as long as I could until my father came to get me.

My *father*.

I don't know what was more surprising: that Dad showed up when I'd least expected him to or that he knew. Everything. He knew everything about my mother. About all the things she had done over the years.

And he was... horrified.

He was apologetic.

He said he hadn't known. He had no clue—which was how I wanted it to be but still—because if he had, he would've intervened. He wouldn't have kept his distance. In fact, the *reason* he kept his distance from me was to protect me from my mother. Because he knew how jealous she was of me, of her own daughter.

And then he said he was there to take me back to New York where I belonged. I belonged at our house, with our family where he'd protect me moving forward. And that family includes *Biji*. Whom he also sprung out of the old age home because he knew how much she meant to me.

It was both heartbreaking and heart-healing that I may have my dad back.

No, actually I was more surprised about the fact that even though the man I'm in love with was at the police station and he was in a similar state as Shep – bloody and beaten and barely conscious – he still found a way to protect me. He still thought ahead and found a way to keep me safe from my mother who was fucking furious when she saw me at their doorstep with Dad last night. Because Coach Thorne was the one who told my dad everything, at *his* request.

So then I spent all night crying and crying that he could do all these things, he could do all these *crazy protective things*, he could go to these lengths for me but he wouldn't say that he loved me.

He'll try to marry me off to his brother under this insane assumption that I absolutely have to have everything that I ever dreamed of, instead of just giving us a chance.

Just a little chance.

Of being together.

For real. Without secrets, without sneaking around.

And now I don't know what's going to happen.

I don't know where we go from here.

Shep texted me a little while ago that he's out but he didn't tell me anything else. And I didn't ask because I'm done asking. I'm done chasing him and running after him. I'm done fighting for this love when I'm the only one with the sword.

I'm *done*.

With him.

With that thought I try to focus on the movie when loud sounds and banging make me jump. And I spring up on the bed.

"What on earth," my *biji* says, looking toward my bedroom door.

I don't even do that.

I don't even look. I jump out of the bed and run to the door. I throw it open, dash down the hallway and reach the landing and...

I have to catch the banister or I would've fallen down the stairs.

Because he is here.

He's at my house.

All tall and broad and battered and bruised.

And he's got my mother pinned against a wall, with his fingers wrapped around her throat. My *mother*.

Oh my *God*.

And then I'm running again. Or rather flying down the stairs. Just as I reach the bottom, I realize there are all these people around him. He's got a couple of guys, bodyguards, trying to pull him away from my mother but to no avail. I notice my dad standing to the side, looking horrified by the blatant display of aggression.

And then there's my mother who just squeaked, her eyes wide and fear-ridden, her hands swatting at Stellan's chest, his wrists.

As he growls, "I dare you to say another thing against your daughter. Because all I need is one excuse, just *one*, to snuff the life out of your sorry little ass. So just –"

"Stellan," I call out.

And then run toward him.

He's only a few feet away but it might as well be miles. And in those miles, I get waylaid by bodyguards, my father, people I don't even look at because my focus is entirely on the man who's trying to kill my mother.

For me.

Finally when I do reach him, I don't hesitate.

I fist his shirt and try to pull him away from her. "Stellan, no. Don't!"

He doesn't listen.

He keeps the pressure around my mother's throat and her eyes are getting wider and wider. And my attempts become urgent. I tug and pull and demand, "Stellan, please. Please let her go. You're killing her, okay? Just let her go. Please."

I'm on his arm now, my fists twisting and twisting in his shirt. "*Please*. She's not worth it. She's not."

And I'm right.

She's my mother and I love her.

But she's not worth Stellan losing his shit over. She's so not worth Stellan doing something drastic over. That I know he'll regret later.

I *know*.

And I'll be damned if my mother—of all people—becomes another burden for him.

I pull on his arm again. "*Please*, baby."

I snatch my hands away then.

I didn't mean to say that.

I didn't mean to use an endearment. And I know it's super crazy to think about this slipup when so many other dire things are happening. My mother's still squeaking and appears to be dying. Men are still trying to get Stellan off her. My dad still looks horrified.

But the moment I call him that, he finally switches his focus on me.

And God, *God* in addition to snatching my hands away from him, I also have to take a few steps back. Because his eyes, gosh his eyes, are lava. They are blazing lava. So intense, so molten, so fucking... *bright*.

Like there's really a wildfire raging inside of him.

Uncontrolled. Unfettered.

Free.

And it's going to eat him alive.

Pair that with his messy hair, his wrinkled clothes from last night, his bruises – good Lord, his bruises, vicious and angry – he looks like an avenging angel. Sent down to earth to destroy everything and everyone who means me harm.

Actually a devil with revenge on his mind.

He roves those burning eyes of his all over my face before finally, *finally* letting my mom go. Not all the way though; he still has his hold on her. But enough that she's not in mortal danger anymore. A relieved breath whooshes out of me at that—which I hate mostly because it's more for his sanity than for my mother's safety.

He notices it, my chest moving up and down with a jerky breath. Then, turning back to my mom who's trying to catch her breath, "Say thank you."

Mom's eyes jerk up to his, a little of her defiance coming back to life. "W-what?"

He leans closer to her and my heart starts to pound again. "Say thank you to your daughter. Because she just saved your life."

"I will not –"

In response, he cuts her off by squeezing her throat. Causing my mother to squeak again.

Then, in a growly, threatening voice, "Say fucking *thank you*."

"Stellan, she doesn't –"

"T-Thank you," she gasps out.

My eyes go wider as I take in my mom's horrified face without being able to utter a word.

Stellan doesn't have such problem as he goes, "*This*," my mother's eyes go back to his, "here, is your lesson number one in how to talk to your daughter and the answer is *nicely*. Should you forget that, I will be back to remind you. And if that happens," he flexes his grip around her throat again, "you should know that I forget things too. Like letting your fucking throat go in time before you choke to death."

With that he lets my mother go and turns to me.

I don't know what happens around us then. I can't tell who goes where; who says what; what happens to my mother. Does my father still look horrified?

All I know is that he comes for me.

He advances on me, his chest dragging up and down, his bruised mouth parted. And I can't do anything except stand in my spot.

Frozen.

Trapped.

He comes to a halt a few inches away and stares down at me without a word.

For a few seconds I don't understand what he's doing. Why isn't he saying anything? Why is he looking at me like that?

Then I notice something.

His hand.

Between us.

Palm up.

As if he's offering it to me.

And then it occurs to me that he is.

He *is* offering me his hand.

Just like his twin brother did all those months ago. At the party that started everything. At least in any real sense. Before that it was a petty girl running after a cold man. But the night of the charity event, I was just a girl and he was just a man and we had a fire between us that we've tried so hard to ignore.

"Come with me," he commands roughly.

And I look up at him.

I want to.

I so want to.

But I'm also so afraid.

I'm also so angry.

And heartbroken.

Is he going to burn me with his fire? Is he going to end me?

I always wanted to die at the end of this story, didn't I? So is this what the end looks like?

"Please," he adds.

Which is what seals my fate.

Please.

I've said that to him a million times, but he's never said it to me.

He's never made himself that vulnerable to say it to me.

So then if this is the end, let it be. If he's going to burn me, then let him. I put my trembling hand in his large, scrape-y palm and he engulfs it in his hot, *hot* grip.

And takes me.

CHAPTER 3

I'm in his room.
 His childhood bedroom.
I know that.
Although given that I've never been in his room before, I don't know *how* I know that, but I do. Maybe it's the walls that are bare and without any personality. Or the fact that the desk sitting in the corner is bare as well and very generic looking. There's also a dresser and a chair by the window. All plain and generic and without a sign of life. The nightstand by the bed where I'm lying is bare as well.
Much like all his hotel rooms.
Except a stack of books in a corner by the window.
As always, they're the only life in this room.
Actually, that's not true. There's another form of life and it's him.
Sitting in a chair, he's slumped over the bed. His head is resting on his arms and his hand is wrapped around mine. As he sleeps.
Even in slumber, I feel like he's the most alive thing in this room.
More alive than even his books.
His back goes up and down with his breaths. Back that's wide and looks like a mountain, and breaths that are deep and somewhat noisy.
Then there's his grip on my hand. It's the same hand that he offered me. Back at my house. The same hand that he took again and wouldn't let go of once we both got in his car, and he drove us here.
To Bardstown.
To his house.
Although I fell asleep halfway over but I have a feeling that once he got me

out of the car and put me down here, in his bed and covered me with his blanket, he went right back to holding my hand.

And then there's the heat of his skin.

It's... hot.

And not just from the sleep or from how long he's been holding my hand for, no.

I think it's him.

This heat belongs purely to him.

And it's so cozy and comfortable and dear and familiar that I go to get away from it. I go to get away from *him* because if this is the end and he brought me here to kill me, then I don't want to make it easy for him.

I don't want to die without screaming and screeching and fighting.

Without giving him a few third degree burns in return.

My struggles wake him up. With a jerk, he straightens up in his chair, his eyes blinking. It takes him a second or two to get his bearings. As if he was in such a deep sleep that he forgot where he was. As if he hadn't slept well in days and now that he had finally managed to, he didn't want to be shaken awake.

Good.

I hope so.

I hope he hated waking up. I also hope that he didn't get much sleep this past week. Because despite what he did last night, he'd started to pull away from me ever since we got back to New York. Which means my sleep was shaky as well. So I'm hoping his was too.

In all of this though, I realize that he still hasn't let go of my hand.

So I renew my struggles.

I twist my hand in his, trying to pull it free.

Which I guess reminds him of the situation at hand because he finally goes alert. At last, his eyes look awake and the first thing they focus on is me.

Propped up on the pillows.

My hair probably all sleep tangled and strewn about, and my eyes stern.

Or at least I hope they look stern.

Neither of us says anything but I still try to jerk myself free from his grip. He looks down at our joined hands and my struggles increase. He breathes out long and sharp, his shoulders undulating, as if preparing himself for something.

Before he lets me go.

The moment he does, I sit up in the bed and he stands up from the chair. He goes to a table on the side, again generic and without any personality and something that I'd missed in my initial perusal. There's a glass of orange juice sitting on it that he brings to me.

"Here," he offers.

I look at it suspiciously. "I don't like orange juice."

"It's passion fruit."

I hate him.

Because I love passion fruit juice. I could drink passion fruit juice till the end of time. And the fact that he remembered... No, actually, the fact that he had passion fruit juice *ready* for me as soon as I woke up as if he's bringing me breakfast—or rather juice—in bed like this is such a normal occurrence, makes me even madder.

First, it's not even morning right now.

Second, this is *not* normal.

He beat up his twin brother last night because I said I loved him.

He got beaten up for it in return as well.

How is any of that normal?

I mean just look at his face.

All banged up and battered. Bruises galore; all of them look red and angry.

Painful.

And like before, on the night of my fake engagement, I feel it. Right in my chest. That pain.

I feel the hurt that he must've gone through.

That he must have still be going through.

So to distract myself, I accept the juice from him and even take a sip as I ask a question I don't really care about. "What... What time is it?"

"Just after three in the afternoon."

I put the juice down on the nightstand. "What am I doing here?"

He studies my face. "Are you hungry?"

"No."

"I could –"

"I'd like to go back home now," I announce. "To New York."

He stares down at me, his face impassive.

Or at least I think it is.

I mean I can't really tell with all those bruises. With that black eye and cut on his lip. With how swollen the left side of his jaw is.

Maybe he's frowning right now, who knows?

Because hey, I said I loved him and he got into a vicious fight with his brother.

"That's not your home," he corrects me after a long moment.

"No, that *is* my home," I correct him back even though what he said was right. "My family lives there. My dad lives there."

"Your mother lives there," he says tightly.

"Who you were trying to hurt by the way."

"Because she hurt *you*."

"Are you going to hurt everyone who hurts me?"

He widens his stance. "Yes."

My heart squeezes. "Then you should put yourself at the top of that list."

He flinches.

And despite myself, my heart flinches too.

My *stupid* heart.

"I –"

"Does it hurt?" I ask, flicking my eyes over his banged-up face.

"Yeah."

"Did you break something?"

He stares at me a beat, probably remembering how we had the same conversation the last time he got into a fight with Shepard over that cell phone. Then, shaking his head, "No."

I fist my hands in my lap. "Too bad."

"Maybe next time."

I fist and *fist* my hands as I say, "Well, a girl can hope but..."

He frowns slightly because I went off script. "But what?"

I debate whether to say it.

Then I just do.

Because who cares?

"But I won't be here for that," I tell him.

"What?"

I nod. "I'm leaving."

That frown thickens.

His mouth parts as well.

Along with his chest that jerks up and down with his breath.

Because apparently he does.

He cares.

I knew that. That's why I said it.

Maybe it was petty, but I think I'm allowed a little pettiness right now. I'm allowed to be angry. I'm allowed to want to hit his already battered face.

What I shouldn't be allowed to want is to take the words I just spoke back.

The words that make him look agitated and dare I say, scared.

"Leaving for where?" he asks, his voice thick.

My heart is pounding in my chest as I lift my chin and reply, "For this drama camp in LA. My professor had helped me apply for it, just after the play. And well, we heard back. They want me. So I'm leaving for that."

"You never..." His chest shudders with a breath. "You never said anything."

"Well I have secrets too."

Again, petty and again, I don't care.

Besides I'm not going to tell him the truth, not now. And the truth is that I forgot. Which is crazy because it's a big deal. It's something that I always wanted: to go after my dream, for someone to believe in me. And I know he does; I know that. Even after everything that's not something I have doubts about. So I would have told him but being on the road, living in a little bubble with him, made me forget everything else.

Even something that I always wanted so badly.

Which just goes to show how crazy I am about him.

And how he repeatedly keeps hurting me.

Not to mention, I wanted to tell him yesterday; that's why I went to the bar. When Shep had texted me that he was there, I was angry. Outside of his regular check-ins over the calls that would last about two minutes, we hadn't had much contact. And not from my lack of trying either. Whenever I called him, I'd get his voicemail and whenever I texted him, he'd reply back hours later quoting that he'd been busy with the championship game.

Which I understood.

Despite getting a bad feeling about it all.

And then I found out—from his brother no less—that he was in Bardstown last night because they had a day off.

Of course I was angry.

I was also afraid that maybe like me, he'd given himself a deadline as well.

That while I was getting ready to tell him the truth, he was getting ready to end things after the championship game.

Which would've been ironic, wouldn't it?

And totally like him.

Just as I was planning to begin things, he was planning to finish them.

And lo and behold, he did.

Which prompts me to further add, "And I can't wait for it. I can't *wait* to get away from it all. I think it'll be good for me. Just me and my passion. My dream, you know? No pain. No heartbreak. No one to hurt me there and –"

"Full circle."

"What?"

I know I've asked him to clarify what he meant. But I don't think he's in any position to respond just yet. Because he's... *burning*.

Not literally of course.

But I think the blazing heat that I'd felt from him back at the house has now spread. It's gone beyond his eyes and has overtaken his entire body. That looks flushed. Darker. His cheekbones. The side of his neck with that vein pulsing. The triangle of his throat that's visible from his wrinkled shirt. Even his forearms look darker, his fisted hands.

"I brought you here," he says, his voice somehow *sounding* hot as well, and rough. "For full circle."

"F-full circle of what?" I ask, my own breaths getting messy now.

"Of my life."

"Your life?"

He shifts on his feet.

He opens and closes his fists.

His breaths turn choppy then smooth, then back again.

It only takes about ten seconds for him to do all these things but somehow I feel like for him, it was days. It was decades. It was all twenty-six years of his life.

Then, with a deep and smooth breath and his fists open, he says, "It all began here. In this room. This is where I grew up. In this house. I was born in this house too. Actually, I was born just down the hallway. They couldn't get my mom to the hospital in time. So me and my twin brother, we were *really* born in this house. Conrad helped from what he tells me. Because my dad wasn't there.

He was never there for anything or for any of us. So it wasn't anything new but anyway. That's not what I'm trying to tell you. What I'm trying to tell you is I may have been born two doors down, but my life started in this room when I was five.

"I was sleeping right there"—he points to the bed—"it was a different bed of course but I heard my father crying in the backyard. Because it was summer and I guess the window was open. So his voice had carried and I went down to find him. I went down and... that was the day I learned who or what I was."

He shifts on his feet again, something flickering through his eyes, something akin to shame and it tightens my chest.

"By now I'm sure you've figured out what my secret is," he goes on, his gaze locked on mine. "I'm angry. All the time. Every day. I'm on the edge, ready to explode, ready to do damage, to destroy things. And I get it from my dad. He was angry too. He was a lot of things: a drunk, a cheater, an abuser. He'd hit my mom. He'd hit Conrad. I'm not sure about the genetics of it all. If things like these can be passed down or if it's just a coincidence, my anger and his. That not one or two but *three* members of the Thorne family share the same trait. My father, Ledger, and me..."

He shakes his head as if waving away that line of thought. "I keep digressing. That's not what I'm trying to tell you at all. What I'm trying to tell you is that when I found out that I was angry like my father, that was the day I was *really* born. *Me*. The kid who grew up to be the man you know now. The Cold Thorn. With his legendary control and coldness. His heart, his insides buried under six feet of ice. And I was born this way because that day I promised myself that even though I share this abhorrent trait with my dad, I will never *become* like him. I will never give in to my anger. I will never succumb to my baser emotions. I *promised*, you understand. So slowly, day by day, I built my life around my promise. I built my life where I'd have absolute control over everything. I designed my own cage with my ironclad rules and a rigid structure. I did things that were safe. I distanced myself from the ones that weren't. And honestly, I thought it was a great decision. I thought it was the right decision. I thought no one would ever find out my secret. No one would ever know that a monster lived among them. No would ever get hurt. *I* would never hurt anyone. But I was wrong."

"Wrong?" I whisper and I don't know how I do that.

Because I think my insides are clenched so tight, my throat is clenched so tight that I can hardly breathe let alone make words.

I'm a tight, *tight* ball of bones and muscles.

A tight ball of emotions.

"It wasn't the right decision."

"W-Why?"

He swallows thickly, his Adam's apple bobbing. "Because I ended up hurting you."

My heart thuds. "You..."

"I kept everyone safe around me," he says, his burning eyes going back and forth between mine. "I protected everyone from me and my demons. And while that was important. What was more important, what was the most important thing to me, I failed at that. I failed at protecting you. I failed at protecting the one person who..."—he swallows again—"*saw* me."

I have to bring my hands down and grab the sheets.

I have to press my spine against the pillows for support as I whisper, "Saw you?"

"In the dark."

"At the p-party that night?"

"Yeah," he says. "But also, you're the first person, the *only* person, to actually see me. *Ever.*"

He ducks his head for a second as if gathering himself and I take the time to slow down my breaths. I take the time to prepare myself for his next words.

Because I know they're important.

And I know they're going to hurt.

Both him and me.

"And that's because I've always been in the dark. I've always been in the cold too. Ever since I was five. And I wanted it that way. I wanted to stay hidden. I wanted to be kept a secret. Monsters are always kept behind closed doors, aren't they? They're thrust down in the basement and left there to die. So that's what I wanted. But you came and you opened the door. You came and you switched on the light. And you found me. You *saw* me in that dark room. You discovered me. And I don't know how you did that.

"To this day I wonder how you could see me when no one else could. When I *made it so* that no one else could. But then again, maybe I shouldn't bother wondering because you're Isadora Agni Holmes. Agni means fire, doesn't it? You're the girl who can melt winter. You're the girl who melted me. You're the element of nature. Without you the world won't function as it should. So it would make sense that you'd see me, wouldn't it?"—he breathes out—"And when you meet someone like that, someone like you, it also makes sense that the life as you know it would change. The life as you know it would *end*. So I brought you here, Dora, because I'd like to bring my life full circle and *end* it. In this room where it all began."

What does that mean?

What does he mean?

What...

"Because I don't want a life where I end up hurting you. Where I end up making you cry. Not once, not twice. But over and over. I don't want a life where I fail to protect you. Where I fail to keep you safe. And so I brought you here so I can end my old life and start a new one," he explains. "A new life. A *real* life. A life that I build around *you.*"

"Me?"

Determination lines every feature of his face. It lines every angle and expanse of his body, his shoulders, his chest. Even his fists that are tightly clenched at his side. Even those thighs that are already arranged in a battle stance.

"Yes. I built my old life around my promise, but this new one, this new life, I'm going to build around you. In *this* life, when you ask me my name, I will tell you. I will tell you that my name is Stellan. Stellan Thorne and people call me cold. But it's a façade. A role I play. Because I don't want them to find out this fire inside of me. This wildfire. This *hellfire*. Where my demons live. Demons that I battle with every single day."

He puts a hand on his stomach, as if telling me where they are. "And when you ask me what that means, I will tell you that these demons come from my past. I will tell you that in my old life I tried to keep these demons caged. I tried to suppress them because I thought they would scare people around me. But I think they scared me more than they ever scared anyone else. I was ashamed of them, guilty of them. So I kept them a secret. But in this new life, I'm going to be brave. I'm going to face them head on. I'm going to not only face them but destroy them. I will end them like they ended my life. And it will take time, but I will do it. I will fucking do it, Dora. Because this new life that I'm building around you has a purpose.

"And it's that I protect you. I protect you above all else. I protect your smiles, your laughter. I protect your happiness, your dreams. Your wants, your needs. Your desires. I protect your emotions and your feelings. I protect that heart of yours. That fire. That big and bright and fucking beautiful fire that found me in the dark. The fire that melted my ice. I'm going to protect it, baby and I'm going to cherish it. I'm going to wrap your heart, your fire in roses. I'm going to keep it safe as you fly without wings. Because you don't need them, real or otherwise. I'm going to keep you safe, Dora."

I think I'm ripping his sheets into shreds with how tight I'm holding them. I'm think I'm going to fuse myself with the bed with how heavy I feel right now.

How... pathetically hopeless.

Because he said all these wonderful things. He said all these lovely things, but he didn't say what I wanted him to say.

He didn't say what I was *dying* to hear him say.

"You're going to keep me safe," I whisper, curling my toes under the blanket.

"Yeah."

"I can keep myself safe," I declare.

"I know."

"So I don't need a bodyguard, okay? I'm –"

"But I'd be lying if I said that's the only thing I'll do," he cuts me off.

"What does that mean?" I ask frustrated.

And as promised, he replies, his eyes roving over my features. "It means that in this new life, I'll do what I couldn't do before. Not freely. Not without restraints. And it's that I will love you."

My mouth parts with a breath.

And he goes on, "I will love you like you deserve to be loved. Recklessly.

Thoughtlessly. Insanely. I will love you without any chains or rules. Without boundaries. Without any sense for myself or preservation. Without any thought for myself or care. I will love you with all the fire inside of me, inside of my heart, inside of my gut, inside of my soul. And I will love you every single day. I will love you every single *minute* of every single day. Every single second of every single minute of every. *Single. Day.*" A pause and then, "It also means that if you're leaving, I'm leaving with you."

"What?"

He shifts on his feet, his spine straight and rigid. "You're leaving for that camp, yeah? I'm going with you."

"You're going with me?"

He nods. "Yes. Where you go, I'll follow."

"You'll *follow*?"

"You've followed me before, haven't you?" he reminds me. "You've chased after me. You've done things for me. In my new life, I'll do things for you. I'll chase after you."

My breaths are slamming in and out of my chest right now. My heart is racing and racing. And I don't think it's a good thing because I'm going to pass out any second.

I'm going to faint.

Because not only he said – finally, *Jesus Christ* – that he loves me, he's saying all these... impossible things that...

He's blowing my mind right now.

"What about your job?" I ask, my voice high.

"I quit."

My voice climbs higher. "You quit?"

"While you were sleeping," he confirms.

"While I was *sleeping*?"

He nods. "It was the very first thing I did when I brought you into this room." Then, with something similar to regret flickering through his features, "I wish I could... leave behind everything that... That makes me the way I am but I can't. So I left behind what I could."

Pain pierces my chest.

Not for the first time either. In fact, my entire body is hurting.

For him.

It's been hurting because all the things he just told me. It's been tight and curled and achy. And I...

I want to go to him.

I want to put my arms around him and hug him. And in his words, I'd be lying if I said that's all I want to do. But something is stopping me.

Something that I can't move past.

"So what are you going to do?" I ask, gripping the sheets even more tightly.

He shakes his head. "I don't know. But I love books."

Yeah, he does.

He loves them so much.

And I always wanted him to go for all the things he loves.

I always wanted him to love *me*.

I slide my feet up and down on the bed, getting restless. "What if I don't want you to follow me?"

"I'll still follow you."

"That's –"

"But for you, I'll keep my distance."

"Distance."

"I've done it before. I can do it again," he announces. "But this time, I won't hide. I won't be careful. This time, you will know I'm there. This time, you will see me watching you. You'll *feel* me watching you. This time, I'm seizing my destiny."

That does it.

That breaks this dam inside of me that I was holding at bay.

My muscles go lax and my voice opens up.

"I'm not your destiny," I scream then and even though it was loud, he doesn't flinch. He simply stares at me as if he gets it. He understands that I need to let it all out and I hate him for it.

God, I love him for it too.

"I'm not your fucking destiny, okay?" I keep going. "I don't want to be your destiny. I don't want your love. I don't… You pulled away from me. For a week. For a fucking week, Stellan. You wouldn't answer my calls. You wouldn't answer my texts. You… And then you came to Bardstown. Without telling me. Without… And then when I came to see you, when I came to demand answers and I told you I loved you and you beat up your twin brother. You beat him up. You…" A sob catches in my throat. "Y-you guys fought because of me. I never…" I hiccup, my vision blurring from my tears. "I never wanted that. I never wanted to come between you two and I know I did. *Before*. But I… And you b-broke your promise for me. You did, didn't you?" I sob. "You made a promise to yourself and your b-broke it for me. You did it to p-protect me. To push m-me away and I'm so m-mad. I'm so mad that I can't even be mad at you. I can't… I'm so…"

Before I know it, I'm lifted off the bed and I'm in his arms.

He's made me climb his body and he's pinned me to his chest. He's also tucked my face in the crook of his neck with his large hand as he rocks me. As he shushes me and soothes. As he whispers things in my ear that are as soft as a feather and as sweet as honey.

But the thing that really gets me, that both melts and stings my heart is that he's hugging me.

Like he always does.

After a week of no contact, after a week of dread that this might be it, he's hugging me so tightly that I want to sink into him. I want to sink my bones into his body and fuse us together.

And apparently, he wants that too with how tight he's holding me.
How tight and solid his arms are around me.
"I came to Bardstown to be close to you," he whispers roughly.
With my face still tucked in his chest, I scratch the side of his neck. "You could've a-actually been close to me by coming to see me."
He flexes his arm around me. "Because like an asshole, I pulled away from you. Like an asshole I was going to let you go. I was going to..."
He trails off but in lieu of his words he tightens his hold around me.
He crushes me to his body as if he thinks I'm going to take off.
I tighten my hold around him too as I scratch him some more. "You hurt me, Stellan."
He grips me even more tightly. "I know. I fucking know."
"You beat your brother up."
"Yeah."
Breaking away, I look up at him. "For me."
His eyes are red-rimmed and his features are determined. "I'll do anything for you."
I fist his shirt. "I m-made you break your promise."
He shakes his head. "You made me keep it."
"What?"
He brings his hand forward and cups my cheek, wiping my tears off. "You're my grounding object." When I frown, he explains, "This thing inside of me, it makes the world disappear. It makes me forget who I am, where I am. It's all-consuming, this thing. But you... you're the thing that gives me an anchor. You're the thing that pulls me back from the edge. You're the *reason* I don't go over. If I focus on you, I forget my anger. I think about you and I don't want to be angry anymore. Your thought is what *saves* my promise, baby. You're my reason. To not be what I am."
My heart clenches. "You're not a monster."
Pain ripples through his features and his fingers flex on my face. "I'm... I..."
"You what?"
He swallows thickly. "I-I think I know but... it's hard for me to believe that."
"You're not," I insist, grabbing his face. "And you're definitely not like your father."
Heartbreak shines in his eyes. "I believed that for years. Ever since I was five, I... I thought I was like my father and I finally know I'm not. I know... But I..."
"Is that why you... you freaked out about my mom. When I told you about her. At the engagement party? Because of your dad. Because of what he did to... your mom."
He grits his teeth for a few seconds before nodding tightly.
And God, I still remember the way he looked that night. The way he almost lost it.
The way he was burning.
All because of his dad.

His evil, *evil* dad.

And to think that he actually *believes* he's like his father? That he's lived his life believing that...

"I'll help you," I say, flexing my thighs around his hips. "I'll help you believe it. I'll help you *believe* that you're not like him."

A flood of emotions moves through his face, his entire body and he shudders. "I know I've hurt you. I've hurt you countless times. I've lied to you. I've deceived you. I've been selfish with you and maybe it's because I'm an asshole. Or maybe it's because I've spent my entire life burying and denying any emotions at all. I've spent my entire life trying to feel nothing. So I know it'll take time but... I'll learn, Dora. I'll learn to feel again. I'll learn to love. I'll learn to care. And I'll learn to do it the right way. You..." He lets out a shaky breath. "You told me once that I don't know how to care for you. I don't know how to do it right and... You could teach me. You could... You could show me the right way. You could... and I'll follow you. I'll follow your lead. I'll... I did so many things I—"

I press a hand on his mouth. "I don't care what you did. Because whatever you did, I would've done the same thing. We're matching souls, remember? And all I ever wanted was for you to see that. All I ever wanted was you to believe that. To believe that you could love me. That we deserve a chance. That's all I wanted from you, Stellan. To just love me and let me love you."

"I love you," he says gravely.

Instantly.

As if the declaration was sitting on the tip of his tongue.

So I take the time to look at him.

I take the time to memorize his features.

The red and purple bruises on his face, his messy hair. That stubble.

I take the time to feel the heat of his body, the strength of his hold.

And I don't think he's ever looked more beautiful than he does right now.

I don't think I've ever loved him more than I do right now either.

I don't think I'll ever forget this moment.

The moment when I tell him, for the first time ever, "I love you *too*."

Before this, I was always the first—and the only—to say it. So I never got the chance to tack on the *too*. I never got the chance to return the feeling and God, it's the most epic feeling ever. Saying it back when someone has said it to you first.

And I guess he's thinking the same thing because my *too* rearranges his features and turns them all loose. It leaves his body relaxed and at ease. And he whispers, "I let you be alone in this. Before. I always left you in the dark with your love. But not anymore. I'll never let you be alone, Dora. I'll never leave you in the dark. You will know that you're loved. *Always.*"

I smile, my eyes welling up. "I thought... When you brought me here, I thought... you were going to say this was it. You were going to end things and it would kill me. I thought I was going to die. I... And I was prepared to die. I was always ready to die at the end of this story, you know. I was—"

"You're not dying," he declares firmly, vehemently. "I'm not letting you fucking die."

I let out a broken laugh. "Well, I didn't mean literally. I meant—"

"I meant both," he declares again, flexing his grip on my bod.

I laugh again. "Stellan, baby, that's crazy. You're not God. You—"

"Aren't I?"

Chuckling, I rest my forehead on his. "You are. You're my god."

He lets out a relieved breath. "So then."

"How about no one dies in this story?" Then, I correct myself, "Well, except the old, grumpy Stellan."

He chuckles too. "Yeah, that sounds good."

"Hey, how about we both die at the same time?" I go excitedly. "Wouldn't that be epic?"

Closing his eyes, he hums, as if he's so relaxed and at peace.

Finally.

"You could write about it, Stellan," I say even more excitedly. "I mean since you quit your job and you're now free to do stuff with the books."

He hums again.

"Oh my God"—I gasp—"How about I act in it?"

"Uh-huh."

Then something occurs to me and I go, "Will you be mad if I tell you I lied?"

His eyes open. "What?"

"You're getting mad."

"Dora."

"Well you just opened your eyes. You were so relaxed before and—"

"What did you lie about?" he asks sternly.

I wrinkle my nose. "So the camp?"

His eyes narrow. "What about it?"

"I do have to leave," I tell him, playing with the ends of his hair.

"But?"

"But I don't go until the summer."

"Summer."

"Uh-huh. I just said that to –"

"Hurt me," he finishes.

I bite my lip. "I'm sorry."

"No, you're not."

I shake my head. "No, I'm not." Then, I explain, "But only because you deserved it. You deserved a little pain and—"

He shuts my mouth with his kiss.

And the moment our lips touch, I melt.

I kiss him back.

Even though it occurs to me that if this is his new life, he should really follow in my footsteps and ask me. Like I asked him.

For a kiss.

I mean it's only fair.

But it's okay.

For now, this is good.

This is great.

Him and me and our kiss.

We have entire lives to figure the rest out.

EPILOGUE

SIX MONTHS LATER...

As always, he stands at the edge of things.
In this case, he's standing at the edge of the roof as he looks out into the night.

I take a few moments to study him, his profile, from a distance. I run my eyes over his tall frame. Tall and broad. So tall that if he were standing under my pink magnolia tree, he wouldn't have to reach his arm all the way up to pluck the flowers; and so broad that he carries the weight of the world on them. His jaw is clean-shaven and his dark, gleaming hair is smoothed back as always. His white shirt is crisp and dark jeans mold to his athlete thighs with perfection.

He looks the same as he did over two years ago when I first saw him.

But there are differences.

Like for example, his shirt is white as opposed to dark like that night. The ends of his hair are damp because he's just had a shower. And he isn't standing in the dark like a thug. Or like he wants to melt into the shadows, no.

Tonight, every inch of him is illuminated by the moonlight.

In fact, he's staring right at the full and bright moon right now.

As he waits for me.

So I call out, "Hey."

He turns to face me and as always, my breath catches in my throat when our eyes clash. There's something about him, you see. Something that simply speaks to me. That makes me go breathless and thoughtless and reckless.

I like to call it destiny.

And these days, he agrees.

I can see it in his eyes.

As they take me in as well.

Going from the *maang tikka* on my forehead to the sparkly *paayal* around my henna tattooed ankles. Of course he stops at places during his perusal. Like around my shoulders where my hot pink and golden sequined *dupatta* goes over, and at my chest where the matching blouse I'm wearing shows off my cleavage. He also takes a long time staring at my bare midriff, at my belly button, at my elaborate *lehenga*, which is also hot pink in color.

I'm not going to lie. I love when he stares at me like that.

Like I make him go all breathless and thoughtless and reckless too.

See? Destiny.

"Sorry I kept you waiting," I breathe out.

He blinks.

As if he was in a trance and my words broke it.

I bite my lip to stop my smile.

And his eyes flare in response.

"You look..." he begins but trails off, his eyes going up and down my body again.

I bite my lip harder and this time he sucks in a breath. Then, letting my lip go and walking toward him, I suggest, "Beautiful?"

He watches me approach him. "Yeah but..."

"That's not the right word?" I tease, slowly closing the distance between us.

He shakes his head slowly. "No."

Smiling, I keep going, "Resplendent?"

"Yeah but no."

"Glorious?"

He shakes his head slowly, his eyes flashing.

"Luminous then," I say as I reach him and stop.

Although I don't think he likes it all that much.

Me stopping where I did.

I knew it and that's why I did it.

Because in a second he's going to do the thing that *I* like. Which is: he reaches forward and yanks me to him, making me go crash against his hard body. As if he can't bear even a couple of inches between us. As if he wants every part of him touching every part of me at all times.

I agree.

We should be touching all the time.

So I sigh at the first contact while he growls, "Mine. You look *mine*."

He bends his head toward me, going for my lips.

But as much as it pains me, I stop him. "No, don't."

His brows draw close. "What?"

I push at his chest. "Not yet."

I hate making him wait. I do. Because for the longest time, he had to watch me from afar. He had to long and pine and *wait.* I had to do those things too. So these days, I try not to make him—and myself—wait for things.

But this is important, so he needs to.

He frowns. "Why the fuck not?"

"You'll ruin my makeup and—"

"You don't need makeup."

My heart smiles but still I protest. "You just have to wait a little because—"

His grip flexes around my bicep. "I did."

"What?"

"All day."

My heart smiles more at that. Because yes, he did. And again, as much as I hated it, it was mostly on my account because I spent the entire day rehearsing for the new play opening next week—for the Bardstown community theater no less; as always my supportive professor recommended me for the role—and so I came home only a couple of hours ago.

Although I will say that he was the one to push me to go on a Saturday.

With classes and homework and rehearsals, I usually try to keep weekends free so I can spend them with him. But since the play is opening in only a few days, they wanted us to come in. I wanted to refuse but Stellan told me that I should go. Because he's always the one who's pushing me to do things. He's always the one reminding me that I have dreams and that I can't forget them for any reason.

If I had my way, I would forget.

Because when it comes to him, I'm okay forgetting everything else.

Not him though. He wants me to fly and God, I love him for that.

But now that I'm back home, all bets are off.

And as he said, I'm his.

"On top of doing your bidding and spending time with my so-called friends," he finishes.

"They're not your so-called friends," I correct him. "They're your actual friends."

They are.

Homer, his high school friend and arguably one of the very few closest people to him; Byron, mostly his high school acquaintance who's becoming his friend. And Ark, again his high school acquaintance who's on the path to becoming his friend as well.

Although I will say that it's going slow.

Because as he said, he went to see them on my command.

While he's the one pushing me for my dreams, I'm the one who's pushing him to live his life. Which includes going out and seeing people such as his friends and having fun.

Because for the longest time, he didn't do that either.

He kept himself away from everything and everyone. He kept himself in the dark.

So it's my mission to fill his life with light. It's my mission to make him live and live freely.

Which reminds me I need to hit him up for the latest gossip about these three. For the record, Stellan is an awful gossiper. *Awful*. Even though he hangs out with these guys—on my insistence—he never knows anything juicy about them.

And there are juicy things to know, believe me.

Like, take Homer, for instance.

He apparently has a fiancée that he got engaged to when he was only fourteen. A fiancée that he doesn't want to get married to. In a way, I understand it. They both had their life decided when they were both kids. But now they've grown up and from what I can see, Maple—his fiancée—is into him. I have only met her a couple of times but I really like her. So I don't get his reluctance and I'd love to know *why* he's dragging his feet. But as I said, Stellan has no insight into it.

Oh and Byron. From the looks of it, his career might be in jeopardy because of all the rumors about his drug abuse. He denies it of course and there's never been any evidence to support such claims but he's always in the news for one scandal or another. And I'd love to know if it's true or not. If they're going to kick him out like they've been talking about?

And then there's Ark. Everyone knows that he owns a security company called The Fortress—my own bodyguards were hired through his company—and is a very busy man along with being very rich. Which obviously means he doesn't actually do any bodyguarding himself. But recently, in a very unprecedent turn of events, he's personally handling the security of one of their clients. Actually, let me rephrase, he's personally handling the security of their client's *daughter*.

Very curious, right?

Who is this daughter? What's happening there? Why would Ark break the norm for her?

But every time I ask Stellan about any of these things, he looks at me like I'm crazy.

I mean, he's the crazy one. How is he not asking these questions? What do they talk about when they see each other?

"But they aren't the ones I wanted to spend my Saturday night with," he says, breaking into my thoughts.

"Did you have fun though?" I ask hopefully.

"No."

"Not even a little bit?"

"No," he repeats like a grumpy boy.

"Stellan," I warn.

He clenches his jaw in response.

"Come on,"—I smack his chest lightly—"tell me you had *some* fun at least. You always like to hang out with Homer and play your boring chess."

He leans down. "Again, not how I wanted to spend my Saturday night. I wanted to come back as soon as you got home. But you wouldn't let me."

First, I want to pause here because he said *home*.

This is the first time he's said it but every time he does say it, I have to take a breath and absorb it. Because it still feels unreal. It still feels so surreal and dreamy.

That we live *together*.

Six months ago when he told me that he loved me and brought me to his house to show me a part of himself that he hadn't shown to anyone, we decided to move in together.

Well, duh.

He wouldn't let me live with my parents—not that I ever wanted to but still—and he of course wouldn't let me live alone, so we compromised and decided to live with each other. And since I wouldn't let him in his childhood home where everything was so real and toxic for him, we decided to get a place close to my college.

Which means I got what I always wanted.

Him.

All his secrets. All his fire.

All his love.

Although right now he looks pissed that I wouldn't let him come back home.

But that's only because I wanted time to get the surprise ready for him.

That's what this is all about.

That's why he can't touch me yet and that's why when I found out I was going to be spending my entire day at rehearsals and couldn't prep for it while he went to the gym—he goes *every single day*; yikes—I had to send him away so I could get everything ready.

"Okay," I try to appease him. "How about I give you your surprise and then you can do whatever you want with me? Because remember? All of this"—I point to my *lehenga* and the table laden with all the stuff I've put together for tonight—"is for the surprise I wanted to give you."

He studies me a beat before letting out a growly breath and easing his grip on me.

Stepping out of his embrace, I say, "Thank you." Then grabbing his hand, I pull him to the table I was pointing at. "Okay, so! Today's a little thing called *Karva Chauth*. Actually, not a little thing. It's a very famous festival in India. On this day, married women fast from sunrise to moonrise for the longevity of their husbands. Don't ask me what the words—*Karva Chauth*—actually mean. Well, my *biji* told me but I completely forgot. But what she also told me that it started long back as a way for women to pray for their husbands' safe return from the war."

It's actually a very sweet ceremony.

Where, as I just said, women fast for their husbands or sometimes for their husbands to be. They get up before sunrise—which I did—and eat something called *sargi* sent to them by their mother-in-law. *Sargi* generally includes sweet fruits, coconut, and other Indian sweets.

Since I don't have a mother-in-law or a future mother-in-law unfortunately, I asked his baby sister Callie to make me something sweet. And since she's a baker, she baked me cupcakes and cookies. Just for the record, she's the sweetest. We've become really good friends over the past few months, and I love hanging out with her. Plus all the other St. Mary's girls of course. Because they all kick ass and for the first time ever I feel like I'm part of an actual family.

Thanks to the love of my life.

Anyway, back to *sargi*.

It's supposed to last the women through the day and until the moon comes up, which is when they break the fast. It usually takes place like this: going up to the roof where the moon is clearly visible. They carry a big plate called *thali* with them that contains a glass of water or something called *kachi lassi*, a drink made of milk and water; a *diya* which is a small lamp and a sieve.

They look at the moon through the sieve and offer it water by tipping the glass a bit and letting the liquid drip down, followed by looking at their husband's face using that same sieve. And then the husband offers the same glass of water to his wife to drink from, and feeds her the first bite of the day, thereby breaking her fast.

As I said, it's all very sweet and romantic and ever since *Biji* told me about it a few years ago—because I saw it in a movie—it's something I always wanted to do. Which is why I insisted that we get an apartment with a balcony and roof access. So I could do the ceremony when the time came.

"Don't freak out, okay?" Picking up my own *thali* from the table, I turn to him. "But I did it."

He flicks his eyes down to the *thali* before asking, "You did what?"

"The fasting. I know—"

"You haven't eaten," he cuts me off.

"No. But that's not—"

"From sunrise to fucking *moonrise*."

"Yes but—"

"Are you insane?" he bites out, leaning over me. "Are you fucking... And you worked all day. All *fucking* day, Dora." He shakes his head. "You take things too far and... And I made you. I was the one who—"

I put a hand on his mouth to make him stop. "I knew you'd freak out which is why I didn't tell you." He goes to say something again, but I press my hand against his mouth and keep going, "But that's not the point. The point is that it's done. I already did the fasting and you can't change that. No matter how mad you are about it. All you can do is help me break it. Are you going to do that or not?"

He stares at me for a few beats, his eyes filled with displeasure, before letting out a growly breath for the second time and throwing out a short nod.

I smile. "Thank you."

When I remove my hand, he commands, "Hurry the fuck up."

I roll my eyes—even though I want to chuckle at his overprotectiveness—before taking the sieve and looking at the moon through it. Then I offer it the water before turning to the love of my life. I look at his beautiful face through the same sieve and my cheeks heat up at the look he gives me.

All hot and blazing.

Possessive and authoritative.

A little bit threatening too.

Because well he is kinda right. I do take things too far where he's concerned.

But it's not my fault.

It's his.

I am the way I am because he is the way he is. I'm wild because I know he's there to rein me in. And he forgets to be free because he knows I'm there to remind him that he can be.

Destiny.

I hand him the glass. "Now feed it to me."

Without taking his eyes off my face, he takes the glass and offers it to me. And without taking my eyes off him, I drink my first sip of water.

And clench my thighs.

Because I can see he likes that.

He likes feeding me.

Then I hand him the *thali* that contains Callie's cupcakes. Because if there's a choice between her cupcakes and anything else, I'm going for the cupcakes. I step up to him and open my mouth, silently asking him to feed that to me as well. He stares at my parted lips for a few seconds, and he does it in a way that reminds me of the way he stares at me when I'm on my knees.

And God, I have to clench my thighs again.

This time *I'm* about to tell him to hurry up so we can do other things when he plucks the cupcake from the *thali* and feeds it to me.

Thereby breaking my fast.

And I don't know what it is but this whole thing, this whole traditional thing that I did for him, makes me feel so content. It makes me feel so happy, so in love with him.

So in love with the man that I hope to one day marry.

But I'm not thinking about that.

I mean, we only just started dating—granted, it was six months ago but still—and there's so much we need to figure out. Although I will say that if we love each other and want to be together, can't we figure things out later, after we're married?

But again, I'm not going to think about that. We're not even engaged yet. He's never given me any indication that he wants to be or...

Okay, Isadora? Stop.

You're not thinking about that. You're going to be happy with what you have.

You're not going to be greedy.

Instead, I'm going to focus on something else that *Karva Chauth* is making me feel.

Hungry and not for the cupcakes.

So I take the cupcake from his hand, set it aside along with the *thali* and lean forward. I give him my weight as my hands go down to his belt and I say, "Now I think you should feed me something else."

He stops me though.

His puts his hand over mine as he steps back, breaking our contact. Before I can protest or even take my next breath, he does something crazy.

Something that I have a difficult time comprehending.

He goes down on his knees.

I look down at him in confusion and ask, "What are you—"

"You skipped a step," he tells me, looking up and into my eyes.

"What?"

"You didn't eat. From sunrise to moonrise."

"Yeah but that's—"

"But you're not my wife."

My heart thuds. "Oh. That... Girls can still do it for—"

"*Yet.*"

I freeze. "I-I'm sorry?"

He stares at me for a few moments, his eyes glittering and molten, his jaw ticking.

God, it's making my heart pound.

It's making my body shiver.

And when he starts speaking, I have to hold on to something—him—to keep my balance. Because I wasn't expecting him to say the things he's saying.

"I... I'll begin by saying that I'm not perfect." He scoffs. "I mean, my name and the word perfect don't even belong in the same sentence. I don't even think I'm a work in progress. I think I'm just... work. A fuck ton of work. A lot of people at this age have already been made while I'm still learning to be *unmade*. From my previous life. I'm learning to forget things. I'm learning. And for a man who thrived on control, who lived and breathed by it, who knew exactly who he was and what he wanted, it's a very strange thing to do. To learn."

He is.

Learning I mean.

Every single day.

Learning to let go. Learning to be free.

Learning to live.

In both small ways and big ways. In ways like going out with his friends. He protests, sure. But when I push him, he does give in. He agreed to be one of Riot's groomsmen at his wedding with Meadow; I was one of the bridesmaids and it was so beautiful, watching our friends get married. He even went tux shopping with Coach Thorne for his upcoming wedding with Wyn; they're getting married next summer.

He tells me things about himself. Without asking, without prompting. Without making it feel like I'm banging my head against the wall. Like the fact he likes mustard but hates mayo. His favorite color is blue. He likes the beach but hates anything cold. Like sometimes when he wakes up in the middle of the night, it's because he has nightmares about his mother.

On those nights he tells me about her. He tells me that when he was little and would hear his mom cry from her bedroom, he'd go to put his arms around her and comfort her. He'd give her flowers on days she'd walk around limping.

So, on those nights, I hug him tighter. On those mornings after, I hug the rose that he gives me tighter too. Because he still does it; he still gives me roses every day.

I mean is it any wonder that I love this man?

Is it any wonder that I forget the world when he's around me?

That I'm so, so proud of him for putting himself out there, for wanting a new life, for taking steps to live in a new way.

He even goes to therapy. Initially he didn't like it and didn't want to do it. But since he'd made me a promise that he'd build his life around me, he went despite his reluctance. And while I'd never push him to do anything that he didn't like, I'm glad he persisted. Because I know it helps him. It eases him—even if a little bit—in his moments of crisis. In moments when he can't remember anything else except his old life.

And there are days like that too.

When he forgets he's free.

When he forgets his past doesn't have a hold on him.

That he *isn't* like his past.

On those days—bad days—I try to be there for him as much as I can. I try to soothe him, comfort him. I even argue with him and fight with him. To show him that I can handle him. To show him that I'm not afraid of him or his demons.

So yeah, he's learning.

And I'm more in love with him now than I was six months ago.

"So really," he continues, his eyes flashing and liquid. "I have no right to do this. I shouldn't be doing it. But the thing is, Dora, when it comes to you, I've always been selfish. And I wish I could say that I'll work on that. I wish I could say that I'll fix this flaw in me. But I promised to tell you the truth. I promised to not lie to you or keep secrets from you so the truth is I can't. I can't work on it. It's impossible for me to work on it. In fact, I'm only going to get more selfish as the times passes. I'm only going to get even more possessive. So much so that maybe one day, I'll really cross that line. That *one* line and kill every guy who looks at you. Maybe one day I'll really strangle your father when I see him because of all the crimes he's committed against you, and I'll do the same to your mother as well because she still looks at you the wrong way."

I believe him.

I absolutely and wholeheartedly believe that he may one day end up doing these things.

Because well he's angry, isn't he?

And while I know he has a better control on his urges than he'd like to believe, I know that it rears its ugly head when he sees someone hurting me.

Such as my parents.

After we moved in together, my father had invited us over for dinner. He wanted to make amends and reconcile things. And since I wanted the same, I insisted that we go. Honestly, I should've known it would be a disaster because it's not as if I wasn't aware Stellan hates my parents or that my mother hates Stellan. But while Stellan was polite albeit reserved, my mother kept staring daggers at him. She kept taunting him about his family, about differences in our status, the fact that he'd beaten up his brother for me. And that according to her, he had no job prospects because he'd just quit and enrolled in college.

In my college no less.

Since he'd decided to quit soccer and pursue a new path, he thought going back to college was a good idea. And since we'd decided to live together, he thought it was best that he enrolled at the same school as me. And let me tell you, my boyfriend is a freaking *genius*. We have a few classes together and oh my God, he knows everything.

Everything.

He always has all the answers, and he can explain things better than the professors. Ever since he started going, I don't think I've ever paid this much attention in class. Usually, I doodle on the margins of my notebook but these days, I listen to everything he says. Not to mention, I've started to do my own homework too. With his help of course but still.

Wow, who knew college could be so fun?

Plus I will *never* look at study rooms at the library without blushing. Or a Sharpie and a desk, for that matter. I mean it's hard not to if one of those things has been inside you—the Sharpie—and the other thing has been under you—the table—while you were writhing and humping the Sharpie that your boyfriend was pumping in and out of your pussy.

While he was inside your ass.

And all because I got a math question right and so he decided to reward me even though we were at the library, and he knows how loud I can be. But it's okay, he clapped his hand over my mouth when my whining got too loud.

All in all, the best decision ever.

But of course, my mother hadn't known that.

So yeah, disaster it was.

The only person who had any fun at that dinner was my *biji*. She'd break out chuckling at random moments or simply smirk and sip her margarita as she watched Stellan giving my mother the cold shoulder. At one point she blurted out, *"Dil khush kar ditta iss khote de puttar ne."*

Which she went on to translate, without any prompting from me, "I don't think I've ever had this much fun in my life. You're not such an asshole after all."

All this to say, I believe him. Even though I made him promise to go easy on my father at least and not engage with my mother at all because like I told him that day, she isn't worth it. She isn't worth destroying our happiness over.

"I may burn down the world with my fire," he keeps going, "and I don't think that can ever be fixed. I don't know if I *want* to fix that. That is the one thing I don't want to fix about myself, wanting to protect you, wanting to do extreme things to keep you safe. So I don't think this is fair, me doing this, me asking you what I want to ask you but I..." He takes a deep breath. "As I said I'm selfish and on top of that, I'm in love. And that would still be okay, me being in love, but I'm in love with *you* and you make me... do crazy things. You make me want to fly. You make me hope. For a future. For a better life. But more than that you make me believe that I *can* have a life. That I *can* have a future. That I *can* live in the light. That I *can* live outside of that room I'd shut myself in. You make me believe that I can live with this fire inside of me. So instead of making you false promises, I'm going to say that I will. I will always live in the light with you, no matter how scary it seems. I will live outside that room, with you, no matter how hard it seems sometimes. But more than that I will believe. *Always*. I will always believe that one day I'll get there. One day I will be the kind of man who deserves you. I will be the kind of man who deserves to cherish you and treasure you and protect you. I will be the kind of man who deserves to love you. But until then, until that day, until the day I've earned you, I'm asking you to take a chance. On me. I'm asking you to let me be with you. Forever."

"F-forever?"

"I'm asking you to marry me."

It takes a few seconds for me to find my breath. It also takes me a few seconds to find my heart. Because I don't think it's in my chest anymore. I think it fell down to my tummy. I think it jumped up to my throat.

I think my heart is everywhere.

Like stardust.

Like the snow.

Falling and beating and throbbing.

It throbs more when I notice something.

A ring.

He produces a ring from somewhere—probably his pocket—and holds it in his fingers between us.

"You have a..."—I fist my fingers in his shirt—"ring?"

His eyes flick back and forth between mine, his face all cut open and vulnerable. "Bought it the day we moved in together."

"But we"—I catch my breath again—"moved in together, like months ago."

"Been carrying it around," he shares.

"In your pockets."

He nods. "Stopping myself from asking the question." He swallows thickly before continuing, "I wish I had taken more time. I wish I'd worked on—"

"No."

He grows cautious. "No?"

"No, I mean I love you. I—"

"I love you too," he says, still looking both cautious and vulnerable.

And oh God, how can he not know? How can he not already know what my answer would be? How can he not know how perfect he is? How wonderful and amazing and so deserving of my love already.

I mean, look at him saying I love you back all because he'd promised me that I'd never be alone in saying it. So, every time I say it, even as an afterthought, he returns the sentiment as if it's forefront on his mind. As if that's all he ever thinks about.

And knowing him, he probably does.

"You're perfect," I tell him vehemently.

He swallows again. "I don't think so."

"You are." I fist his shirt again. "And you're not that old."

He frowns. "What?"

"You said, back there, that"—I shake my head—"people your age have things figured out and all that. You're only twenty-seven."

He is.

We celebrated his birthday last month and I don't think I will ever look at vanilla cream cheese frosting the same again. Not after how he smeared the frosting on my nipples and my pussy before eating me out. And then how I smeared it on his dick and licked it off him.

"Kinda close to thirty," he corrects me.

"Are you serious? You're not close to thirty. And even if you were, it wouldn't matter because as I said, you're perfect and I love so much."

"I love you too."

God, he's crazy.

"And I will marry you," I finally tell him.

Still holding the ring in his fingers, he goes still.

His chest stops breathing and he stares at me unblinking.

I shake him. "Stellan?"

He blinks. "You will?"

"Yes."

"You're sure?"

"Yes."

"Because I... I looked at you and you were so... You didn't eat all day for me and I... I just... I couldn't stop myself but—"

"Will you put the ring on me and kiss me already?"

And like the rule follower he is, he does.

He obeys me and puts the ring on my finger with his big, usually-graceful-but-clumsy-in-this-moment, hands.

I look down at the ring—a princess cut diamond with red rubies circling it—and smile. "We're engaged."

"Yeah," he breathes out, his hands coming to rest on my bare waist.

As if he needs support to hold himself upright.

I look at him; he still looks a little dazed. "And it's not fake."

At my words, any dazedness on his features goes away and his eyes flash possessively. "Absolutely fucking not."

I chuckle. "I'm never taking it off."

"You're not allowed to take it off," he tells me, flexing his fingers on my flesh.

"Even when you're being bossy and annoying," I point out.

"And neither will I."

"Neither will you what?"

"Take off my ring," he promises, "when you give it to me at the wedding."

"We're going to have a wedding," I say, my eyes wide, as if it's only now sinking into me.

"We absolutely fucking are," he agrees vehemently.

I grin. "I can't wait." Then, gasping, I add, "Can we do it tomorrow?"

His jaw tenses in response. "No."

"But—"

"We will wait."

"I don't want—"

"Because you deserve a perfect *Indian* wedding, and it takes planning."

I stare at him for a beat but give in because he's right. "You know I want an Indian style wedding?"

"You've made me watch enough of those movies to know that yeah I know."

"Hey, they're good movies."

"They are," he agrees solemnly.

"You're going to have to wear traditional Indian clothes, you know?"

"A *sherwani*," he goes. "Yeah, I know."

"You know what they wear at the traditional Indian style wedding?"

"It's a simple Google search," he murmurs.

It is but...

Holy shit.

My boyfriend—fiancé—is so fucking hot for knowing that. For *researching* that. Although I shouldn't be surprised, should I? He *is* a scholar. Oh and a sherwani is a long-sleeved coat that grooms wear over a pair of flared trousers. It is fitted and goes down to the knees.

And oh my God, I cannot wait to see Stellan rocking that, and he *is* going to rock it, believe me.

"I can't believe you know that. You're so fucking sexy for knowing that," I breathe out.

Which makes him chuckle and add, "Well in that case, let me tell you all about how at the wedding, we'll be taking seven rounds around a holy fire, agni in Sanskrit, so we're tied to each other for seven lives."

I clench my thighs, my core pulsing. "Oh my God, stop *talking*."

"And since I won't be satisfied with just seven lives, I'll marry you in each life for the next seven. So we'll be tied every time I'm born."

Ugh.

How can he be both sexy and romantic at the same time?

I'm dying.

He's killing me.

Then, something else occurs to me and I say, "If we're going to be tied every time we're born then you're going to work on your gossiping skills."

He frowns. "No."

"Come on, Stellan. I want to know what's happening with Jupiter and Shepard."

Because something *is* happening there.

And despite all his friends leading a juicy life, this piece of gossip is something I'm the most interested in. I wish I could ask Jupiter but since I've been the source of such grief to her this past year, I'm trying to respect her privacy. So I keep my mouth shut when we hang out.

But Stellan doesn't have to do the same when he hangs out with Shep.

Which, I'm happy to report, he does pretty frequently.

More frequently than hanging out with the other guys.

In fact, they see each other every single week. Well when Shep isn't traveling for the games. But if he's in New York, come what may including a grueling practice session, the twin brothers have a standing date to meet up at The Horny Bard.

I love it.

I absolutely freaking love how they're trying to work on their relationship, and how much Stellan enjoys it. Because every time he comes back from his date with Shepard, he's visibly happy and light.

"What's happening is none of our business," he states firmly.

"It is so," I protest. "If they get married, she'll be my sister-in-law."

"They're not getting married," he states even more firmly.

"But—"

"He can't stand her."

I look at him like he's crazy. "Is that what he told you?"

"Yes."

I keep looking at him like that. "Seriously?"

"Yeah."

I still look at him like that. "Oh my God, you have no clue, do you?"

"Clue about what?"

"He's crazy about her."

"That's –"

"That's why he said that," I share excitedly.

"I think you're delusional."

I put both my hands on his cheeks. "Oh my sweet baby, you have so much to learn."

His eyes flash again. "Do I now?"

"Yes, you do." I nod sagely. "He's doing the same thing that you did. You pretended that I annoyed you when you secretly liked it."

His lips twitch slightly. "I did like it."

"See? He likes it too. In fact, the other day when we did the get-together," I keep sharing. "I think he was staring at her. I got the feeling. I mean, of course when I asked him he denied it but I could've sworn that—"

"Can we stop talking about my brother?"

I look at his sheepishly. "I'm sorry."

"Good."

"I think you should get off your knees now," I tell him. "I said yes. I'm yours."

His grip tightens. "I think that's the very reason I should stay on my knees. *Because* you're mine."

"What does that—"

He explains it to me then.

Not via words but through actions.

When he lifts up my lehenga, spreads my legs and gets his mouth between them. And since he's mine as well, when he's done eating me out, I finally get my turn to get down on my knees where he properly breaks my fast and feeds me.

My wildfire Thorn.

THE END

BAD BOYS OF BARDSTOWN

You Beautiful Thing, You
(Bad Boys of Bardstown 1)
Ledger and Tempest's story!
Buy Now

Oh, You're So Cold
(Bad Boys of Bardstown 2)
Stellan Thorne and Isadora Holmes' story!

A Wreck, You Make Me
(Bad Boys of Bardstown 3)
Shepard Thorne and Jupiter Jones' story
Pre-order Now

Bad Kind of Butterflies
(Bad Boys of Bardstown 4)
Ark Reinhardt's story

For you, I fall to Pieces
(Bad Boys of Bardstown 5)

I'm Hopeless, You're Heartless
(Bad Boys of Bardstown 6)

Add the series to your TBR

OTHER BOOKS BY SAFFRON A. KENT

The Unrequited

Gods & Monsters

Medicine Man (Heartstone Series Book 1)

Dreams of 18 (Heartstone Series Book 2)

California Dreamin' (Heartstone Series Book 3)

St. Mary's Rebels Series

Bad Boy Blues (SMR book 0.5)

My Darling Arrow (SMR book 1)

The Wild Mustang & The Dancing Fairy (SMR book 1.5)

A Gorgeous Villain (SMR book 2)

These Thorn Kisses (SMR book 3)

Hey, Mister Marshall (SMR book 4)

The Hatesick Diaries (SMR book 5)

ABOUT THE AUTHOR

Writer of bad romances. Aspiring Lana Del Rey of the Book World.

Saffron A. Kent is a USA Today Bestselling Author of Contemporary and New Adult romance.

She has an MFA in Creative Writing and she lives in New York City with her nerdy and supportive husband, along with a million and one books.

She also blogs. Her musings related to life, writing, books and everything in between can be found in her JOURNAL on her website (www.thesaffronkent.com)

www.ingramcontent.com/pod-product-compliance
Lightning Source LLC
LaVergne TN
LVHW041738060526
838201LV00046B/848